THE BLOODLESS QUEEN

Also by Joshua Phillip Johnson

Tales of the Forever Sea
THE FOREVER SEA
THE ENDLESS SONG

*

THE BLOODLESS QUEEN

THE BLOODLESS QUEEN

JOSHUA PHILLIP JOHNSON

DAW BOOKS
New York

Copyright © 2025 by Joshua Phillip Johnson

All rights reserved. Copying or digitizing this book for storage, display, or distribution in any other medium is strictly prohibited. For information about permission to reproduce selections from this book, please contact permissions@astrapublishinghouse.com.

This is a work of fiction. Names, characters, places, and incidents are products of the author's imagination or are used fictitiously. Any resemblance to actual events, locales, or persons, living or dead, is entirely coincidental.

Jacket design by Faceout Studio, Elisha Zepeda

Book design by Fine Design

DAW Book Collectors No. 1966

DAW Books
An imprint of Astra Publishing House
dawbooks.com
DAW Books and its logo are registered trademarks of Astra Publishing House

Printed in the United States of America

Library of Congress Cataloging-in-Publication Data

Names: Johnson, Joshua Phillip, author.
Title: The bloodless queen / Joshua Phillip Johnson.
Description: First edition. | New York : DAW Books, 2025. |
Series: DAW Book Collectors ; no. 1966
Identifiers: LCCN 2025007434 (print) | LCCN 2025007435 (ebook) |
ISBN 9780756419196 (hardcover) | ISBN 9780756419202 (ebook)
Subjects: LCGFT: Science fiction. | Novels.
Classification: LCC PS3610.O3567 B58 2025 (print) | LCC PS3610.O3567 (ebook) |
DDC 813/.6--dc23/eng/20250224
LC record available at https://lccn.loc.gov/2025007434
LC ebook record available at https://lccn.loc.gov/2025007435

First edition: July 2025
10 9 8 7 6 5 4 3 2 1

For Rachel
For Agnes
For Harrow

There lies the port; the vessel puffs her sail:
There gloom the dark, broad seas. My mariners,
Souls that have toil'd, and wrought, and thought with me—
That ever with a frolic welcome took
The thunder and the sunshine, and opposed
Free hearts, free foreheads—you and I are old;
Old age hath yet his honour and his toil;
Death closes all: but something ere the end,
Some work of noble note, may yet be done,
Not unbecoming men that strove with Gods.
The lights begin to twinkle from the rocks:
The long day wanes: the slow moon climbs: the deep
Moans round with many voices. Come, my friends,
'Tis not too late to seek a newer world.
Push off, and sitting well in order smite
The sounding furrows; for my purpose holds
To sail beyond the sunset, and the baths
Of all the western stars, until I die.
It may be that the gulfs will wash us down:
It may be we shall touch the Happy Isles,
And see the great Achilles, whom we knew.
Tho' much is taken, much abides; and tho'
We are not now that strength which in old days
Moved earth and heaven, that which we are, we are;
One equal temper of heroic hearts,
Made weak by time and fate, but strong in will
To strive, to seek, to find, and not to yield.

—From "Ulysses,"
by Alfred, Lord Tennyson

New England Harbor, September 29th, 1999

Arthur Miracle whistled as he killed.

Today, it was an old Ernest Tubb tune, one of his mother's favorites. In his memory, she sits in his grandfather's old rocking chair beside the window, the soft lines of her glowing with afternoon sunshine, singing, "Let's say goodbye like we said hello, in a friendly kind of way." Back then, he'd just been Arthur Meyer—Art, to his few friends. Back then, he'd been another poor kid in a tiny, faded white house in a row of faded white houses in Union City, Georgia.

And now?

Arthur Miracle let his shoulders get in on the swing of his whistled song, feeling good. He was only a few years gone from that dump of a house, but that dirty kid with just a few grubby T-shirts to his name was gone, popped out of existence by this person he had become, mighty where he had once been weak, rich where he had once been poor, and much where he had once been less.

"Nine o'clock," came the voice behind him, jangling against the melody of Arthur's tightly puckered lips. Silas—Skyward Silas, to use his half-witted fencer name—always talked like this on runs into the Harbors, like they were all kids playing commando in the tall grass instead of actual warriors, *actual* superheroes fighting at the border between the human and faerie worlds. Silas played at this whole ding-dang thing, as Arthur's mother used to say.

But Arthur Miracle *embodied* it.

To his left—his nine o'clock—came a faerie, moving like a drunken dancer, weaving around the thick trunks of the trees clogging the

Harbor. In worse light or under the influence of more drugs than even Arthur had zipping along the bloody highways of his body, the faerie might have looked human.

In this noon light, though, and with only the barest bump of the stuff before he took off with his team across the fence and into the Harbor, Arthur saw the faerie for what it was: broken, bestial, disgusting, inhuman. Its slantwise face dripped and drooled toward one shoulder, and teeth had begun sprouting from its lips and chin like flowers gone rogue from the garden's confines. One arm hung limp and loose at its side, the fingers grown long enough to trail along the leaf-strewn grass at its heels.

It ducked and dodged forward, aiming in its widdershins way for Arthur, who moved ahead of his small team, the leader. The TV people, the ones his agent called "the media," had begun calling him Mr. Miracle, the Man Who Can't Be Stopped, the Indivisible Two.

All that nonsense. *So much shit in the wind*, Momma Meyer might have said. Arthur Miracle was enough.

The faerie feinted, feinted, and then moved to strike, and Arthur felt a smile pulling at the pucker of his lips, fraying the song he continued to whistle.

"Arthur!" a voice called out behind him, but he didn't need the warning. He didn't need the extra eyes. He liked to work alone, preferred patrolling on the equinox by himself, the comforting rumble of his bike rebounding against the tall buildings and along the empty streets.

But for a job like this—crossing into the Harbor and breaking down the door between this land and whatever the hell lay beyond—Arthur had gathered the strongest fencers the United States had to offer. None were even in the same league as him, of course, but no one was, not in America or in any other country. But this team was good enough to play support for Arthur as he attempted—oh hell, as he *did* what no one else had ever done.

In each of the borderlands between Earth and the land of Faerie, a great tree rose—the Threshold Tree, the final barrier to the world of the fae. It was as yet untouched and unopened by any of the superpowered, primed-up fencers immune to the toxic effects of the Harbors. Each year, as another crop of weak humans transformed into faeries and ran their giggling gallop into those borderlands, those Harbors, they disappeared through that Tree. No human had ever seen the other side.

Arthur would be the first.

He'd found a closed door, and that just couldn't be.

The faerie cut in close, and Arthur Miracle, whistling still with the ghost of his recently dead mother in mind, unknotted the creature with no more than a gentle tip of his head, as if nodding to a friend across the street.

The faerie, which had been mid-leap, its ugly grace airborne, seemed to catch a stray wind and simply blow apart, its every strand and stitch floating free, turned weightless and weak. Hair, skin, blood, bone, tissue, muscle—all of it fluttered away in long, impossibly thin threads, a haze of color diaphanous and lovely. As the wind took them farther and farther away, the tiny strings of being that had once knotted together to form the faerie became less and less until they were gone.

Something to nothing. Arthur's terrible power. His *glorious* power.

His team moved up around him, the six of them all outfitted in their own ways. The three from the Lone Star Harbor down in Texas: Skyward Silas, the Maniac, and the Dowager Complete. Two from the Southwest Harbor: Arkansite and Graven the Last. And then there was WarSpeaker, from the Florida Harbor.

Six of the best the United States had to offer. Plus Arthur himself, so seven in all. A good number, the mathematicians had told him. Prime. Powerful.

But it was just him, Arthur knew. It was him there, at the front, making this happen. And it was the rest of them behind, cleaning up the faeries he missed or let through, the ones he couldn't be bothered with.

It was Arthur and that damn Tree. And it was the rest of them along for the ride.

The others had their weapons out, iron swords and chains, War-Speaker with her strange iron-bladed axe, the Dowager Complete with the coal-black blades she summoned with her primacy.

"I thought there would be more fae on this path," the Maniac said. He'd painted his face to look like a whirlpool. He looked like an idiot.

"Most of them probably already crossed through the Tree," War-Speaker said, using her axe to slice the heads off a stand of small, strange flowers nearby. Weird shit grew in these Harbors, or so the scientists said.

"I won't complain about fewer bogeys," Silas said. He flipped up the lenses of the sunglasses that covered most of his face. "Makes the mission easier."

"I've been killing them from a distance," Arthur said, not bothering to look any of his team in the eye. The Tree was supposed to be just beyond the next few ridges, according to the partial maps he'd been able to get for this Harbor. The few fencers who had made it this far into the Harbor—about twelve miles in as the crow flies—hadn't made it out again.

"You can do that?" WarSpeaker, not for the first time since Arthur had gathered the crew together for this historic run, spoke with some awe in her voice. She was the youngest among them, barely twenty, according to her file. Juliet Michaelson was her name. Her *true* name.

Arthur winked at her and said, "I can do any damn thing I want."

The Dowager Complete pulled out a water flask and, after taking a gulp, passed it around. Arthur shook his head. All morning, they'd been making their slow, plodding way forward, cautious and careful, but he was done with the waiting. Done with the tactical pauses and the calls to "fan out" and the consideration of the maps that he'd memorized despite the fact that he could feel the draw of the Tree. He wanted to turn to them and say, "Can't you sense it? Can't you feel it in your teeth and your hands and your fucking *guts*?"

He knew what the psych evals and thinkpieces about him said: working-class kid raised by single mom after deadbeat dad walked out. It was all so fucking cliché, some neat, easy box for every damn person in the world to stick him in and explain everything he had done and would do.

No, this was Arthur's expedition, and it would be something new, something strange, something that broke that damn box around him for good. The goals, the objectives, the strategies, the reasoning—it was his. And the glory, when it arrived as inevitably as the golden sunrise on the horizon, would be his too.

The Harbor was all soft, grass-covered hills and trees that looked normal from a distance and odd up close. Creeks and ponds cut through and dotted the landscape from time to time, but the scientists had warned the fencers to avoid them. No one yet knew what liquids sloshed through those spaces or how safe they were. All attempts to capture and return them to a lab had resulted in the carrier's death.

But as they'd gotten closer to the Threshold Tree, the land of the Harbor had started to change, as if it were responding to that pull in Arthur's body, the hills growing taller and sharper, like hooks burying themselves in his skin, sliding in and urging him forward. The streams and creeks and ponds had grown louder, much louder than they should have been on such a quiet, calm day. No birds flew overhead. No creatures large or small—save the fae—moved in the grass or among the tree branches.

"Put the water and food away," Arthur said, looking around at the group of six, their weapons stowed or dropped on the ground. "It's time."

"I just need to eat something," Arkansite said. Though she was older than most of the team, she still acted like a teenager, pouting when she didn't get her way or giggling during meetings at inappropriate times. She was on the team only because of her primacy, which gave her the ability to fly.

"Later," Arthur said, pulling in a breath through his nostrils and letting it straighten his back. He could feel the blood rushing through him, urging him forward. "We move now."

She protested, and Arthur expelled the air from his lungs as he turned the food pack at her feet, the baggie of sandwiches in her hand, and even the bracelet on her wrist—some bit of cloth braided into a many-colored memento—into tiny bits of gossamer nothing.

Arkansite yelped and launched herself backward, as if she were under attack. With a straightening of one leg, she was suddenly airborne, and even as he laughed at his own work, gleeful at his control and mastery in only cutting away the three items and not a single stitch of Arkansite's skin, Arthur marveled at her primacy. There was just something impossible about human flight. It offended the natural order of things. It was wrong on some deep, fundamental level.

And Arthur loved that.

"Arthur!" It was the Dowager Complete—*Alexis Oliver*, Arthur reminded himself. She had styled herself the group mother and killjoy, and he had no doubt she'd be the group tattletale after all of this was over. "What the hell are you doing?"

"Oh, come on," he said. "I'm just goofing a little." As if to make his point, he drew a pair of finger guns from imaginary holsters and shot at a tree on a nearby hill. "Pow, pow," he said, and the tree exploded in a two-fold fit of puffed-up matter, hazing to pastel glory as it lifted and expanded and dissipated. Left behind was a twisting statue of intertwined fae in agony, not carved into the trunk exactly but simply allowed to remain by Arthur's precision. The world thought of him as a great hammer—*their* great hammer—but he could be a sharp, small knife, too, with cuts tiny and perfect and devastating.

"You shouldn't be so cavalier this close to the center of the Harbor, Arthur," the Dowager Complete said. *Hissed*, Arthur thought, imagining her as a coiled, reproachful snake. "Our primacies drive the fae insane, the nearer we get to the Tree."

"Our primacies *always* make them nuts, *Alexis*," Arthur said, *pow-pow*ing another tree at least half a mile off. *Poof*, it went, and he smiled at his good work.

"No names!" Silas said, shocked.

"*This* is what the briefings were about," the Dowager said, disgust slithering around in her voice. "You know, the ones you skipped. Where we talked about the new research on names and safety measures as we neared the Tree."

Pow-pow.

"Tell me," Arthur said.

"The fae can use our true names, Arthur. They're so much stronger than the average person, so having or not having one of their names doesn't make a difference, but for us, it's everything. Every advantage we have—iron, primacy, primes—is *gone* if a faerie has your name."

He'd heard all of this before—the folklorists always perked up with old stories about faeries like elves or pixies who steal a little kid's name and then own his soul. Sounded like a load of horseshit.

"What else?" he said, scanning the horizon for his next victim. Alexis, the Dowager, huffed but continued.

"All of the tests and reports said the fae activity would increase *exponentially* in response to primacy use once we were close to the Tree. And they also said that the primacies themselves would get harder to control and more erratic. I believe the specific phrase they used was *a kid holding a fire hose*. Didn't you at least read any of the materials they gave you?"

The specific phrase, Arthur thought, hating the way she said *that* specific phrase. *Thanks for the specifics, Mrs. Oliver.*

He sighed, but when Arthur turned back to look at his little team, Arkansite having returned to earth, he found it wasn't just the Dowager Complete looking miffed. All of them, even Skyward Silas, his little military man, were casting eyes downward in disappointment or fear or even anger.

Arthur kicked for a moment at a tiny mound of dirt nearby, breaking it open to reveal a thin spiral of vegetal growth inside, the strands swirling and bobbing as if they were underwater. Everything was so strange in the Harbor but somehow never in a comforting, magical way. It was always slightly sinister, just ever so *off*, like the mirrors of a funhouse showing a version of you that wasn't quite right.

"I'm sorry," he said, hoping he sounded genuine. "You're right. I know it's—"

But his apology speech was cut short when, from a nearby hill crowned with a ring of small saplings, a group of six or seven fae appeared, each one babbling something nonsensical and eerie, their eyes—those that still had eyes, anyway—fixed on the group of fencers.

"Toward the Tree—fight as we go!" Arthur shouted, and those down-in-the-dumps looks disappeared. Good. A little fear, a little focus was just what they needed.

Arkansite took again to the sky, rising up and away from the clash that was coming. The others charged forward, and Arthur—the leader, the strong right hand and strong left hand both—moved to put himself between the group and the oncoming fae, who, he had to admit, did look a little crazier than normal.

He was hit all at once by the interwoven wall of their voices, each one a thread he couldn't follow before it was subsumed by others.

". . . durst she not disclose her . . ."

". . . precious relicke in an arke of gold. . . "

". . . were to her presence brought . . ."

". . . to her presence . . ."

". . . he might present . . ."

". . . his queen . . ."

". . . unto his queen . . ."

The fae, their transformations having turned them into humped, halfway things, ran and leapt in maddeningly evasive routes, at times seeming to fly or hover over the ground. One of them dipped below the soil as if it were water, breaking through in a splash of dirt and rock and plant matter some ten or twelve feet closer.

Arthur felt a shock of sweat pulse from the skin along his neck, and a cold stab of doubt arrested him for a moment. Had Alexis—the Dowager—been right? These fae moved like none he'd ever seen—had he done this?

"Pow," he said, gesturing with a free hand. "Pow, pow, pow."

But the fae weren't so easily caught now, and Arthur saw only a single spray of disembodied color float lazily up—the others dodged and wove and dove around his invisible efforts.

"Run!" he shouted, flinging more of his attacks toward the enemies but haphazardly now.

The group legged forward, and Arthur found himself suddenly and surprisingly grateful for the fitness work all the fencing organizations had begun to implement for their people. The fencers of ten years before—untried celebrities with minor power and major social capital—would have been run down and ripped apart already.

"Watch out!" he shouted, catching a sudden flicker of movement off to the left. "Alexis! Dowager! Behind you!"

The Dowager Complete turned and her hands blurred in the air, splitting and splitting until she looked like a goddess, many-armed and many-handed, each clutching a shiny black dagger. This was why Arthur had picked her—she wasn't the strongest fencer by any real metrics, but her ability was cool as hell, and after he'd seen video of her carving up a pack of fae last equinox, he knew she would be perfect.

Arthur let out a cheer, forgetting for a moment the *"specific phrase"* and her talk about his missing meetings, but the cry died in his throat.

The faerie cutting in on the Dowager lifted its own voice in glee and cried "Alexis! Oliver!"

Its words thickened in the air around the Dowager, as though she were suddenly moving and striking in liquid glass, swimming in the stuff. Her many arms slowed and slowed until she was totally still, and Arthur realized the rest of the battlefield had followed suit, fae and fencer alike watching in anticipation or horror.

Pow-pow went Arthur, unknotting the fae with the Dowager's name. No one on his squad was dying today, not while he drew breath.

The fae had other plans.

As one, the remaining creatures shouted the Dowager's true name, and the force of it was like nothing he had ever experienced. He felt pressure inside his mind and along the strong lines of his limbs, threatening to cause his collapse, his mind folding in on itself even as his body did, too. He screamed at the pain, throwing up his arms and squeezing his eyes shut.

The pressure climaxed, and Arthur thought all was lost, and the seed of fear he'd been carrying that day, that whole week, blossomed somewhere deep inside.

Someone was shouting, and someone was singing, and his skin felt grainy and loose, and when the pressure left, it happened all at once, so suddenly and completely that Arthur felt its ghost still pressing on his skin and sanity.

He opened his eyes to find the fae leering at the Dowager, her body faceup on the ground, stiff in death. Her arms, just two once again, were crossed over her chest, and her broken legs lay at unnatural angles on the grass.

Her eyes were open and stared sightlessly skyward. Her mouth hung askew in a silent scream that would never end.

The fae, standing around her like mourners at a funeral, shivered and their arms blurred through the air, splitting and splitting until each creature was surrounded by a swirling chaos of limbs.

They had stolen her primacy. First her name and then her ability.

"Go!" Arthur shouted, unknotting one of the many-limbed fae as he surged forward. *The mission*, he told himself. *Finish the mission.*

The rest of the squad followed, though Arthur saw the looks of horror, shock, fear on their faces.

And the fae followed too, screeching their nonsense to the air, arms aswirl around them.

"Unto his Faerie Queene he might present—" one said from the slantwise gash of its mouth, and Arthur cut its strings and watched it float away, its frenetic babble still hanging in the air.

"The Tree!" someone shouted.

Arthur turned and found his prize.

The Threshold Tree. Huge and imposing, the branches like huge arms, harsh white and knotted, reaching high into the air. The bark was covered in a maddening chaos of etchings and scripts and drawings running over and through one another, a palimpsest a hundred times over. A thousand. A thousand thousand. And the curves and lines seemed to move in Arthur's vision, swimming and scuttling when he wasn't focusing on them and yet holding still—too still—when he did.

Littered around the Tree's base were countless bleached shells, like religious adherents who, having flung themselves at the feet of their god, died there, prostrate and low.

A shout of joy—pure joy—ripped from Arthur's mouth. The cry of a child, untainted by the world. This was it. *Finally*, this was it. The brush of tall grasses against his pants, and the faerie wind singing against his ears, and the sky, mottled pink and purple above, even the fae in pursuit behind them and the terse, fearful shouts of his team: all of it was right and good. They had lost the Dowager, and that was terrible, but somehow it was right, too. Nothing gained if nothing lost.

"Forward to the Tree!" he said, and they surged, Arkansite above them, a sword in her hand.

Arthur cut the strings of two more many-limbed fae as they approached, hurling his attacks back without accuracy or care. They were there, finally.

He was there.

"Defensive shell!" he called out, signaling the only real tactic they'd all practiced together.

Twenty yards away from the Tree, the team of six formed up in a rough arc, and WarSpeaker used her primacy to congeal the air before her into a thick, opaque, oily substance—something like glass but not, the scientists and mathematicians at the Fencing Bureau said. Whatever it was, it would keep the fae out and the team in.

People would write about this. They would sing songs and make movies and comic books about what was to happen. Poets and playwrights and movie stars would imagine what it was like to be him in this moment, the chattering, maddened fae held behind that slick wall, his team exhausted and frightened, and all of it so much background noise to the true spectacle—Arthur Miracle and the door.

They would give him a monologue, but he said almost nothing.

They would show him looking around to check in on his people, but he did not.

They would show his thoughts scattered or ruminative, but he did not think.

Arthur whistled again, another of his mother's favorite tunes—Hank Williams wailing out "Hey, Good Lookin'"—and ripped the Tree apart.

It did not puff and it did not fuzz. There was no soft, idyllic haze of un-mattering that clouded the air around the branches.

A deep-bone bass tone exploded out from the gash he made in the huge trunk. Shards of the Tree accompanied the wave of harsh, wide sound, as if carried by it, and Arthur watched in silent, stupefied glory as a lance of palimpsest white, big around as his arm and twice his height, caught Skyward Silas low in the abdomen. Another blur of shrapnel collided with WarSpeaker and sent her flying into the barricade of her own making—which shattered with a sound sharp and awful.

The team members were screaming, screaming, screaming, but their voices were tiny boats on the deep, tempestuous waters of that bass knell. Fae chattered and unnatural magics swirled in the air around him, but Arthur looked through his door in reality's skin and saw.

Another world, disordered and strange. A sky burning a pale, angry yellow. Great stretches of thin, flimsy clouds that turned the gargantuan creatures flying there into horrifying outlines. Hills topped with cairns of dark red stones. Trees that leaned together into tight speys, their leafy heads slamming against one another in a fury of bark and wood.

And straight ahead, a castle on a hill.

"I am here," Arthur said, walking forward through the violence and chaos, barely feeling the ground beneath his feet. "I have come."

Someone is in that castle, he thought. *There is someone there on the battlement, awaiting me. I am expected. She is expecting me.*

Arthur Miracle walked through the Threshold Tree, which knit closed behind him, once again whole and perfect and strange.

PART 1

Love's Opposite and Equal Number

Chapter 1

In the House of Always Giving, black-clad mourners stood from their pews and cast teary glances at the shrouded figure in the pine box before them. A man in priest's robes stood on the dais nearby, and words of exhortation and hope sprang from his lips in well-practiced rhythms. Organ music rose and fell, and a choir, packed tight on the stone risers behind the altar, sang hymns to the Queen Beyond and Her endless, mysterious grace.

In a pew at the back of the sanctuary, Calidore stayed seated and did not sing. He looked occasionally at the people standing and weeping, their faces distorted by memory's fogged lens, but always he returned to the casket and the man inside it.

His father. Cliff. Dead of a heart attack.

Cal thought again of his last conversation with his dad, troubling at the memory like a kid unable to let alone a scabbed-over cut, impeding the healing process and rewarding himself with low, stinging pain.

It had been months since that last interaction, and though he'd tried each day to wring meaning from their conversation, Cal had come up empty each time. Short and stilted, they'd mostly talked about small things: the weather and Cliff's work, baseball and Minnesota road work.

But his father had asked about Winnie, and through their life-long estrangement, Cal had loved him a little for that.

Cal smiled at the sweet and sharp lines of the memory, his father's voice crackling over the phone. He'd been driving at the time, heading out to another roofing job. "And how's Winn?" he'd asked. "Is she liking kindergarten?"

Never mind that she was in first grade. And never mind that she never went by Winn. It was Winnie or, when she was in trouble, *Winnifred*

Maude. Cal didn't care about that. His father was trying, in his own misguided way, to be there, and that was something. Not a lot, but not nothing.

"I can't help thinking your dad would've hated all this pomp and nonsense," Evangeline whispered from beside him. She wore a black dress with long sleeves and a scarf that, though warm inside the building, she had not taken off. It almost covered up her tattoos; only a few numbers showed high on her neck, rising from and then falling below the ruffle of the scarf's fabric.

Cal nodded at that. He wore a suit that didn't fit him very well anymore. The waist cut in painfully against his hips, and the fabric around his thighs was uncomfortably tight. But it was black and somber, and he hadn't had the time or desire to find a better-fitting one.

The collar of the white shirt beneath the suit coat covered his own inky numerals, the thorny fives and stentorian sevens that ran along the skin of his neck, the span of his chest, up and down his sides and arms and legs, curving and curling along the length of his body.

"Our dear friend Cliff went too early," the high priest was saying. He spoke with unnatural pauses between his words, as though he was reciting the thick and sweet syllables of poetry to an adoring, attentive audience. And perhaps he was, because some of those in the congregation responded with murmurs of approval and gentle *hmm*s of approbation.

"Too early for one so young, yes," he continued, his voice rolling out. "And too early for a Sylvan! Thirteen days, my friends, my fellows, my *folk*! Thirteen days from today, the autumnal equinox will be upon us, a special day for the world, historic and important, but for such as we? For those who walk under our Queen's steady and unerring gaze in this place, the fall equinox represents our chance at *salvation*!"

Spittle exploded in flecks as he spoke that last word, and Cal grimaced in disgust.

"Our friend Cliff died as he lived: human," the Priest said, turning this into something sad, almost disappointing. "But had he lived until the equinox—had his battered, weary heart taken him to that day of salvation, he would instead have risen as one of the Queen's chosen few and taken his holy place in Her court. We, all of us here, whether you come to this place as a believer in the Faerie Queen's light or have not yet found your way to Her—we all know the truth of the autumnal equinox. Those who die do not truly die but persist, transformed into the Blessed!"

He smiled out at them. But there was nothing Blessed about what people turned into, nothing holy or beautiful. Not Blessed but *Wretched*, Cal thought, feeling a shot of gratefulness that his father's heart had given out before the equinox.

"Reborn as fae," the Priest continued. "Some may fear these transformations, and some among us may even hate such changes." The man's eyes moved around the congregation, and did they move to the shadowy back where Cal and Evangeline sat? Did they linger there for a moment?

"But we here know this simple exchange—a human life into a faerie one—for the rapturous thing it is! Our Queen takes all souls that pass from this earth, but those who pass on the equinox are especially favored with a new, charmed life, and we are saddened, deeply so, that our friend and brother Cliff, who so labored for the Queen's goodness in his human life, did not achieve that dream of an equinox rebirth."

Cal ground his teeth and closed his eyes, wishing he were anywhere but there, listening to anything but this fool priest babble about things he didn't understand.

"Daddy," a small voice said, and Cal looked down to the floor, where Winnie sat, a coloring book in her lap and a fistful of crayons held in one hand. Her eyes, brown and beautiful and wide, held his with serious import. "Look."

It was a big sanctuary—ostentatiously so, Cal would have said—and the high priest was braying loudly to the half-filled room about Her grace and Her goodness, so Cal wasn't worried about making a scene or Winnie drawing attention.

He slid slightly sideways on the smooth wood of the bench and came face-to-face with Winnie, who showed him the picture she'd been working on: a centaur holding up a bouquet of flowers.

"It's for Grandpa," she said.

"It's really nice," Cal said, giving her shoulder a squeeze and planting a kiss on her forehead. "He would have loved it."

"Yeah," Winnie said, her voice sad. As she returned to coloring, she leaned her head into the back of the unoccupied pew in front of them, the wood of which was scuffed and scratched and had the half-erased but still visible hieroglyphics from a child bored in church. When they'd arrived that morning for the service, Winnie had immediately dropped to the floor and said, "It's a perfect little cave for me."

Cal wished he could fit down there, too, but he didn't think the fabric of his pants or the middle-age ache in his hips would allow for it. Instead, he settled on leaning forward and pressing his forehead firmly into the pew ahead, his eyes closed.

"Okay?" Evangeline asked, putting a hand on his shoulder, pitching her voice low.

"Yeah," Cal said, his head still down. "Just, you know." He gestured around, and Evangeline gave him another pat on the back.

"And now," the high priest, whose name was Hamp or Harl or something like that, said, his voice ringing off the stone arches and marbled plinths of the space, "we say goodbye to our good friend and faithful brother, Cliff. Never forget, dear friends . . ."

He paused, and even Cal raised his head, his eyes taking a long moment to focus on the colorfully robed man up at the altar, the smooth cream of the fabric over his chest emblazoned with the image of a hand stretching out, presumably in friendship, though Cal had always found it hostile.

"Our Queen has a wrath like the sea in a storm," the High Priest said, his smile grubby and greasy. "But She has a grace like the sky and the sun, and it is waiting there for you and for me."

The singers behind him took their cue and started up a tune as four men in less-garish robes came forward to heft the pine box with Cal's father in it.

"Our *Queen*? Oh, fuck off," Cal muttered, clasping his hands tight in his lap and looking down at the floor.

"Yeah, fuck off," Winnie echoed from below.

"*Winnifred*," Evangeline whispered, frowning down at their daughter. Their policy on swearing for Winnie was simple: swear words were not verboten but should be used with care and, in general, were probably best deployed in the safety of their home.

"But Dad—" Winnie began before quieting under her mother's glare.

"You're right, sweets," Cal said, straightening up and nodding to her. "I shouldn't have said that. My fault."

"We invite you all to join us at Brookside Rush Cemetery for the interring of Cliff," the high priest said as the pine box exited stage left, heading for whatever hearse the Sylvans used to cart their dead. The room had begun to fill with the soft sounds of quiet, respectful chatter.

Cal spotted relatives he hadn't seen or spoken to in years, maybe decades for some of them.

"Do you want to go to the cemetery?" Evangeline asked. People had begun to filter past them in somber ones and twos, casting curious looks their way but not stopping to talk.

"I don't know," Cal said, watching his father's pine box until it was gone from the room, carried through a set of tall oaken double doors. "I guess so."

Evangeline looked past Cal to the man sitting a pew over from them. His suit, like the two other government agents waiting outside in the car, was a nondescript but appropriate grey. He'd had to remove the gun and earpiece he normally wore, but Aleph looked plenty intimidating still for those who could see past the calm, serene demeanor he wore like a mask.

He sat close enough to intercede should anything go wrong, but far enough away to give at least the illusion of privacy.

Now, though, he caught Evangeline's eye and nodded when she said, "We'll head to the cemetery." He stood and walked to the large archway that led into the sanctuary, stopping briefly at the end of his pew to smile and let a few tearful mourners pass him by. Cal was sure one of those people was his great-uncle Roy, a man who had sat across from him at the dinner table for many holidays, laughing and telling a young Cal inappropriate jokes.

Great-uncle Roy, much aged, looked at Cal with the barest flicker of recognition before it disappeared and he moved on, a slight wrinkle of confusion creasing his liver-spotted brow.

Did he see the murky shapes of those same memories? Could he hear the boy Cal had been laughing at his jokes? Could he even hold on to that slippery fact that Cliff had had a son, or had the government's memory work loosed too many stones in the part of his mind where Cal had once lived?

They waited to leave until the room had safely cleared, with only a few stragglers hanging around the altar or clustered in the seats. Winnie had packed her coloring supplies in a tie-dyed canvas bag and was humming a song to herself as she walked, her hand small and warm in Cal's.

"You're the fencers, right?" It was the same voice of song and sermon from the last hour, though gone was the projected grandiosity with which the high priest had spoken. Cal turned to find the man—*Harp*, he remembered now—standing in the aisle, hands folded across his belly in what he almost certainly imagined to be a wise, elevated pose.

Beside him, Cal felt Aleph step closer, his attention focusing on the robed man before them.

"We are," Evangeline said before Cal could speak. "But we're just here today as family."

Harp offered them a wide, magnanimous smile.

"I understand. Of course. We appreciated the government's forewarning about your attendance today." He turned that smile on Cal. "Your father would have been very happy to see you here, fencer Calidore."

Cal nodded but didn't trust himself to speak.

"It was a really lovely service," Evangeline said, gesturing around at the soaring sanctuary, at the high, arched ceilings and the polished columns. "And you have a beautiful building."

"Is this your first time in our House of Always Giving?" Harp asked, feigning genteel surprise. He, along with his army of concealed surveillance cameras and always-monitored points of entry, knew damn well they had never been in there before. Almost no government agent of any kind had.

"Sure is," Cal said, hating the flippant, childish lilt of his voice.

A trio of women passed by, their appraising glances taking in Cal, Evangeline, Aleph, and Winnie. One by one, they touched gloved hands to Harp's elbow or shoulder or arm, whispering "A wonderful message" and "He would have loved it" and, in the case of the final woman, "Such a shame—he was so close."

Harp took all of this with that same knowing smile—a *smirk*, Cal decided, *an ugly smirk*—and a slow nod.

Cal let his eyes drift up to really take in this place where his father had spent so many of his later days.

Above the altar, set high into the otherwise-unbroken stone of the wall, was a triptych of stained-glass windows, aglow with the late morning's light and rapturous with color. The first and third were alive with the spread of a huge, white tree, its myriad limbs hosting leaves in autumnal finery, each red and goldenrod made doubly beautiful by the sun's illumination.

In the center, dominating the largest of the three windows, was the deity of the fools who worshipped in the House of Always Giving, the deity of Cal's father who, because his heart attack took him just a few weeks early, he would never get to meet.

The Faerie Queen.

The skeptics, though, had another name for her—the Bloodless Queen—and it was a name they imprisoned in a *maybe*, an unproven possibility. They gave papers and talks and wrote books on the Bloodless Queen *theory*.

In the window's confines, the Bloodless Queen might have been any character from western mythology. Her skin was the same pale white as the Threshold Tree rendered to her right and left, but her own raiment was an earthy, dark green with lines of dark black that repelled the sunlight and counterpoints of brilliant gold that shone.

Her mace, held up beside her head in a position that someone had clearly cribbed from an ancient portrait of Zeus, glittered with shards of many colors. Her other hand, free and empty, extended forward, the mirror image of the stitching on the front of Harp's robes.

Cal stared into her sunlit eyes, one a forest green and the other a bright, seafoam blue, and felt a smug vindictiveness wash over him at the thought that even if this place's whole mythology were true, even if there were some magical fae queen on the other side of the Harbors turning everyone who died on the autumn equinox into a murderous faerie— even if that nonsense were true, she—She—hadn't gotten Cal's father.

"We ought to be going," Evangeline said, taking the opportunity to move toward the exit. She pulled on Cal's arm, and he turned away from the Bloodless Queen's stern, stoic gaze.

"Your father will be missed around here," Harp said behind them, and Cal couldn't stop himself from turning. Harp was looking at him, that smile back on his badly tanned face. "He was a wonderful member of our community. And he talked about you betimes. When he could remember you, of course."

"*Betimes?*" Cal asked, his voice a higher, louder pitch than he wanted.

Harp wiped away a droplet of sweat emerging from the carefully styled hair at one temple.

"It means *occasionally*," he said, chuckling.

"I know what it means," Cal snapped. Nearby, Aleph tensed, a creature in the deep grass preparing to strike. But before Cal could say more, and before Aleph could intercede, Winnie spoke.

"I like your dress." She was holding Evangeline's hand now, the tie-dye bag slung over one shoulder. She'd worn her headband with the cat ears for the day, so her normally messy locks of brown hair were somewhat restrained.

"Oh. Well. Thank you very much," Harp said, that smarmy smile disappearing for a brief moment before he put hands to knees and bent to grin at Winnie. "But these are actually my *robes*." He drew the word out, giving it the importance of a new parent speaking the name of their child aloud for the first time.

"It looks like a dress," Winnie said, running one hand idly in circles across her stomach. "It's pretty, but I think it should be even prettier."

"These *robes*," Harp said, emphasizing the word again, "are actually quite special and very old. They're called folk finery, named after the citizens of our fair queen."

More likely, they were robes stolen in design from early Catholic priests and simply reimagined with faeries in mind. Swirls of leaves were stitched into the weird poncho/cape thing covering Harp's broad shoulders, and along the edges of this and other articles of his clothing were gold-threaded symbols that Cal didn't recognize but looked as though they might have been found in wingdings. But swap those symbols out for crosses and make that outstretched hand on his chest into some

Christian image, and Harp could have been a Catholic just finished with mass and thinking about lunch.

Hard to come up with a new aesthetic for a religion when you don't invent it until the 1980s, Cal supposed.

"They don't look so old," Winnie said, and Cal loved her for that skeptical curve of one eyebrow, for that scrunching of one side of her face, and for her childlike willingness to call bullshit on bullshit. "They don't even have any stains or anything."

"We really should be going," Evangeline said again, tugging on Winnie's arm. "Thank you for a very nice service."

Cal followed them, walking beside Aleph and keeping his eyes forward, even when Harp spoke again.

"A happy autumn to you, fencers," he called from the sanctuary. "And a happy equinox."

The cemetery sprawled, its gentle hills toothed with tombstones, a few of the slabs garlanded with the gifts of mourners. Autumn sunlight lit the grass and caught the leaves, turning fall's palette fiery and bright.

To Cal, it looked sad. A place to be forgotten.

"Do you want to talk to any of them?" Evangeline asked.

"I don't think I do," Cal said, looking over at the assembled swarm of his family, most of them estranged, a few barely recognizable.

Cousin Todd, bald now and sluicing a glob of spit into a repurposed pop bottle, the divot of tobacco pushing out his lower lip. Grandpa Lawrence, still living somehow, his every feature the same but shrunken, as though he were being slowly dried out by life and would someday collapse in on himself. Aunt Delilah, in whose crushing hugs even a very young Calidore had recognized the thick waft of alcohol.

Relatives from a family he had long since left behind stood around the newest, brightest tombstone in the cemetery, the letters looking as though they had been milled just that morning, every edge crisp and clean. Cal wondered briefly how it would feel to run his fingers along those letters. Were the edges sharp enough to cut? And if they were, how long until time and the movement of the seasons wore them down to smoothness?

"That's all right," Evangeline said, nodding and looking down at Winnie standing between the two of them. "We don't mind just hanging out right here, do we, sweets?"

Winnie looked up at her parents and shook her head. She had never met any of her father's relatives save one, the man settling into his forever rest below the tombstone she would have liked to examine had it not been in the middle of that pack of strangers. She, too, thought of running her fingers along the letters recessed into the stone, wanting to feel the smooth runnels and examine the neat edges.

"Thanks," Calidore said, putting an arm around his daughter and pulling her close for a moment. He felt again the worry that they should not have brought Winnie to this—funerals were no fun for anyone, kids especially, and she hadn't even known her grandfather that well. A few Christmases and the sporadically remembered birthday had been the sum of her visits with him.

Instead, he had been present in her life as a series of toys given at those occasions—a little car that she'd used from age one to the present, age almost seven; a stuffed dog she still slept with and had tucked under one arm now after insisting Grandpa Cliff would have wanted her to bring it; a box of dominoes that had once been a thousand strong and had become, with time, closer to 975 or so.

Calidore kicked at a loose tuft of weeds, thinking back over his own broken relationship with "Grandpa Cliff," waiting for the memories of his absent father, the harsh words they'd exchanged throughout the years, the missed performances and games, the calls that didn't come and the support that could never be counted on—waiting for any of it, or maybe all of it, to swell inside him and bring the tears he'd been waiting for all day, all week, since the phone call from his estranged aunt telling him that his father had died and yes it was terrible and you never know when the Lord will take one of His children home and who could have seen a heart attack coming so young and would he come to the funeral and you know, honey, how much your dad loved you, don't you?

"I'm going to climb that tree," Winnie said, squinting off at a small maple tree growing up the hill a little ways away. She passed her cat-ear headband to Cal. Despite being almost seven, Winnie had inherited and then perfected the look that Evangeline so often wore: curmudgeonly, vaguely grumpy, critical. Her eyebrows, like her mother's, formed truculent lines above bright brown eyes, which she directed toward the maple tree, its leaves a shower of crimson and orange. "Is that okay?"

"Sure, sweetie," Evangeline said. "Just be careful, yeah?"

Aleph moved to stay between Winnie and her parents, his steps and posture so casual and at ease that he might have been just another mourner, though he'd regained his earpiece and gun since the service.

The government protected its assets, and it had few assets worth more than Calidore and Evangeline.

"I didn't realize your dad was so active in that church," Evangeline said, her eyes, like Cal's, following Winnie's run up to the tree, her careful consideration of its height and girth, and her ungainly attempts to climb it.

Cal nodded, thinking again of Harp's smile and his familiarity with Cliff. He wanted to hate the high priest, with his faux-regal rags and his talk of the Queen beyond the fence. But he couldn't help but feel a creeping guilt about the fact that this man, robes and all, had been there with and for Cal's father when Cal himself hadn't. Harp had known his dad, had even said things about him during the service that had surprised Cal. Cliff had been saving for a boat, had started volunteering at the food bank, had recently been on an airplane for the first time in his life—and Cal hadn't known any of it.

"I never really heard him talk much about being a Sylvan," Evangeline said.

"Me neither." Cal spun his wedding ring—iron, of course—around on his finger, feeling the gentle tug as the metal caught and released against his sweaty skin. "I didn't really know anything about him, I guess."

Evangeline stepped closer, entwining one of her arms with his.

A squawk of excitement rang out from the tree, and both parents looked up to see Winnie, her dark grey dress caught on five or six different branches, fabric stretching or already torn. She waved at her parents, hand emerging from the autumnal shroud of the leaves.

"Do you think we've stayed long enough?" Cal asked, waving back at the tiny figure in the tree.

"Sure. Yeah." Evangeline looked at her watch, an intricate thing made of various metals carefully interwoven. "Do you want to go over there at all? Say goodbye?"

The small crowd around the tombstone had begun to scatter, though slowly. Uncles and aunts, cousins and siblings, greats- and steps- and in-laws nodding conversations to a close as they stepped away, the grave that held their mournful prayers and the remains of Cal's father now pushing them back to their homes and jobs, their lives, which would go on.

"Outside of you and Winnie, he was the only one here I actually might have wanted to talk to," Cal said, shaking his head. Between the slacks- and dress-covered legs beginning to disperse, he could see the small tombstone, the flecked crystals of the stone glowing in the caught sunlight. "I can just imagine him standing here, jeans and a button-up shirt, hair slicked back, pissed at having died so close to his holy day."

Cal hadn't stopped thinking about those final moments of his father's life, wondering if his old man had been aware enough to realize he was dying less than two weeks before the equinox, less than two weeks before that "sacred time."

Less than two weeks before the day when dying meant something different, something stranger.

Evangeline, who understood silence and its uses, leaned close and wrapped an arm around Cal.

"Momma! Daddy!" Winnie was hanging upside down this time, her knees bent around a low-slung branch, hair a waterfall of light brown curls cascading endlessly toward the thick, well-tended grass below her.

Aleph, perhaps judging the risk as having decreased significantly with Winnie's increased proximity to the ground, had stepped away and was looking now at the assembled congregation of mourners.

"Let's just get her and go," Cal said, leaning into Evangeline before setting off toward their upside-down daughter. "I haven't talked to most of those people in ten or fifteen years. I'm not going to start now."

Winnie's caws of laughter as her parents retrieved her from the tree seemed sacrilegious in the relative quiet of the cemetery, but Cal felt his spirits lifted.

"Bad news, Evangeline," Cal said, lifting Winnie up in a hug. "It looks like someone stole our sweet daughter and replaced her with this chimpanzee."

"Oh, no," Evangeline said, "maybe she escaped from the zoo! Should we return her?"

"No!" Winnie shouted.

"I think that would be best," Cal said, nodding seriously at his wife. "Maybe they'll even give us a reward. I—"

"You're Cliff's boy, aren't you?"

Cal looked up, his breath catching suddenly at the sound of that voice, so familiar. It sounded out from his memory, too, a voice calling him by his former name, the one given to him by his parents. Welcoming the person he had been to Christmas morning or calling to wish him happy birthday.

"I am, yes," Cal said, straightening and smiling at this woman who stood a cautious distance away. She wore a skirt and blouse, both black with small white flowers sewn in a pattern along one side. In her hands, she clutched a dark blue purse, holding it against her chest like a shield.

The effects of the memory work she had undergone were apparent in her uncertain gaze, the curious tilt of her head—the same process that all of Cal's family, and all of Evangeline's, too, had experienced. Where there had once been that young person in their memories, there was now a hazy silhouette, half-remembered moments and experiences, each one stripped of that original name, and as if those few syllables were the cornerstone on which the rest of the memory depended, most everything else had fallen apart, too.

"You used to love watermelon," the woman said, squinting up and away at the sky for a moment as she grasped at memory, a deep-sea diver using the last of her oxygen to retrieve a bit of glinting treasure half-seen in the black muck at the bottom. "Is that right?"

She was old, much older than the last time Cal had seen her, hands threaded with bruise-colored veins, the stoop and slope of her shoulders more pronounced.

Cal nodded, his eyes flicking for a moment to Aleph, who had walked with casual silence behind the woman, standing close enough to intervene should he need to.

"Cliff's boy," the woman said to herself, eyeing Cal. "Which makes me . . ."

"My grandmother," Cal said quietly.

Winnie watched the whole of this exchange with a curious stillness, something she had learned very young. Her parents had strange jobs and spoke with strange people, and she was less likely to be sent off to her room or passed to a babysitter or handler if she stayed quiet, part of the background, watching and listening.

"Your grandmother," the woman said, nodding. She took a cautious step forward, and then another. Cal's grandma held out a hand to Evangeline, who took it. "Hello, dear. I don't think we've met. I'm Doreen, Cliff's mother."

"It's nice to meet you. I'm so sorry for your loss."

"Thank you." Doreen smiled, and took a moment to wipe at a fresh wave of tears, before saying, "And who is this little pumpkin?"

Winnie took this moment to bury her head in her father's shoulder, at once aglow with and afraid of the attention from this new person.

"This is Winnie. Winnifred," Cal said, turning so a single shy eye was visible.

Doreen waved a hand and said, "Hello, little Winnie. It's very nice to meet you. I'm your great-grandma."

A twist of doubt pulled at Doreen's face, and she looked up at Cal and Evangeline.

"Is Winnifred her real name?" Doreen asked, lowering her voice and tipping her chin up as if she could cast the words up and over Winnie's ears.

"Yes," Cal said, offering a small, sympathetic smile. "They only do the new names and memory work for fencers." He brushed a hand along Winnie's arm, empty of the thorny, chaotic numbers that would have covered her skin had she been a fencer like her parents.

"It's funny," Doreen said, almost wistful. "I have these foggy half-memories of you as a boy, but I can't remember your name. That's no surprise, of course, but I can't even remember what they did to me to make me forget. And when I try to reach for those memories, it feels like walking into a fog."

Cal felt a surge of gratitude for this conversation, which existed outside of that other one, his father's death. This, hard and strange as it might be, was a distraction from that tombstone and the man—cremated, of course—beneath it.

"I'm sorry about the lingering effects; they can be unpleasant," Cal said, his face softening into one he'd practiced many times in the trainings he and the others had gone through. The Bureau offered a set of guidelines for fencers interacting with the world around them: Be kind but slightly disengaged. Apologize for the continued effects of memory work but not for the central act. Do not make physical contact. Do not proactively discuss the lost name. If you encounter protests, be sympathetic but distant. Deescalate, and aim for, if not acceptance, at least silence. "And I'm sorry about your loss."

"*Our* loss," Cal's grandmother said, her voice going harsh and cold.

Aleph had stepped closer, his feet silent on the thick grass. Though he continued to look around the graveyard with what seemed to be casual disinterest, his hands hung loose and ready at his sides, prepared should this interaction turn ugly. He spoke a quiet word, inaudible over the wind and Doreen's heavy breathing, and the agents at the car a few hundred yards away stood suddenly at attention, their heads swiveling in the direction of their charges, their assets.

"You're right," Cal said, turning his body just slightly away from Doreen to shield Winnie. "I'm going to miss him."

A few people who might have been Cal's cousins were walking back to their cars and looked over at Doreen and these strangers with curious glances, perhaps remembering that hushed-up fact that Cliff had had a son—still did, maybe—and he was one of those fencers. But that bit of knowledge grew murky and slippery, sliding from memory as easily as a slip of silk from numbed fingers, and they continued their walk, muttering about the loss, what a loss, and feeling secretly grateful that they were leaving the quiet, oppressive silence of this cemetery.

"You're going to miss him," Doreen said, looking from Cal to Evangeline to Winnie, eyes hard and wet. Her thin lips trembled as she worked to calm herself.

All morning, they had heard the same words passed back and forth—every speaker at the church, even Harp, and every mourner walking the paths between the pews, everyone at the cemetery—all of them chewing on and spitting out the bits of overused comfort. *What a sad day. I can't believe he's gone. So soon. Such a shock. I don't even know what to say.*

Speaker after speaker, mourner after mourner overheard as they passed that final pew on the right, used the same language, all of it banal, all of it empty save for that one bit of truth no one could say: *There is nothing where he used to be.*

"I'm sorry," Cal said again, reaching for but unable to actually say any more of that stale language.

"I'm sorry too," Winnie said, peering around Cal's shoulder at her great-grandmother, voice tiny and unsure.

"Oh, sweetie," Evangeline said, leaning close and putting a hand on Winnie's back.

Doreen pulled in a ragged breath, stifling a sob. She smiled at Winnie before looking back over her shoulder at the tombstone, the last bit of her son left on the earth.

Perhaps she thought of Harp's message and his sadness about the timing of Cliff's death. Perhaps she, too, wondered what might have been if he'd waited a few more days to die. Perhaps she thought of her son, dying instead on the fall equinox, his pock-marked skin grown smooth and clean in death, his knees no longer popping and creaking with effort as he ran and leapt, his wide mouth echoing all the while that uncanny, awful laugh of the Wretched.

For Cal and Evangeline, who heard that noise each autumn and thought of it every other day of the year, it was no romantic thing to imagine it, no religious exultation to hope for.

After the keys turned in 1987, after the Reagans and that damn book, after the War of the Wretched and the treaties, after the discoveries of the folklorists and mathematicians, the world's governments, its systems, and its people had to contend with a simple truth, unbearable and strange: those who died on the autumnal equinox did not truly die.

A man in a car crash would rise from the wreckage, miraculously unhurt, it seemed. A cancer victim whose body had let go would find herself standing with strange strength suddenly, her skin taking on a healthy glow for the first time in months, perhaps years.

Those who might have died of old age or accidents, disease or sickness—a father who had smoked and drunk and eaten himself into a heart attack's dream—would not die but continue on. The basic processes of their bodies stilled and stopped and yet they endured, growing strong and strange, their minds and spirits changing. Their eye color would shift into the uncanny grey of some infants' eyes before the color has settled on brown or blue or green.

The Blessed, some—fools like Harp and his congregation—called these equinox dead.

The Wretched, those who understood the horrors they might cause called them.

Fae, the folklorists would determine in the early nineties.

And their laughter as they grew more and more curious, more and more fae, less and less human, would ring out on the streets and in the fields on the equinox, those days when the world stayed inside and fencers like Calidore and Evangeline worked.

Perhaps that laughter—some romanticized, lionized version of it, watered down and made palatable by people who did not go out on the equinox—was in Doreen's mind as she looked at her son's gravestone.

Perhaps she wished he could have waited to die so that he might have gone on, gone strange, endured.

"I'm sorry again," Cal said, speaking to his grandmother's back. "We need to get going."

He set off toward the car, not waiting to hear her reply if she had one, Evangeline next to him and Winnie held against his chest. She was almost seven and too big to carry like a child anymore, but he held her anyway, needing her strength much more than she needed his.

Behind them, Doreen said something, her voice high and distressed.

"Just keep walking," Evangeline said, her voice calm, as it always was in moments of tension and conflict.

All around them, the wind sang through the trees and against the jagged, uneven stones of the memorials. To Cal, it sounded like rest.

A History of Fences and Fae by AK Senga, PhD

Published in 2027 by University of Minnesota Majestic Press
Excerpt from Introduction: "Nancy Reagan, Ulysses H. Wright,
and *The Last Thylacine*"

This story has many beginnings.

Here is one: Alexander Grothendieck was born in 1928, became one of the world's best mathematicians early in his life, and in 1970, with several of his friends, formed a radical environmentalist group called Survivre et Vivre. This group, after little more than a year, wrote the book that would destroy modern civilization.

Another: In 1983, First Lady Nancy Reagan was given Survivre et Vivre's book and read it. The next week, she shared it with her husband. The following year, the First Lady accompanied her husband on a historic diplomatic visit to China. While there, she joined Paramount Leader Deng Xiaoping in a closed-to-press meeting not listed on any official itinerary or schedule. In that meeting, Nancy Reagan gave the book to the paramount leader, who read it and shortly thereafter passed it to China's president, Li Xiannian.

And one more: In 1984, after reading a book his wife shared with him, Ronald Reagan became a crusader for environmental issues such as biodiversity loss, carbon emissions, and native-habitat preservation. This man, who had once said of the giant redwoods native to his state of California, "If you've looked at a hundred thousand acres or so of trees—you know, a tree is a tree; how many more do you need to look at," surprised the world when he made it his administration's key objective to "save and protect the world's natural resources and environmental splendor." More surprising was his coordination with leaders from China, the then–Soviet Union, Japan, Germany, England, and several more nations to introduce the Harbors Act of 1985, which set aside half of the Earth for these goals of environmental preservation and restoration. The larger countries able to set aside their land for these Harbors did. Legislation thought impractical and impossible passed through government chambers with baffling ease and concerning speed. Political journalists and policy wonks, government watchdogs and smaller allied nations watched with growing alarm as the world's largest countries united with startling coordination behind the Harbors Act, freely giving up their natural resources for the abstract goals of biodiversity and climate.

What could turn the leaders of the world into sudden environmentalists and bring about international cooperation and coordination on a scale previously thought impossible?

The book was *The Last Thylacine*, a slim volume of 107 pages written, typed, and printed by the members of Survivre et Vivre, though scholarship suggests Grothendieck himself was the true driving force behind the project. The cover featured a cartoonish Earth split in half, one side sprouting towering skyscrapers and sleek homes, the other side gone wild, with massive flora tangling its surface and rising high, obscuring glimpses of animals and birds and bugs of all kinds. Due to printing costs and internal disagreements among the group, only a handful of copies were ever produced.

"Half for us, and half for them," the cover copy said, offering a simplistic articulation of the group's central argument, namely that rates of biodiversity loss and rampant deforestation were existential threats to all that was good on the planet, and the only real way to combat these threats was to let Earth heal itself by giving half of the land back to nature.

The United States created ten Harbors in support of this effort, most masses of land crossing one and sometimes two state lines. The Midwest Harbor, for instance, a pivotal setting for later sections of this text, is a swath of land that includes some of western Minnesota, southern North

Dakota, and northern South Dakota. In all, the US Harbors were created by fencing off huge portions of Idaho, Wyoming, Minnesota, the Dakotas, Texas, New Mexico, Alaska, and California—and smaller portions of Nevada, Mississippi, Alabama, Florida, and New England. In all, just over two million square miles' worth of Harbors were designated and fenced off in the United States between 1985 and 1987. The Reagan administration cannibalized national and state parks and, when necessary, relocated families and businesses, often to the consternation of ranking members of his own party—consternation that quickly quieted after private meetings with the President in which a certain small book was passed around.

And on September 23rd, 1987—the autumnal equinox—the countries of the world finished their work on the fences that outlined their Harbors. Like each time zone celebrating the New Year in sequence, these countries locked the gates of their Harbors at midnight, ringing in autumn with the sound of keys turning and the joyous shouts of the revelers and partygoers.

Of course, once the deaths began, those joyous shouts went quiet.

Chapter 2

The next morning began, as always, with riddles.

Winnie rose before the sun, walking with solemn steps into her parents' room. Accompanying her was Tennyson, the three-year-old Landseer Newfoundland. Winnie had a hand buried up past the wrist in Tennyson's black-and-white fur. The sound of their steps—hers a soft whisper and his a louder scratch as long, carefully filed claws pulled and rasped against the carpet—merged into the soaring breaths of Calidore and Evangeline, both still asleep.

"Wait," Winnie whispered to Tennyson as they came alongside the bed. The enormous dog, who, standing on all fours, rose to Winnie's shoulders and who, at last weigh-in, topped out at just north of 165 pounds, dropped into a sit where Winnie pointed and let his tongue loll out, releasing a wave of ropy slobber into the scruff of fur around his neck and toward the ground. He watched the slender, wiry girl creep toward her parents with steady, unfaltering love.

This was their routine, and Tennyson played his part with commitment. His dog bed lay at the foot of Winnie's bed, so he woke with her each morning, let her lead him to the parents' room, and waited while she received her instructions. When she raced about the house with excitement, he would be there with her. When she found her prize, he would be there to sound a single, bass-thump bark in celebration.

Winnie stepped around the dirty clothes dropped on the floor and spared a glance at the crossed swords hanging from the wall, well out of her reach, the dull metal obscured by the leather straps and sheaths hanging around and in front of them. Those swords meant work to Winnie, meant her parents going off to do the jobs everyone talked about sideways around her, as if they thought she couldn't or wouldn't understand. Those blades meant the one day each year when her parents were gone from the beginning of one bedtime to the end of the next.

But right now was still the time before the machinery of the day moved, before schedules and tasks emerged to set people into motion.

Even at six, Winnie understood that these pockets of time were precious. She stepped closer to her father, his arm flung out and hanging just off the bed. Behind him, her mother was a series of low hills swathed in shadow.

Winnie shivered in anticipation.

"Secret Agent Dawnlove reporting for her mission," Winnie said, and she listened to the pleasing change in her parents' breathing as they woke, the stretching groans and quaking of the bed as they both turned to her.

"You've returned again, Agent Dawnlove?" Cal flicked on a bedside light and blinked at his daughter through eyes smeared with sleep.

"I thought your last mission would have been too much for you," Evangeline added, sitting up and pushing glasses onto her face.

"No mission is too great for me," Winnie-Secret-Agent-Dawnlove said. When she'd first found out that her parents had different names from the ones they were born with, names that they had picked out earlier in their lives to hide their true names from the fae and the world, Winnie had demanded to choose her own, one that would let her "be a powerful secret hero just like Momma and Daddy." She'd started with Sky and then moved to All Things, and then Bright Heart. Dawnlove was the most recent iteration. Cal and Evangeline had not told her that, for fencers, once a new name was chosen, it could never be changed.

"I never doubted, Agent Dawnlove," Cal said, muffling a yawn with the back of one hand. He gestured to the bedside table, a government-issued piece made of light-colored wood and sporting polished iron handles on the drawers. Atop it, beside Cal's glasses and a half-full glass of water that said *It's beginning to look a lot like Christmas!* on it, lay an envelope bearing only the words *top secret* in dark green ink.

Winnie wore a grey onesie with an attached black-and-gold tutu—an outfit she would change out of before school, but one she started each day in. Clip-on purple earrings, three on her right ear and none on her left, were a new addition.

"Your task this morning, Agent Dawnlove," Evangeline said, leaning over Cal and fixing her daughter with a stern, calculating gaze, "can be found in this cryptic message sent to our agency from beyond the known worlds. Solve it, if you can."

Solemn and resolute, Winnie took the envelope and removed the single sheet of paper inside, which bore more writing in that same green ink.

Every night before bed, Cal and Evangeline put together a new riddle or set of clues or puzzle for Winnie, ending their day with a promise to the next.

With trouble on only a few of the words, Winnie read the message.

> "I rest below the watery spout,
> In a place where trash goes in and out,
> Up in the pipes, I'm waiting there,
> For Agent Dawnlove, bright and fair."

Thrice through Winnie read it, shifting from one foot to the other, eyes blinking rapidly as she committed the words to memory and considered their meaning. The next clue, which Evangeline had placed, waited for her below the sink, taped against the drainpipe. Another envelope with another riddle, which would lead her to another and then another, before ultimately depositing her at the location of her breakfast—overnight oats and a small clutch of raspberries—waiting for her in the fridge.

When the answer came to her, Winnie released a shriek of joy and took off, Tennyson a mass of black-and-white fur in her wake. His tail, huge and hairy, waved like a proud flag carried by a standard-bearer, marking Winnie's progress down the hallway and then the stairs, before it was lost to view.

"She's getting better," Cal said, settling back against Evangeline's warmth. "No more *d*'s and *b*'s switched around. And she got *spout* on her first try."

"They've been working on it a lot at school," Evangeline said, nuzzling into Cal's neck and breathing him in. "Mrs. Iverson said she's read all of the books on the green shelf and has been asking about the pink."

Winnie's first-grade classroom was full of classification systems like this: books of increasing difficulty striated in colors, math worksheets catalogued with a hierarchy of animals, one that rewrote kingdom and phylum, genus and species according to new and strange rules. *What could be harder than a lion math problem, Momma?* Winnie had asked over spaghetti dinner one night, the devastating condescension of a first-grader firing behind her words. For Cal and Evangeline, it was like learning the world anew, and they found a kind of joy in it.

Downstairs, that same first-grader loosed another joyous screech, and Cal said, "I guess she found the next one. I wonder if she'll be able to read it herself."

For Cal, who had grown up with books as his best, and often only, friends for most of his life, the looming prospect of Winnie becoming a reader excited him more than he cared to admit. He knew the stories about parents living vicariously through their kids and forcing them to take the same paths the parents themselves had, and he was committed to avoiding that unhappiness.

But he couldn't help imagining their little family of three all sitting on the couch on some rainy day, leaning against one another, each buried in their own book, stopping occasionally to share a funny bit or great line.

His own father hadn't been a reader—had been proud, in fact, to never have finished a whole book in his life—save for the Sylvan Scriptures of his religion, which didn't count, not according to Cal. Growing up, before his tattoos had come on, before he'd gone away to school and before he'd been pulled from his family's memories, Cal had disappointed his father in every way possible: terrible at athletics, uninterested in improving, and happier to spend a day inside reading regardless of which baseball tournament or cookout or street dance was happening.

Cal let out a breath, stopping the pity party in his mind before it really got going.

"How are you doing?" Evangeline pulled away from him enough to look into his eyes. "After yesterday."

After the funeral, they'd come home and ordered pizza, spending the rest of the day watching movies, napping, playing board games, and listening to the Twins game on the radio. Neither Cal nor Evangeline liked baseball much, but Oddry, the head tech at work, was always talking about it, and Cal's father had loved baseball.

Listening to the announcers call the game, idly chatting about swing planes and shift parameters, spin rates and who's been throwing junk, gave Cal the strange sensation of sitting beside his father in the car just as he had as a boy, a book in his hands as his dad smoked cigarette after cigarette and listened to the ball game, pounding a work-hardened hand against the wheel when things went bad and slapping a thigh when they went well.

He'd turned the game off after a few innings. The Twins had been losing by five.

"I'm all right," he said, meeting Evangeline's dark brown eyes. "Really, I am. I'm sad. But I didn't know him all that well, not for a long time."

He sat up and took one of Evangeline's hands in his.

"I think I always hoped we would find each other again in his later years. Have that relationship we didn't when I was a kid. I've been sad since I got the news, but I think I'm most sad about the space inside me where a relationship with my dad should be."

Cal held up a hand, baring the inky numerals crowding his arm from the wrist up.

"That part was empty way before I came into my prime and became a fencer."

Evangeline squeezed his hand and leaned close as a booming bark sounded from downstairs.

"You had a shit father," she said, frowning. "But you're a great dad to Winnie. I'm sorry you didn't have that."

Cal dropped his eyes, feeling them begin to fill with tears, his vision of the white sheets and navy-blue comforter with the silver flower pattern beginning to wobble.

"Thanks," he whispered, just as Winnie raced back up the stairs, her mouth stained the red of raspberries. Tennyson trailed her, flag tail waving, mouth open in a grin.

"I have defeated the riddles and now I'm the master secret agent of the world!" In one hand she still held the spoon she'd used to eat the oats, the silver of the metal flecked with remnants.

"Good work, master secret agent," Cal said, blinking away the tears and giving Evangeline's hand a quick squeeze. "But your most difficult challenge awaits, for you have stepped unthinking into the torture chamber . . . of . . . the Tickle King!"

Cal sprang from the bed, arms going wide to engulf his daughter, who screamed in delight and bright peals of laughter. Tennyson released another subsonic woof before joining the fray, bucking up and down on his hind legs and nosing Cal and Winnie where he could.

Evangeline sat on the bed, smiling, catching and reflecting the joy of her family.

After Winnie left for school—riding in the same bulletproof van she did every school day, Aleph at the wheel and accompanied by another agent who would escort her into the school and stay with her during the day—Cal and Evangeline had a quiet breakfast, her reading the paper and him reading a novel. Tennyson was a snoring mass of fur at their feet.

They stayed that way for a time, caught in the soft spell of the morning, coffee scenting the air and the occasional turned page sounding like a sigh.

Tennyson broke the peace when he sat up abruptly and let out a deep, chesty bark followed by a string of growls that sounded like a motorcycle gang approaching from a few streets over.

Evangeline checked her watch and cocked a curious look at Cal.

"They're early today. It's only 8:15."

Someone knocked at the front door.

Cal marked his place with a slip of paper Winnie had given him—it was a drawing of her wearing enormous sunglasses and pointing at the sun, which wore an angry face—and stood.

"Maybe it's the Jehovah's," he said, smiling, "come to save our souls and rescue the money in our savings."

"Or the Sylvans," she said, laughing. "Come to ask what our plans are for the equinox."

"Don't joke about that," Cal said, but he was chuckling too.

When he opened the steel-reinforced door—its weight impossible to move without the power hinges attached to it—he found not the pleasant faces of proselytizers but the smooth, expressionless face of Aleph, who was in the act of surveying the yard and nearby houses. Tennyson shoved his face between Cal's legs to inspect Aleph, though he immediately dropped to the ground to let the agent pet him, which Aleph obliged for a moment.

"Everything okay with drop off?" Cal asked, stepping back to let the agent into the house. It always felt odd to him, playing through the farce of domestic normalcy, the agents knocking and waiting for one of the family to open the door, as if the property, the lawn, the house, and nearly everything in it weren't government property, with Evangeline, Cal, and Winnie serving as tenants. Even Tennyson was technically categorized as a "work implement" by the government, though the Newfoundlands trained and used by the fencing bureaus were more often thought of as weapons, just like the swords Evangeline was already heading up the stairs to retrieve, just like the guns carried by Aleph and the other agent sitting at the wheel of the car idling in the driveway.

"Just fine," Aleph said in his monotone voice, stepping inside and closing the door. His pristine black suit now bore the hairy evidence of an interaction with a shedding Newfoundland. "Winnie entered the school at 7:52 without incident. Her teacher confirmed receipt, and coursework has been ongoing since. Two-digit numbers and finger-painting zoo animals today, I believe."

Cal nodded. If something had happened with Winnie's drop-off, they would have known already, would have known immediately, of course. Someone at the school would have called, or one of the people assigned to Winnie would have alerted them. He just liked hearing the flinty, expressionless government agent capable of immense and nearly consequence-free violence say things like "finger-painting zoo animals."

"Oddry wants to see all the fencers," Aleph continued. "Full staff meeting at nine."

Cal looked down at the newspaper Evangeline had been reading, which was still headlining stories about the protests around the New England fence. Nothing had gotten violent yet, but things seemed to be trending in that direction enough that President Tuchman was scheduled to appear, both for a speech and a sit-down with leaders of the embattled Fencing Bureau and the protestors. The headline read, *Protestors Block Traffic as Debates Grow Heated Over Fencing Budgets and Failing Energy Infrastructure.*

"Is it about that stuff?"

"Not that I know of, sir," Aleph said, glancing at the paper and shaking his head. "Oddry didn't say, and I haven't picked up any rumors."

"Great, a surprise," Evangeline said, coming back downstairs, her sheathed sword in one hand, Cal's blades in the other. She'd changed out of her pajamas and now sported the standard off-equinox outfit of the Midwestern fencers: black suit, black undershirt, black shoes that looked dressy but were just fine to run in.

"Maybe it's a happy surprise?" Cal said, heading for the stairs to change out of his own pajamas.

"So close to the equinox?" Evangeline called after him, absently petting Tennyson, who sat beside her. He was large enough that, sitting, his head rose past Evangeline's hips. "I don't think so."

Ten minutes later, Cal and Evangeline were in the back of the car as it left their small neighborhood, Tennyson curled up at their feet on the extra-spacious floor of the vehicle. So close to the equinox, he went everywhere with them.

"I can't believe you're wearing that," Evangeline said, looking again at the T-shirt Cal had on beneath his government-issued black blazer.

"Oddry is going to love it," he said, offering a smug smile and patting a hand against the shirt, which featured a blindfolded angel holding up a sword, her wings limned in glow-in-the-dark green and dripping bright red droplets of blood that fell to the ground below her to spell out *CHEMOS*.

Oddry, the head tech and administrator in charge of all major equinox operations for the Midwest Branch of the United States Fencing Bureau, was an ardent lover of the heaviest, gnarliest, amelodic, atonal, arrhythmic music on offer. His office regularly thrummed with sounds that bore only the faintest familial resemblance to music of any kind—singers aping the sounds of demons and pigs, their voices set against the high, raging storm of drums and the whipsaw jag of guitars.

A small man, Black, thin, built like four lengths of rope tied to the trunk of a sapling, Oddry would work strange hours in his office—there from three to seven in the morning but gone then until 2:15 in the afternoon, when he would return, eat three or four bags of chips from the vending machine, and work in thrash-metal disharmony until eight p.m. He turned his music down when someone needed something from him, but never off. It thrummed like the heartbeat of his office, distant or near, sternum-shattering or temple-pulsing, but always beating.

Evangeline, who had come to the Midwest Harbor from the Publix Harbor down in Florida where the operation was run with clockwork, private-money-chic efficiency, had been shocked by Oddry at first—his refusal to follow most of the written or unwritten rules of the workplace, his clothing (which often made Cal's CHEMOS T-shirt seem tame by comparison), his music, and his total disregard for the orders that came down from the central fencing agency: the United States Fencing Bureau.

But Oddry, it was said, was a genius. He'd started working for the fencing bureaus at nineteen and invented half of the equipment used each year on the equinox as well as having a hand, if not total control, in the design of nearly every fence in the United States and several across the world. Now, closer to sixty than fifty, he could afford to be an eccentric curmudgeon.

Like Evangeline, he'd started at a bigger Harbor, with better pay and all the fame a person could want.

And like Evangeline, it had turned out he hadn't wanted any of it.

At the peak of his career, when he could have led any fencing organization in the world, including the big bureau itself, Oddry Mulligan quit his high-powered New York fencing job and moved to America's lowest-funded, least-publicized, and longest-prime-per-fencer Harbor.

In the *New York Times* interview before his exit, the reporter had asked, "Why are you leaving it all behind, Mr. Mulligan?" to which Oddry had said, "What a stupid fucking question."

The interview did not improve thereafter.

A History of Fences and Fae by AK Senga, PhD

Published in 2027 by University of Minnesota Majestic Press
Excerpt from Introduction: "Nancy Reagan, Ulysses H. Wright, and *The Last Thylacine*"

The Last Thylacine was never published on a large scale, and only a dozen copies ever existed. All were disposed of and rendered unreadable, the last of which was destroyed on September 23rd, 1987 by Nancy Reagan herself, who penned the following short letter to her husband before burning the book in the fireplace and driving off in one of the family's cars. She was never seen again.

> Ronnie,
>
> I have woken as if from a deep sleep. The past few years slide away from me now, and I see my actions and yours from a great distance. The meetings. The debates. The delegations and the dinners. Ronnie, what were we thinking?
>
> The book has returned to us. Rajiv sent it back, unread, with a kind note. I cannot say how grateful I am that he did not read it. He might have fallen under its spell as we did. As you still are. It has infected so many, enthralled so many. I do not know why I have emerged from its hold now, but I will use this chance to do what I should have done that day in 1984 when the book found its way to me.
>
> I will destroy it. And hope that in doing so, its power over you and so many other world leaders will be broken.
>
> You are, as I write, away at the ceremony to celebrate the locking of the New England Harbor. I told you I was too under the weather to go, and for that lie, I am sorry.

I'm going to our spot. I'll wait for you there, and I'll be praying that when you join me, it will really be you, awake as I am. Together, we'll find our way through this.

With love,

N

Chapter 3

On the way in to work, riding in the back of the government vehicle assigned to them, Cal and Evangeline talked of small things, mostly Winnie, never using her name—never needing to.

"Did you see her art from yesterday? Another unicorn-snake."

"I don't know how many more of her knock-knock jokes I can take."

"We should really clean her room this weekend before the Long Day."

Winnie was the only "she," the only "her" they were ever thinking about, so why use her name? Every conversation about her was the continuation of one they'd been having, together and in their own thoughts all the time, every day.

They passed most of the drive this way, laughing at that funny thing she'd said before dinner, the way she used to point at Christmas lights and think they were magical creatures—not faeries, never faeries—living in trees and on houses, her refusal to eat broccoli because "it's just little trees and I don't even eat trees!"

The unease that had begun to stir in Evangeline's chest when Aleph told them about the unscheduled meeting with Oddry stilled somewhat as she fell into those easy memories of Winnie.

Outside the car, the houses and businesses of Majestic rolled by. After a block of one- and two-story homes at the edge of the town proper, all painted in drab colors made more glum by years of changing seasons sucking away any vibrancy they once had, Clark's grocery came into view, its gabled windows festooned for the upcoming equinox, goldenrod and maroon streamers catching in the wind. Next was Tip-Top Hardware, with its cartoon mascot Tip painted on the front, balancing an overlarge hammer in one hand and offering a wink to customers that Evangeline had always found disconcerting.

A new clothing store called loveYOU, owned by the Sylvans though not sporting any obvious religious iconography or slogans, dominated one corner at the stoplights along Main Street. Their clothes promised a "return to modesty and grace" for the women of Majestic and the surrounding area, according to the large sign out front. Evangeline gave the building the finger as the car moved through the intersection.

"Wow," Cal said from beside her. "Not very modest or graceful, love."

Evangeline, raising her eyebrows, turned the gesture to Cal, who laughed and raised his hands in mock surrender.

There remained in Cal's smile something sad, and Evangeline could imagine his thoughts returning to his father, the melancholy coloring every bit of joy he felt in talking about Winnie or laughing with her. She could see the grief in his eyes and hear it in his laugh.

It made her glad in a way she would never admit to him. Grief was natural—the necessary response from the body and the mind to true and deep pain. Evangeline's own parents, her mother especially, had raised her to be in touch with all of her emotions, never judging or discounting them. Although she'd never fallen into the well of her mother's obsession with spiritual transcendence—which had, in practice, often looked like nothing more than taking drugs and walking around barefoot—Evangeline *did* find in herself still a tendency to accept emotions, even those deemed troublesome or bad by the world. Perhaps even *especially* those.

So, she took Cal's hand and squeezed it, and felt glad for his grief. She would not rush it along, and she would not demand its utility be made known. It would be yet another wave on the ocean, and they would both rise and fall with it.

Evangeline turned to look out the window again, letting the slow slide of Majestic's main street occupy her attention.

Opposite loveYOU sat the Bean, Majestic's coffee shop, haunted at all hours by faculty and students from the university metastasizing on the northern side of town. Cal and Evangeline often took Winnie there on Saturday and Sunday mornings. The shop boasted a huge number of board games, some with all of their pieces still intact, and the three of them would play the mornings away while the parents drank overpriced coffees and Winnie slurped down the Bean's famous Cookie-Crumble-Custard Shake.

Today, though, the normally quiet sidewalk in front of the Bean held several people, each of whom was brandishing a sign at cars passing by.

$$$ FOR SCHOOLS, ROADS, AND ENERGY

$419 BILLION . . . FOR WHAT???

WHO NEEDS BIG BROTHER WHEN WE HAVE
THE US FENCING BUREAU

DAYS WITHOUT ELECTRICITY THIS YEAR: 55
OF MBUSFB ADMINISTRATORS: 113

DOWN WITH THE FENCES
THIS IS **OUR** LAND

"I didn't know they were here, too," Cal said. "I thought all of the protests were happening on the East Coast."

"Me, too," Evangeline said, trying not to stare too openly at the protestors as they drove by. Nothing on the car marked them as fencers or employees of the Midwest Branch of the United States Fencing Bureau, but she'd been reading about how protesters had been harassing fencers, and she didn't want any part of that. "Look at that last one. They actually think we should tear down the fences."

"Can you imagine what the death counts would be if we did that?" Cal sounded horrified.

"It's been too long since any of the really bad stuff happened," Evangeline said, turning to watch the protestors slowly disappear behind them. "Some of those people weren't even born in the same century as when Reagan made his deal and destroyed the world."

Everyone got the same history lessons in school, of course—Evangeline had been surprised that Winnie's first-grade classroom would have a unit on the Harbors and even fencers. Kids learned about the Harbors Act, about the book that had swayed Reagan and the other world leaders, about the fences and the fae, but they learned it *as history*. As past.

Sure, they might learn that. In 1994, groups in the Midwest had tried to pull down the very fence Evangeline and Cal worked to service each year. Kids in a tenth-grade history class might be tested on what happened after their teacher, underpaid and overworked, told them that yes, several citizen groups attacked the fence one early summer day, cutting out or tearing down huge sections of the barrier in the name of freedom or liberty or some other abstract concept.

Those same kids might need to write an essay about how many of those citizens lived—zero—and what really happened. They might pen paragraphs synthesizing the information they found: the Harbors that each fence surrounds emitted some force toxic to anyone not covered in the magical tattoos found on each fencer, and those fences, which began as decorative, symbolic things in the eighties, became functional after that first equinox, holding back the vast majority of that lethal, eroding force. The greater the amount of iron and old wood used in the fences' construction and maintenance, the greater the efficacy of the fence as a protective barrier, though even a pure iron wall would not keep all of the deadly radiation in.

Yes, those students might write, it was still unwise for an unprimed person to venture too near a maintained fence because some of that toxicity managed to seep through and collect just outside the fence's perimeter, but it was nothing like the deluge that emerged from the Harbor that day in 1994.

All eighty-two members of the group styling themselves "Rising Liberty" died before the day was out—died, really, before their breath had even stopped. From the moment the fence was breached and they were awash in whatever invisible and deadly radiation came from the Harbor, they were as good as gone even if they didn't feel the effects yet. By the time they had all been apprehended and brought to the nearest hospital, most were already dead, their skin hardened and rough, their eyes gone a solid white, and their limbs broken with new-grown joints.

But all of that learning and work would be done within the supposedly safe cocoon of history, and what an easy thought it was to imagine the people and issues of today as distinct from those in the past.

Evangeline didn't know she was going to speak again until she did, the words coming out cautious.

"I know they tell us in training to be sympathetic but distant toward protestors. Don't engage, stay polite, all of that stuff. But I *am* sympathetic."

She raised a hand to quiet both Cal's surprise and Aleph's sudden interest from the front seat.

"No, I don't think we should tear down the fences or fire all the agency administrators or anything like that. The 'this is our land' people are terrible. The Venn diagram of them and the idiots who regularly encourage people to 'go back to where you came from' is almost definitely a perfect circle."

She tipped her head to the side, thinking of the news reports she'd been reading the past few weeks—not the fiery, dramatic ones about the protests but the real reporting about the issues behind the protests. And thinking, too, about how even the people of Rising Liberty had mostly come from poor communities who perceived their tax dollars going to fund a fence they didn't need or understand.

"They are right that power outages have been increasing, and funding for schools and roads—infrastructure, really—isn't keeping up with the country's wear and tear. They're wrong about the solutions, but they're right about at least some of the problems."

Aleph seemed satisfied with that answer and returned his focus to the drive. Although most agents were instructed to refrain from interacting personally with their charges save for moments when safety demanded it, Aleph had been assigned to the family for long enough that he had become more than a bodyguard or security agent. Not a friend but more than protective potential violence in a suit.

"I guess you're right," Cal said, using that dubious tone he always did when feeling his way along a new idea, changing his mind to accommodate it.

It was one of the things Evangeline loved about him: he held ideas with conviction and consideration, but he was, in his heart of hearts, a doubter, secretly worried that he might be wrong about much, if not most, of what he thought about the world. He was a person with the constant, niggling worry that he had overlooked a crucial piece of information.

It could lead to indecision on his part, and it made him one of the most gullible people Evangeline had ever met, but on his best days, it meant Cal really could see the glow of the world through another person's eyes.

"It's frustrating," Evangeline said. "If we do our jobs correctly, and if they follow the rules, then the equinox comes and goes with no major injuries or destruction, and because we get the funding we need and do our jobs well, most of these people have never seen any real catastrophes or deaths, and the history of those things happening fades further and further back."

"If we're successful," Cal said, nodding now, "the world looks the same after the equinox as it did before, and it's easy to start thinking maybe all this money and energy put into fencing agencies isn't necessary. When the Wretched aren't killing both of your parents and unzipping your dog like a gym bag, you might forget that they were really all that dangerous at all."

"And then if the government is spending tax money on fencers and fences and bureau administration?"

"But . . . no, hold on," Cal's sympathetic nodding was replaced by a grimace of revulsion. "They show videos every year, all around the world—even here in Majestic—they show videos of fae destruction and violence, and they tell stories about what happened in the past. They even talk about it in Winnie's class, remember? Mrs. Iverson told the story of the Sixteen Souls from oh-three—she smoothed out the details because it was first grade, but still. It's not like the old stories and evidence of fae danger are gone."

"Government propaganda," Aleph said, his deep voice a surprise. He kept his face ahead and expressionless, sunglasses obscuring the emotion in his eyes, but the sarcastic note in his voice was plain enough. "The government wants to keep its citizens scared, pliant, and paying. So, they blow up the scary stories, circulate them, and make everyone hide during the equinox so they don't see how harmless it really is."

"That's . . ." Cal's mouth hung open as he searched for words to capture the foolishness of such a belief.

"Scary," Evangeline finished for him, looking out the window at the town passing by.

"But someone is putting that nonsense out—manufacturing the doubt and conspiracies," Cal said. "People don't just believe that kind of thing without it coming to them prepackaged, right?"

"Those two senators from Ohio are always putting this kind of stuff out without ever saying it directly," Evangeline said. "Ellman and . . . Graeber or Graver or something like that."

"It can't just be them, though," Cal said. "Who would benefit from something like this?"

But of course he knew. They all did, and as the car moved out of the city center of Majestic, Cal and Evangeline cut their eyes eastward to where the tall towers of the House of Always Giving rose above the homes and businesses around it.

The church of the worshippers of the fae. Cal's father's church. The worshippers called themselves many things: the folk, the friends, Sylvans, the Queen's vassals.

In the years after eighty-seven, as humanity pieced together what had happened and what they were dealing with, a small group of people had responded to the revelations of the equinox with a kind of religious ecstasy. They believed that those who died on the equinox and became faeries were holy, chosen by a Queen beyond the fence, and while other religions might offer solace through the faith in a never-seen, never-heard god or goddess, the world now had proof—true, bloody, visceral *proof*—of a power beyond humanity that did exist.

These people came together to form a new religion: Sylvanism, which worshipped the Faerie Queen and the equinox. They called their churches the House of Always Giving, and in the early days of their belief, those spaces were home to many fits of mass suicide on the equinox, the Queen's vassals undergoing the transformation into fae as a group, cups of poisoned wine falling from their hands as the strange and wild changes were already beginning.

The government entered into an uneasy truce with the House of Always Giving following several years of these mass suicides, each of which resulted in hordes of fae terrorizing the towns and people around them before eventually escaping into the nearest Harbor and disappearing into whatever worlds or lands existed there. In this agreement, the government would allow the House of Always Giving to maintain its status as a protected religion, free to proselytize and sermonize where and when its members wanted, tax-exempt and safe from the greedy paws of the government, and the Sylvans would refrain from what the government documents called "intentionally induced or assisted acts of deadly harm on or near the autumnal equinox."

The House of Always Giving had been growing the last few years—Cal's father was just one of the many converts who had found his purpose and meaning through worshipping the fae and their Queen. Each equinox, he would join the other faithful as they cloistered together and hoped for their own death.

Evangeline squinted at the receding towers of the House of Always Giving as Aleph took them onward, thinking of Cliff, his kind eyes and large, well-worked hands, attending that church, singing their songs and believing their beliefs, sure he had hit on the truth of the world.

For a town its size—just north of five thousand on a day when the weather was no good for fishing and everyone stayed home—Majestic should not have had a Main Street nearly as busy or populated as this one, but thanks to the university and the fence, what should have been another forgotten Midwest town instead had the only stoplights in the county (four), a movie theater with two screens, a bowling alley, and seven restaurants.

Of course, it also boasted the standard parity of bars and churches (eight of each), and the same windblown, run-down architecture found in any of the little towns scattered throughout Minnesota, Iowa, and the Dakotas.

Before the fence went up, Majestic was just another one of those towns, a place small enough that you could hold your breath while driving through and have enough air left in your lungs afterward to sing a line or two of your favorite song.

After the fence, though, and after that first equinox, the government set about creating the University of Minnesota Majestic—the research arm of the Minnesota system, a school focused on the few areas of study relevant to the fence and the Harbor beyond (mathematics, engineering, folklore, history, and literature). And the people who came to staff and attend the school along with the slow, quiet influx of government agents, bureaucrats, and mathematicians swelled the population and the offerings of Majestic to something beyond the average Midwestern tumbleweed town.

"Okay, let's think this through. Oddry calls a full staff meeting twelve days out from the equinox," Evangeline said, mumbling almost to herself. "Could be normal business, but probably not, and if not, that means surprise news, almost certainly of the bad sort. I'll bet it's a funding cut, a press push, or a transfer. I don't know which would be worse."

"Yep," Cal said, grinning. "Aren't we the lucky ones."

This tendency of Cal's to give every conversation or sour note a banal little button, the conversational equivalent of a palate-cleanser during a fine meal, was a constant annoyance—the "We'll see" and "Who could say" and "So it goes" phrases that he seemed to utter at the end of most discussions, a gift from his mother, who'd had the same habit. He couldn't sit with discord or unease, had to tie off each loose thread in a conversation with a punt to the future or a sardonic joke about the present.

"You really don't know anything, Aleph?" Evangeline asked, meeting the agent's eyes in the rearview mirror. "No little hints?"

"Nothing much," Aleph said. "Only that Oddry sounded quite angry when he called the meeting."

"Angry is his base setting," Evangeline said, turning to look out the window again. "He wakes up angry."

"Remember last month when he was going to pick up yo-yoing?" Cal leaned forward, elbows on knees and hands pulled into fists underneath his chin. "And then two days later, we found all of his yo-yos smashed in the garbage out back?"

They all had a laugh at that, but Evangeline's mind returned once more to this meeting, so close to the equinox. It was a puzzle that would be solved for her soon enough, but she worried at it, sure that something odd was going on.

The car moved out of Majestic, the buildings falling away once more as Main Street transitioned into County Road 28, known locally as Harbor Way. Off to the north, huddled on the hill that loomed over Majestic, was the university, its blocky brick buildings framed against the noon sky.

Just ahead was the Shop, so called by everyone who worked there, in part because "Midwest Branch of the United States Fencing Bureau buildings and offices" didn't zip from the lips as easily, and also because "the Shop" made it seem like a small, knowable space, nothing strange or unexplainable happening behind the doors. Simple, material things happened in shops. Cars were fixed, maybe, products made. People might sit around Formica tables, drinking bad coffee while sharing stories of peewee soccer games or farm yields for the year.

Calling it "the Shop" meant the engineers and builders who worked there didn't fix and maintain the fence separating this world from the fae realm. It meant the fencers who worked there were not magical warriors carrying prime-numbered tattoos and the attendant horrifying powers. It meant body counts were not discussed at those Formica tables, which were not Formica at all but steel and iron. It meant no one there even knew what the Riparian was.

Calling it "the Shop" meant there were no mathematicians inside. None in the offices. None in the laboratories. And none several floors down, where rooms were longer than seemed architecturally possible, where the silence was too much, where the lights were too bright, where the numbers scribbled on and etched into the wall would not stay still. Where the prime priests mumbled and muttered to themselves, words holy and sacred.

Of course, the buildings were far bigger and more impressive than any "shop" could ever be. Huge granite arches and glassed facades rose into the sky, catching the autumnal sun's light and reflecting it a thousand times over.

What some might see as a single, monolithic government building was actually three distinct buildings, each several orders of magnitude more expensive than any thirteen structures in Majestic put together.

The business portion of the MBUSFB branch was the central tower, the Bluestem Building, which was seventeen floors of clean, neat rooms filled with computers and whiteboards and people talking over spreadsheets and printouts.

To the left, extending from Bluestem like a tessellating nightmare of glass and iron was the Tactical Headquarters. Unlike the sturdy, steady walls of the central tower, the Tactical Headquarters—what Cal and Evangeline really meant when they talked about "the Shop"—was a geometric jumble composed of fractal polygons fitting together, imperfect and impossible, each edge measured thrice to ensure its primality.

This, the Shop, bristled with edges and angles, chaotic at a glance but ruled by an iron logic: prime lengths and prime angles. Any who died inside on the equinox would soon find the Shop a prison, its bars composed of base mathematical elements, indivisible and unyielding.

The car pulled to a stop at the curb in front of the Shop, and Cal and Evangeline were met with the sounds of Oddry's metal music growling from the open bay doors. What melodies there were writhed and died beneath the stomping boots of the angry, heavy rhythms.

"I thought Oddry wasn't even supposed to be in today," Evangeline said, pulling out her keycard to show the guards out front, who waved them through. "He should be away on vacation for another day, getting some rest before the Long Day."

"Delivering bad news probably *is* restful for him," Cal said. "Oddry was practically giggling when he told us that Tempest King was leaving despite the fact that he was our second-strongest fencer and had all that good press."

"That asshole," Evangeline said, face wrinkling in displeasure at the memory. "I hated that man. Out of all the fencers I've ever met, I don't think any of them have been even half as vain or self-loving. He was in the paper this morning, actually. Apparently, he's been elected speaker for the fencers up in New England. They got a quote from him for the story on the protests, something about"—Evangeline conjured the Tempest King's smug voice from memory—"*the huge importance of listening to the people of this nation even as we work to protect them.*"

"What an asshole," Cal said, though he was smiling at her impression.

Evangeline felt the lightness of the moment leave her as she looked past Cal at the third part of the MBUSFB building, the structure neither of them talked about when they could help it, not since that morning nearly eight years previous. The sky had been so overcast that day, the wind bitter and biting.

Unlike the Shop and the Bluestem Building, the third part of the complex was a single-floored building, and it looked like a Cold War bunker, windows slitting up the sides in narrow strips and a wall that bulged out, as if it might repel Soviet attacks and belch out gunfire in return, withstand nuclear radiation and communism all at once.

Her first time—her *only* time—in that building, Evangeline had been standing around with the other new recruits when Cal had made a joke early on—his way of dealing with the nerves, she would come to realize. He'd said something about the windows serving nicely as archer slits in case the world went to hell and the barbarian hordes attacked.

The calculating silence that followed should have warned him of what was to come, but he had simply grinned at the other fencers. Evangeline, feeling bad for him, had offered a charitable chuckle.

And then they'd stepped into the elevator.

The real secret of that third building was below, where seven floors spread like rotten roots underground, long concrete hallways, walls made of chalkboards, computer terminals punctuating the monotony. Evangeline had only seen the fifth basement floor, where she'd been asked to step out for her tests, and Cal had only seen the third, but that had been enough for them.

It was the calculators' building, where primes were studied and examined, pursued and caught. Where the mathematicians worked in darkness and silence.

They called it the Sieve.

Evangeline finally wrenched her eyes away from it as their car pulled to a stop, and she followed Cal and Tennyson into the entrance of the Shop—a tall, well-lit space functioning as a massive garage with a few offices, meeting rooms, and workspaces near the back. Along each white wall were scores of hand tools, most designed by Oddry himself, hung neatly in well-organized rows or groups. They reached all the way to the ceiling some forty feet above, and ladders on rollers and tracks clung to the walls, waiting for one of Oddry's machinists or techs to scurry up for some obscure, ultra-expensive tool. It was the Library of Alexandria but for gearheads.

Vehicles of all kinds—cars, trucks, vans, and tactical technology—were parked in the wide-open space, some in the process of having work done on them, others prepped already and waiting for the equinox, when they would be used for more than twenty-four hours straight.

Evangeline and Cal, with Tennyson between them, walked through one of the open bay doors and around the vehicles, shouting hellos and waving to the techs who saw them, many of whom they'd been working with for several years.

Any other dog might have required a leash around such activity, if they could even handle the stimuli at all, but Tennyson was a fencing hound, trained from birth and bonded to his fencers. At home, he might play with Winnie and nap prolifically throughout the day, but when it was time to work, when Cal and Evangeline put on their swords, he became what his training had prepared him for.

Every squad of fencers had at least one hound that lived with its leader and accompanied the squad on the equinox. Some squads, especially at the wealthier fences, had two or even three Newfoundlands assigned to each. The dogs were like big teddy bears for nearly every day out of the year. Only on that one day in the fall did they show their true capabilities, just like the fencers they lived with and supported—as if the autumnal equinox were the key to the bundles of potential and power locked away inside them.

The music from Oddry's office in the back was audible, the sounds abrading the air from the huge speakers he had mounted on the walls, positioned for "superior acoustic quality."

"God," Evangeline said. "It sounds like how chewing gravel would feel."

A voice emerged from the chaos, screaming and growling indecipherable lyrics, doing violence to melody and language alike. Filling in the space around it, waves of sound crashed against one another, bass and drums and guitars slamming together into noise, unrelenting and furious.

"He must really be angry this time." Cal had lost some of his levity and now carefully shifted his blazer around to reveal more of the heavy-metal-band shirt beneath.

They cleared the lines of vehicles, shoes squeaking against the waxed, polished concrete floor. Ahead, the door to the meeting rooms stood slightly open.

"Ready?" Cal asked, unbuttoning his blazer to fully reveal the CHEMOS shirt. He reached down to scratch behind one of Tennyson's ears.

"Once more unto the breach, teacher's pet," Evangeline said, walking through.

Chapter 4

"This might be the year we all actually die," Oddry said as he walked into the room, flanked by three of his techs.

A soft chuckle rose from the assembled fencers and staff members, though Oddry's expression of long-suffering annoyance didn't change. He wore a brown button-up that was a few sizes too large and a pair of long khaki shorts that terminated in torn wisps of cloth mid-shin. His hair had receded to a close-cut crown, leaving the top of his head bare save a patch in the front, which Oddry kept longer than the rest and would fiddle with while working on challenging technical problems. Currently, it spiraled up and away from his skull like an asymmetrical horn.

For anyone else, this might have been a look that signaled a time of deep distress, but for Oddry, it was as close as he got to an aesthetic standard. Disheveled, mismatched, and chromatically confused.

"Cuts?" one fencer called out from the back, a younger man called Gloaming. His primacy had to do with manipulation of light.

"A surplus?" said another, the Stone Weaver, one of the four in-training fencers. She would shadow Cal and Evangeline's squad during the upcoming equinox but not be responsible for either any fighting or any shepherding of the Wretched. Evangeline had watched her in training and been impressed, and though the Stone Weaver hadn't yet had a chance to show her full primacy, having only just gotten her tattoos last equinox, she could apparently see for miles in any direction and make out shapes and movement even through barriers.

The mere suggestion of a surplus conjured a laugh from the wary group, and one of the hounds in the room sounded a soft bark, as though she, too, found it funny. Tennyson, who was sitting beside Evangeline, looked at her, his expressive brown eyes seeming to ask whether he, too, could bark. Evangeline sank a hand into the thick fur around his neck and shook her head.

Along with the fencers, there were several techs and a few liaisons from Central Bureau in the meeting, all packed into the room, which was shaped like a rectangle, with Oddry standing at the lectern in the front. High white walls rose on all sides, and behind Oddry was a huge screen showing the floating logo of the Midwest Harbor: a stalk of wheat and sword crossed over one another, a clear progeny of the proletariat's hammer and sickle.

The only one in the room who didn't laugh at Stone Weaver's guess was a woman sitting at the way back of the room, behind the final row of fencers lounging in their chairs, outside of the purview of the meeting. She watched, observed, but did not participate. And when everyone else laughed, she stayed still and silent.

A mathematician, one of the Sieve workers, wearing the white-and-black lab coat of her order. On her lap was an open notebook, the glint of a pen in one hand. No matter the meeting, no matter the participants, the Sieve workers always sent an envoy to sit in. Officially, this was to "maintain open channels of communication between the practical and theoretical work of the Midwest Branch of the United States Fencing Bureau," or so the emails between different departments said. Technically, the "practical" workers—fencers and techs, administrators and engineers—were always welcome to send envoys to meetings held in the Sieve, but almost no one ever wanted to go, and the mathematicians were not forthcoming with their own schedules, often burying them deep in the labyrinthine organizational system they used to keep their digital files.

This mathematician wore a name tag. "Sister Marla."

Sitting next to Sister Marla was a fencer called Incident, the only one in the room who wore her weapons at all times. Every other fencer in the room had, in the early days of their career, chosen weapons that fit their fighting style and build—all of them laced with iron and crafted perfectly for their individual style and strengths—hanging in a locker out in the Shop proper. Only Incident carried hers year-round, a triangular shield with sharpened edges, each one covered now with a guard. She was tall, with long arms and legs, white skin and whiter hair.

Over the top of her bureau-issued polo and coat she wore a well-polished necklace, the thick chain around her neck pulled down by the gnarl of a heavy wooden pendant, lengths of oak worked into the shape of a hand, the fingers all sprouting silver, metallic thorns. The symbol of Cal's dad's church, the worshippers of the fae. The House of Always Giving.

Tiny scars covered her skin, complementing the dark numerals of her prime, each one a tiny sliver of white, like a waning crescent moon caught just before abandoning the night sky entirely. A symbol of her devotion to her faith.

In between blowing on a steaming cup of coffee, Incident whispered quietly to Sister Marla, and whatever she said brought a smile to the mathematician's face.

"It's our math friend again, sitting with the only one in the room who can stand her," Cal said, nudging Evangeline and nodding toward the pair in the back. The mathematician, Sister Marla, had been the envoy at their last four or five meetings. "Do you think it's punishment for them to attend these? Maybe she forgot to carry the one in some all-important equation and this is her penance."

But Evangeline wasn't looking at the mathematician, one of whom she called the "number pushers." Instead, she had half-risen from her seat and was scanning the room, her dark brown eyes flicking from table to table as she mumbled to herself. Her hands, flattened against her legs, were balled into fists that soon disappeared as she flicked one finger out at a time.

Cal frowned a moment before realizing: *She's counting.*

They sat at one of the smaller round tables with the Stone Weaver and the other member of their three-person squad, a fencer called Nero. She had been in high school in the early 90s when her tattoos came on, and her favorite class had been history with Mrs. Elgin. With a need to pick a fencing name and a recent unit on the Roman emperors in mind, she'd gone with Nero.

Now, she was a mid-forties mom of five kids who, while the rest of the room offered jokey guesses to Oddry's mystery, was looking at her laptop, which showed the football practice schedule for her two oldest kids—twin boys named Aldis and RJ. Aldis sometimes babysat Winnie when Cal and Evangeline had the rare date night or work trip.

Another laugh rattled the room, gaining in confidence as more jokes were allowed to be made without Oddry shutting them down.

"Any guesses, Nero?" Cal asked, speaking low enough for only those at the table to hear.

"I'm gonna kill this coach," she said, looking up, her Southern drawl thick as syrup. "This asshole's scheduled practice for the *day before* the equinox! Every got-damn person in the world starting to close up shop, and this tiny man is running the boys? No, sir."

Nero's hands flew over the keyboard as she channeled her frustration into a scathing email.

"Piss," Evangeline said, hissing the word under her breath as she dropped back into her chair. "It's Effie."

"What?" Cal said, bewildered.

"Yes, it is Effie," Oddry said, his voice cutting through the pleasant guesses and guffaws the meeting had turned into. He had been watching Evangeline, nodding along as she put it together. The other fencers and techs quieted as Oddry spoke again.

"As of this morning, Fencer Effervescence has been transferred to the Harbor of the South. She has already packed her things and"—Oddry checked his watch, a large-faced contraption with gears visible under the hands—"is en route to the airport right now."

Empty silence followed this pronouncement. Transfers happened, of course—Evangeline had transferred there from the Publix Harbor, just like others had transferred in and out: the Runner and Nero from the Lone Star Harbor, String Theory from the Southwest Harbor, and Daughter Courage—the Midwest's newest in-training recruit—from the Harbor of the Icy North in Alaska.

But so close to the equinox, to the Long Day? After an entire off-season of training with her squad, working on maneuvers, scouting their territory, drilling techniques, and building rapport?

"This is bullshit, Oddry." Ordinal was one of the longest-serving fencers in the Midwest coterie, and with Effie gone, they would now have the second-shortest prime, which made them the second-strongest fencer in the room, at least on paper.

In reality, Ordinal was an aging punk, their wispy mohawk showing an advancing line of grey roots beneath the faded green dye. Teeth yellow from too many cigarettes and too few brushings, with sun-faded tattoos blotting the space on their arms, legs, and neck that weren't covered in the darker numerals of their prime tattoo. One ear sagged against the weight of the thick metal hoops punched through it, and twin diamonds glittered at either side of their lower lip.

Cal had once asked Ordinal if it had hurt to get their lip pierced, and they'd smiled that tobacco smile and said, "Not enough to stop me from doing it again."

When Winnie first met Ordinal, sometime after her fourth birthday at some off-season fencing event in the spring—hot dogs and kiddie pools and grass cut for the first time following a long winter—she'd asked the grungy, tatted fencer if they were part snake. And when she had reached her grubby kid fingers out toward the two piercings, glittering in the sun like fangs, Ordinal had waved off Cal and Evangeline's attempts to stop her, allowing Winnie to tentatively poke at the diamond-crusted rings.

"I don't think any of my ancestors were snakes, but you never can tell with folks like my family," Ordinal had said, smiling down at the young girl. "Do you think I'd make a good snake?"

With a solemn nod, Winnie had said, "Yes, because you have lots of colors on your skin like snakes and sharp teeth like snakes."

Ordinal had laughed at that, mouth wide, joyous, and said, "Yeah, kiddo, I guess that's right. And I'll tell you a little secret so long as you promise to keep it in."

Winnie had nodded, full of all the import and gravitas a child could muster. She'd crossed her heart with one finger.

"My primacy—my power, you know—lets me fit between small things," Ordinal said. "Squeeze in between cracks and little openings where folks aren't supposed to go. Just like . . . ?"

Winnie thought for a moment and then gasped. "A snake!"

Ordinal had laughed again and wrapped Winnie in a big hug.

Ordinal's prime ability allowed them, on the autumnal equinox, to disperse the material of their body over short distances, which meant they could squeeze under door frames or through air vents. Cal once witnessed them pass through a locked screen door like a spray of rain, shimmering into a billion bright molecules before collapsing back into themself on the other side and slamming a fist into the man on the other side.

"Orders from *Central*," Oddry said, turning the word into a curse. His eyes flicked back to the mathematician in the back of the room for a moment.

"She was supposed to be on my team this year," Ordinal said, looking around in disgust. "We'll have to rework all the routes, all the approaches, our order of operations, everything. Are they at least giving us anyone in return?"

The muscles along Oddry's jaw flexed, and he looked as though he had plenty he wanted to say, but he only shook his head.

This time, it was not just Ordinal expressing their frustration. Cries of dismay mingled with disbelief and outright anger from everyone, including Cal and Evangeline, who had known Effie professionally and socialized with her a few times outside of work. Even Nero took a break from her email to offer a weary sigh to the ceiling in Effie's honor.

The only one in the room to show no great emotion—indeed, no emotion of any kind—was the mathematician, Sister Marla, in the back, who wrote quietly for a moment in her notebook before returning to her impassive observance of the meeting and sharing a few whispered words with Incident, who was also on Ordinal's team but didn't seem too perturbed by the news of Effie's transfer. She didn't even seem surprised.

Everyone knew of the great split at each Harbor: the fencers and techs who fought against the Wretched each equinox and against the Central Bureau every other day of the year; and the mathematicians who worked closely with the Central Bureau every day of the year, especially on the autumnal equinox. The relationship was an uneasy one during even the best of times.

Oddry gave some rope to the grievances before glaring those assembled back into silence.

"I got the news late last night of her transfer. I did everything I could to keep her or at least get a replacement, but the folks in Central rejected both. I was asked—forced, really—to say nothing until now."

Someone, Ordinal maybe, started speaking again, but Oddry silenced them with a hand and a shake of his head.

"Nothing else to be said or done about it now. I'll talk with Effie's squad later this morning about revisions to your plans for the Long Day. For now, let's actually use the time for something productive instead of whining at each other."

"We didn't even get to say goodbye," someone said.

"Don't we usually have a farewell party when someone leaves?" another asked.

"We stopped doing that after the Tempest King transferred," Oddry said, looking up from the computer with annoyance. "Now leave me alone for a minute while I get this machine to act right."

As Oddry attacked the keyboard, the fencers turned to those nearby, most muttering darkly about Effie's transfer.

But Cal was thinking about the Tempest King.

"Remember that international fencer gala?" he said, smiling at the memory.

"Scotland?" Nero asked, arching one eyebrow.

"Scotland," Cal agreed.

"What?" the Stone Weaver asked, looking around. "What happened?"

"A big, grand man made a big, grand fool of himself; that's what happened," Nero said, chuckling and returning to her computer.

"You haven't had one of these yet," Cal said, turning to the Stone Weaver. "But every four or five years, all the fencing agencies from across the world get together at these big galas. Promoting unity and peace and all that. Anyway, the last one was in Scotland. They were celebrating major renovations on their Harbor—you know the one patrolled by the Thistle Guard."

"I used to have a picture of the Thistle Guard up in my room," the Stone Weaver said, grinning. "I thought they were the coolest."

"They *are* the coolest," Nero said, not looking up.

"So, there we are in Edinburgh at this fancy party, and all the big-name fencers are there, including Jiangshi Chaoren, and Tempest King walks up to her and starts bragging—loudly—about how many Wretched he bagged during the last equinox, like it was all a video game and he was the high scorer."

"The man was and is a twit," Evangeline said. "An arrogant, idiotic twit. And Jiangshi Chaoren treated him like it in front of every major fencer and government official in the world."

It had been a big night: fencers from around the globe, accompanied by top government officials, business leaders, and swarms of hangers-on. A castle had been rented out for the event, the great stony chambers echoing with laughter and music and speeches all night.

The American contingent had all worn red-white-and-blue pins and identical sets of clothing—black suits and ties for those who preferred that; black, sleeved dresses and heels for those who preferred that.

It was a nice statement, Cal and Evangeline had both thought, even if it was meant to conceal a lie.

The truth, much like it was for any other country or territory big or wealthy enough to have more than one Harbor, was the fencers of the United States were of two classes. On the top were those fencers stationed at the major Harbors: the Southwest and Northwest teams, the unionized groups around New England and Chicago, and the private fencers of the Florida area.

And on the bottom were the understaffed and underfunded coteries working and fencing the two Harbors in the Midwest and the Harbor of the South. Unionizing efforts had failed several times over the years, and no private company wanted anything to do with Harbors or fencers that regularly got either no press or bad press. The powerful fencers, those with thousand- or ten-thousand-digit primes, ended up at the top-class Harbors quite quickly, even if they somehow began at the Midwest or Southern locations.

"It's like baseball," Oddry had said to Cal and Evangeline one day, sipping and grimacing at the coffee he always seemed to have in hand. "You might get a promising player who starts out with the Minnesota Twins or the Kentucky Cranes, but as soon as that promise comes to fruition, one of the owners of those rich teams—the fucking Yankees or the Dodgers—swoops in and makes an offer no self-respecting player can turn down. The Twins? The Cranes? The A's? They might as well be spelunking in the couch cushions for spare change, for all the good their counteroffers might do."

Cal and Evangeline had both read the NYT interview, and neither had brought up that he'd come from the fucking Yankees to the couch-spelunking Twins.

At the gala, despite their unifying uniforms, the fencers of the United States had broken apart almost immediately—the wealthy and powerful congregating together at a set of big tables that seemed to ring with laughter and light. The poorer fencers, modern superheroes in any other situation but B-rate banalities there, mingled and munched on appetizers.

The Midwest coterie had stayed mostly together, Cal and Evangeline content to chat with their fellow union-less, underfunded friends, but not Tempest King—a man who thought he should be fencing for a better Harbor—batting fourth for the Yankees instead of playing right field for the Twins.

He would strut around the Shop, lounge grandly in any meeting, and happily talk over anyone, regardless of their position or seniority. And all because his prime was a few hundred digits shorter than that of the next-closest fencer, which happened to be Evangeline.

"These digits," Tempest King would say, running a finger up one arm held just slightly flexed for any of the younger female employees not yet wise to his maneuvers. "They're the shield between you and the Wretched each year."

At the gala that night, surrounded by the greatest and strongest fencers in the world, Tempest King had dropped into a seat next to Jiangshi Chaoren, China's most famous fencer, and the only one in the world—still alive, that was—whose prime was fewer than a hundred digits. Seventy digits, in fact, a one followed by sixty-eight zeroes and ending in a nine. Unlike the tattoos that crawled and crowded over Cal and

Evangeline's skins, both of their primes numbering in the hundreds of thousands of digits, Jiangshi Chaoren had only a small, short tattoo that began just under her chin and wound around her neck like a snake, or a scarf, or a noose, the zeroes like gems.

Evangeline and Cal had been standing nearby, looking at one of the displays—a gaudy, glossy thing with pictures and news clippings from around the world titled BUILDING FENCES: THE EARLY YEARS—and so, they had front-row seats for the brief conversation.

"So, you're the famous Jiangshi Chaoren."

"Yes."

"I saw clips of your work last equinox. You're almost as fast as me." Tempest King's primacy was speed, superhuman and impossible. Most fencers kept quiet about their primacy, a unique power granted to each fencer by their tattoos, not wanting or not allowed by their fencing organization to disclose something so private and powerful.

Tempest King, as in all things, was happy to bawl loudly about his ability to any who would listen at any time.

Jiangshi Chaoren's agents—wearing the same gun-concealing suits as Cal's, Evangeline's, and every other fencer in the castle—moved a little closer. This was meant to be an evening of international cooperation and celebration, but with so much power and wealth concentrated in one place, anything could happen.

Jiangshi Chaoren, who was in her late twenties and yet held herself with the kind of steadiness found in those who had fame thrust upon them too early, cocked her head slightly at Tempest King, her eyes dark and unreadable.

And then she had smiled, pitying and kind, and it was like watching a set of floodlights banish the darkness and all the rodents it held.

"I'm sorry," she said finally, speaking quietly and with an accent. "I am not giving autographs tonight. But thank you for being a fan."

The slick smile on Tempest King's face, framed by the thin goatee he'd begun growing, slid away along with his confidence. He stared at the Chinese fencer for a moment before getting quickly to his feet and muttering something about needing to see a friend from Europe. The spots of color high on his cheeks, as well as his quick retreat and low profile for the rest of the night—including a subdued wave and sickly smile when his name was announced during the evening's roll call—had been, for Cal and Evangeline, more delicious than any of the upscale hors d'oeuvres they'd eaten, including the crab cakes that had nearly made Cal weep with joy.

When his transfer call had finally come, Tempest King had asked for—demanded, really—a going-away party. Cal and Evangeline had attended, out of obligation more than any desire to fake a sad goodbye to the man they'd all loathed, but the dreaded farewell had never materialized.

Around ten p.m., Oddry had shown up to the party, which had taken place at the Shop on the government's dime, and announced that Tempest King had already left. He'd caught a plane the day before without telling anyone, and Oddry had only found out because the final billing approval had just come across his desk.

Tempest King's last gift to the Midwest coterie had been to skip his own going-away party. Good riddance and good luck. He'd been transferred to the New England Harbor, finally getting the attention, pay, and fame he felt he so badly deserved.

"There!" Oddry said, pressing a final key and nodding with satisfaction at the screen. "Eyes up here."

The wall he stood in front of lit up as projectors kicked on, and suddenly, a massive, zoomed-in map of the Midwest Harbor and surrounding towns was visible on the white wall. It was a map that occasioned most of these meetings, its lines and boundaries as familiar to Cal, Evangeline, and the other fencers as those of their home states or the squiggles of their signatures.

Each neighborhood of the nearby towns—Majestic, Winthrop, and Klontarf—had lines cutting them into smaller pieces, like gerrymandered districts represented on a political map. Numbers floated inside these neighborhood sections, showing how many people lived in each area and in each home. With a simple click of the mouse, a person could see who those people were—name and age, any medical notes, and a location within the house where they would be (or should be) for the duration of the equinox.

"The surveillance state's wet dream," Oddry muttered, casting a look over one shoulder, and Cal found himself thinking of that protestor on the sidewalk, sign held up in a gloved hand—WHO NEEDS BIG BROTHER WHEN WE HAVE THE US FENCING BUREAU.

Outside of these three towns and the Harbor sprawling across the space between them, the scope of the map contracted, rendering hundreds of miles in the same space that a single street in Winthrop had taken up. Out in the distance was Minneapolis to the east and Fargo to the northwest, Sioux Falls down to the southwest. Bright blue lines, like highways but cutting across fields and roads, rivers and woods, ran from those larger cities to the Harbor. It was along these lines—fae ways, some idiot poet or scholar had termed them in the early nineties—that those who died on the equinox would travel, their frenzied rush collapsing together onto those magical pathways until reaching the Midwest Harbor, leaping over the great fence that surrounded it and rushing on into whatever lay beyond.

Fencers stationed at and around the Harbors handled the majority of the equinox activity since the Harbors were the final destination of all the fae anyway, but a large group of unaffiliated fencers, often called rovers or rangers, covered what they could of those swaths of land distant from a Harbor. A team of thirty or forty fencers might be assigned to all of Montana, cutting up the massive state into smaller—but still impossibly large—chunks for each fencer or pair of fencers to cover. The rest was left in the hands of local law enforcement, their own numbers bolstered each equinox by national-guard forces.

The projected map of the Midwest Harbor was a mostly blank space on the otherwise intricate and detailed map. A red line traced around it, representing the fence, busy with buttons that, if clicked, would reveal a legion of relevant technical and maintenance information about when a stretch of fence had last been fixed, what cameras were in operation on and around it, which fencers were assigned to its patrol, what materials it was made of, the ground and air temperatures, et cetera. In the face of something so misunderstood and mysterious as the equinox and its strange, perennial magic, the government demanded reams of technical information, useless as it may have been.

Like the carpet in the room—dark grey with geometric patterns in black and white, like the government orders lining the hallways—"We are here to support YOU!" and "OSHA and CBUSFA approved!", like this building and the people who worked in it—all whispered "control" in a desperate, quaking voice.

The truth was inside that crimson line, found in the vast darkness of the Harbor itself. No attempts had been made to render hills or trees (since even physical landmarks seemed to shift and change with unnatural speed and intention). Only a few known and dependable paths carved through the hundreds of square miles of space inside the fence. The clickable bits of information clustered around the fence itself and were almost nonexistent in the center of the Harbor.

Save for the very center, of course, where a small circle interrupted the grey space of the map. The title next to it read *Threshold Tree*.

The Harbor at large remained relatively unexplored and uncharted save for the spots just inside the fence. Like children exploring the shallows of a lake that grew deep, cold, and strange, the fencers of the world did their work just inside the comforting curve of the giant fence that surrounded their Harbors, carrying out scientific explorations or frivolous mapping attempts fifty or one hundred or maybe two hundred feet past the fence. Save for a few carefully planned and overly supported expeditions deeper into the Harbors, no one went that far anymore.

Of course, in the early days, when so little was known, fencers went farther. A mile. Two. Five. A few of them went in under government orders. And a few of them went in on their own, curious and full of idiotic bravado.

Most died.

Of the fencers who had made it out alive, only a bare handful had returned with a semblance of sanity and capable of giving details that did not border on the impossible. And by then, it had become clear to everyone, including the governments of the world, how precious and finite a resource the fencers were, and the near-suicidal exploratory missions past the fences and into the Harbors had ended.

After signing on to the Midwest coterie, both Cal and Evangeline, their first date still months away, had gone through a rigorous orientation program meant to prepare them physically, mentally, and spiritually for their work as fencers. As part of that preparation, they had watched the footage of the only fencer to have gone into the Midwest Harbor and returned.

The year had been 1988, before anyone understood the power of true names or the need to keep them secret for fencers. Cal had not realized this when watching the tape, so when the doctors and government officials interviewing the fencer had called her "Pauline Ende," he had turned to the orientation leader—a much-younger, just-as-grouchy Oddry—and said, "She picked 'Pauline Ende' as her fence name?"

But that confusion quickly disappeared from his mind as he watched Pauline describe her three-day journey through the Harbor in a low, guttural voice that always seemed just on the edge of fraying away to sobs. Most of what she said made little sense—castles built into stones that could fit into your hand and that drifted away like dandelion fluff when you blew on them; stars in a suddenly dark sky that sang to her of many worlds, many ways; a trio of suns that circled above in a rapid dance that left contrails of light, the three-body problem solved; earth that was not earth and rivers that were not rivers.

Pauline could not answer questions directly, and she held both hands in front of her face throughout the whole interview, two fingers freshly missing from each, shielding all but her mouth, which barely opened when she spoke, making it hard to see the fractured and broken teeth inside—one of the many gifts she'd received from her time in that strange, unmapped land.

Cal and Evangeline talked about everything in those bright, early days of their courtship, Cal a fresh signee at his first fencing job and Evangeline new to the Midwest Harbor. What luck to meet in a job such as this, to find another person who would understand the stresses and responsibilities of work that shouldn't exist, work that pulled them away from family and friends—a small price to pay for saving the world, they were assured by every government official and marketing campaign.

They shared their pasts and their hopes for their futures—their future—and they talked endlessly about fencing, about the Harbors, about Reagan and his '87 disaster, about the Midwest fence and its constant repairs, about the other fencers and their lives, about the techs and mathematicians and the Wretched, the equinox dead, the fae.

They opened the books of their lives to one another.

But only once did they discuss Pauline Ende and her interview, both of them weeping, both of them shuddering as they remembered that horrified, horrifying voice uttering impossibilities. When Evangeline mentioned the one moment when Pauline had dropped her hands from her face, revealing the changes wrought to her nose and eyes, her cheeks and ears and scalp, Cal had vomited, and that had been the end of their remembering.

Fencers talked about Pauline Ende and Dante Whitewith, Tantalina

Marsh and Kwame Boyls in secret, pleading tones. Each of them was a warning of what might happen if a fencer strayed inside a Harbor, if a fencer broke protocol. *There are worse things than death*, those sad, awful memories said. They were cautionary tales to frighten adult and child alike, and talking about them felt like picking at a still-healing wound. Compulsive. Habitual. Necessary. Harmful.

Of course, there was another fencer whispered about, his name not a warning but a curse. So hated was he that even his prime number was taught to children with a slash through it.

2

Remember this, that slash said.

Remember him, that slash said.

When Winnie returned home from kindergarten the year before, proudly showing what she called her "numberwork," Cal and Evangeline had smiled and nodded and felt good at seeing the work of her shaky hand in writing out *1-10*, the *2* viciously slashed.

"News from the globe," Oddry said, clicking a few buttons so that the map projected on the wall zoomed out to one of the whole globe, though not one any of the fencers had ever seen before beginning at the Midwest Harbor. Unlike every other fencing organization in the United States, Oddry refused to use the standard map of the world, one that, he said, "obscured the true size and shape of nearly every country and projected a skewed sense of Anglo-European importance."

Those maps, called Mercator maps, apparently, were summarily destroyed upon Oddry's assumption of his role as head technician of the Midwest Harbor. Depending on the administrative report that one read, Oddry's map-based purge cost the Midwest Harbor between a few thousand and tens of thousands of dollars.

Cal, when he started at the Harbor and saw the curious maps that replaced the Mercators, had asked Oddry about the financial need for such a switch. Oddry had glared at him as though Cal were a bit of food waste dribbling out the bottom of the compost heap.

"Sometimes, we should keep our questions inside" was all he had said.

Africa was a vast half-moon up in the top left corner of this rectangular map, with Europe and Asia beside it, Australia down below them. North and South America were angled off the coast of China. *"Angled* is a word that suggests a certain perspective about the world," Oddry might have said, but neither Cal nor Evangeline could get it out of their heads. It looked as though Alaska were reaching out for China across the Pacific, North and South America sliding down at a southward angle behind it. Antarctica was a blob of white in the bottom right corner.

The borders of countries were traced in a muted grey and labeled with faded letters. More important, and what every fencer in the room immediately began to scrutinize, were the amorphous shapes etched in bright, glowing blue, cut into most countries on the map.

They were the shapes of the Harbors of the world, more important each autumn than any national borders or state lines.

"Reagan's gifts," Oddry said, clicking a button and making the Harbors glow brighter, the national and state lines, like missives from history's atrocities, fading almost completely. "Reports from other fences around the world show our total number of fencers roughly maintaining since last year. No major news to report, and only a few minor stories."

He looked down at a sheet in front of him, reaching up with one hand to fiddle with the remaining bit of hair at the forefront of his head.

"Venezuelan fencers faced a slight uptick in the number of threats last week—letters, some crude online posts, and one fencer had her house broken into, though it's possible they didn't know she was a fencer and only knew she was wealthy; the Ghanaian fencing bureau finished construction on a new technical building last week; twelve fences worldwide have finished major repairs; and nearly all of them—ours included—have finished minor repairs. The Thistle Guard in Scotland have been following some protests at a few of their legislative buildings, but nothing violent yet."

"What about the protests here?" Cal asked.

"The large-scale protests in New England are under careful observation," Oddry said, turning a glare toward Cal. "The Central Bureau has plenty of shock troops to break up those hordes of innocent people asking their government to help them; don't worry. If President Tuchman manages to turn this mess into an even bigger mess, which would surprise me almost as much as you forgetting to fill out expense reports, fencer Calidore, then the muscles with mallets will be waiting."

"No, I mean the protestors *here*—in Majestic. We saw four of them on Main Street this morning." Cal's relationship with expense reports was an old hobby horse for Oddry, but Cal didn't engage.

"I saw them too," Gloaming said. "I can't remember the last time we had protestors in Majestic."

A rumble of agreement followed that. Anyone who lived in Majestic quickly came to understand it as the quintessential Midwest town: forgotten by progress of almost any kind, naturally resistant to change good or bad, and full of people so passive-aggressive, they could have a pleasant dinner with you at five and be piling mud on your name with the next-door neighbor by seven thirty. It was not a place where protests happened, because it was not a place of protest.

When winter came, the people of Majestic zipped up their coats and grimaced into the bitter winds. When the annual summer festival— Sunflower Days—saw the town festooned in decorations and bursting with activity, the people of Majestic had their fun and didn't make too big a deal about it. When storms and straight-line winds a few springs before had ripped up trees and knocked out power for the better part of a week, the people of Majestic squinted at the damage, shook their heads, and complained—quietly, amongst themselves—about the cleanup. Like Cal, they had a habit of tossing uncertainty and unhappiness out into the ether with phrases like "Well, what are you gonna do?" and "Ain't that just the way of things?"

They didn't protest, not because they had nothing to protest but because they had long since been taught that such things were garish and ugly, the purview of East Coast elites and attention-seeking politicians. Keep your head down, enjoy the simple things, and don't whine—these were the tenets worked deeply into the DNA of the Midwest, and nowhere was that so true as Majestic.

Oddry's look of curmudgeonly rancor softened somewhat, and his eyes narrowed in consideration. With one hand, he patted at the breast pocket on his billowing brown shirt—an old gesture from when he'd smoked.

"The Midwest Bureau is monitoring these *four* protestors," he said, speaking more slowly now. "But more importantly, we've been monitoring the organizations they participate in or represent, chief among them the House of Always Giving."

A dark muttering sounded at that, joined in by Cal, who offered his own litany of mumbled curses.

"Shut it," Oddry said with a grimace. "Yes, the House of Always Giving has been a legislative and political enemy of ours in the past, but our position these last few years remains the same: maintain a positive working relationship with the Sylvans, and I'm happy to say that we've made a breakthrough recently—thanks primarily to the efforts of Fencer Incident."

Oddry gestured back to where Incident rose from her seat and took an actual bow to the lack of applause from her colleagues. Perhaps the most eccentric fencer in the Midwest, Incident had gotten a reputation for, among other things, being a devout Sylvan.

"Because of Incident's work as an ambassador between our two groups, the Majestic chapter of the House of Always Giving has invited a delegation of fencers and staff to tour their building and join them for..."

Oddry glanced down at his notes.

"Conversations of goodwill and holy friendship."

"How miserable do you think he was while saying that?" Cal whispered to Evangeline.

"So, fencer Calidore," Oddry continued, glaring at their table. "I appreciate you volunteering your squad for this important and necessary mission of holy friendship. I'll work it into your schedule."

"Great work, sweetie," Evangeline said quietly, a sarcastic smile pulling the corners of her lips up. This was classic Cal—his mouth leading him happily into consequences obvious to anyone but him. Nero, to her left, frowned at Cal and gave him a thumbs-up that turned after a moment into a middle finger.

Oddry resumed his updates, the meeting once more falling into a stale routine.

"Look," Cal whispered to Evangeline after a bit, his whisper sliding under Oddry's discussion of the specific construction projects outlined for the next year. Cal nodded at the center of the map still projected on the wall above them, to where Russia sprawled across much of the space. Twelve Harbors dotted its expanse, the largest number of any country and the greatest total landmass given in response to the Harbors Act of 1985.

Evangeline scanned the Russian harbors, noting the long names that she could barely pronounce and thinking of the Russian fencers she'd met during her time, until she saw what Cal had—a blinking red dot, small in comparison to nearly everything else on the map, hovering on the eastern edge of the fence surrounding the Belovo Harbor.

"He's still there," Cal said, his whisper cutting under the continued updates from Oddry. "That's three weeks. He *never* stays that long in any place."

"It," Evangeline said, glancing at Cal and catching his eyes. "*It* never stays anywhere that long."

"*It*, yeah," he said, shaking his head. "Still, it's weird, right?"

"Something to share with the group?" Oddry asked, the change in his voice and the break in the monotony of his updates sending a sliver of ice into Evangeline's back. She and Cal looked up to find Oddry leaning over the podium and glaring in their direction.

"We were just commenting on the position of the Riparian," Evangeline said, glad for the dimmed lights as heat flashed up her cheeks. "It's odd that the Riparian hasn't moved in the last few weeks. It might not have what anyone would consider *normal* movement patterns, but it doesn't stay put like this, not for a long time, anyway."

"It's been at least three weeks, right?" came Ordinal's voice.

"Almost four!" said Cal, sitting up straighter in his seat and looking around, clearly relieved for the conversation to move past the bureaucratic faux pas of talking with his wife during a meeting.

"Is it really so strange?" Nero asked, closing her laptop and giving the projected map her full attention.

"Yes, it is," Evangeline said, nodding.

"The last time it stayed anywhere that long was . . ." One of the secondary techs, sitting at a table along one wall, typed at a laptop for a moment before finishing. ". . . ninety-nine. When . . ."

"Don't fucking talk about it," Ordinal said, leaning forward in their seat and pointing at the tech with one cigarette-stained finger, the nail at the end chewed down to a ragged white line.

The tech, a young man named Cormac, quailed before that jutting finger and the middle-aged punk staring at him behind it.

"Enough," Oddry said, sharing his displeasure with the whole of the room now instead of just Cal and Evangeline. "The Riparian is not the focus of this update. I have a whole sub-team of analysts following it closely, and I know the number badgers over in the Sieve are watching it too."

Oddry glanced up at the black-and-white-clad Sister Marla, who had paused whatever arcane proof she had been working through on her notebook to watch this conversation with interest.

"*Mathematicians*, Oddry," she said. Her voice was low and raspy; it conjured images of long, dark hallways filled with chalk dust and endless whispering in Evangeline's mind. "Have done with your diminutives."

"Technically, it's a hypocoristic," Cal said, turning in his seat to glance back.

"No one cares, Cal," Evangeline muttered, frowning at the gee-whiz grin he offered her. Cal had been in the first year of a PhD program in literature when his prime had come on, which meant Evangeline often had to put up with what Calidore called his "party-trick knowledge" about nonsense linguistic oddities and literary histories. Even his fencing name—Calidore—had been plucked from the lines of an epic poem Evangeline had never heard of called *The Faerie Queene*. She'd tried to read it in those early dating days when they were glimmering mysteries to one another, but she'd stopped after a few hundred lines. When she'd told him it just wasn't her thing, he'd only shrugged and said he liked it enough for both of them.

"Thank you, Fencer Calidore," Oddry said. "But your wife is right. No one cares."

That got a loud chuckle from Incident in the back, who opened her mouth wide to laugh. She made eye contact with Evangeline and gave her a bright wink.

"I wish the Ripper would come our way so we could kick its ass!" shouted one of the in-training fencers sitting near the front, a young guy, curly hair held back from his face by a red-and-black hairband, as if he were a European footballer. A few of the younger fencers, all sitting together with him in a clump, laughed at that.

"Oops," Evangeline said. It was the word she uttered anytime she saw someone in trouble, as if the universe had made a little mistake, what her mother Roxanne called a "whoopsy," a little gaffe that surprised and embarrassed Evangeline to see. Like what a person might say when they see a stranger step in a fresh pile of dog shit on the sidewalk.

Oops, like *You just beefed it*.

Oops, like *You're about to see why*.

"Newbie idiot," Ordinal said from nearby, though under their breath.

"My lord," Nero said, rubbing at her face with both hands.

"Fool," Incident said, leaning forward in her seat.

Even Tennyson seemed aware of the problem; he let out a quiet whine and shuffled his feet to sit closer to Evangeline.

Oddry stared at the loudmouth fencer, a recently primed guy in his fourth month of work named the Devil of Smoke and Flame. (Not, Cal had whispered to Evangeline after meeting him for the first time, a name he could blame on having picked as a child.)

"I can't watch," Cal whispered, dropping his forehead until it touched the table with a soft *thump*. Tennyson sniffed at him and then put his own enormous head onto the table, too.

Moving around the podium, Oddry stalked forward, moving quickly enough for his too-large button-up shirt to billow slightly. The sleeves were rolled up unevenly to leave bare his wrists and stretches of his powerful forearms. Those hands, so technically gifted, were splayed wide at his sides now as he moved forward.

He stopped close enough to the Devil that he might have been the next to high-five the fencer. When Oddry spoke, it was in a low voice that would have gone unheard if the room hadn't gone silent as a winter night.

"*The Riparian*," he said, carefully articulating the name. "If you don't want to use that name, it has others. *Pyotr of the Pools. The Little Tear. Zenithal.* A billion other names. The Russians call it some foolish thing about dark ice. You've never dealt with it before, so I'm going to give you a pass right now instead of sidelining you for the Long Day, which I'd gladly do even with Effie transferred."

"I—" the Devil started, but Oddry shook his head.

"No. You're listening now." He leaned forward, putting a hand on the table. "You think the Riparian is a big bad guy and you're a superhero whose destiny is to save the day and destroy the villain.

"You've read the books and articles about how it moves through shadows as if they're doorways, crossing hundreds or thousands of miles as if they were just a single step. You've sat through briefings—some given by me—describing the effects it has on fences—destroying them sometimes by force and causing serious structural decay simply by its presence. You've read about how it appears, and in your tiny brain you probably think it's funny—a being whose coming is foreshadowed by streams and rivers carving through the ground where none were a moment before? Water from the air coalescing into tiny droplets that hang frozen in place or trickle slowly up trees?"

The Devil was looking uncomfortable now, the frat-bro grin on his face gone sour.

"You've seen the pictures and probably thought, in your pubescent comedy routine, that the Riparian has four eyes and you used to call the nerds you picked on in school 'four-eyes,' and here you are now, touched by the indivisible god and granted immunity to the cancer of the Harbor, given abilities Stan Lee could only have dreamed of."

Oddry's countenance had gone slack, his voice empty of emotion. Haunted.

"Those eyes *never* close," he said. "To be caught in their gaze doesn't just kill you; The Riparian *debrides* you, pulling parts from your body out and structurally undoing your body like the knot of tissue and bones and organs that you are. It's faster than you will ever be, and stronger, too. We had a fencer who outran it once, and that son of bitch was the fastest person *ever*—and he barely made it away before getting turned into spare parts. Like you, he was a cocky asshole; unlike you, he had the sense to respect the Riparian.

"It moves under a haze of shadow that no light can pierce, and so, when it attacks you, if you're dumb enough to get caught on the business side of the fence with it, you'll be trapped with a twenty-foot-tall being of seemingly infinite power who you can't see, can't look at fully without fear of being undone, and of whom we've never been able to achieve anything other than a blurry, hazy photograph."

Evangeline cocked her head at that. It wasn't technically true, of course. There were the pictures of *before*, the ones not burned or deleted from servers.

"What will you do, I wonder, when your cocky self swaggers in past the gate, your primes alight, your primacy in its full power, and Pyotr of the Pools appears on ground that was, just a few moments earlier, totally dry but is now running with fat rivers and blotted by toxic ponds? What will you do when it traps you against the wall, your coterie unable to help because they're dealing with the incoming fae who have gone mad in the presence of the Harbor and the proximity of their demon, and then suddenly Pyotr of the Pools pulls out its shears to cut your thread? When your body walks out of the gate and leaves you behind, the two no longer bound? Will they high-five your picture at the funeral after we capture and destroy your corpse?"

The Devil of Smoke and Flame opened his mouth to speak but nothing came out, and Oddry nodded.

"Respect for your enemy might be the difference between living and dying, and even if it isn't, it's the difference between you looking like a waste of space and not, so call it by its full name."

The only sound as Oddry returned to the podium was the scratch of Sister Marla's pen as it skated across the notebook page once more.

What do you think Sister Marla is working on? Cal wrote on his own pad of paper, pushing the message toward Evangeline.

Proof for the existence of a soul? Calculations for fae court power? Plans for world domination? Evangeline wrote back, one eyebrow rising into a soft arc.

I bet it's a grocery list, and she just wants us to think it's something mathy and important.

Oddry continued the meeting, talking about slight tweaks and changes to the government regulations that so often weighed down fencing work. He did not mention the Riparian again, and the Devil of Smoke and Flame did not speak up.

Cal and Evangeline settled into the rhythm of the updates and bits of administrative nonsense, passing the time with their notes slipped back and forth.

Can we even run a full coterie with 15?
I don't think my shirt is going to make up for how pissed off Oddry is.
Look at Ordinal—I think they fell asleep.
What do you think she's doing right now?
Did you see this picture she made? I'm going to hang it at my desk.
I miss her.
Me, too.

A History of Fences and Fae by AK Senga, PhD

Published in 2027 by University of Minnesota Majestic Press
Excerpt from Chapter 3: "The Fencers"

The historical precedents of the Harbors Act and the immediate geopolitical consequences of the autumnal equinox of 1987 covered, let us turn to what some scholars[1] have called "nature's response to our attempts to save her."

The fencers.

Today, it is impossible to avoid sight or sound of the fencers of the world. They adorn most billboards, feature in many commercials, and are regular guests on news programs and in government hearings. In 1987, though, when so much attention was rightly given to the chaos following that first autumnal equinox of the fae, very few people knew or cared about this other, seemingly more banal occurrence.

On September 23rd, 1987, approximately 545[2] people across the globe woke to find tattoos covering their skin. At first, these tattoos were thought to be merely random, chaotic assortments of numbers placed over the necks and chests and limbs and backs—everywhere but the faces—of these people. However, in time, and with the help of doctors and mathematicians, these tattoos were analyzed and found to be connected, with every numeral constituting one larger number, always prime, and always unique.

One number, never replicated from fencer to fencer, and always prime. Some were 500 digits. Some were 500,000 or 6.7 million. Questions

---

[1] e.g., Gallard, Tanisch, Flower, and Istis.

[2] Reports in those early years are spotty, and we cannot be sure how many fencers died or did not report their tattoos. We know of at least 545 people who were primed that first equinox, and by the mid-90s, surveillance systems and reporting procedures were clear enough that new fencing numbers became more dependable and more easily found.

about the origins of these tattoos quickly disappeared when it was discovered the primed individuals were resilient to the ill effects of the Harbors.[3] While the average person will experience negative health effects by prolonged proximity to a Harbor and certain death if foolish enough to venture past the fence and into a Harbor, one of these tattooed people can spend any amount of time near or even inside a Harbor without any deleterious health consequences.

Very quickly, the governments of the world snatched up any of their citizens sporting these curious tattoos. These people became scientists and construction workers alike, employed—and in most cases coerced—by their governments to explore the inside of the Harbors and perform repairs on the fences. In early 1988, the BBC reporter Gunderson Wright called them "fencers," and the name has since stuck and become an essential part of our lexicon.

A few months after that first equinox, a Brazilian fencer named Ivone Chaves was walking through one of the Harbors in her country picking plant specimens for scientific analysis when she was spooked by a nearby tree with glowing aerial roots. Without thinking, she leapt away. Ivone said later that she intended to jump only a meter or so, but in fact she leapt over forty meters away, crashing down into the grass and spraining both ankles.

What government officials and scientists realized shortly after this episode was this: the prime numbers tattooed on these fencers' bodies did more than confer resistance to the toxic effects of the Harbors. They also granted abilities, as unique as the numbers themselves, and the lower the prime number, the stronger the ability. These special powers became known as primacies.

With a single jump, fencers went from workers in armor to superhe-

---

[3] For in-depth scientific studies of the toxic radiation released from the Harbors, see the recent work of Gilstadt, Churche, and Khumalo.

roes, capable of fixing the fence during the winter, spring, and summer, and battling the fae each autumn, wielding powers impossible and arcane. Countries boasted of their fencers and the numbers of digits they had. China proudly showcased their top-tier team of four fencers, each of whom had a prime number in the low thousands of digits.

Manipur had, for several years in the early nineties, the most powerful fencer in the world, a woman named Leima Karam. Once the world realized how important it was to keep the true names of fencers from the fae, however, she went by the fencing name Tiger of Panthoibi[4]. Her prime was 79, the lowest the world would see until Arthur Miracle in 1996.

---

4 Deane's 2003 study of the Manipuri fencer, *With Claws and Teeth*, remains the only book-length work dedicated to this significant figure. As of this writing, the Tiger of Panthoibi remains one of only three fencers known to possess or have possessed a prime under 100.

Chapter 5

Oddry ended the meeting in his usual way—"That's all I have to say, so leave"—but amidst the zipping of bags and cracking of backs as the attendees stood, he motioned to Cal and Evangeline and said, quieter, "You two stay."

So, they waited around, greeting the other fencers, petting the other hounds, and commiserating over and over about the Effie news.

"Completely unreasonable," Evangeline said, nodding solemnly at Ordinal.

"Totally fucked," Cal said to Nero. "Don't forget the squad meeting in a bit."

"I'm very sorry to hear about your father, Calidore," Incident said, stopping on her way out. She extended one hand up and toward Cal, fingers splayed wide. The gesture of her religious order, the House of Always Giving. An open hand, extended in friendship beyond the borders of the known world. It was the same open hand that hung from her neck and that had been stitched into Harp's robes. The same likeness that was carved in Cal's dad's tombstone, next to his name and the dates that bookended his life.

Even the skin of her palm, soft and untouched by her prime, was littered with those crescent scars.

Cal nodded and mumbled an almost inaudible "Thank you."

"He was a kind man," Incident said, dropping her hand and trying to catch Cal's eyes. "I only met him a few times at House events or during worship, but I liked him. He had a nice smile."

"I'm sure you're sorry about his heart not quite making it to the equinox too, huh?" Cal clearly meant for it to come out loose and jokey, but instead, he spoke in a loud, bitter voice, the sound grating on Evangeline's ears and drawing the attention of those left in the room.

Incident's eyes flicked to Evangeline and Oddry before returning to Cal.

"Sorry again," she said quietly before leaving.

"She's trying," Evangeline said, tipping her head to one side as she nudged him. "In her own way."

Cal blew out the spent breath from his lungs and nodded.

When the other fencers and their techs had finally cleared out, Cal and Evangeline approached the front of the room, where Oddry was finishing up giving one of his assistants a list of tasks.

"I should punish you two for passing notes during my meetings," he said, turning to them and waving away his assistant. "Make you read them aloud like they did in school. Except I bet they're all about that cute little girl of yours, aren't they?"

"Usually," Evangeline said, smiling.

"Call for you, sir." It was another of Oddry's junior techs, a younger man with a goatee and thinning brown hair, peeking in around the doorframe. "Williams from Central."

"Nope," Oddry said, shaking his head and wagging one finger. He turned back to Cal. "How are you doing? The funeral was okay? Nice CHEMOS shirt, by the way. Teacher's pet."

Cal grinned, though there was something soft and defenseless about it.

"It was all right. The memory stuff, you know. It's hard with family. And I didn't even know him very well, not really."

Evangeline put a hand on his back.

"He was still your father. I'm sorry," Oddry said, the angry set of his mouth shifting for a moment.

"Winnie got to climb some trees, so at least she had a good time,"

Evangeline said, keeping her eyes on Cal, who looked to be blinking away the tears that seemed to never quite leave the edges of his eyes.

"Is it going to be a problem for you to visit the Sylvans?" Oddry asked. "I wasn't thinking when I—" he began, but Cal waved it away.

"I'll be okay. Thanks, though."

The room was cavernous without the sounds of the fencers and the limpid light of the projector still haunting the wall. It was silent and still outside of this old argument, and Evangeline felt suddenly as though she were in a great arena, the crowd watchful, anticipating the next move, the monster lurking just out of sight.

"Is Winnie back to school today?" Oddry asked, apparently immune to the sinister enchantment of the empty room.

"Two more days until the equinox break," Cal said, clearing his throat. He could be like this: quick to weep and quick to stabilize. "She was excited to practice her numbers in class today."

"What practice does my goddaughter need with numbers?" Oddry looked offended, and his voice rose. "I've never met a more agile thinker or mathematician, present company *included*."

"Hey!" Cal said, grinning now, his melancholy banished for another little while.

Evangeline, though, followed Oddry's eyes, which looked beyond her and Cal and were instead fixed on the person in the back of the room, the person who had not left with the others. A chill swept up the back of Evangeline's legs and along her spine as she turned to see Sister Marla, still in her seat. Her hair was cut close to the scalp on one side of her head and grown long elsewhere, the curls a jumbled mess of auburn and grey.

Her eyes were down, filled with the white expanse of the oversized notebook page on which she was writing, the scratch of her pen a near-silent whisper in the tall room.

"Silence is better than unmeaning words, Oddry," Sister Marla said, not bothering to look up.

"Shakespeare?" Cal ventured.

She did look up now, fixing the fencer with a grim-eyed look of annoyance.

"Pythagoras."

"He was going to be my next guess," Cal said, turning back to Oddry and Evangeline with a cheery, aw-shucks smile, the one Evangeline knew he used to cover nerves and anxiety in public. Early on in their relationship, she had realized how fractured and delicate Cal was down deep. Maybe it had been Cal's father's influence on him as a boy. From the stories Cal told about him, Cliff sounded like a boogeyman to young Cal, prodding him to be something else, mocking him for being what he was. Cal grew up hating and loving his father all at once, desperate to snub him and make him proud at the same time.

Evangeline found her thoughts drifting toward her own parents, two people who had loved each other earnestly, who had ridden the merry-go-round of life together in sun and snow. Losing Evangeline's name had been hard for them, but they had persevered, accepting the necessity of it eventually, even if they never truly understood. She still visited them regularly, and they loved seeing Winnie and Cal—Evangeline, too, despite the abyss between them where her true name had been, the black void of it pulling always at the loose threads of their memories.

"You ought not speak so ill of the Central Bureau, Oddry," Sister Marla said, standing and closing her notebook with a sharp *snap*. "It's not appropriate."

"We're charged with protecting and shepherding a near-third of the entire Midwest in less than a week, and they took one of our strongest fencers without warning, Marla," Oddry said, the grouch returning in full force. "They deserve the criticism."

"*Sister* Marla" was her only reply to Oddry as she walked toward the exit, though she paused in the doorframe for a moment, one hand resting on the faux wood of the post. "I am glad to hear the children are still practicing their numbers. In each numeral is the world's past writ. Do not forget your promise, Oddry."

She looked as though she wanted to pet Tennyson, who regarded her from where he sat between Evangeline and Cal, but ultimately decided against it.

"Why do they always have to say such weird shit?" Oddry asked as Sister Marla left.

"You say plenty of weird shit, Oddry." Evangeline looked up at the clock and sighed. "We should get moving, Cal. Those folks from the university are coming, and we have the squad meeting at ten."

"Your squad meeting has been rescheduled," Oddry said, chewing at his lower lip for a moment. "It's why I asked you to stay late. I'll be meeting with Ordinal later to go over this, but I'm breaking up their squad and reassigning the members to other squads for the Big Day."

He held up a hand, forestalling Cal and Evangeline's immediate cries of shock.

"We can't get around it. We don't have enough fencers to field four squads—we barely have enough to field three. You two and Nero will get one from Ordinal's squad, plus your trainee, to form a group of five. That gives us three squads of five each—good, prime numbers all around."

"*Three* squads, Oddry?" Evangeline gestured up at the map, which showed the Midwest Harbor, its border tracing an uneven, amorphous shape that extended into Minnesota, North Dakota, and South Dakota. The Dakota Fencing Bureau was in charge of the western portions of the fence, a far-larger section than Cal and Evangeline's group covered, but they also had some sixty fencers and a staff of techs at least three times what the Midwest had.

Still, despite that, the Midwest Bureau was in charge of almost ninety miles of fence and three fae lines that drew into it. On the equinox, hundreds of the Wretched would be running those paths, leaping along the tributaries and joining the larger avenues, all coming together onto one of those three fae lines leading to the Harbor and to the strange, unmapped land beyond.

Though the tributaries were too myriad to merit individual names, the three large fae lines were labeled: *The Nettled Path*, *The Lost Way*, and *The Grand Road*.

"It'll be fine," Oddry said, grimacing as he looked up at the map.

"It'll have to be. Each squad will move with five."

"Some of them are just kids, Oddry," Cal said. "Stone Weaver is, what, *nineteen*? And she's had her tattoos for less than a year. She's not ready, and she's the *best* of the trainees."

"She is the best, and Evangeline is the strongest of our fencers, which is why I'm assigning Stone Weaver to your new squad, which will take the Grand Road for the equinox."

"What about the rotation?" Evangeline asked, frowning. Since her time at the Midwest fence, she'd never worked an equinox where the squads didn't take turns on the Grand Road, which was the largest of the three fae lines and the one most prone to what the handbook called "Anomalous Fae Mischief" and what most fencers called "action." It was a grueling place to work the equinox, and most squads spent no more than a few hours patrolling it, pushing the fae back toward the Harbor, often by force.

"We're going halfsies this year," Oddry said, glancing down at his watch. "Your squad gets the Grand Road for the first half of the Long Day, and then you'll take the Nettled Path for the second half. Gloaming's squad will take the Grand Road after you."

"This is *dumb*, Oddry," Cal said. He'd lost the humor and levity that usually lifted his speech. "A squad of ten experienced fencers might hold and patrol the Grand Road for twelve hours without too many problems.

We're a group of four—five with a trainee—who haven't been training together, and one of us shouldn't even be working this equinox."

Oddry sighed, and Evangeline felt dread creep up her spine.

"Who are we getting from Ordinal's crew, Oddry? It better be Ordinal if we're going to be taking the Grand Road that whole time."

"Ordinal's leadership is needed on another squad, unfortunately," Oddry said, not meeting either of their eyes. "You'll be getting Stone Weaver, who needs far less training than most others—she's been putting up strong numbers this year. Additionally . . ." Oddry reached up and began twisting the hair on his brow, pausing to chomp at his gum loudly. Was he nervous? Hadn't he already delivered the bad news for the day? "You're getting—"

"Please," Cal said, realization hitting him like a truck a moment before it reached Evangeline. "Please, do not say the name I think you're going to say."

"Anyone but her, Oddry," Evangeline said, rubbing at her face with one hand. "Give us two trainees instead. Please. We'll even take the Devil of Smoke and Fire. Just not . . ."

Oddry glared, first at Evangeline and then at Cal, before speaking.

"The reassignment decisions have already been made. Your job is to accept it. Your squad will consist of you two, Nero, the Stone Weaver, and"—he looked down at a sheet in front of him—"An Incident on a Train Involving Two Goats and a Copy of the Holy Book."

"She came up with that name when she was *thirty*, Oddry! Thirty!" Cal began to wander around, stepping into and out of the circle of the conversation, as he did any time he was truly agitated. "It's one thing if you're twelve when your primes come in and you come up with 'Dr. Superstar Lightning Man' or whatever, but Incident was *thirty years old* when she decided her fencing name should be that."

"She's a capable fencer and has as much experience as both of you together."

"She's plenty capable," Evangeline said, nodding. "But you saw her during the meeting. Sitting by Marla, whispering together. You know she was the one who leaked our fence redesign plans to the mathematicians last year, just like you know she takes every scrap of intelligence and technical planning from our squad-only meetings and passes them along to the mathematicians *and* to the Sylvans. She's not trustworthy, Oddry."

"You—" Oddry began, but Cal picked up where Evangeline left off.

"She barely listened to Effie and Ordinal, and she's been with their squad for three years! There's no way she'll take directions from Evangeline, much less me or Nero. And, and!"

Cal held up a hand, splaying it wide and holding it in front of Oddry's face.

"She's a faerie worshipper! She shouldn't even *be* a fencer."

"Enough." Oddry's voice had gone hard. "This is not a conversation we are having. The assignments are made, and you will take Incident on your squad. We make do with the fencers we have, and right now, the Midwest, the United States, and the entire world—save those fuckers in Scotland, for some reason—are desperate for fencers. Even if it weren't *completely illegal* to fire someone for their religious beliefs, I still wouldn't do it with Incident. We need her, and not just for fencing. She's the whole reason—*the only reason*—we were able to set up this meeting with the Sylvans. They've invoked their nonsense about religious liberty every time we try to poke around in their activities near the equinox, and our dumbass government just goes along with it."

He stopped and took a breath.

"Incident is the key to our developing *relationship* with the Sylvans, and she'll need to go along on this visit, and since she's in your squad now—*she is*, Calidore, so stop looking at me like that—because she's in your squad, you get the honor of attending this historic meeting," Oddry said.

"Wait," Cal said, shaking his head. "I thought we were being sent as some sort of punishment for me talking during the meeting. You were going to send us all along, weren't you?"

Oddry pulled a pack of gum from a pocket—the kind kids chewed, big cubes of bright blue, dusted with white, wrapped in psychedelic smears of red and green. Oddry popped three pieces in his mouth and began working at them with the patience of a cow chewing its cud, staring at Cal the whole time.

"I saw an opportunity and took it," he said finally, offering a rare grin before growing serious again. "But I really am sorry about the proximity to your father's funeral there. I'm sure you didn't like being at that church yesterday, and I won't send you back if it's going to be an issue. I can make up some bullshit administrative work for you, and the rest of the team can go instead."

"I'll be fine," Cal said, shaking his head, though he didn't bring his eyes up to meet Oddry's.

"Good," Oddry said, popping his gum. "Because I need you to do more than just deliver goodwill and cheer, and I'd like the whole squad to be there for it."

"This isn't going to be a friendship-building endeavor?" Evangeline asked.

"Yeah, right," Oddry said around the blue bolus puffing out his right cheek. "We'll never be friends with them. Your agent told me you had a little tiff with their head priest before you left the funeral—did you get the feeling that we were heading toward kinship with them? That possibility left the room when those idiots started worshipping an imaginary lady beyond the fence."

"You really don't think the Faerie Queen is real?" Cal asked.

"No, and I don't think Santa is real, either, Calidore," Oddry said, blowing and popping a huge bubble.

"But what about that footage from ninety-five? And the articles and books and research?" This was an old debate, much chewed without ever losing its flavor. Did the fae operate under some grand authority that existed in those unplottable lands beyond the fences, some mysterious Queen who controlled the equinox dead, grabbing them as they turned from human to faerie? Or were the fae simply mindless animals, operating on alien instinct, magnets with arms and legs and odd abilities pulled toward the fences and the Harbors beyond them?

Evangeline cut in before the debate could get up to speed.

"Can we get back to business? You want us to go on this friendship visit, but it's not really a friendship visit, so what is it? What do you want us to do?"

Oddry stalked over to the door, the slap and chomp of the gum the only sound as he looked out into the hallway. Satisfied by what he saw, he came back.

"In addition to the official schedule for the visit, which will involve a tour of their facilities—most of them, anyway—and a sit-down with their head honcho, Gregory Harp, I want you to plant some iron in their sanctuary."

"You . . ." Evangeline was blinking rapidly at Oddry, her mouth working but no words emerging.

"I'm not finished," Oddry said, holding up a hand and pushing his gum into his lower lip, a pitcher staring down at a slugger ready to take him deep. "I want you—"

He pointed jagged-nail-tipped finger at Cal.

"To plant some iron in their sanctuary and get caught doing it."

Cal started to laugh, the ridiculous joy of it a happy distraction from that slow pain he'd been feeling since finding out about his father.

It was ridiculous. And impossible. The House of Always Giving forbade the presence of iron in their buildings throughout the year, but especially near the equinox, when it could harm any of their members "lucky" enough to die and find their faerie rebirth.

To bring it in would be bad enough. To be a fencer on a supposed friendship-making mission, the first of its kind, bringing iron into the House of Always Giving would mean legislative crisis and cultural war. There wouldn't be four protestors on the corner of Steiner and Main after this—there would be forty going on four hundred.

"They'll kill us," Evangeline said, finding nothing to laugh at in what Oddry had said. "And if they don't, the government will."

Oddry held up his hand once more to stop Evangeline's objections.

"While he is doing that, and in the ruckus after he gets caught, I want you"—Oddry's finger shifted to Evangeline now—"to take pictures of their entire internal setup, steal their records, and escape from the building, which they will lock down as soon as anyone realizes something is wrong. I need someone who can get their records and get out."

"Jesus, Oddry," Cal said, his laughter drying up as this plan moved from consequence-heavy tasteless prank to actual theft.

"Listen," he said, lowering his voice and leaning toward them. "This is not from me. It comes from higher up. If you cannot do it, I will find others who can, but it should be you—you understand why?"

Evangeline looked from the tattoos on Cal's arm to her own. She thought of the powers those tattoos offered them—the unique powers that had been waxing as the equinox neared and would begin to wane afterward.

"Yes," she said.

"Good. I will instruct your agents—Aleph and Fosse—in the plan. They'll have blueprints and details to share with you. Thanks to their obsession with old-timey shit, the Sylvans keep paper records of everything: budgets, plans, members. Probably write it with quills dipped in oxblood or something. We want anything you can get but especially member lists and financial information. And I want photos of their room and setup—the whole room, got it? Don't worry about legal repercussions—this order is coming from the top, and there's no heat they can't shield you from."

"But—" Cal began, but Oddry stopped him with a sharp gesture before nodding toward the hallway, in which footsteps and voices sounded. A moment later, two more of Oddry's techs poked their heads in.

"Calls for you, sir. Central and the Sieve, both high-priority."

"I'll decide what's 'high-priority,'" Oddry said, though he dropped his head in such a way that Evangeline understood their conversation was over.

Oddry hawked the glob of gum into a nearby trash can before sucking in a few calming breaths through his nose.

"Show me some pictures of my goddaughter," he said, turning back to Cal and Evangeline, "before I have to listen to these blowhards talk about whatever bullshit they have for me. I need something happy in my life."

Cal and Evangeline both brought out their phones and spent the next few minutes swiping through a gallery of Winnie's previous week.

"There she is on the playground. She almost threw up after spinning on that thing."

"She wore that unicorn crown for three days before losing it."

"Here she is, painting."

"Her favorite book. We always have to read it before bed."

"Here she is, drinking out of that weird straw you got her."

"Here she is, napping with Cal."

"Here she is."

"Here she is."

The Shop was a swarm of activity when Cal and Evangeline emerged, Tennyson trotting between them. Released from Oddry's meeting, the techs and engineers returned to their work on the vehicles with vigor, the symphony of their tools filling the wide, bright space. Pneumatic drills and arm-powered hammers *whiz*zing and *clack*ing, pressurized pumps lifting their *chunk-chunk* rhythm up like a prayer, the shouted words of the workers breaking through in a call-and-response verse, and, once he'd returned to his office, the holy thrum of Oddry's music behind it all.

"I need to put up Winnie's art at my desk, and then we can head over," Cal said, pitching his voice loud enough to be heard over the noise.

Evangeline gave him the A-OK sign and, Tennyson in tow, moved off to chat with Nero, who reacted exactly as Cal and Evangeline had when given the news about the expansion of their squad.

"You have to be shitting me," Cal heard Nero say, her voice blending nicely with the sounds of the Shop. He chortled as he set his bag down on his desk—one of many set up in the fashionably open-office style standardized by the Central Bureau. Evangeline's desk, just another thin, long table, was pushed up against his so they faced one another in the odd moments where they were both seated at their desks at the same time.

Hers was surprisingly chaotic, pens lying about haphazardly, hiding inside stacks of papers or sticking out of half-read books. Two bookends that might have introduced some order instead lay on their sides together to form a little platform on which Evangeline had balanced a used teacup, the string of the bag still hanging over the edge, stained brown and long dried. Framed pictures of Cal, of Winnie, of Cal and Winnie and Evangeline herself, punctuated the mess, marking out the corners of the desk and leaning against stacks of books and other used mugs.

When he'd first met Evangeline, Cal had assumed her clarity of thought and purpose would have extended to the world she kept around her, and he'd been shocked—pleasantly so—to discover she was colossally, fantastically messy. She treated the hamper like a mere suggestion for dirty clothes. Dishes once used could be used again so long as they weren't too dirty and an obligatory statement about saving water was voiced. Bookshelves required no order or organization and could hold, in addition to the randomized books, any number and type of oddity or knickknack, tchotchke, or memorabilia.

Between their desks was a pane of tempered glass, curved along the top like a rising sun. Both Cal and Evangeline had filled their sides of the glass with artifacts from Winnie—colored and painted pictures, random bits of writing practice from school or ten-word letters she'd written to them, and drawings of fantastical creatures in Winnie's distinctive style (huge eyes, tusks regardless of species, and always featuring a floating halo over their heads). They maintained a tiny window amidst the spread of Winnie's work, although the glass didn't reach so high, and they could have stood at any time to see one another.

Cal pulled open his bag, set it on his neat, organized desk, and removed the newest piece of Winnie art for the Cal side of the divider: a four-panel comic she'd made a few days earlier, using only red and brown crayons, about a young girl who learns she's a dragon rider and saves the queen dragon from monsters made of darkness called "Night Teeth." Cal had long ago run out of free space for Winnie's art, and he'd decided to just add new pieces on top of the old, like a city built on the sinking foundations of itself, climbing higher and higher. On slow days, and even on fast ones, he liked to lift the newer pieces and move back through a curated history of Winnie. Her early belief that only art made with the color green mattered. Her practice writing her name, struggling always to remember that there were only two *n*'s in *Winnie* instead of the four to seven she liked to write.

He taped this new one up over a half-sheet of paper showing a group of flowers with happy and sad faces that Winnie had drawn a few months earlier when she'd been just sick enough to not attend school but healthy enough to watch movies and color all day.

Cal smiled at the memory as he added the new art. The papers covering the pane of glass had grown thick, months and years of memories all combined into a strange palimpsest.

Along the edge of his desk, Cal had neatly faced and organized books, those texts that sat in the overlap between his own interests and relevancy to the fences: Spenser's epic, of course, Sir Orfeo and the other Breton lais, Yeats and Kipling, Muir and the speeches of Roosevelt the elder. To anyone else, it might have seemed a hodgepodge of disconnected literatures stuck together at random, like the books on the shelves of a showcase house, purchased for the leather of their spines instead of the contents of their pages.

But for Cal, who had no intention of leaving the ideological clutches of his time as an English graduate student, life was best lived with a carefully curated book list to inform it. Other people might approach large projects or moments in their life by pulling friends in close or accruing economic resources, reaching for comfort in any form or seeking advice from mentors in their lives.

If pressed, Cal would have said he did the same—the only difference was that his mentors were people he'd never met except through their books and poems, some published just a few years earlier and others like time capsules, buried in the pages of books from decades or centuries earlier. He liked to imagine these authors and politicians, environmentalists and poets reaching out from time's river, passing him a missive as they rushed by on leaky boats, or as he did. It was comfort and wisdom all at once.

The newest book on his desk, held at the end of the line by a bookend shaped like a sword, was a piece of nonfiction by one of the professors at the local university, AK Senga. She was an historian, newly hired for, according to the back of her book, her "revolutionary approaches to the field of fae new histories." The youngest in the department at the local university by about twenty years, Senga had apparently already been causing trouble, calling into question the methodologies and conclusions of all her senior colleagues. Just as she had been hired for her exciting, radical ideas, it looked as though she might find her way to being fired for them, too.

Cal grabbed Senga's book, *Cold Iron and Fae Bargains: Insights from a New Historical Approach*, and headed off to where Evangeline, Nero, and the Stone Weaver were waiting. He'd read the book over the past few weeks, at turns cringing at the studiously academic tone of Senga's writing and laughing at the cutting criticism she employed toward her own field.

"Did you bring a special pen, too?" Evangeline asked as he neared. He stuck his tongue out as the group of them left the Shop, tracing the shrub-lined walkway to the Bluestem Building.

Compared to the crooked angles and mismatched polygons of glass that made up the exterior of the Shop, the Bluestem Building was a study in symmetry and right angles. Upright, made of concrete and featuring flat-faced walls with rows and columns of springline windows. Up and up it went like this, every floor consistent with the number of windows (thirty-seven on the front and back of the building, thirteen on the sides).

People in suits walked in and out of the building, shades of navy and black shuttling between meetings and talking on phones. These were the money people, the workers sent from Central, the marketing and PR specialists, the administrators and project managers, the government oversight specialists.

The people who pretended to be in charge every day but the one that mattered.

"Is this the fewest number of fencers the Midwest has ever fielded?" the Stone Weaver was asking as they rounded an aggressively landscaped area with tiers of different-colored stones—bright white and fading to slate grey as the tiers rose—packed in around a few carefully curated stands of big bluestem, each one a bare handful of stalks rising into the air and waving fitfully about.

"Just about," Nero said. "Back in ninety-three, they had a major fencer shortage, and a few places got hit worse than others. This was one of them. I think they could only field twelve fencers then, but that's when they had Origins as their strongest fencer, and she was worth about six people all on her own."

She glanced at Evangeline, the Harbor's current strongest fencer, and said, "No offense, dear. You're worth four or five yourself."

Evangeline waved away the compliment. She cared so little for those power rankings and historical hierarchies of strengths and primacies, despite the very legitimate claim she had to a spot on them. Cal slid his hand into hers and smiled at her.

"Origins?!" the Stone Weaver said, turning wide eyes on Nero. "Did you know her?"

"My god, how old do you think I am?" Nero said, putting one hand to her chest and recoiling from the Stone Weaver, although she softened after a moment. "Origins was before my time by about ten years. I hadn't even gotten my prime when she was at her height, and she passed not long after I became a fencer. But I saw video of her in my early training. She was amazing."

Evangeline grinned over at Cal. This was one of their conversational hobby horses—the way that almost every interaction between and among fencers drew inevitably toward the pantheon of fencers past, as though those revered figures were black holes pulling all attention back toward them, their names like prayers whispered back and forth between the worshippers: Origins. Pabulum. Tabitha Runaround. Riot Sky. Extinction Event. The Long Rainbow.

The Stone Weaver shook her head in awe, looking even younger than her years. Short and thin, with dark hair and light brown skin, she'd been pulled from her senior year of high school the morning she woke up with the tattoos all over her body, her skin feeling like it had just been rubbed by ice cubes. It was the same feeling every fencer in the world experienced when their prime came in. Numbed. Chilled. Shivery and uncertain.

Nero was the Stone Weaver's opposite in many ways, tall and fat, closer to fifty than forty, and weathered by the winds of enduring experience.

But talking about Origins and the other figures from their personal fencer pantheons, these two might have been close friends from way back, happily tripping into one another's sentences, finishing the other's thoughts and cackling with delight at their jokes and observations.

"Oops," Evangeline said as she looked beyond their little group toward the front doors of the Bluestem Building, where a lone figure waited, like a stone rising from the currents of those moving around her, unmoving and uncaring. Unlike the suits entering and leaving the Bluestem Building, who either looked straight ahead or down at the ground, speaking into cell phones or focused grimly on reports held in front of their faces, this figure stood totally still, her face raised into the autumn sunshine, eyes closed, a beatific smile on her face. A cigarette in one hand trailed a tail of smoke into the air.

Incident.

"*She's* coming?" the Stone Weaver asked. Evangeline had broken the news to the other members of their squad, but none of them had realized Incident would be joining them so immediately.

"It'll be fine," Evangeline said, offering her best parental-reassurance smile. "She'll be weird and say some off-putting things, but Incident is harmless, and we need some squad cohesion, so let's try to bring her in, okay?"

Cal gave a thumbs-up as the Stone Weaver said "okay" in a dubious voice. Nero only grunted, the look of disgust on her face fading only slowly. Tennyson gave a low, sighing *woof.*

"My team!" Incident shouted when she saw them, sweeping her arms wide and nearly backhanding a suit walking by. "My squad! My *coterie!*"

This last she pronounced with a thick, stereotypical Parisian accent, mucus scraping across the roof of her mouth as she ground out the syllables through her nose.

"I hate her so much," Nero muttered, raising a hand in greeting.

"Squad unity," Cal said out of the corner of his mouth before fixing a smile to his face. He was thinking of Incident stopping by on her way out of the meeting to offer her condolences for his father, her hand spreading wide.

He ground his teeth and hoped it didn't show in his smile.

"Hello, Incident," Evangeline said, shaking the other fencer's hand. "Welcome to the squad. I'm glad we're going to have you with us. Let's go in, shall we?"

Chapter 6

"Sorry we're late," Evangeline said as the squad walked into their second meeting room of the day. This one was designed in corporate-boardroom-chic, complete with faux-wooden floors, high-backed chairs, tasteful lighting, and a table shaped like a bloated rectangle. It was one of many such rooms in the Bluestem Building, which seemed at times to exist exclusively for the purpose of having meetings in increasingly soulless spaces filled with geometrically questionable furniture.

Evangeline, after a few glasses of wine or a healthy pour of whiskey, would sometimes riff on what she called the "boardroom bros" of her previous Harbor in Florida, who structured their social hierarchy by the rooms they had their meetings in and how often (and by whom) they were redesigned. Cal had spent many a happy night with side pain from laughing so hard at Evangeline's impressions of the high-powered lawyers and tech bros who scuttled through those gilded halls and perched in those art nouveau–inspired boardrooms.

Waiting for the squad in this room—"understated, nü-modern, and tasteful," Evangeline might have called it in the boozy throes of her impressions—were three people, two men and a woman, talking passionately over one another, loud enough that none of them heard Evangeline's apology as they entered. Like the fencers, these three, professors from the local university, wore the uniforms of their office: thick sweaters going to rags around the necks and cuffs, collared shirts beneath, and ill-fitting khakis (for the two men) or a dark, floor length skirt (for the woman).

"—aren't taking into account the canonical interpretations!" one of the men was saying as the squad entered, his voice booming out with the long practice of someone who'd spent his life lecturing groups of uncaring twenty-year-olds.

"The canonical interpretations themselves are the problem, Gene!" This was the woman, AK Senga, the same one whose book Cal had been reading and now clutched behind his back.

"Methodology! No one teaches sound methodologies anymore!" The third man was rapping his knuckles on the table to punctuate his words, his brow furrowed and eyes scrunched shut in anger. Luckily, the others had their eyes open and stopped their argument mid-stride when they noticed the fencers.

"Apologies," the first man, Mr. Canonical Interpretations, said. His hairline had given up the fight long ago and retreated to the fringes of his head, where he kept the greying hair close-cropped, the same as the dark grey beard that covered his cheeks, chin, and upper lip. Silver-rimmed glasses framed eyes that were sharp blue and angry. "A small academic disagreement." His name was Gene Hayward, and he was the chair of the history department at the University of Minnesota Majestic.

"We understand completely." Evangeline offered that same parental smile and waved away the apology. "Didn't you tell me the last time we met that professional disagreement was the occasion for progress?"

The anger in Hayward's face vanished as he let out a boisterous laugh, tickled to have his own wisdom offered back up to him. "The *catalyst* of progress, I believe, but yes! You've a wonderful memory, madame fencer."

Evangeline let out her own laugh and gestured to the chairs for her squad. Cal caught her eye and smiled. Among all the ways Evangeline amazed him, this was perhaps one of his favorites—her ability to navigate situations with big, unyielding personalities in them, like a sailor cutting a perfect path between Scylla and Charybdis.

"Our squad has changed slightly since our meeting last year," she said, gesturing down the line of her fencers as she sat. "You remember Calidore, my husband, and Nero." Cal and Nero nodded. "This is the

Stone Weaver, one of our in-training fencers. She'll be joining our squad this equinox and possibly seeing some action."

The Stone Weaver waved, and the professors on the other side of the table each murmured their congratulations and welcomes.

"The newest addition to our squad is"—Evangeline looked down at the notebook she'd brought with her—"An Incident on a Train Involving Two Goats and a Copy of the Holy Book. She's not new to the Harbor, but we've had some restructuring of our squads, and we're very happy to have Incident join us."

Incident nodded at the academics before her and said, "Hello, apostates."

"And Tennyson, of course, is a familiar face," Evangeline said, patting the dog, who sat just beside her chair, his head resting on the table as if it were made for the purpose. His eyebrows, like mechanized things, twitched and arched as he looked from Evangeline to the academics and back again, over and over.

"This is the Stone Weaver's first research update, so could you please introduce yourselves?" Evangeline asked, pushing straight past Incident's jibe.

"Of course, Evangeline," Hayward said, ignoring Incident and smiling at the Stone Weaver. "I'm Professor Gene Hayward, dear. Scholar of history, in particular the long-latter twentieth in America, with particular emphases on political history and theory, fae-fence histories, and the Reagan administration. I believe one of my books is still required reading for new fencers, yes?"

It was, which he knew. The Stone Weaver smiled and nodded. What he didn't know, of course, was that Oddry didn't actually enforce the reading for any of the new fencers, which meant none of them ever turned a page in Dr. Gene Hayward's seminal text, *A Bold New Reagan Brought Low*.

Hayward sat back, satisfied.

"Hello," the other man said. He was short and thin, with a weak chin, wide eyes made wider by his thick, dark-rimmed glasses, and a head of disheveled brown hair that had seen neither comb nor shampoo in too long. He idly spun a golden pen on the open notebook before him. "I'm Dr. Terry Olson Breck, professor of history and folk-fae studies at the University of Minnesota Majestic, specializing in the history of folklore and fae representation in literature, intellectual thought, and philosophy. I am the current Escher-Lockley Writer-In-Residence in Majestic, and I'm completing my manuscript, *The Forgotten Fae*. Lovely to meet you and offer whatever help I can."

The final professor, AK Senga, was younger than her colleagues by far—probably in her late twenties. Her hair was brown, though it looked like she'd tried to dye it purple and blue at some point, the shoulder-length strands a muddled mix of brownish-purple, brownish-blue, and brownish-brown. Freckles dotted the bridge of her nose, and a complementary spray of acne covered one half of her jaw. She held a fountain pen at the ready, her fingers dotted and smudged by blue ink.

"I'm Adalynn," the woman said, nodding around at the fencers. She caught Cal's eye and held it for a long moment, looking at him with an expression he didn't understand. "I'm new at UMM this year. I'm in history."

An expectant pause followed this introduction, but Adalynn Senga apparently did not want to discuss her research focus (which Cal knew to be in the history of mathematics and its relationship with faerie folklore). She frowned down at a loose stitch on her sweater and said nothing more.

"*Assistant* Professor Senga is a welcome addition to our department," Hayward said after a moment, unctuous. "She brings a certain . . ." His hands had been laced together across one knee, and he unclasped and flicked them in front of himself now. "... *energy* to her teaching. And scholarship. Very refreshing."

Adalynn stiffened at this, understanding—as everyone else at the table did save perhaps the Stone Weaver—the insult it was.

"Speaking of your scholarship," Cal said, bringing out the only social weapon he had. Unlike Evangeline, who could see the truth and lines of power in complex social situations, Cal was a social blunderer, often saying or doing the wrong thing, misunderstanding what was really going on before and around him. His only saving grace, he had come to know, was to lean fully into his social clumsiness and be genuine, honest, and kind.

So, he smiled a guileless smile, first at Hayward and then at Senga as he lifted the book onto the table and slid it halfway across to the woman.

"I was wondering if you'd sign your book for me? I, well, we"—Cal gestured at Evangeline—"just finished it—we were reading it to each other before bed the last few weeks. We both liked it a lot. Especially the chapter about Grothendieck. What a guy."

The oleaginous smile on Hayward's pale face curdled as Senga leaned forward with a soft cry of delight.

"Of course I'll sign it." She pulled *Cold Iron and Fae Bargains* to herself and signed on the title page, her fountain pen sounding with a pleasant rasp against the paper. "This is silly, but I haven't actually signed one of these yet. No one really buys academic texts except libraries, and they usually frown on people writing in their books."

"I have to know," Cal said, catching the book as Adalynn slid it back across the table to him. "That story about Grothendieck living in that tiny town where he ate only dandelion soup, but then the people of the town would bring him cakes and things—is that true?"

Cal opened the book to the page—he'd remembered which it was because of the number, 239. Prime. His messy handwriting dominated one of the margins, written in pencil, one of the many Winnie kept around the house. Evangeline had been reading when they'd reached the part about the once-forgotten mathematician, Alexander Grothendieck, wilting away in his self-imposed hermitage.

Cal, who'd been happily drowsing and moving steadily toward sleep, had asked Evangeline to read it again, blinking away the heaviness of sleep as she read once more about his final days in a small village in the Pyrenees, burning away as he saw deeper than anyone ever had into the realm of mathematics. He had been infamous by then, his work as a founding member of Survivre et Vivre having had such a hand in the creation of the Harbors, his connection to the Reagans, to *that* book, having been revealed, but still he'd hidden away at the end of his life, unknown by those around him.

And on the door of his small house—a hut really, based on firsthand accounts—Grothendieck had carved a final cryptic missive to the world: *I am become the sleepwalker.*

His body, Adalynn's book reported, was never found, although he'd been far too weak at the end to leave his hut, much less disappear into the brush and wilderness around the village.

Government forces from each of the world's major powers had descended on the village when it was finally discovered that it held—or had held—Grothendieck, but none had been able to discover anything, at least not anything they had disclosed.

After hearing it a second time, he'd taken one of Winnie's pencils—green and black with a dragon design and topped by an eraser shaped like a rocket—and written *NO FUCKING WAY* in the margins.

"As far as we know," Adalynn said, a small grin pulling up one side of her mouth. That inscrutable expression had once more returned to her face as she looked at Cal. "It does seem that story is true. I was granted access to some archives that support it, and I snuck into a few others that verify it, too. Sascha Grothendieck *did* disappear to that village sometime in late 1990 or early 1991 and live there for a few years alone, working on a grand theory, one that utilized the languages of mathematics, philosophy, spiritualism, and what he called the original tongue, all to explain the fae—which he referred to as 'a mathematical problem only the rising wave could solve.'"

"He was amazing," Cal said, shaking his head. "But also terrible. He leaves his wife and three kids, and then a new wife with another kid, all to go be the tortured math guy in the woods, and people bring him cakes for it?"

Adalynn shrugged.

"He was complicated. A genius. And an incredibly selfish man. Those two things were probably related."

Hayward *humph*ed as he placed a spread hand on the table, reclaiming the conversation.

"Much as I think we would *all* enjoy a thorough discussion of our junior colleague's extraordinary work," he said, nodding soberly, "we are here to deliver the newest findings from the fae-folk research sector to our heroes on the ground, are we not?"

He rapped on the table with a fist, and as if that were the signal, the three academics began unloading the faux-leather bags on the floor at their feet, bringing out notebooks and heavily annotated articles, academic texts thick and thin, prints of ancient artworks, mathematical schema, and pages of glossed poetry in Old and Middle English.

The table grew crowded, like a Thanksgiving feast for intellectuals, the texts covered in words and phrases like *counter-systemic hegemony* and *teleological ontologies*. One article, pushed out by the expanding materials, was titled "Repressive Return: A La-fae-nian Analysis of Faerie Libidinal Economies." Evangeline eyed this one and tried to hide a frown.

"These are only a small sample of the exciting work—criticism and primary texts—that have been finding relevance this year," Dr. Breck said, patting the pile of books and articles with soft, open hands, the motion somehow childish. "The field is booming, and we're excited to guide you through the major theoretical and scholarly thrusts of the past twelve months."

Evangeline opened her mouth, but Hayward swept in, picking up on the end of Breck's sentence like a trained musician sliding in seamlessly for his solo.

"We've pruned away the immature and, frankly, dilettantish scholarship that has begun to grow along the edges of our field," Hayward said, and did he cast a brief glance at Adalynn's book held in Cal's hand when he said it? Evangeline thought maybe he did. "What we have for you today is the best of the best, only that scholarship which has been published in the most prestigious journals and undergone the most rigorous scrutiny."

He pulled an article from the papery mass and flicked it.

"The field was stunned this year by this article, and if you are to understand any of the numerous breakthroughs we've had, you must understand this—written by our colleague from New York University, Professor Winston Ernest. It's titled, 'The Numinous Queen: A Historical Reading of The Queen Beyond The Mist.' In it, Ernest makes several key arguments, one using my own approaches, I should say, and he—"

Hayward was looking down at the article in his hand, beginning to flip through and run a considering finger along his annotations, so he couldn't see Evangeline trying to get his attention, the apologetic smile on her face growing more and more strained, until she had to interrupt him.

"Before you get too far into your presentation, Professor Hayward," Evangeline said, finally catching his eye as he looked up, startled, her own sorrowful mask returning in full force, as if she were a parent about to break unfortunate but necessary news to a child—which, Cal thought, wasn't so far off from the truth. "I want to apologize and let you know:

because of the last-minute changes in our squad and the need for intensive and immediate training to prepare us fully for the equinox, our meeting today has been shortened to only thirty minutes. We were just informed on our way over—I'm truly sorry."

Dr. Breck actually gasped at this, while Hayward simply stared at Evangeline, his mouth still open from the sentence he hadn't yet finished. Only Adalynn seemed unfazed by this information. She crossed out a few lines on the notebook in front of her but otherwise seemed perfectly fine with the usual three-and-a-half-hour meeting being cut down by so much.

In truth, it had been Oddry's small gift to them, a tiny offer to soften the blow of Incident joining their squad. Every group was required to meet with the local research experts at several points throughout the year to "get abreast of any new and significant developments in the relevant fields," and the updates were almost uniformly wastes of time. But they were required, and only a serious and unforeseen circumstance (such as a major organizational shakeup less than a week before the equinox) could trump that requirement.

"Well . . . I . . ." Hayward blinked and shook his head, trying and failing to come to terms with this information.

"There's simply too much," Dr. Breck said, in a hushed tone, as though he were surveying the ruined remains of a natural disaster. "Thirty minutes."

Incident, the smile widening on her face, began to chortle, the sound high and slightly mad. Next to her, the Stone Weaver was looking around, confused and uncomfortable.

"Dr. Senga?" Evangeline prompted as she uncapped a pen and held it ready over her own notebook. "Perhaps you could give us your best summary of the key ideas in the field this year, just to get us started."

"Of course," Adalynn said, blinking for a moment and then beginning with a sharp nod. "As my colleagues suggested, we've had a truly remarkable year in terms of new and diverse ideas entering the field, but key are these three, I suppose."

She tapped the list before her with the end of her pen.

"One: the confirmation through both mathematical and literary means of our long-held suspicion that the Harbors themselves have at their core some kind of portal or doorway to a shared fae realm. Despite the Harbors dotting the globe so far from one another, they're best thought of as doors that all happen to lead to the same room. What that room—the fae realm—actually is, no one knows for certain, of course, but the proximal placement theory, as scholars have taken to calling it, has been explored with enough disciplinary and methodological variety to confirm it."

Hayward raised a hand, perhaps to disagree with his *junior* colleague, but Adalynn rolled on.

"Two, and this comes primarily from our colleagues in the animal sciences but is supported by robust textual evidence: the fae are best thought of as animals."

"Blasphemer!" Incident took a turn at shock and dismay now, actually rising from her chair to glare down at Adalynn, who shook her head and raised her cheap pen in defense.

"Oh, no, I'm sorry—it's not meant as an insult. These scholars don't use animal as a pejorative to describe something *less* than human. Quite the contrary, actually!" Adalynn brightened with a smile, and Incident slowly sank back into her seat. "What they really mean is that we cannot project our own human logic and thought processes onto the fae. Just as anthropomorphizing a moth or a moose can very quickly lead to misunderstanding and error, we also shouldn't anthropomorphize the fae. They do not act human because they *aren't* human. Many folklore scholars have suggested this from the beginning, but animal sciences scholars have supported this reading by arguing the fae lines you all will guard this equinox are nothing more than migration routes, for instance.

Other important work was done investigating the little we know about fae magic, their hunting practices, and the mischief they cause on their way to the fae lines."

Cal snorted at that. *Mischief* didn't even begin to cover what the fae got up to each equinox, the violence and destruction, the senseless, almost-gleeful way they delivered death. But what would scholars know about the truths of the Long Day when they spent it carefully locked away in their homes, forbidden from going outside or putting themselves in any danger—what could anyone other than the fencers and techs and emergency medical workers know about what the fae could really do?

"I will let your near-insult pass," Incident said, pointing at Adalynn with two fingers. "Your scholarship reveals the truth even if it uses clumsy language: the fae are greater than us, and as we cannot fathom the Queen's mind, neither can we fathom her subjects' actions."

"Please continue, Adalynn," Evangeline said, sighing and looking down at her watch. "You had a third key finding from this year?"

"Yes," Adalynn said, nibbling at her lower lip for just a moment as she sifted through the piles of paper in front of her. The piece she pulled forth bore a simple title: "The Sleepwalker and the Queen."

"Absolutely not," Dr. Breck said, waving his hands as he saw which article Adalynn held. "I'm sorry, fencers, but I *must* put my foot down here. This drivel should never have been published at all, and that Adalynn here is willing to not only spend her own time reading it but also be prepared to offer it to you as serious, impactful scholarship is an insult to our field and our institution. Gene, surely you agree?"

Dr. Breck turned to Hayward, who was nodding, a troubled, sad look on his face, as though he were about to tell a child, *This is going to hurt me more than it's going to hurt you* before a punishment.

"You've put it very well, Professor Breck," Hayward said after a long moment. "I hope you will forgive young Adalynn—she is still finding her way in academia and in our department, where the standards for scholarship and research are famously high. We intended to bring her along today so that she might be a shadow, learning from this meeting and *observing* without the responsibility to summarize a whole field she is still acquainting herself with in a professional capacity. Much like the young Stone Weaver here"—Hayward gestured, magnanimous and smiling, toward the youngest of the fencers before him—"a bundle of potential and possibility, no doubt, but still learning the craft, yes?"

The Stone Weaver nodded, her lips pushed together into a thin line, her eyes down on her lap.

"So, so," Hayward said, rubbing his hands together, "perhaps I could return to my overview and, in particular, the key findings from Ernest's work. You'll find some incredibly exciting revelations . . ."

But those revelations were destined to remain unrevealed, because Evangeline once again interrupted Hayward, putting out a hand across the table, her reach pulling up her sleeve and revealing the inky mess of numerals crowding her skin there.

"Professor Hayward, I appreciate your wisdom on this, but I'm afraid it was my boss, Oddry Mulligan, who requested Professor Senga's presence here at this meeting, and I was given explicit instructions to hear from her. The Central Bureau is keen to know more about her research agenda and sense of the field. If we have time at the end, we would love to hear your interpretation, though. And you, too, Mr. Breck."

Hayward became a fish on dry land, mouth opening and closing in a dumb play for air. Breck, too, had nothing to say, merely looking around in astonishment, perhaps deciding whether to be more insulted by getting shunted to the "Any additional thoughts?" slot at the end of the meeting or by Evangeline calling him Mr. instead of Dr. or Professor. He might have seen it as a slip, but Cal knew better, and he knuckled away the smile that threatened to spread across his whole face.

"Professor Senga?" Evangeline asked, nodding at her.

"Sure. Right," Adalynn said, glancing quickly at the two professors on her right before focusing on the article she still held in her hands. "The Sleepwalker and the Queen.

"This piece, published in a special issue of the *Journal of Math Histories* focused exclusively on Alexander Grothendieck, tracks his early history—long before he became a famed mathematician, founded Survivre et Vivre, or co-authored *The Last Thylacine* with his fellow activists. The author of this essay is Talia Diop, a historian—"

Hayward scoffed at this.

"A *historian*," Adalynn continued, "at the University of Edinburgh who published *the* definitive biography of Grothendieck. In this essay, Diop recounts Grothendieck's early years as the child of two activists. He was a boy who, by his own accounts, was quite odd—for instance, he spoke only in rhymes for a time as a child, a detail that should not be ignored when it comes to his hand in fae history. Diop, though, pays particular attention to Grothendieck's time in an internment camp at the age of twelve in Vichy, France, where he was kept with his mother. His father, we know, was shuttled around between camps for a few years before being killed at Auschwitz."

Adalynn flipped through the essay, which looked to be far longer than the average twenty- or thirty-page academic article. She stopped on a page filled with several passages underlined.

"Diop is careful in her analysis to avoid the all-too-familiar antisemitic trope often employed in considerations of Grothendieck's history—him as a scheming mastermind behind much of the world's folly. Instead, she sees him as man manipulated from an early age by forces far beyond his own understanding. A blade thrown by an expert hand. Grothendieck's life is a marvel in many ways, but Diop has found what might be the most amazing—and, for your purposes, significant—moment of all. While at the Rieucros Camp, a young Alexander met two women, one young and one older, prisoners just like him. The young girl was named Maria; the older woman is a person Grothendieck referred to as 'lovely, beautiful Diana,' though records of the camp show no one there with that name. Scholars wrote off Diana's inclusion in Grothendieck's recounting as the necessary imaginations of a child facing terrible conditions, including his mother growing sick—she contracted tuberculosis at that camp and would succumb to it years later. It seems an easy leap to assume this twelve-year-old, imprisoned in this camp with his mother and separated from his father, created Diana as a coping mechanism, either at the time of his internment or in his later years while recounting the events in writing, and who could blame him?"

"It's an easy leap because it's *obviously* the truth," Hayward muttered, the words ground out between his teeth. He'd collapsed in on himself, arms folded across his chest, head down, jaw working.

"This has been the working and widely held belief—a *certainty*, really—for many years." Adalynn was growing excited, her words coming faster and faster, and even Hayward's obvious anger seemed to have no effect on her. She was leaning forward in her chair, eyes wide and bright, Diop's essay held before her.

"In Grothendieck's writing, he describes the three of them becoming friends, or at least friendly, talking and sometimes eating together. The key recollection, though, for Diop, comes when Grothendieck describes how one day Maria taught him a truth about circles: that they are simply a collection of points equidistant from another point."

Adalynn tapped out some dots in a rough circle in the margin of the essay to illustrate the point.

"A simple, anodyne lesson between two children in horrible conditions," Adalynn said, "but that night, as Grothendieck recounts, Diana came to him 'glowing as though caught up in the moon's light itself.'" Adalynn read from the essay now. "'She took my hand and led me from where I was sleeping, out into the bare emptiness of the camp itself, and there on a patch of sandy ground, she traced Maria's circle, teaching me about it many pristine and wild things. She recited poetry to me, much of which I did not understand. 'Ulysses' by Tennyson. *Sir Orfeo* in Middle English. The beautiful Diana offered me much, and told me that, for the right price, she could offer me everything. It was an easy price to pay. I returned to my bed with many thoughts, chiefly of mathematics and the shape of the world. In the morning, Diana was gone.'"

Adalynn looked up, surveying the fencers before her.

"This passage has long been discounted as either the trauma response of a young boy or the growing senility of an older mind. It is clear, of course, that by the end of his life, Grothendieck had begun to lose his grip on reality, which has led many scholars to discount his writings entirely, save for the pieces that can be externally verified.

"However!" Adalynn held up the essay, papers rustling like wings in her hand, "Diop makes a startling argument, one that proceeds from a simple question: what if Grothendieck is telling the truth? What if Diana really was there? If she really was there, then we must ask who she was and how she escaped registration and the camp itself!

"Perhaps she was another revolutionary, like Grothendieck's parents, caught up in a world conflict. Maybe she was just a regular citizen, like so many others, her life ended by a brutal regime whose record-keeping could not even remember her. Or perhaps the young Grothendieck was shown kindness by one of the guards and gave to her a fantastical name since she did not give her own? This could be, though Diop *is* careful to point out that we have no records of any female guards at the camp.

"But what if the truth is stranger yet?" Adalynn looked around at the fencers before settling on Cal, her face twisting with that expression again, and Cal understood it this time to be delight, the kind a person might have before revealing a present they've been long anticipating giving to a friend.

Not just delight but expectant delight.

"Diop draws a connection between this Diana and a character in Edmund Spenser's famous poem, *The Faerie Queene*." Adalynn turned the page on the essay and read.

"Grothendieck refers not just to 'Diana' several times in his remembering but to 'beautiful Diana,' a repetition that begs our attention turn toward Spenser's infamous character Belphœbe, a representation of Queen Elizabeth, the metaphorical faerie queen herself. 'Belphœbe,' of course, translates to 'beautiful Diana,' the name an epithet for Artemis—a goddess with connections to the moon (consider the fact that Grothendieck's Diana is described to us as aglow with lunar light).'

"Diop's argument is clear and compelling, if not conclusive," Adalynn said, setting down the essay. "Perhaps this mystery woman discounted by so many scholars in the past, this *beautiful Diana*, was the Queen of Faerie herself, emerging from the fae realm to seed into the receptive mind of young Alexander Grothendieck the very ideas that would lead him to fame, to madness, and to pen the very book that would go on to ruin the world!"

"This is *nonsense*," Hayward said, his neck red with rage, spittle speckling his lips. "Never, in *any* historical or folkloric account, do we see even the slightest hint that the Faerie Queen even exists—I'm sorry to say it, madame fencer." He held up an apologetic hand to Incident before continuing. "The so-called Bloodless Queen Hypothesis is, academically speaking, only that—a *hypothesis*, and a flimsy one at that! And even if the Faerie Queen *does exist*, we have no folkloric or literary evidence that she has ever left her thornéd halls or the fae realm, much less stepped across the fence!"

He slammed a hand down on the table to emphasize his point.

"These textual readings," Dr. Breck said, his agitation expressing itself in the speed of his speech, "are without merit or concrete contextual veracity, and in-so-far as they exist within the scholarship, they are nothing more than the work of B-rate academics—*children* with large vocabularies—playing a what-if game with the fate of the world and the integrity of our field!"

Breck sucked in a breath, his eyes wide and hands shaking.

Hayward looked to be readying himself to launch again into invective, when Tennyson barked, the sound deep and frightening, like thunder that presses on the sternum and promises violence to come. The hound still sat at Evangeline's side, though he'd raised his head from where it had rested on the table to better consider the two men seated across from him.

He did not snarl, nor did he bare his teeth. These men would know what a fencing hound could do, especially so close to the equinox. Had they not been on the other side of the table, they might have seen the black-and-white pattern of Tennyson's coat seem to shift and swirl slightly—not the hairs but the coloring itself, splotches of black expanding and contracting, runs of white stretching and cutting new courses along his back and sides.

Evangeline paid no attention to either the sudden academic antagonism or Tennyson's silencing bark. She kept her eyes down, scribbling notes for a long moment before finally looking up.

"Thank you for this update, Dr. Senga," she said, smiling. If Cal's conversational technique was a feckless smile and trusting innocence, Evangeline's was this: tactically ignoring or brushing past that which she did not want to grant validity through her attention. Cal could often not resist rising to an argument, whether it was from a coworker or from Winnie, who was expert at baiting him into a losing conversation.

But Evangeline chose her battles with care and patience.

"I suspect our people will be very interested in what you've offered us here. We will have access to Diop's article, I assume?"

"Yes, of course," Adalynn said, flustered after the outbursts from her colleagues and the conclusion of her scholastic revelation. "I brought copies, if you'd like to take them."

"We would, thank you," Evangeline said, smiling at her and taking the proffered essays.

"I'm sorry to ask," Adalynn said, eyes returning to Cal, "but it seems too strange a coincidence—this connection to Spenser's poem through Grothendieck's writing and your own name—*fence name*, I mean—taken also from Spenser's poem."

This was dangerous territory, and Cal felt the slightly shameful thrill of schadenfreude slip from him as he waited for the inevitable question, one of the forbidden few that hung like a miasma around fencers, tempting interviewers and friends alike, pulling at the restraint of anyone who happened to meet one of the tattooed heroes of the world.

To mock a fencer's name, to hold it up as reverent, to speculate about its importance or laugh at its supreme silliness—all of these were fine, even to a fencer's face. Cal suspected that, by the end of this equinox, his own restraint would be ground away and he would openly harangue Incident about her fencing name, the length of it, the pomposity of it.

"I was doing a PhD in a field of literature no one cares about, and *even I think your name is pretentious!"* He could already imagine himself shouting the words at Incident. And while it would degrade the squad dynamic some, it would break no rules, official or unofficial.

But what Cal would never do, and what he knew Adalynn was about to do for him, would be to ask Incident *why* she chose that name, or perhaps *why* that name had chosen her. A few fencers, early on, spoke of the phenomenon—the feeling after their tattoos had come in that they were standing in a gallery of art but that each piece of art was a name, hovering before them. Some shone bright as a sunrise; others twisted with dark horrors; some stretched to fill the imagination and lift the spirit; some clutched deep down in the stomach, where shame and guilt lived.

Some were the chosen names of children—Space Princess or Killer Storm Hero Man—but the selection itself, the stroll through that endless gallery with the dark recesses inside it—*that* was holy, never to be talked about, never to be divulged if it could be helped.

Cal's full fence name, Calidore, was plucked from that gallery, and he had delighted in recognizing it as coming from Edmund Spenser's sixteenth-century epic poem, one that he'd studied in graduate school and loved despite its (and Spenser's) faults. Calidore, in Spenser's work, was the knight of courtesy, though a younger Cal, reading the poem for the first time, had loved how this knight was not one of grand deeds and glorious battles but one who often criticized and questioned the very truths about knighthood that he embodied. He was a figure of contradictions, and Calidore felt right taking on that name, not to embody it perfectly but to add yet more contradictions to it, to further tangle the knotted truth of it.

His own primacy, of course, only added to the perfection of the name.

"I was wondering—" Adalynn began, tiptoeing into the taboo topic.

"That's all we have time for, unfortunately," Evangeline said, snapping her notebook shut and smiling around at the scholars before her. "Thank you again for an informative presentation, and I hope to have much more time for you during our next meeting. One of the building attendants will be along to help you out."

"Thanks for signing," Cal said, holding up Senga's book as he followed Evangeline to the door, the other fencers just behind.

The sounds of an argument, one fought with weapons like "postmodernity," "liminality," and "hagiography," trailed behind the fencers as they left the room and moved down the long hallway.

"That was terrible," the Stone Weaver said as they reached the large central staircase around which the Bluestem Building was designed.

"That was pretty standard, actually," Nero said, shouldering a bag and nodding at a man walking by, ensuited and texting on a phone that looked tiny in his large hands. He stopped and stood aside for the fencers, offering Nero a grateful smile to even be noticed by her.

"They always fight like that?" The Stone Weaver pulled an energy bar from a pocket, unwrapping and eating it in a single, cheek-stuffing bite. So close to the equinox, with her primacy ascending, she was hungry all the time. They all were, and so the bureau supplied the fencers with food of all kinds, though especially these easy, on-the-go bars.

"Always," Incident said, squinting up at the autumn sun as she planted a cigarette in the corner of her mouth. "They sniff at the Queen's doings like dogs examining a work of art, and like dogs"—she lit the cigarette and pulled in a deep breath of it, and her next words were accompanied by the tumble of smoke from her lips—"they can't help but bite and scratch one another in their idiocy."

A History of Fences and Fae by AK Senga, PhD

Published in 2027 by University of Minnesota Majestic Press
Excerpt from Chapter 3: "The Fencers"

Before continuing, a note about names and naming.

With the discovery and confirmation that the equinox dead were turning into faeries, it followed that names—true names—could prove dangerous if discovered by the fae. For the average citizen, who spends the autumnal equinox today sheltering in place in their homes, this has become an almost-moot point, but for the fencers who, starting as early as 1988, tangled with the fae each year, their names became a resource as valuable and vulnerable as an energy grid in a winter storm.

Fencers in those early years took on fencing names, but they were nothing more than public monikers, and those old, true names continued to exist in government documents and the minds of friends, family, and acquaintances. The Tiger of Panthoibi's mother continued to call her Leima. The most powerful US fencer of those early years—until Arthur Miracle came along—went by the fencing name Odin's Rage, but at his first press conference, the journalist Peter Jennings opened the questions by saying, "Hi, Douglas. Thanks for your service."

It wasn't until the early 2000s that the intergovernmental workgroups focused on memory work developed the first processes for actually removing names from the mind. In 2002, scientists at Stanford reported the successful modification of one woman's memory; everything remained the same for her except for the newfound inability to remember the name of the test subject, a Texan fencer going by the moniker Firebrand.

In what seemed no time at all, the true names of fencers were being scrubbed from internet databases, school records, and old print archives, but more importantly, they were being scrubbed from the minds and memories of friends, family, teachers, coworkers, and anyone else who had known them.

A curious note before moving on: in those early days, fencers themselves underwent the modification procedures, but every single one of them emerged with the memory of their true names still intact. It was, scientists discovered, impossible to remove someone's own name from their mind.

But what fencer would willingly give their enemy the keys to their own destruction?

Chapter 7

The phone rang as they were leaving the administrative building, and Cal hung back with Evangeline while she talked.

"It was fine," she said in response to Oddry's questions, her eyes going distant even as she waved goodbye to the squad. Tennyson, too, watched the other fencers go but stayed beside Evangeline. "Yeah. Senga pushing the Bloodless Queen Hypothesis. Somewhat convincing. Yeah."

Oddry, she mouthed to Cal, and then a second later, *science trip*. He gave her a thumbs-up and wandered over into the nearby landscaped patch of prairie grasses. If Oddry was calling to send them on a science trip—what he called "experimental peregrinations"—then Cal and Evangeline would be in the Harbor before the end of the day, scraping tree bark and pulling up plants, ripping out handfuls of leaves and scooping up soil.

"The science nerds want more plant samples before the equinox," Oddry said into her ear. "Something about autumnal proximity and growth patterns."

"How many should we send in?" Evangeline watched Cal and Tennyson poking around in the patch of landscaped bluestem, so much like the grasses that grew beyond the fence in the Midwest Harbor, although each of the samples fencers had brought back from the Harbor for scientists to study over the years had turned out just slightly wrong. Tiny variations in the DNA structure or coloring or stem makeup or root system. Little things that looked to have been changed.

"Just the two lovebirds should do it," Oddry said, and Evangeline could hear the bubblegum in his mouth. "We'll have folks out there, me included. In and out, no problem. You okay with that?"

"That's fine," she said. "I was worried you might want the whole squad."

Oddry paused for a moment and then said, "Yeah, sorry about that. How's group unity? Everyone getting along?"

"Incident, you mean? She was okay with the academics. A little weird, but her usual stuff." Evangeline smiled and nodded at Cal, who was trying and failing to play hide-and-seek with Tennyson in the tall grasses.

Oddry paused again, and Evangeline felt a tick of worry at that. Oddry Mulligan was not a man for pausing.

"She's not really the one I'm worried about, fencer."

Tennyson boomed out a deep, playful bark from the grasses, and Cal answered with a yelp of his own.

"He's just having a hard time with his dad," she said, turning away from Cal even though there was no way he could hear her from where he was. "He'll be okay. He and Incident are a lot alike, which doesn't make it easier."

"They're what?"

"You know—both big personalities, both anxious around other people, both true believers in this thing we're doing." Evangeline could hear her own mother in her head, and she spoke in that voice. "They're leaves on the same tree."

"This kind of team-leader-social-science-people-smart stuff is why those big suits up in the northeast want you, you know?" A click on the other line was the only warning Evangeline got before Oddry's music—at a lower volume than normal—began to rage in the background. "Everyone thinks it's because of your short prime and your primacy, but this is really it. You see people for how they are."

"I guess so," Evangeline said. Why deny it? Midwest faux modesty had never suited her with its understated arrogance and implied swagger.

"Is he going to be ready for the Long Day?" Oddry asked.

"Yes."

"And you think he can handle this Sylvan thing? Really truly?"

Evangeline didn't want to pause, but she could hear her quick *of course* and knew it for the lie it would be.

So, she took a breath and felt herself at a crossroads, her ties to Cal leading her down one path and her professional responsibilities sending her along the other.

"I'll be there with him," she said finally. "And so will the rest of the squad."

"Fine, fine," he said, and if he understood her response as the non-answer it was, his voice gave no indication of it. "Get on over to the fence. Just a few samples should do it—from that same colony of vines. You know the ones they mean?"

"I sure do," Evangeline said. How many times had they pulled leaves and berries and vine fragments from this particular patch? Her own squad had done it five times, maybe six. "Must be something interesting in there for the scientists."

"Those weirdos could look at a pair of old shoes and claim they're the most interesting things on the planet. I've seen your samples—they look like regular vines to me. But the scientists need *something* to stick under their microscopes."

"Sure," Evangeline said. "See you there in a bit."

"In and out," Oddry said. "Nothing fancy or weird. No hiccups so close to the equinox."

Evangeline hung up, still thinking of that patch of vines—one of ten thousand bits of odd, fae nature growing inside the Harbors. Why the research folks were focused on this bit instead of one of the others was beyond her. They mostly looked like regular plants to her, too, although it was like that at all of the Harbors. What had begun as nature preserves for the sake of the Earth and biodiversity had morphed into something else, something close enough to the known natural world that it might go unnoticed, its oddity unrecognized.

In the massive Southwest Harbor, there were trees that had once been giant sequoias. Their location and type and age and coloring had all been carefully studied, mapped, and noted before the fence had gone up. Conservation biologists, botanists, ecologists, soil and air scientists, and researchers of all kinds had worked to compile that data for the Southwest Harbor, and yet only a few years later, when fencers had gained government approval for regular scouting missions into the Harbors, one such mission returned with clippings, bark samples, and root samples from six of the giant sequoias, those same scientists and researchers were baffled.

None of the trees were sequoias, not anymore. One had all the biomarkings of an elm despite the fencers swearing it still looked—as did all of them—like a giant sequoia. Three others were identified, after much work and many confused calls to other plant specialists, as *Sigillaria*, a plant supposed to have gone extinct during the Permian period. Other specimens studied—bushes and flowers and vines—were identified as odd, impossible amalgams of extant but distant plants and extinct species from hundreds, thousands, or millions of years ago. More than a few were simply unidentifiable.

Evangeline let her memories of these scientific impossibilities run through her mind as she walked over to Cal and Tennyson. How funny was it—or maybe it was irony, actually; she could never remember—that the Harbors, meant to preserve the disappearing world, had ultimately ended up resurrecting an old one and maybe creating a new one.

In the Midwest Harbor, just a mile or so over to the west from where she stood now, fencers—including Evangeline herself—had brought back bits of plants that held long strings of animal DNA, their leaves covered in leopard spots or rough like a gecko's skin. One tree that Cal had sworn was a maple based on its leaves—palmately lobed leaves, he'd excitedly told everyone after learning it from one of the scientists—

turned out to be just that, save for the tiny streams of bison blood trickling through the leaves.

The vegetation was chaos inside the Harbors, a mix of impossible, old, and impossibly old.

Of actual animal life, there was no sign.

"Another peregrination?" Cal asked, meeting up with her as she walked out toward the parking lot, away from the path that would take them back to the Shop.

"Vines again," Evangeline said.

"There's Aleph," Cal said, waving toward a black truck rolling slowly toward them. "I'm surprised Oddry is having us go in so close to the Long Day. It couldn't wait until after?"

Evangeline held open her hands, as if to say *Who knows?*

Autumn was singing soft in the wind, and the light of the sun promised warmth without heat. It was perfect, and Evangeline took a big, deep breath, holding all of it—light and air and the crisp edge of the world—in her chest.

Cal took one of her hands, lining up his arm with hers, his hip with hers.

"I love you," he said.

"I love you, too."

Tennyson, as if sensing he had been forgotten, nosed his wet snout into the tangle of their hands, and Cal leaned down, running a hand through the Newfoundland's thick fur.

"I love you, too, Tennyson," he said, and Tennyson gave him a sloppy kiss in return.

"Let's take a trip after this equinox," Cal said, bringing himself upright and smiling in that happy-go-lucky way he often did. "Go to the ocean or Europe or China. Paris. Nebraska. I don't know. Somewhere."

"Winnie has school," Evangeline said, but already she could feel the *yes* inside her. A trip sounded great—perfect, in fact. Get away from Majestic, from the fence. Evangeline, ever dutiful, would speak aloud the reasons it couldn't work, of course, not to convince Cal that they shouldn't do it but to pay tribute to the obstacles they needed to circumvent to make it happen. "And there's always the rush of fence repairs we have to help with afterward."

"We don't have to go right away," Cal said, opening the door of the truck as it stopped before them. The cab itself was plenty roomy for the two of them plus Tennyson, and Aleph at the wheel, and the bed held all manner of tools, technology, and weaponry. "We could wait until winter. Winnie could miss some school, but who cares? It's the beginning of first grade—it's a successful day if no one eats paint or forgets the color blue."

Evangeline pressed a hand to her chest in outrage and shock at this. They'd spent many long nights during those first years after Winnie was born talking about where they should send her to school. Given the length of Evangeline's prime and the overwhelming power of her primacy, it was not out of the question for the two of them to transfer to another Harbor if they really wanted, and they spent many days looking at early education programs in the South and along the West Coast. Evangeline refused to return to the Southeast, but with so many other Harbors in the US, especially in more-populated and less-rural areas, they had plenty of options.

But in the end, they'd settled on staying in Majestic and sending Winnie to the tiny school just outside of town, built initially as an experimental charter school but purchased eventually by the school district when it became clear there just weren't enough wealthy families interested in experimental education in the Majestic area. The school was fine—full of mostly good teachers and only a few stinkers, and led by people who really cared about the students.

And maybe, they thought, Winnie would grow up and understand that life wasn't a big competition to be won by accruing little badges that read things like *Ivy League* and *prestigious, elite*. Maybe she would understand that swimming forward along time's stream, high on her own supply and certain, *utterly certain*, that the universe had a center and she was it, was a shitty, childish way to live. If Winnie could learn to live among anyone—even, *gasp*, people neither prestigious nor elite—then, Evangeline and Cal had reasoned, she might find that elusive good life everyone always said they were after.

Evangeline and Cal heard from fencer acquaintances and friends at other Harbors who sent their kids to elite private schools, taught by the finest minds money and power could buy. Little Susan, who had almost aced some high-level aptitude test after a grueling second-grade year. Bryce, who was having his art shown professionally in New York City as a capstone for his sophomore year in high school. Samuel and Tara, twins, who had enrolled at a rigorous boarding school in rural New York that, according to their parents—a fencer named Alekazhar and her partner, a surgeon named Anna—had been attended by several senators-to-be and more than a few future Nobel laureates.

With these burgeoning egomaniacs in mind, Cal would feign shock at discovering that Winnie's first-grade teacher, Mrs. Iverson, didn't even have a PhD, and Evangeline would stare in dismay at a bag that returned home with Winnie that didn't contain any "calculus for the young genius" worksheets. The parents would flutter around the house, peering at Winnie's drawings and whispering to one another that she'd never get into Yale with such simplistic lines, and when Winnie struggled with adding two one-digit numbers together, Cal would *tsk tsk tsk* and say, his voice mournful and weary, that advanced physics might simply be out of reach for her.

It was a way for the parents to ask one another *Are you still okay with this decision?* and for the other to say *absolutely*. That secret language, the language of laughter and silences, of body language and old stories and slantwise truths, had been Evangeline's favorite part of building her relationship with Cal. Learning how he spoke and what it meant when he went silent, what honesty looked like for him and what face unease showed—all of it felt like a gift from the universe, a special, secret thing she got to learn and know and hold.

They saw more protesters on their way through Majestic, more signs criticizing the government, the Fencing Bureau, and the fencers themselves. The influence of the House of Always Giving was there, lurking behind the large, angry letters, forming the thoughts that had gone into making them. The Sylvans weren't the fire itself; they were the wind, giving the blaze fuel and reach.

"It's getting worse," Cal said, watching as a group of protestors clustered around a woman standing up on a box, holding her own sign.

FORCED IMPRISONMENT "FOR YOUR SAFETY" IS STILL IMPRISONMENT.

"A senator from New York—Carlton Thael—came out in support of them just a few hours ago," Aleph said, a single slight curve in one eyebrow the only admission of a perspective on this news.

"*Officially* in support?" Evangeline asked. There had been quiet, indirect support from politicians, but had any of them actually come straight out and stood behind the protestors? She didn't think so.

"Yes," Aleph said, turning the truck onto the street that would take them out of town and toward the Harbor. "His office released a statement, and he gave a press conference afterward. It was during your meeting with the professors."

"Oops," Evangeline said, turning to watch the edge of Majestic melt away into corn and soybean fields.

"He's a Sylvan, right?" Cal asked and received a nod from Aleph.

"He's the senator who led the vote to let the Sylvans break ground on that facility in New York—the one that's technically within the parameters of the Harbor-adjacent land." Evangeline fogged the window a little as she spoke. The autumn air outside had turned cool, like an emissary from winter, warning the world true cold was on its way.

"I remember him now," Cal said, thinking back to the headlines from the previous year. "He's the one who spearheaded the project to drill in Alaska."

Aleph dropped his voice to a low, clipped mumble, the perfect impression of Carlton Thiel, and said, "If we have irretrievably granted our Harbors to the fae, then it is only right that we may make full use of the Earth remaining to us."

A moment of stunned surprise filled the car after this, and then both Cal and Evangeline were laughing.

"That was dead-on, Aleph!" Cal said, still giggling.

"I didn't know you did impressions!" Evangeline said. "Who else you got in there?"

"Shelly says I do a pretty good Bob Dylan, and I used to get my son giggling with my Kermit the Frog impression." Aleph's normally stoic face softened into a smile at the memory, and they spent the rest of the ride to the Harbor poking and prompting at Aleph until he relented and put his remaining impersonations on display. Even Tennyson enjoyed the show, loosing a few subsonic barks and wagging his huge tail.

They left Highway 19 and turned left onto a road called Fence Way, a wide gravel road girded by signs proclaiming it to be a MAJOR HAZARD ZONE and NOT FOR THE PUBLIC. After a mile or two of open skies and long crop fields with their neat lines and orderly rows, a thick spruce wood sprang into being along the left side of the road, and it was through this that Fence Way wound.

The sudden transition from field to wood had always felt jarring to Evangeline. Every Harbor had its own shift like this one—a sudden dip away from the land into a valley where the Harbor was located or a curve into mountainous terrain where the miles of Harbor hid. But in the Midwest, where the sky was an endlessly open vault above and the horizon was only ever a distant, unbroken line, the sudden shock of shaggy evergreens swallowing sky and horizon alike never lost its surprise.

On Fence Way, the sounds of the outside world disappeared, but more than that, it felt like the possibility of sounds and movements and events went too, as though the open sky and endless flat fields of the Midwest might at any moment explode with birdsong or a murmuration of starlings tracing arcane language against a backdrop of distant thunderheads.

Cal liked to go for runs on a road that cut a straight line between two cornfields, and during the later days of summer, when the heat of the sun felt thick and warm, Evangeline would sometimes ride her bike along with him and listen to the sound of the wind stirring corn husks already going dry and thin. She couldn't help but think that that sound, which was not just a sound but a movement and a collision and a scraping and a dancing—she couldn't help but think that it needed the openness of those fields, that it was the product somehow of all that space.

Driving along Fence Way, her knees drawn up and held tight by the circle of her arms, Evangeline looked out at the encroaching crowd of spruces and thought that the possibility of sound or movement or happening was gone, edged out of existence by those thick, sloping branches and their baronies of blue-green needles.

The gravel road moved back and forth gently, as though mimicking the soft curve of a river, until finally the trees broke away on either side and the world opened again.

Aleph brought the truck to a stop, and the three of them got out, each bringing their gaze eventually around to the huge structure before them.

The fence.

It rose ahead of them, still fifty yards off but imposing nonetheless. A structure woven of wood and iron, steel and osmium. Static and lifeless, yet it writhed all the same, every curve and twist of it an illusion of stability. Almost forty years before, in 1987, when the fences were first built, they were simpler things, some chain-link and some iron slats, but all barely functional and—save for the gates where pictures were taken during the locking ceremonies—ugly.

At first, the fences had been functional only if one imagined their purpose was to deter the average drunk hiker or curious fishermen. This was land set aside for nature's purpose, for wilderness to flourish. For the wild to exist again. There were no trails, no service stations or water pumps inside the miles and miles of preserved land harboring the threads of biodiversity and nature that the world had come together to protect.

It emerged in the ensuing years that the Reagan administration had had plans to monetize the Harbors by selling exclusive and expensive access to groups ranging from interested scientific parties to wealthy thrill-seekers and trophy-hunters. Their plans were altered, of course, after the first equinox and the realization around the world that the Harbors were no natural things, but it remained the case that those first fences were closer to the chain-link jobs lining the edge of peewee baseball and softball fields all over America than anything serious or formidable.

Now the fences were form and function entwined, huge and well maintained and built to deny attempts at trespass from the outside as well as the inside.

This one, the Bluestem Fence surrounding the Midwest Harbor, had been built to withstand the climate of Minnesota, North Dakota, and South Dakota—rounded edges to defy the ever-present wind and winter-resistant construction to weather the frozen violence of the Midwestern cold season. The Redwood Harbor down in California had a fence built with waves of bluish metals and iron posts shaped like trees spiking up into the air. The Lone Star Harbor sprawling over hundreds of miles in Texas was crowned by the upturned horns of thousands of bulls. Evangeline and Cal had gone to see those other US Harbors during their early training, back in the days before their house, before Winnie, before settling down here.

Each of the fences, no matter where it was built, was exactly thirty-one feet high and nineteen feet thick. In some places, the walls were topped with crenellations and towers. In Russia, home of the highest number of Harbors for a single country, their walls were capped with towers swirled and colored like those of St. Basil's Cathedral, a nod to their architectural past and their aesthetic superiority.

"Why can we not be both beautiful and formidable?" Gorbachev had asked in the lead-up to the autumnal equinox in 1987, when the world still looked to these Harbors as symbols of international cooperation and grand human progress.

In the end, the rest of the world had agreed, and in the ensuing years, the United States, along with every other country, had turned their crummy chain-link or wooden-slat or rope-and-pillar fences into true symbols of national pride and power, work done exclusively by fencers immune to the toxic energies of the Harbors. It was as though, to truly galvanize a population thrown into the grips of terror by the horrors of the equinox, countries had to wage an aesthetic war against the fae and the Harbors just as much as they waged a physical one.

The Bluestem Fence was maybe one of America's least aesthetically impressive fences, and the Harbor beyond—appearing to be a seemingly monotonous field of native prairie grasses broken only occasionally by a large tree—was one that, even in 1987, average people found underwhelming.

But both Cal and Evangeline had stepped foot into that Harbor before—not for too long, and never very far—and they knew how deceiving the docile, quiet stretches of tallgrass prairie could be. It was as though the Harbor was pretending to be something that people expected, holding over itself an illusion that might soothe and calm the people who, throughout the year, stood safely back and peered through binoculars at it.

Step over the threshold of one of the gates, though, and the illusion slipped, like a mask shaped into the likeness of a beautiful person held over the face of a monster, and with each step, the mask twitched and fell further away, until there was only monster and nothing human.

Today, Cal and Evangeline would look beyond that mask at the monster beneath.

"Oddry's over in the huts," Aleph said, gesturing off toward a cluster of small, low-roofed huts set a hundred and fifty feet from the fence itself. Workers from the Bureau used them to take readings and keep equipment, and though techs were not allowed to spend more than four hours at a time so close to the fence—to prevent "possible unknown deleterious effects," according to the official handbook out of Central—they were still a bustling place most days.

"Bye, Tenny," Evangeline said, pressing her face into Tennyson's massive one and ruffling the fur around his neck. He was off for a final tune-up with the vet. Normally, any expedition into the Harbor, even a short one, was accompanied by a Newfoundland, but this would be a quick jaunt, and the vet checkup was necessary.

"Bye, sweet guy," Cal said, planting a kiss on Tennyson's nose and giving him some ear scratches.

They waved at Aleph as he drove off before walking over toward the huts.

A few of the buildings were home to stores of materials for patching and repairing the fence, which the fencers would spend the off-season doing, their primes protecting them from the very well-documented deleterious effects from the Harbor. Some held extra weapons fencers might use in a pinch. Others housed spare microscopes and the long-range binoculars favored by fence workers.

One, Evangeline knew from experience, housed an emergency room, carefully stocked with every bit of life-saving medical trickery a doctor could need. She'd taken extra first aid and medical training classes herself to use some of those machines in an emergency. Fencers who fell during fence repairs or cut themselves on the endless bladed whorls of iron at the top of the fence could find aid in that hut.

Similar clusters of the small, weathertight buildings existed by the North Gate—locked and barred and unstaffed for many years now—and the Western Gate, which was managed by the Dakota offices of MBUSFB and their fencers.

The wind was a constant out there, always gusting out from the Harbor, always cold. No matter the day and no matter the weather, a chilly wind blew out from the Midwest Harbor, one that shook the trees Cal and Evangeline had just come through and ruffled the grass they walked over now but seemed to have no effect on the tallgrass prairie inside the fence, which was uncanny in its stillness. As if it were waiting for something. A beast about to pounce, all attention and potential.

"It's beautiful out here," Cal said, smiling up into the wind and sunlight.

"I like it better in winter," Evangeline said. "It's quieter. The snow is like a big piece of insulation around the weirdness of this place."

Cal kicked at a clod of dirt poking up through the grass.

"That's true. Plus, if it's winter, that means we had another successful equinox and don't have to worry about another one for half a year." He looked over toward the fence. "Still, there are so many fae in the winter who haven't gone through yet."

Evangeline nodded at that. Everyone who died on the fall equinox became a faerie, and all of them disappeared into their closest Harbor by the end of the day or shortly thereafter, but not all went through the

Threshold Tree immediately. Some loitered in the Harbor interior—a fact only discovered by those early fencers who explored the Harbors without any safety mechanisms or scientific understanding on their sides.

Some of the fae, though, meandered around closer to the fences, staring out at the world, gibbering or singing to themselves, climbing trees or building strange structures out of rocks.

Eventually, all made the journey through the Threshold Tree, and the longer they stayed out, the less energetic and dangerous they became, but still—Evangeline would take those early winter months when movements beyond the fence told of the fae still kicking around in there. At least it didn't feel then like it did now, so close to the equinox. Charged, tense, like a bottle balanced *barely* at the edge of a table.

They found Oddry in one of the larger huts, working with a few of his techs at the wall-mounted table that traced the perimeter of the room.

"I think it's going to be a big floppy flop," he was saying as Cal and Evangeline stepped into the center of the open, peak-roofed room.

"The earlier tests looked promising." A tech, a twenty-something kid with dyed red hair and thick-framed glasses named Burke, frowned down at the item they were both fiddling with.

It looked like a cell phone from the eighties, cinder-block thick and geometrically unimaginative. The cover was a matte black and looked well worn, the spiderweb of scratches and scuffs covering every inch of it. There were only a few keys where the regular grid of 0–9 should go, but it had the microphone and speaker slits and a thick, stocky antenna reaching up from its top.

"Are you planning to call in for your Wham! tickets on that thing?" Cal asked.

"Leave the comedy to your betters, fencer Calidore," Oddry said with a glare.

"I thought it was a fine joke, sweetie," Evangeline said, smirking and bumping her hip into his.

"Let's not encourage him," Oddry said, hefting the cell phone in one hand. It looked heavy.

"New tool?" Evangeline asked.

"Yeah," Oddry said, holding the brick out to Cal and Evangeline.

"What do you want us to do with it?" Cal asked, running his fingers over the surface.

"In addition to getting more of those plant specimens, you're to bring this hunk of junk into the Harbor and try to make a call with it once you're further than a hundred and fifty feet in," Oddry said, watching with plain disgust as another one of his employees, Laszlo, worked with tweezers and a jeweler's loupe at a scaled-down version of the entire Midwest fence. The tech was swearing under his breath as he tried to leverage a nearly microscopic sliver of wood into place on the model.

"But electronics don't work in the Harbor," Evangeline said, taking the phone from Cal. "Is it just because it's old that you think it'll work?"

"Just stop, Laszlo," Oddry said, glaring over at his tech. "Go do something else."

"But promotion wanted a model by—" Laszlo the tech began.

"If I have to watch you try to glue that piece of wood onto that dumb thing for another second, I'm going to chew my fingers off. Go do something else for a while."

Laszlo gave his model one last look before setting down his tools and joining a few other techs, who were working on what appeared to be a disassembled computer. Oddry returned to the conversation.

"It's not old tech," he said, running a well-chewed fingernail over the surface and pulling a thin rasp from the material. "And it's not really a phone. More like a walkie-talkie. It connects to that one Burke has over there."

Burke held up a matching block.

"And it's going to work because . . ." Cal began.

"To be clear, *I* don't think it's going to," Oddry said, holding up one hand to stop Burke from speaking. "My very-junior colleague Burke, however, thinks it will."

"Clearly, I'm missing something," Cal said, looking around, his cheeks going slightly red. Evangeline knew how much he hated feeling like this—like truth had been hung out to dry and everyone could see it but him. Cal had told her about how his father had liked to laugh at his ignorance of the world, not as a parent might delight in their child's creative understanding of life but with what Cal would later come to understand as cruelty. Cliff was a man who could not find much in the world to leverage himself into a position of superiority, so he used his son to reach what heights he could. He would taunt Cal, playfully at first and then not, withholding some bit of information just out of his reach. *You don't know who the president is?* Cliff would ask in horror. *They don't teach you anything at school, meathead?*

Once, during one of their rare date nights, Cal had admitted to Evangeline that all of his time in graduate school and all the intellectual work he'd done there—the deep dives into archaic authors and obscure literary movements, the long nights reading and rereading poetry that yielded little in the way of meaning or sense—all of it had been his own attempt to tell himself that he wasn't that little boy Cliff had laughed at and called stupid. "I just did it to prove to myself that I was not my father and I was not the child of my father," he'd said.

She'd wondered later that night if he'd only believed that lie during his time in graduate school or if, somehow, he'd gone on believing it since.

"This walkie-talkie-thing is from the mathematicians," Oddry said, popping a piece of candy from one pocket into his mouth. "They designed it all. I didn't have a hand in any part of it."

Evangeline leaned close, studying the abrasions and scratches on the comm device.

"And what makes them think it'll work beyond the fence?" Cal asked, looking to Burke for clarity.

"It's not scuffed," Evangeline said, holding the device up to her eyes and squinting. "It's carved—engraved, I mean. Tiny numbers. It looks like a—"

"The mathematicians think they found a prime," Oddry said, the candy socked away in one of his cheeks giving him a slight lisp. "It happened a few months ago, I guess. One of them found a live prime and caught it using whatever mathematical powers and numerical prisons they have down in the lower levels of the Sieve. They carved it on that hunk of junk and want to see if it protects the technology just like those tattoos protect you."

Evangeline said nothing. Could say nothing.

They'd tried this before, the mathematicians. Carving primes on technology and weapons. Tattooing them on willing participants. Encoding them into the guts of simple machines. And then throwing their experiments across the fence.

It never worked. The tech broke down, rusted and aged as if it had been recovered from an ancient, waterlogged tomb. The machines sparked and spat and died. And the participants came back with the same symptoms as any unprimed fool who ignored the warnings and broke into a Harbor: lesions along the arms and legs and inside the mouth; a high-pitched melodic noise that no one else could hear ringing in their ears; spots in their vision that swam and resolved only to return later.

And eventually, internal bleeding. Hardening of the skin. Loss of teeth, toenails, and fingernails. Organ failure. And finally, of course, death.

So little was known—really known and understood—about how and why the primes found the fencers they did, but the mathematicians in service of the fencing bureaus had studied the process from the very beginning, and early on, a mathematician named Brother Tom had said something at a press conference that had chilled Evangeline then and now.

When asked what it was the mathematicians at the bureau were finding about prime numbers, Brother Tom, grinning his yellow smoker's grin, had said, "Primes are mysterious. No formula yet exists to reliably find these numbers. We've made progress, but it's a challenging, fundamental problem in mathematics."

And then Brother Tom had leaned close to the microphone and said, "Primes, you see, like to hide."

There was something about that smile, each tooth outlined in the dark black residue from thousands of cigarettes. And something, too, about primes being more than just numbers on a page. Mathematicians spoke of finding primes, but according to the trainings and some hushed conversations Evangeline had had with some administrators, including Oddry, that process was more than just writing the number down and verifying that it was a prime. It involved, she had learned, something like understanding the number's true essence—something much more like finally seeing who a person was after years and years of knowing them. The mathematicians talked about these numbers as if the numerals themselves were only the door, and their correct arrangement the key. Everything interesting, everything that might be sought and caught, they said, existed through that open door.

It frightened Evangeline, down on a level she didn't care to think much of, to imagine primes—her own included—as having personalities and characters, desires and intentions. To think of those mathematicians down in the Sieve as hunters, seeking those primes that had somehow grown rich and wild with energy.

What if they caught one?

And what if they caught hers?

"A real prime? This isn't just some number carved into a walkie-talkie?" Evangeline asked, disbelieving.

"They claim it's real," Oddry said.

"They always say that," Cal said, looking now at the walkie-talkie with contempt.

"They do," Oddry said, "which is why I think you're holding a future failure in your hand. But . . ."

He ran a hand over his scalp before giving that tuft of hair at the edge of his forehead a twirl.

"But what?"

"Sister Marla was different when she delivered this tech. The number badgers are always saying weird shit and pretending they know arcane truths, but she was *really* excited when she brought this to me. Much more than she's ever been in the past. Like she'd just found out it was her birthday or something."

They chewed on that for a moment, and Evangeline fought the sudden urge to hurl the walkie-talkie—the apparently *primed* walkie-talkie—at the concrete wall. She didn't know how her primes worked, no one really did. But this, if it was the advance the number-crunchers promised, was wrong. Distasteful. Sacrilegious.

"We're losing daylight," Oddry said, crunching through the candy he'd been sucking on. "You should get going."

"You've looked at the Riparian data, right?" Evangeline asked.

Oddry nodded.

"He's still in Russia?" Cal asked, and Evangeline clenched her teeth at the flare of discomfort hearing that "he" caused her.

"*It*," she said, widening her eyes at him.

"Sorry, sorry," he said, but his look said clearly, *What's the big deal?*

"I checked the data myself just before I came over here," Oddry said after a thick moment of silence. "Three sightings from the Russian mathematicians in the last day."

"*It*," Cal said, emphasizing the word, "has to still be in Russia, then, unless *it* has suddenly developed the ability to be in two places at once."

Oddry was staring off, though, not listening to Cal.

"I thought maybe . . ." he began but didn't finish.

"You thought maybe?" Evangeline asked.

"Nothing," Oddry said, shaking his head. "Nobody really understands how the Riparian operates, so we won't question it. Still, those vines are just inside the gate, right?"

"Right," Evangeline said.

"Good. Go grab a few of them and try that dumb walkie-talkie. If you leave it in there, I won't tell anyone."

Chapter 8

The Eastern Gate was a wicked thing.

A mess of metal, all long, twisted bands of iron, sharpened and curled into something menacing and cruel. Bladed edges spilled out over the top like the tangled tines of a farmer's cultivator. Worked through this chaos of banded metal were large steel posts set into crosses in each door of the gate.

One of the doors stood open now, and it was toward this Cal and Evangeline walked. The doors of the Harbors were closed except for times when fencers were sent on exploratory missions or internal fence repairs.

And, of course, on the equinox, when all the gates on all the fences around the world were thrown wide to welcome in the new fae.

"Iron?" Evangeline asked as their boots crunched against the gravel.

"Check," Cal said, tapping the sword at his waist. Neither of them wore the same blades they would bring on the equinox, but it would be enough. With the Riparian still lurking around in Russia, and with no fae still lingering around in the Harbor, they shouldn't have any problem.

"Sample canisters?"

"Check." Cal held up the metal tubes they would put the cut vines in.

"Let us go then, you and I," Evangeline said, giving him a smile.

The gravel disappeared and was replaced by thick, springy moss as they neared the gate.

"Fencers going in!" came the mandatory shout from the sentinel on watch—a man who sat in the hut positioned nearest to the gate, still a cautiously safe seventy feet back.

"Safe going!" The response was a muffled echo from all of those techs and scientists who happened to be working at the fence that day.

Cal and Evangeline passed through the open gate, and the power of the Harbor reached out to them. Much had been written about the pain, the disorientation, the dread of walking through a Harbor's gates as an unprimed person.

For fencers, it was a gentle pressure and nothing more. It made Evangeline think of sitting safely inside during a rainstorm.

Across the threshold, the Harbor *stretched*. What had looked like a few acres of prairie grasses lorded over by the occasional tree from the other side revealed itself to be instead a few square miles of the tallgrass prairie native to this part of the world.

The land for the Harbor had been carefully measured in the mid-eighties during Reagan's great push to establish the nature reserves around the United States and the world. With a perimeter of just over 260 miles, the Midwest Harbor was supposed to have an area of over 7,300 square miles.

But the truth every fencer knew is that the Harbors flexed and expanded within those numerical confines. Midwest fencers had made extensive efforts in the early nineties to map out the Harbor, and their work had shown that, from the inside, the space of the Harbor had to have been well over 25,000 square miles. More, perhaps. It always seemed to be changing, like some hibernating animal stretching and grunting, resettling itself for a long sleep, dreaming strange dreams.

Cal and Evangeline passed a supposed oak tree, familiar to them by now, that grew leaves in the shape of book pages, the veins of dark green swirling into a cursive script as yet uncracked by the linguists and philologists of the world. As they followed the path around this tree, Cal reached out and pulled off a few leaves, stuffing them in his pocket. When Evangeline glanced at him, he shrugged and said, "Maybe this is the day I understand what it's saying."

Ahead, the path forked, and snugged into the split was a tree stump, the rings on its surface jagged and chaotic, like the sound waves of a thrash metal song, all peaks and valleys. The stump had been there from the beginning, perhaps cut by some fae force or grown that way, a complete organism all its own.

The fencers cut left at the fork and walked along the Blazing Star Path—a dirt track lined by perfectly spaced blazing stars, liveried in purple and standing taller than any earthly plant of that kind should have. The close-set flowers, fuzzy and fragrant, looked like bugs' eyes up close, compound and all-seeing. Fencers and scientists had discovered in the early 2000s that those towers of purple and lavender could be squeezed to release a foul-smelling liquid with properties not yet understood, mechanized, or profited from.

"There they are," Evangeline said, pointing toward the rise of a hill nearby. At the base of the hill, prairie grasses gave way to a wide, empty area of earth, the soil charred black from a fire never seen by any fencer or scientist.

Upon this soil, someone or something had stacked smooth stones into six- or eight- or ten-foot-tall cairns, each one giving the appearance of precariousness, though nothing Cal or Evangeline or any other fencer had ever done had successfully knocked one down.

And on these cairns, growing up from their foundations and garlanding the discs of stone like holiday lights strung along the struts, were thin, thready flowering vines. Blossoms so dark gold, they were nearly amber. Each one composed of exactly four petals. Never three. Never five. Rip one off and another appeared in its place as soon as you looked away.

"Individual petals, whole flowerheads, and three-inch segments of the vine," Evangeline said, pulling out their instructions from the bureau scientists, who would take the samples like bits of some lost deity's broken body, handling the capped tubes with holy attention becoming zealous obsession.

"Check," Cal said, pulling out a knife and stepping close to the vines, leaning against the cairn as he set about his work. One by one he lopped off flowerheads and flicked them into the tubes Evangeline held open, clearly enjoying the experience of looking away as he did so before returning his gaze to what should have been a beheaded nub poking out from the vine but was, always, a perfect, symmetrical flowerhead.

Sometimes, he would throw the same flowerhead or petals into the tubes over and over. Sometimes, he would vary the specimens. Did it really matter? Would the scientists be able to tell the difference? Evangeline didn't think so and didn't really care all that much.

"Is it warmer than usual?" she asked.

"Is it?"

"I think so." Evangeline capped another specimen-filled tube and shoved it into the small bag they'd brought. "Or maybe it's not heat, but *something* feels strange."

They'd spent hours in this part of the Harbor, and though it changed some from time to time, Evangeline still recognized some of the landmarks—that stand of three interwoven trees and that small circle of turtle-shaped stones. Everything was as it should be, *where* it should be, according to whatever bit of instinct or intuition she was feeling at now—but still, this felt off. Something there was *wrong*.

"It feels normal to me," Cal said, holding his tongue between his front teeth for a moment in concentration as he slid the knife through a curling reach of new-growth vine. "Or at least as normal as a nature-reserve-turned-faerie-graveyard could feel to a prime-tattooed superhero fencer like me."

"I'm serious," Evangeline said, taking the specimen and capping it again.

"You think it's the Riparian?" Cal started skinning one length of the vine, the blade of his knife wet with whatever juices flowed inside it. "Oddry has that team of techs monitoring the data and . . . *its* movements. They would have let us know if it were here."

"It's not funny, you know—constantly using the wrong pronoun."

"It's just a mistake," Cal said, focusing on the vine with unwavering intensity all of a sudden.

"It's not, though," Evangeline said, still looking around. The air around her felt thick and scratchy. "You keep calling the Riparian 'he.' It's not a person anymore, Cal. There's no person left in there."

Cal stopped his cutting and looked at her now, and Evangeline felt the smallest of victories as she saw that he would not just let this go, not just pooh-pooh it with one of his little nostrum phrases.

"It's just nice to think," he said, overemphasizing each word, "that there might be a little bit of humanity in there still."

"It's a fantasy." Every fencer was taught this, drilled on it in their early years. The transformation purged the fae of their humanity, and fencers couldn't do their work, not effectively, if they believed otherwise.

"We don't know that!" Cal huffed out a breath before saying, quieter, "No one can know that."

"You can't go down that road, love," Evangeline said, trying her best to make her voice reasonable and friendly. "You can't give them that. How can you defend yourself with any force or conviction against one of them if you think there's a person in there still? What if you have to put one down?"

"It *should* be hard, Evangeline," Cal said, though his voice softened somewhat in response. "We shouldn't just get to kill those things every equinox without batting an eye."

"You haven't ever killed one, Cal." The air around her might as well have been sparking with heat and energy. And still, she let her eyes move around, monitoring the area, aware of her surroundings, ever the leader. "You've hurt them, and you've caused plenty of damage, but you haven't ever killed a faerie. I have, and I know how hard it is. You don't have to tell me."

"That's not what I'm saying," Cal said, sucking in a breath through clenched teeth. "I'm sorry. I just mean . . . I *want* to believe that there's still something human inside them. I'm still going to do my job, and I'm not going to blink when it comes time to act. But what if it were me that turned? Wouldn't you want to still see me in there?"

"No," Evangeline said. "No. I think that might kill me."

Cal stared at her but said nothing.

"They've done tests, Cal. All those messed-up experiments in the early nineties—it's just not true that there's anything left in there. It isn't."

"Who cares if it's true or not?" Cal said, but the fight was gone from him. "Who cares if it gives someone hope?"

And what could she say to that?

Cal returned to cutting the vines, and Evangeline returned to capsuling and sealing them, her eyes continuing to rove.

That tree was where it should be.

That stretch of hazy grasses was just that shade of purple last time.

That bush reminded her last time of a pyramid, and it still looked like that.

She looked and verified, looked and verified, looked and . . .

"What is it?" Cal asked, holding out a length of paper-thin skin to the spot where the capsule should have been if Evangeline hadn't just been staring off toward the center of the Harbor, toward where the Threshold Tree stood, miles off and out of sight.

"Look," she said, and Cal followed her gaze along the idyllic fields of prairie grasses and flowering plants, out toward the Threshold Tree's shadowy bulk in the distance.

"What am I looking at?"

"Cal, *look*." Sweat had broken out on the back of her neck and along the ridge of her shoulders.

"I don't . . ." Cal began.

"On that hill. Just to the left." Evangeline pointed with one hand but pulled out her sword with the other.

Finally, Cal saw it—the grass on the hill, more of whatever lived in the Harbor that was pretending to be real grass, was *moving*.

"What is that?" Cal asked, dropping the length of cut vine and trading the small knife for the sword.

The grasses shifted and stirred along the hill, their movement as gentle as hair in water, caught and caressed by an unseen current.

"Wind," Evangeline said in a voice small and afraid.

The invisible breath of a fae wind in this place where the grasses and the trees and the dirt and the vines and the rocks seemed always so still, so watchful.

Cal released a long, low moan of terror.

This was wrong. This was all wrong.

Evangeline fumbled in the bag, the dull *click* of metal tubes sounding from within, and pulled out the walkie-talkie, its surface marred by the artificially added prime.

Get control, she told herself.

"Go toward the gate," she said. Her voice had dropped to that low, calm husk it became when she stopped being Evangeline, wife of eight years and mom of almost seven, and instead turned into Fencer Evangeline, strongest of the Midwest Coterie and fifth-strongest living fencer in the world. "Move with purpose and caution."

"Okay, yeah," Cal said, but his feet weren't moving, and he was still staring at that wind that ran currents through the grasses, setting the long blades dancing. Hills and slopes and stretches of flat land that they had seen so many times—on fence fixes or scientific jaunts like this—grew strange and other and horrifying, and all because of a wind that shouldn't have been gusting.

"You better work," Evangeline said to the walkie-talkie in her hand. "Break for Oddry. Come in. Oddry, can you hear me?" She pushed Cal forward, breaking whatever spell the Harbor had over him and sending him moving at a trot toward the exit.

When the thick brick of primed technology spat and crackled and answered, Evangeline felt her stomach retract into a point of pain. And when Oddry's voice came through the speaker, confirming that he was there, Evangeline looked up in time to see one of the cairns, taller than her by at least five or six feet, wobble and fall.

"I'm here," came the voice of their head tech. And then: "I can't believe this fucking thing works."

"We're retreating," Evangeline said, slinging the bag over her shoulder and beginning to move. "Something's wrong in here."

The stones fell around Evangeline's feet, toppling against one another in a series of gentle *click*s that made a perfect rhythm, like hands clapping together. The vine that had been growing around the cairn, the same one Cal had been slicing parts off of only a few moments before, writhed and died, the long green of its body curling in suddenly upon itself, like an insect spooked into a defensive twist. Veins of grey raced along the plant, rot spewing from inside and beginning to ooze out, and one by one the blossoms, those beautiful amber-gold blossoms that made Evangeline think of fields of corn in the fall, the husks a gentle whisper waiting for the wind to sound—those flowers began to close and retract, liquifying as they did so and becoming a single golden drop of viscous goo dribbling from the dead or dying vine.

"Evangeline!" Cal's shout sounded distant and frightened, and Evangeline was surprised to see him twenty, maybe twenty-five feet away. His voice had echoed as if emerging from a deep well. But there he was, sword in one hand, concern on his face.

"I'm coming," she said, but she wasn't, because the stones at her feet were singing to her, rubbing their rough bodies against one another to make a kind of music that sounded to Evangeline like screaming, like terrified screaming coming from all around her.

"Evangeline!" Cal shouted, and she took a step, just one, but soon there followed another, and another, and then she was following Cal forward, and he was saying something, wiping with his free hand at the tears running down his face. Had he heard the screaming too?

The wind felt like breath, alive with a recently devoured meal and hot against the back of Evangeline's neck, and when she turned, she saw the Threshold Tree even though she shouldn't have been able to, not at this distance. It was not a huddled group of boughs rising into the hazy green of foliage as she had seen in artist renderings but instead, the huge white tree appeared to her as bared teeth, their sharpened edges grinding against one another as whatever dark gullet behind them exhaled that fetid wind.

Something was back there.

Some*one* was back there.

"Evangeline!" Cal must have been running, because he was out of breath and sweating—no, not sweating, but covered in rain.

"What?" Evangeline muttered. "It never rains here." The language was almost immediately vestigial, springing from a confusion that vanished as she looked, *really* looked, at the water in the air.

Not falling as rain might have, but hanging, as though confused about gravity and weight and purpose.

Know the Riparian by its fruits, the training leader had drilled in to Evangeline when she'd started fencing, forcing the new crop of fencers to recite the little rhyme over and over until it lived on their breath.

Droplets hanging in the air,
Toxic water where once fair,
Unending eyes bring horror and pain,
Obscured by haze of blackened rain,
Shears it carries, rusted through,
To separate body from the truth of you.

The rhyme eddied through Evangeline's mind like a leaf in the air, unhurried and chaotic, and she felt the collision of memory and moment inside her, pulling her back and forward. A child in her home, frightened of the dark. The newly minted fencer, wide-eyed as she learned of her foe. And the mother, the wife, rushing forward through grasses slick with condensation, toward a gate that hung open, its spray of metal tines and blades at once imposing and flimsy, enormous and fragile.

Evangeline might have remained caught somewhere in that liminal space if it hadn't been for the walkie-talkie, which fizzed and cut through her reverie with its own kind of wrongness.

"—out! Get out! You . . . the fuck out . . . Get . . . !" Oddry's voice crackled in and out, but the immediacy of it and the uncanniness of a piece of tech functioning inside the Harbor wrenched Evangeline back to the moment. She regained her stride and nodded to Cal, who let go of her arm.

Side by side they ran down paths they had walked many times on scientific endeavors, sometimes just the two of them, often with a few other fencers. Always those paths were dry, packed dirt, established by whatever fae magic haunted the Harbors long before any fencers walked them.

Now they were dotted with stinking, toxic pools of water that both fencers dodged with adrenaline-heightened fear, knowing the stories of what could happen to a person—primed or not—touched by the Riparian's poisonous puddles.

In all of their training as fencers, all of the information sessions filled with secret and not-so-secret information about the Riparian, one directive had been offered to them over and over, by teachers young and old, experienced and fresh: *Do not try to fight it. Do not imagine it is just another fae, larger and stranger but under your power as the other Wretched are.*

The Riparian destroys.

It rends.

It has never been damaged, never been hurt, and certainly never been killed. *Primacies capable of ripping apart the fae or teleporting them into a parallel universe seem to have limited or no effect on the Riparian.*

If you see it, run.
If it sees you, run.
Do not fight it.
Do not engage.
Run.

"Go, go, go," Cal was chanting under his breath, and Evangeline felt that single repeated word press against the rhyme still flitting through her mind, smothering it with the simple urgency of fearful running.

The gate was within reach, no more than fifty feet away, and the grasses around them had begun to dissipate in favor of the thick moss and dirtpack that existed so close to the fence.

We're going to make it, Evangeline thought. *We have to make it.* She thought of Winnie, and she ran.

And when she looked back over her shoulder, she saw the Harbor, still once more, though marred as yet by the hanging drops of water and the curling rivers and stagnant pools.

Empty of that huge, cursed shape. Empty of the Riparian.

They exploded through the fence and were swarmed by the waiting techs and even a few fencers who'd been called in as support. Oddry was there, and even with his shouting and rage, he managed to get Cal and Evangeline safely into one of the huts and in the care of doctors who would check them over for injuries of any kind.

As they were walked in that direction, Evangeline looked back once more through the open gate, but the Harbor had gone still again. A crouched, waiting creature, eyes trained on its prey.

PART 2

A Handful of Stars

Chapter 9

"Tell them—*in Russian*—that their numbers are lying to them. Tell them—*in Russian*—that we've seen the signs here and almost lost two of our fencers. No, no, I don't give a shit about that. I need actual confirmation—*in whatever fucking language you can get it in*—the Riparian is there. Yeah, I've got my people looking here. Yeah, that would make sense, wouldn't it, Cassian? Except now I can't trust the fucking numbers here or anywhere else because *TWO OF MY FENCERS ALMOST DIED AFTER WE TRUSTED THE NUMBERS*. So, stop telling me to look at the numbers. I want someone somewhere in the world to put eyes on the Riparian and *only then* to report back. No more radiation levels or light readings or wood-degradation tests or any of that other shit. Eyeballs and monster—got it?"

Oddry, who had been pacing in the small space between Cal and Evangeline in the medical hut, ended the call and set about shadowboxing the bunched-up curtain hanging near the foot of Evangeline's bed. The doctors who'd been in the hut, as well as the three or four who'd rushed to get there in the wake of what happened, continued their work monitoring their two patients, drawing blood and taking readings on eyesight, sensory response, and anything else they could think to do. The big scans—to check for cancer and internal bleeding and bone degradation and all the other frightening, invisible damage the Harbors could wreak—would come later.

"We didn't actually see . . . *it*," Cal said, holding up empty hands, several of the fingers capped with monitors. "Just the signs—that's happened before, right? It doesn't mean the Riparian is necessarily in the Harbor."

Cal felt an ease and confidence now that the worst was over, but he knew Evangeline was the opposite. The whole thing had been such a mess, and she sat there now with veins full of adrenaline, a heart rate that was still too high, and fear without any action to guide it. She was energy lacking an outlet, and she hated that feeling.

"Yes, it has happened before, and yes, the presence of the signs isn't a guarantee that the Riparian—*it*, as you say, fencer Calidore—is around." Oddry twisted and pulled at that horn of hair at the front of his head, wrenching it so hard Cal thought it might finally give it up and come all the way out. "But 98% of the time—98.6, my dweeb techs tell me—it *is* there when its signs are. Thunder and lightning. That sort of thing."

"Mr. Mulligan," one of the doctors said, waving the clipboard in her hand to get Oddry's attention. "Both of the fencers are clear. All the tests came back with good news. Nothing sustained, and no foreign entities growing in their bodies."

"Gross," Cal said, shaking his head at that last.

"I had a foreign entity growing in my body for about nine months," Evangeline said, glaring at Cal. "I got through it."

"Calling your child a foreign entity should be grounds for legal action," Oddry said. "And no jokes right now."

He turned to the doctor.

"Any follow-up tests they need to do?"

"No."

"Any special care they need to take between now and the equinox?"

"No."

"Any reason they can't proceed on the equinox as they had planned?"

"No."

"Excellent. A pack of happy negatives. Up you get, fencers. Back to work."

Cal hopped from the bed and began putting his jacket and shoes back on. Evangeline moved more slowly.

"We're going back to business as normal?" she asked, wriggling her foot into one boot.

"As far as I'm concerned, this *is* normal," Oddry said. "You went into the Harbor, you got some specimens, you came back out. The anomalies are mine to worry about, and if they're going to impact your job, I'll let you know."

He looked at his watch and frowned.

"You've got training today, right? Assuming these signs aren't bullshit, I expect we'll have the Riparian in our Harbor by the equinox, so training sounds like exactly what the doctor ordered."

The doctor, who'd been packing up her stuff near the entrance to the medical hut, said, "To be clear, I didn't order that."

"Thank you, Doctor," Oddry said, making a shooing gesture toward her without even turning around. She exited with a snort. "Training it is."

"Are we going to talk at all about the fact that the mathematician's phone worked?" Evangeline asked, eyeing the thick, metal device sitting on the brightly polished medical tray nearby.

"No, we're not," Oddry said. "In fact, I'm going to take care of that right now."

With a quick look around to ensure they were alone—easily confirmed in such a small space—Oddry took the walkie-talkie and smashed it against the concrete wall of the hut, holding it firm by the thick rubber of the antenna and swinging it over and over against the wall until it became pieces on the floor.

"That might be the most surprising thing I've seen today," Cal said, finding Evangeline's eyes and smiling.

"Listen and don't talk. Don't talk now, and don't talk ever about this. The mathematicians, under the guidance of several key politicians, have been working on technology to pull energy from the Harbors. The politicians are motivated by their belief that it could fix our badly ailing energy sector, and the mathematicians are motivated by whatever weird shit they're always motivated by. I find the entire idea idiotic and horrendous, but I've allowed some of their testing to happen here—which they insist *needs* to happen here because of our small size and distance from major population centers—because I didn't actually think it would ever work. No one—those number freaks included—knows how the primes work, and I thought this thing would fizzle out like the thousands of other essays they've made."

He bent down and gathered up a handful of the technological detritus, holding it out to them.

"I'm going to report to the mathematicians that their tech broke during the peregrination and that it's not clear that it worked at all."

"But it did work," Evangeline said. "And there had to be people around who heard it work. It'll get back to the Sieve folks, right?"

"Maybe," Oddry said, dumping the shards and circuit boards and bits into a bag and dropping down for another scoop. "My techs were the only ones nearby, and they know what to do. But I don't trust what they're up to. I've seen some of the schematics they've drawn up—big pipelines running through the fence and into the Harbor where they pull in the magic of that place. When have pipelines ever been a great idea? One of them even suggested running a line all the way into the Threshold Tree. Do you want that?"

"No," Cal said immediately, and any ease he'd been feeling disappeared. They hadn't yet talked about what had happened in the Harbor—not really. Sure, they'd reported the facts to Oddry, but Cal hadn't told Evangeline what he'd heard in there, what the Harbor had shown him. And the idea of "running a line" into that place horrified him on a level he could barely access.

"Me neither," Evangeline agreed, looking at Cal with some concern.

"Good," Oddry said. "Their plan has a billion things that could go wrong, and they can't even get into the Harbor without fencers, much less past the Threshold Tree. Last I checked, there are about four fencers total alive today who might have a chance at getting past the Threshold."

"Yeah, but she's one of them," Cal said, nodding at Evangeline.

"And are you going to help the mathematicians suck magical energy from the fae realm and use it to run electric stoves so some person can make pasta?" Oddry asked.

"No, I'm not," she said.

Evangeline didn't like thinking about the Threshold Tree. Early in their relationship, Cal had brought it up a few times, especially after discovering that her short prime number combined with her primacy likely gave her the power to break through the Tree. But even then, his head full of love's early fog, Cal had realized how frightened of the Threshold Tree Evangeline was, how the stories of the fencers who'd attempted it and died—or, in one case, done much more than die—affected her.

For him, with his prime number several hundred thousand digits longer than hers and a primacy that offered nothing in the way of getting past the Threshold Tree, the issue had only ever been a fun theoretical one.

But for Evangeline, who'd been hounded by people from all corners of the Bureau and beyond when the initial tests revealed how strong her primacy was and what kind of power she really had, the question was more immediate and real, and though she'd rebuffed each and every scientist and politician and administrator, Cal knew the thought of the Tree had snagged in her mind, like a burr caught and then worked deep down into her skin.

The Threshold Tree was a challenge she hated and rejected and yet couldn't stop thinking about.

"Good," Oddry said. "So, we won't do anything to help them, yes? I'll take care of this junk, and you two head off to training. I'll let you know if anything changes."

The training grounds stretched across the wide, grassy area behind the three Bureau buildings, each one like a small coliseum—built to enable and encourage violence. Only fencers, their protective agents, a few techs, and the fencing hounds were allowed in the grounds.

For most of the year, they sat fallow, hoarding snow in the winter and rainwater in the spring, host to some light cardio and weights once the weather turned nice enough for such activities outdoors. The Bluestem Building had a large gym in the basement for fencers to use during the winter months, though only a few actually went.

The true purpose for the training grounds, the reason for the high, steel-reinforced walls etched with burns and deep scratches, for the wide, empty spaces and the dummy houses built along replica streets all inside the confines of the coliseum—the real reason these training grounds existed was for the small period of time each year when the primacies of the fencers, the unique powers granted them by whatever magic imparted their prime numbers, came within their reach.

The Stone Weaver, whose primacy had to do with her sight, could see better than the average person for most of the year, able to pick out a pileated woodpecker doing its dodge-and-weave dance up and down a tree some two hundred yards away.

But on the equinox, as autumn signaled its arrival in color and cool nights, her ability grew to something impossible, something supernatural. Unnatural. Her eyes could see across hundreds of yards, could pick out the softly stirred air from a moth 350 yards away, could see *behind* and *through* the walls of a house if she squinted.

These powers ascended in the days before the equinox and then descended afterward, like a tree finding the temperature and humidity right, finally, for the buds dotting its branches like barnacles to open and flower. Whatever power moved inside fencers responded to the turn of the earth and the changing of the seasons.

The Stone Weaver's primacy did not require the massive, protective walls of the training grounds to keep people safe as she practiced with it each year on its ascent.

The primacies of others, however, did.

"They must already be out there," Cal said as they pulled their gear from the lockers in the changing room attached to the training ground.

Nero and the Stone Weaver's lockers were both packed with their street clothes. Incident, too, was already out there—she wore her training clothes at all times and had gone straight out to the field, according to the locker-room manager.

Tennyson lay near the exit, the mass of him seeming to expand into a puddle, his head flat on the ground and his long upper lips spreading out to either side. He might have been sleeping if not for his eyes, which were fixed on Cal and Evangeline. He sensed that he'd missed something during his vet visit—all good, according to Dr. Montrose—and he was not happy about it.

"I'll call," Evangeline said once the changing room was empty. On the walk over to the training ground, they'd gotten a voicemail from Winnie's teacher, asking them to call her. Mrs. Iverson hadn't said anything specific in the message except that there had been "a little accident, nothing to worry about."

Cal and Evangeline had spent the time since worrying, all thoughts of their disastrous Harbor visit vanquished by the specter of elementary-school strife.

"Before I do, though—are you okay?" Evangeline was peering at him in that same way she had during their talk with Oddry—concerned and confused. "It seems like that really shook you up."

"Oh, a near miss with the Riparian isn't supposed to shake a person up?" he asked, smiling and raising his eyebrows in jest, but his hands had begun to sweat again, the palms slick with it. Casually as he could, he wiped them off on his pants.

"Don't joke," she said. She was still angry from their talk in the Harbor, and he didn't really blame her. He knew it was dumb to hold out on a sliver of humanity in the fae and even the Riparian. And not only dumb but against every bit of training and protocol they'd ever received.

But sometimes a person needed hope even when—*especially* when—the outlook was grim and nearly certain.

Cal opened his mouth to apologize for what he'd said in the Harbor, and instead, he found himself telling her the truth. About how it hadn't been the Riparian that had rattled him but those stones.

"Stones?" she asked, shaking her head.

"From the cairn," he said. "The ones that aren't supposed to fall."

"Oh. Yes," she said, and Cal saw they had affected her, too.

He told of how the sound they made, that rubbing, clicking, soft noise had reminded him, suddenly and desperately, of his father Cliff and the way his hands, similarly rough, used to slide against one another at the end of a long day while he watched TV, finding what small joys he could in the bodies of young athletes barreling down a field or shooting a ball.

His father, who had first found drink and then found drugs and then found religion, who once pushed Cal—then only a boy and not yet named Calidore—up against the wall outside the bathroom, one of those big, rough hands pressed hard into Cal's tiny chest.

There in the Harbor, he'd heard his father's stony voice speak, the same as the voice in his memory that told young Cal to "figure it the fuck out" because no son of his was going to quit a sport and let his team down.

"It felt like the Harbor had access to every part of my memory," Cal said, sniffing and knuckling away the tears falling again. "It reached right in and ripped me up."

Evangeline took his hand and held it, saying nothing, and after a moment, Cal nodded.

"I'm okay. Thanks for listening. And I'm sorry about what I said in the Harbor, about *it*."

Evangeline lifted his hand and kissed it, the way a knight might have offered compliments to a lady. Cal grinned and returned the gesture.

"Let's see what happened with our little troublemaker, shall we?" Cal said, and Evangeline nodded.

The phone, which Evangeline put on speaker and held up between them, rang twice before Mrs. Iverson answered.

"Hi, Evangeline and Cal. Thanks for calling me back."

"Of course. What's going on?" Cal asked, hoping the anxiety didn't make him sound too brusque. They liked Winnie's teacher a lot—she was patient, good with the kids, kind, and genuinely seemed to love her job. And both he and Evangeline were very aware of the unique landscape of their situation. Because fencers were a limited resource—one that governments could not yet manufacture or bring about of their own power—the fencers themselves wielded immense power and leverage. Some acted like celebrities, demanding increasingly large salaries, opportunities, and material wealth. Others became social tyrants, requiring their governments to grant them access to television and movie opportunities, establishing and maintaining vast legions of followers on the various media platforms.

If Cal or Evangeline offered even the slightest public criticism of Winnie's school or her teacher, MBUSFB and the United States government would have the school changed or Mrs. Iverson fired and buried under nondisclosure agreements by the end of the day. All because of their tattoos.

"Think of it like supply and demand," Oddry had once said while sitting on the floor of their living room, playing ball with Winnie, only a toddler then. "Thanks to Reagan and that book, the world has a demand for fencers that we've never seen met. You're the supply, and because we're always in short supply, and because those number badgers down in the Sieve haven't yet figured out how to catch more primes, you can basically ask for whatever you want, and within the very furthest bounds of possibility, the government will probably give it to you."

In his first year as a fencer, Cal had flirted with that power, demanding his own bit of vanity: lavish apartments filled with old books. Before he'd met Evangeline, Cal had spent his off-equinox months traveling around to rare-book sales, haggling and bartering and always getting the books he wanted.

The expense reports—nothing more than an empty gesture by the government—were filled with his increasingly nonsensical justifications for the outrageous sums he paid for the purchases.

Only after meeting Evangeline and seeing himself in her eyes had he understood how like the vainglorious fencers he hated he had become. Every fencer he'd ever met had gone through that period of being corrupted by the power of the position. He felt grateful to have found a lifeline in Evangeline so early.

"We had a little accident on the playground," Mrs. Iverson said, her voice fuzzing slightly across the line. So close to the Harbor, only the very best tech worked perfectly and with any dependability, especially as the equinox neared. The magic of that vast, fenced-in landscape—a great doorway, according to AK Senga's research report from that morning—worked like a chaotic weather pattern on technology, sometimes diminishing its efficacy and quality, and sometimes disrupting it completely. On the equinox itself, any calls made within a mile of the fence would sound like static and rainfall, and any voice heard in that susurrus would be one best ignored.

"Is Winnie okay?" Evangeline asked, hunching forward toward the phone. The lights in the changing room were set into recesses above the tall, faux-wood lockers, rendering the circular room in soft illumination. The bright screen from the phone was a harsh contrast to that peaceful ambience, rendering Evangeline's face in a garish blue-white.

"She's okay, yes," Mrs. Iverson said. "There was a disagreement on the playground with a friend who wanted to play on a piece of equipment Winnie was using."

Cal could almost imagine her standing off to the side in her brightly lit, colorful room as the kids worked on their letters or numbers, scrawling simple sentences across the pages of construction paper with the blunt edges of crayons, overseen by protective agents and a few assistants. If pressed, both Cal and Evangeline might admit to Winnie's school, with its abundance of teachers and resources, protections and opportunities, as being the newest form of their poisonous power as fencers.

"Was it the digger?" Cal asked, smiling a little as he caught Evangeline's eye. "She loves that thing."

"It was, yes. It's Winnie's favorite toy, and she had been on it for a little while when this friend asked to use it." The school calling all the children "friends" had been strange for Cal at first, but he'd become used to and even fond of the term. Let "classmates" and "colleagues" and "peers" come later. Let them be "friends" for now.

"Winnie said no," Mrs. Iverson continued, "and this friend got a little upset and tried to grab the digger. Winnie was surprised by it and fell off. It's all sand there and only a short way down, so she wasn't hurt."

"Oh, good," Evangeline said, releasing a sigh. "That doesn't sound so bad."

"*That* wasn't." Mrs. Iverson's voice grew cautious. It was still the beginning of the school year, and despite the three or four interactions she'd had with Cal and Evangeline, she still didn't really know them. Were they the kind of fencers people talked about? Tyrants who floated above the world and stepped on those who got in their way? Narcissistic egotists without an imaginative or sympathetic impulse to be found?

"Uh-oh," Cal said, though quietly enough that Mrs. Iverson didn't hear him.

"Winnie was quite upset about falling, and she threw sand at her friend's face and then pushed them down. One of our aides intervened, but her friend did get some sand in their eyes."

Cal felt as though the air in his lungs had gone stale, and his body stilled at Mrs. Iverson's words.

"Should we come and get her?" he asked.

"You can get her if you'd like," Mrs. Iverson said, an edge of relief underlying her words. Maybe these fencers weren't the monsters she'd heard about. "But I think it is probably better for her to stay the rest of the day, if that's okay. We talked with Winnie about what she did, and she's already apologized to her friend. She's actually making them a sorry craft right now."

"Is the other student okay?" Evangeline asked, her face turned down into a frown.

"They're okay—we washed their eyes and they're doing fine."

Cal found himself wondering which of the other kids it was. The school couldn't tell them, of course, but he had at least seen the other kids in Winnie's class a few times at pickup or in the pictures of classroom activities Mrs. Iverson sometimes emailed out. Maybe it was that one kid with the long blond hair, the son of some state politician. Or one of the girls Winnie said always ate together and wouldn't let anyone else sit with them.

It was so easy to imagine any of those kids as actors in this instance, and already Cal could feel his mind twisting the vision he had of the conflict, putting mean words into the other six-year-old's mouth as they approached Winnie, making her flung sand into a purely defensive act, the push a pure accident as she tried to get out of the way.

He shook his head and exhaled the stale air from his chest. He didn't want to be that parent whose child was an angel surrounded by demons. But why would she do it?

"We'll talk to Winnie when she gets home," he said, putting a hand on Evangeline's shoulder and giving her a gentle squeeze.

"This kind of thing does happen," Mrs. Iverson said. "We'll watch Winnie with this friend for the next few days to make sure it's just an isolated incident. I know how busy a time it is for you right now, especially with the equinox coming up, so please don't worry too much about this."

In five days, Cal and Evangeline, along with the other members of their squad and every other fencer in the world, would become the arcane warriors their tattoos promised they were. As the rest of the world shut and locked its doors, as the streets emptied and all but the most critical services and businesses closed for the day, Cal and Evangeline would walk the ways, finding, fighting, and shepherding the fae toward the Harbor that beckoned them. They would wield powers wild and dangerous to battle the Faerie Queen's newest vassals.

And right now, neither of them could think of anything other than their almost-seven-year-old pushing another child down on the playground.

"Thanks for letting us know, Mrs. Iverson. It's important to us that Winnie can treat her classmates with kindness, so we'll talk with her about it tonight." Evangeline was smiling and nodding at the phone, as if Winnie's teacher could see her.

They sat in silence for a moment after the phone call ended, Cal's hand still on Evangeline's shoulder.

"It's from that ninja movie you two were watching," Evangeline said finally, raising an eyebrow.

"Ninja movie?"

"You were both watching some movie with ninjas where, in one of the fights, someone throws sand into someone else's face. Remember? I was out gardening and came back in to show you the potatoes I'd dug up, and you two were watching that?"

Cal groaned and shook his head.

"*The Last Sword of the Mountain*," he said, remembering the movie now. "I do remember now. I can start the talk with her tonight."

"Yes, you can," Evangeline said, standing up and buckling her sword back on—one long single-edged blade, her weapon of choice. "Let's get out there."

The why of it—the real why of Winnie being so cruel to another child—still gnawed at Cal, whose imagination had begun to fill in details about that other child, the words they might have said to Winnie, the way that, earlier in the day, they might have taken the scissors from her workstation without asking, just to be cruel, just to be mean to Winnie, and why would *that kid* do that?

Cal buckled his own swords—two mid-length blades, one on each hip—and followed Evangeline out of the changing room and out into the fresh air of the training ground.

Along one side of the huge, open-air coliseum was a row of houses built along a street, two single-stories, three two-stories, and an apartment building all constructed for training simulations.

Cal had once tried to get everyone to call those collections of buildings in each of the five training grounds "the simulacra," but only Nero had gotten the reference and even she had thought it was stupid, so they were just called "the training houses."

On the other side of the training ground was a large stretch of fence, an exact replica of the one that encircled the Harbor less than a mile away from where Cal and Evangeline stood right now. Thirty-seven feet tall and made of steel, stone, concrete, and iron, the Midwest fence bore an artistic tracery of the tallgrass prairie along its outer side, the stems and shapes of big bluestem and reed canary grass, prairie groundsel and rattlesnake master etched into stone and concrete as a tribute to the wondrous landscape that had once dominated this part of the world.

Given the history of the fences and Reagan's duplicitous brand of environmentalism, the tribute to a biome destroyed by "progress" was a cruel joke but one that most in the world ignored or simply didn't understand.

Between this stretch of replica fence and the row of training houses was a yawning stretch of grass. On the opposite end from where Cal and Evangeline emerged was Incident, her form obscured by a dark miasma swirling and churning around her, an inky tempest that stretched and bulged and whipped in response to every gesture.

Nearby, the Stone Weaver was working with one of the techs, a man named Ross, who had set up a series of eye-exam-type tests at increasingly great distances. The Stone Weaver would glare at the board and then speak quietly into the walkie-talkie in her hand, which would crackle a moment later with Ross's voice, letting her know how she'd done. Evangeline had told Cal that on the equinox, the Stone Weaver's eyesight was strong enough to leave impressions in the things she focused on, as though her vision had actual weight and force.

"Like the little dents a hailstorm leaves on a car?" Cal had asked.

"No," Evangeline had responded. "Like the dent in a car door a baseball bat leaves. Apparently, it takes her a little while to focus on the thing, but imagine a slow-moving, unstoppable baseball bat being pushed through your body, and there's nothing you can do about it."

Cal shivered at the thought as he did some quick stretches and looked toward the center of the training ground, where Nero was working out her primacy, which involved the creation and manipulation of bubbles. In a motion so practiced it looked natural, she would raise a hand to her lips, middle finger and thumb pressed together, and blow a stream of air through the circle made there. Out would come a filmy bubble, the oil-slick rainbow of its color visible along the edges and when the sun caught it.

During the rest of the year, those bubbles might be the size of a fist or maybe a soccer ball, but now, so close to the equinox, Nero was producing bubbles like wrecking balls.

But their size was not the only impressive quality of these creations.

"Heave-ho!" Nero shouted as she hefted one of the bubbles, a gargantuan thing half as tall as she was. It seemed to weigh nothing to her and clung to her hand like the soap-and-water variety Cal was familiar with, yet when she hurled it, pivoting around once like a discus thrower about to launch, the bubble flew through the air as if it weighed more than air and soap and slick, and when it collided with a wooden wall constructed by one of the techs for this very purpose, the lumber exploded from the force, splintering and shattering as if struck by a train.

The bubble caught on one of the now-jagged spars of wood and sagged, its shell slagging like metal in heat, losing its form and deflating with a slow droop.

"Bull's-eye!" Nero said, pumping a fist and high-fiving the tech who had built that wall and the thirty or so others standing nearby. That bubble had been a roundish thing, closer perhaps to an egg than a perfect sphere but recognizable as a bubble.

Most she made were that way, but Cal had seen Nero blow a bubble shaped like a club and use it on one of the Wretched after having her sword knocked away.

"They're much more like the kinds of balloons you can twist and make into dogs or swords or whatever," Nero had once said about her primacy. "They just happen to look like bubbles in their base form."

Evangeline jogged a little ahead, windmilling her arms to loosen up. Tennyson, his mouth open in a wide smile, eyes alert and locked on Evangeline, followed behind. Ahead were a number of obstacles built for fencing hounds in particular—not just the usual hoops to jump through and ramps to run up but mannequins holding all manner of weapons near structures large and small. Other mannequins, smaller and unarmed, were tucked away in some of the structures or set on the ground behind groups of two or three of the armed figures. A few had faces painted on and pastel-pink fairy wings attached to their backs—some tech's funny joke.

"Set." Evangeline gave the command with a line of gravity running through the word. It was the voice she used exclusively with Tennyson when training or on the equinox. Cal could do a rough approximation of it, and Tennyson would listen to him in lieu of Evangeline, but hers was the command he preferred.

Tennyson, who'd been in the act of scratching at an ear with his back foot, mouth still wide and drizzling slobber, straightened at the command, setting his feet wide apart and snapping his jaws together. Another of those subsonic growls rumbled forth, like war machines on the horizon.

His coat, a Rorschach riot of black and white, shifted and ran, the two opposing colors seeming to turn liquid and dynamic, rivers of white and evolving organisms of black, expanding and contracting. A person could fall into a trance, staring at that piebald monochrome kaleidoscope, the patterns writhing and changing endlessly.

"Retrieve!" Evangeline commanded, and Tennyson ripped forward, tearing up pawfuls of grass as he leapt into the midst of the fae mannequins bunched around a child, snapping at one of them before slamming his hindquarters into another, taking a hand off the first and knocking over the second. His coat was a mesmerizing swirl now.

With a gentleness Cal always found strangely touching and melancholy, Tennyson picked up the child mannequin, carrying it by the back of its red MBUSFB shirt, the clothing caught in his snaggly bottom teeth. As he escaped from the tangle of fae simulacra, Tennyson reared on his back legs and raked a flurry of claws down the front of two more dummies, pulling long strips of the matte material from their chests with a furious rending sound.

When Tennyson trotted back with the child dangling from his jaw, straight to Evangeline's side, less than a minute had passed.

"Safe," Evangeline said, putting out a hand to catch the child mannequin before showering Tennyson with compliments, pets, and a few treats from the pack she wore around her waist. The technical, BUSFA-approved term for this was a "tactical midriff sack," but Cal and Evangeline both called it what it truly was despite the Kevlar material, double fasteners, hidden iron knife, and the GPS locator chips embedded in the sack and band.

A fanny pack. A tactical fanny pack.

"I'm going to practice for a bit with Ubah, and then we can trade?" Cal gave Evangeline a wave as he jogged over to a spot near where Incident was training. A few techs had begun staking out a wide path through the center of the training ground, marking out a simulation of the Grand Road—the largest of the fae lines this side of the Midwest Harbor and their assignment for the first half of the equinox. Once all the fencers had warmed up and were feeling good, that was where they would practice their drills and maneuvers for the remainder of the day.

"A fine day for the Queen's gifts, Calidore!" Incident's voice emerged from the black swarm of particles whirling about her, and Cal could just spy her form inside, standing completely at ease. She reached her arms out and lifted her face up into the sunshine, smiling and taking in the day; the inky twister mimicked and extended her gesture, turning her sub-six-foot wingspan into something closer to ten or fifteen feet.

Cal gave her a thumbs-up but said nothing, hoping she might leave their interaction at that, but no luck. She pulled the storm of darkness in tight around her, looping it into a few tight coils of power, and trotted over to him.

"We received word of your ordeal in the Harbor," she said after giving him a small, formal bow. "Are you well?"

She talked like a theater major working a summer job at the Renaissance Festival. Soon, she'd be dropping *thee* and *thou* and *forsooth*, and Cal might really run away screaming then.

"Just fine," he said. "We thought it was the Riparian, but no sighting beyond some of the signs. I don't suppose you have a special name for the Riparian in your faerie church, do you?"

"Oh, yes," Incident said, meeting his eyes. "We speak of him often."

"In rosy, hopeful tones, I'm sure," Cal said, picturing his father in one of those pews, holding his holy book close, chanting some pseudo-arcane nonsense. Incident sat nearby, hands held up in rapturous adulation. Praise to the Riparian, the Queen's guard dog.

"There are some who love the Little Tear," Incident said, and Cal was pulled from his imaginings by her voice, which had grown suddenly soft. "They speak of him as an angel of death and deliverance."

She had been looking up and away, over toward where Nero worked her primacy, but now she turned back to Cal, finding and holding his eyes.

"But there are others," she said, a near-whisper now, "who hate and fear him."

It, he thought with a sudden, sharp clarity, Evangeline's voice echoing in his head.

"I'm glad you are well," Incident said, and if she had been different, it was gone now, replaced with her usual oddity, the high-pitch carry of her voice rolling over him. "It would not do for our squad leader and her primed paramour to be down for the Holy Day!"

With that, she gave him a wave and moved back to her practice area, the strands of black particles unwinding from around her in grand, lazy arcs.

Something had just happened, something Cal was too addled or too thick to figure out. He'd never exchanged more than two or three words with Incident in the past however many years they'd both been fencing for the Midwest Harbor, and now he'd gotten condolences about his father and . . . what? A bit of vulnerability about her church? Her beliefs?

Cal exhaled, letting the weirdness of the brief conversation leave him. He needed to train, and he could feel his primacy shifting inside his mind now, beginning to shiver and roil like water contemplating a boil, the nonsense words flaring and dying along the synapses of his brain.

Ubah, a tech Cal often trained with, was waiting for him. She stood next to a few tubs filled with what looked like kids' toys: balls, foam gliders, remote-controlled cars and drones. And then a few items that were not toys: knives, whips, guns.

"Hello, sir," Ubah said as Cal approached. She was a young tech, Somalian-American from Minneapolis and freshly graduated from the University of Minnesota Majestic. She was new to the role and still stiff with professionalism. Working with Oddry would break her of the habit before too long. A few weeks back, Ubah had been over to Cal and Evangeline's for a barbecue along with the other techs assigned to their squad, and she'd told them about how proud her parents were of her work, how they'd come out to visit and taken pictures of Ubah next to all of the buildings, all of the signs, and even one—from a very safe, very great distance—of Ubah with the fence and Harbor in the background.

"You don't have to call me *sir*," Cal said, although he knew she'd continue. "Ready to throw stuff at me?"

Ubah smiled, deep dimples appearing on her cheeks.

"Absolutely. Should I start with the softer projectiles?"

Cal nodded and, as she pulled a few of the softer balls and gliders from the tubs, did some quick stretches.

"Did you ever do anything really mean or cruel as a kid?" he asked, pulling one arm across his chest and then the other. "Back in your early years, I mean? Six or seven?"

Ubah, who was looking down the line of a foam glider's wings, making sure they were flat and straight, brought her eyes up and gave Cal a questioning look.

"Probably," she said. "I don't really remember. Why?"

"No reason," Cal said, sitting down on the grass and attempting to touch his toes. Inside his imaginings of this other kid as a villain and instigator, rotting at the core of his thoughts like fruit gone bad, was a twisted bolus of shame.

He understood kids could be little monsters, and he understood they could be genuinely good people. And he understood that these extremes were overly present in kindergarteners, who could wake up as completely different people with completely different psyches from one day to the next, everything from their dietary preferences to their optimism about the world's continuation could change.

Mrs. Iverson had said "these things happen," and Cal understood that, *knew* it. But somewhere deeper down he believed—or wanted to believe, which was just about the same thing—that Winnie was special. If asked, he might have denied it or, with closer friends, admitted it with a laugh and caveat that he knew every parent felt that way, believed it deep down.

But she *was* special, had to be. How could that girl who had once been a cheeky, chubby infant and now read short books on her own and solved riddles each morning and laughed at silly jokes and refused to eat carrots and drew pictures of Tennyson that she taped to the wall by his food bowl and danced to the jazz records Cal liked and the classic rock Evangeline did—how could that little girl *not* be special?

Maybe, Cal reasoned, his shame grew from that same poisoned root as so many other parental failures: vicarious living, the conceited belief that your child's life was a reflection of your own, their choices yours, just as their successes and failures were yours too.

If Winnie could do such small, cruel acts—unprovoked, it seemed, despite what Cal wanted to believe—then was his shame less to do with her and more to do with himself?

The thought made him physically recoil, not just for the ugliness and cosmic vanity of it, but because it reminded him of his father, Cliff, who had been the father on the sidelines of whatever sport Cal had been trying that year, shouting at his son to "Run faster, damnit" or "Hit that kid; smoke him" or "Look at the ball, look at the ball—" In his mind, Cal heard all of these shouts again, felt the deep, childish shame at knowing he had disappointed, was disappointing, and would continue to disappoint his father. Cliff's voice in his head, using Cal's name—his *real* name, the one he'd gone by before his tattoos came in and the memory work had happened—that voice dripped with scorn and criticism and shame, his and his son's, shame that Cal was not a better reflection of his father.

Shame that Cal was not better than everyone else.

It was a flawed inheritance he'd gotten from his father, but it would die with and in Cal. He would not continue it.

He did believe Winnie was special, but it was not the tenuous, self-centered belief Cliff had had, the one that had, at its center, a truer belief that he himself was special.

Instead, Cal believed—*wanted* to believe and willed himself to believe—that Winnie was special, and that special people could do cruel things. That special people could be unremarkable sometimes. That special people could live mundane lives because of their contexts, their circumstances, their situations.

Cal pushed against his imagination to see that other child, the one Winnie had hurt, as special.

And he worked, too, to hold his father in his mind, to see and remember him as a flawed, frustrating man who was also special, also interesting, also deserving of attention and curiosity and kindness. The man who had responded to his son's tattoos and career as a fencer by joining the very religion that worshipped the beings fencers fought every equinox.

"Sir?" Ubah asked, looking at Cal with some concern. She held one of the long gliders in her hand, the Styrofoam and plastic shaped like a white passenger plane with blue and red trim lines painted on. Some tech, maybe Ubah herself, had written *It's gonna be a bumpy ride!* on the side.

"Sorry." Cal rose and gave her a smile that he didn't quite feel. "I'm good. Ready to go."

Ubah watched him for a long moment, eyes squinted slightly in thought. All of the techs who worked with fencers were trained to monitor them for any signs of mental or physical degradation and had ironclad instructions to report any such signs to their superiors. Fencers might have the chance to live rich, privileged, famed lives, but they were fundamentally government property, prized assets that could not fall into disrepair and dysfunction.

"My dad's funeral yesterday," Cal said, looking down and away. "Messed my head up a little bit, that's all."

"Of course," Ubah said, nodding. "And I heard about the stuff at the Harbor, too."

"You too?" Cal asked. "Did one of Oddry's techs send a mass email or something?"

Ubah shrugged and said, "Do you want to train later?"

"No, no." Cal shook his head and did a few deep knee bends. "I'd rather have something to distract me from the moping." He smiled, and it was real this time. "Let's mess with time and space."

Ubah flashed her own grin in return and flung the glider off at an angle, away from the other training fencers, toward the simulacrum fence itself. The light plane caught a whiff of wind and banked up and to the left, really moving with the force of Ubah's throw.

Cal focused on the plane and spoke.

"Down the Spindle-River running, we leapt and aloughed a lark-long runneling of twist-spun weeds encumbered along the tombs of the lysitis-lord Tiniel, first singer of dusk and last bearer of the mighty thristine Desire. The sky, candy-cane red rhymes singing with the sun, and yet the low terrocracy of launderers laughed and laughed to see our progress. When from the under the long-rocks of time, a . . ."

A nonsense story, filled with nonsense words and images spilled from Cal, a messy torrent of gibberish and non sequiturs, describing places that were and would never be, impossible images rendered in nonsensical sentences. Always this gibberish was in his head, not yet formed into words but moving in the shadows at the back of his mind, waiting to be let out so that it might collapse into what Cal called his "hollow grammarie."

The words distorted the air around the glider, like heat vapors on a summer day filming the air with their strange density. A shifting, amorphous globe of thick space—not air but the space itself—wobbled into being around the glider, fuzzing the sharp lines of its wings and tail.

The sleek speed of the glider vanished in that distorting frame, and the plane slowed without losing altitude or changing its course in any way. It still gained height, the gentle curve of its flight path unchanged—it simply moved much slower, as though it were cutting through thick, swampy water, pulled by watery friction.

". . . and without a withy, an osier, a willow wand witchy and wisterious, the warlordling came to the pristiac shores of the common lake. And there he died. The end." Cal finished, throat dry and forehead already beading with sweat. The effort of holding in his primacy every day, of not letting the hollow grammarie come flooding out of him, was nothing compared to the strain of forming and deploying it intentionally, of shaping the space of the sluggish time to slow down a single object or person, much less a few of them. As the equinox neared, the scope of his power would grow, just as his control would.

The bubble of distorted time and space dissipated, releasing the glider from its power. The plane continued its upward curve until it had lost enough momentum. It twisted and twirled down before burying its nose in the grass a few inches deep.

"Very good, sir. How did that feel?" Ubah was already rustling through one of the tubs for the next projectiles.

"Just fine," Cal said, taking a drink from one of the ubiquitous water bottles stationed around the training grounds. "Let's ramp it up."

Ubah's smile was bright as she lifted a handful of lawn darts from the tub, each an arm's length long and tipped by dull metal points.

"Good?" she asked.

"Great," he said.

One by one, Ubah hurled the darts up in the air, and one by one, Cal slowed them on their paths, a few on their ascent and the rest on their descent. At first, Ubah tossed them in an arc away from where she and Cal stood, and the two of them could witness the hollow grammarie blurring into being a short distance away.

The final dart, though, described an arc that was narrow and tall, its destination dangerously close, and as Cal began spitting his nonsense, he stepped underneath it, eyes up and following its path, the grammarie bubbling into being directly above him. When the dart hit the perimeter of Cal's primacy, it must have been going twenty-five or thirty miles per hour, and though Cal might have leapt out of the way, it would have been close, the hovering distortion hanging just a few feet above his head.

He clenched a fist against the sudden flood of fear and spoke faster, the gibberish almost unrecognizable even as a language, and in response, the shape of his grammarie grew more distinct, more real. The dart, upon entering it, didn't simply slow down but for a moment *stopped*, as if stuck in a strange floating mass, something solid and real, and the shaft of the dart buckled under the strain caused by its first third having no speed and its back two-thirds moving at thirty miles an hour. The physical conflict ripped the plastic and rubber toy apart, sending shards in several directions.

When Cal stepped aside, ended his nonsense tale, and let his hollow grammarie dissipate, only the metal tip and a few bits of still-attached plastic fell where he'd been standing. The rest festooned the nearby grass like tiny streamers flung high at a lawn party.

"Excellent!" Ubah said, surveying the wreckage. "I didn't know you were going to push it that far so quickly. I'll put on my protective gear before we move on to the heavy stuff!"

Ubah jogged off toward a small shack. Next up would be the heavier items—baseballs thrown at him, metal pipes flung and swung his way, and eventually guns, fired first at nearby targets and then, finally, at him.

Cal looked over toward Evangeline, who was running Tennyson through increasingly strenuous and complicated scenarios and obstacles. Soon he would switch with her, first giving Tennyson a big drink of water and some time to cool down before getting back at it while Evangeline stretched and worked her own powers. After that, the squad would come together to practice together on the simulated Grand Road. They would ride together in one of the open-air tactical trucks that Oddry's techs were getting tuned up for the equinox, running through scenarios where one or two or all of them needed to leap out, training their various talents together. Evangeline, Cal, and Nero had already done this, though not with the Grand Road, but they would need to integrate Incident and the Stone Weaver into their squad strategies now. Who would take the lead if they came upon a single wandering Wretched? A group of them? Who would go into buildings first if a Wretched was known to be inside? If one was *suspected* to be inside?

A million different possibilities and eventualities flitted through Cal's mind as he looked beyond Evangeline at the stakes marking out the approximate dimensions of the Grand Road, and though he should have been thinking through the responses to such situations, he couldn't get his thoughts away from Winnie, his bright, beautiful, kind girl, hurling sand into some other bright, beautiful, kind child's face. What should he say to her tonight? What perfect words—the opposite of his hollow grammarie—could let Winnie know that this was not okay, that he and Evangeline still loved her, that she could not act like this, that it was never okay to hurt someone else—except when it was, of course, except when someone was doing something *really* bad, or except when Cal and Evangeline left every equinox and hurt lots of people? Or things that were very recently people?

Faced with a world where hard-and-fast rules were bound to get a person hurt at some point, what could Cal say to Winnie? Not just truth but wisdom?

As Ubah returned, protective goggles huge on her face and a Kevlar suit now covering her body, Cal wondered idly what his father, Cliff, would have said to him as a boy if he'd done such a thing. Probably he had—what kid didn't engage in cruelty?—and probably Cliff, who at that time had not yet turned to the House of Always Giving or the worship of a Faerie Queen who probably didn't even exist—probably that younger Cliff would have been too drunk to give much of a shit on principle but would have let Cal know somehow, through his words or his silence, that Cal had disappointed him, had embarrassed him.

"Ready, sir?" Ubah asked, bringing the long, dark barrel of a shotgun up, the stock positioned snugly against one shoulder. She aimed the gun at a target nearby, her finger held clear of the trigger, eyes on him.

Cal gave a thumbs-up and focused on the gun, which shifted slightly as Ubah aimed, and then barked its report into the air.

Chapter 10

"Pizza party!" Winnie raised her clenched fists and thin wrists up to the sky as she got out of the government car that served as her bus. Her backpack, a large pink thing that looked like it could hold Winnie herself in it, jounced and bumped against her back and legs as she raced across the lawn to where Cal and Evangeline waited on the porch.

"Pizza party!" Cal shouted in return before Winnie vaulted up the steps and into a big family hug. This was their tradition each Monday after school and work, once Winnie finished with her after-school program (painting with Mr. Paley) and Cal and Evangeline had a chance to shower off the sweat and grime of training: pizza from Winnie's favorite restaurant in Majestic, Cooley's Pizza Pub, a movie playing in the background, a board game dominating the parts of the table not covered in greasy slices of pepperoni, and, of course, a special guest.

"Hi, Tenny," Winnie said, breaking from one hug to leap into another, wrapping her arms around Tennyson's thick neck. The Newfie, who had been ripping apart mannequins and leaping in and out of a moving tactical truck not more than ninety minutes earlier, fur aswirl in a black-and-white storm, now leaned into his girl, mouth open in a slobbery smile, tongue lolling out as Winnie scratched that special spot just above one of his ears.

Evangeline waved to Aleph, who sat behind the wheel of the car and gave his own wave in return. The car glided away down the street, and Evangeline smiled at the illusion of privacy, the brief belief she could hold that their house—a red two-story Craftsman on a quiet street outside the small city of Majestic—was really theirs, that the small rambler across the street and the two Cape Cods on either side of them were home to families or elderly couples or single people all trying to make their own ways in the world instead of the agents who lived in those houses, monitoring the outputs of the surveillance equipment installed throughout the entire neighborhood.

How nice it was to imagine that their door was not capable of stopping bullets or battering rams because it didn't need to be. What a fantasy, a *wonderful* fantasy, it would be to get Winnie's bike from the garage and walk beside her while she pedaled down the sidewalk, just the three humans and the dog, talking about their days, laughing about what they'd experienced, all without agents trailing behind and calling ahead on their devices, without the government's presence just barely visible at the edge of their sight.

How light would she feel, Evangeline wondered, without the deep, trained-in certainty that she could call out to a nearby agent at any point of the day using one of several means? What would that uncertainty feel like? Would it be terrifying? Or would it be exhilarating?

The illusion, what little of it she could conjure, disappeared as the agent on duty across the street, Maris, emerged from the house and took a seat on the porch, nodding to Evangeline as she did. Maris would stay there for a few hours, creaking in the rocking chair and looking to all the world like a woman just enjoying the fall afternoon on her porch, a cup of iced tea beside her along with a novel that she might open at any time.

But she wouldn't open that novel, and beneath that cozy red sweatshirt, tucked into the band of those jeans, was a gun that Maris would use without question on any threat or perceived threat to the government assets living in the government housing across the street from her.

Evangeline gave Maris a wave and walked inside, closing the door behind her.

In the living room, Winnie was unloading her bag onto the floor, showing Cal the art she'd made during her after-school program and the crafts she'd made during school itself. As Evangeline stepped into the room, Winnie held up a picture she'd made of a rainbow, the seven bands of its color all filled with numbers: the red band packed with *1*s all the way up to the violet band filled with *7*s, all in Winnie's careful hand.

Only the orange band was not filled with numbers—a single *2* was written in the center of that section and had been violently crossed out, the number barely visible beneath the lines.

"So, I did red, then orange, then yellow, then, ummm, then the rest of them," Winnie was saying to Cal, gesturing at the picture and losing the thread of what she was talking about as her eyes found Evangeline. She did this often when she got excited, her speech getting tangled in the mess of stimuli around her, the at-times diverging threads of her thoughts, and the too-quick jumble of her words. "Momma, look, I made a *number rainbow*, and I told everyone that my mom and dad have all of these numbers tattooed on their bodies but in a much, much longer way."

"I love it," Evangeline said, taking the artwork. "It's fridge art, for sure."

The other items in Winnie's bag included a new book for the reading program she was doing, a bracelet her friend Ramona had made for and given her, a blue folder containing instructions for parents about how the equinox break would work, and a pair of socks she'd gotten wet during recess from accidentally jumping into the stream that ran along the edge of their play area.

"Accidentally, huh?" Cal raised an eyebrow at his daughter, who in turn raised both of her eyebrows in the indignant, unfairly maligned expression of a true martyr and said, "How could I know that I was going to jump into the stream when I had my eyes closed?"

"And you had your eyes closed because . . ." Cal said, fighting to keep away a smile.

"Because we were playing baby bunnies, Dad," Winnie said, looking at him with pitying condescension. "Ramona said all baby bunnies are born blind and only get their eyesight after their first birthday."

"Ramona really knows a lot about rabbits, huh?" Evangeline asked, dropping down on the couch. Winnie's best friend, who'd been over to the house for play dates constantly during the summer, was a wonderful kid who lied with as much gusto and confidence as a politician, but unlike politicians, she only lied about insignificant stuff like this, which Cal and Evangeline didn't mind at all. Evangeline suspected Ramona didn't even know she was lying, and who was she to question the confidence of a kindergartener?

"She knows *everything* about them." Winnie gathered the innards of her backpack into a stack on the carpet of the living room. She followed a strict schedule after school, even on pizza-party days:

1. Display the day's victories to Mom and Dad.
2. Play a game of Mom Chess
3. Have a cold snack while Mom and Dad read a book to her.
4. Color with Tennyson until dinner.

Mom Chess had become part of their routine the previous year when Winnie found Evangeline's old chess set in a closet and demanded to be taught the rules. Cal had been at work the whole day, so it had just been the two of them, mother and daughter squaring off across the chessboard, and somehow, in the way of family magic, it had become their special thing. Nothing exclusive, and Cal often liked to sit nearby and watch the games, but it was, all the same, Mom Chess. Evangeline and Winnie.

"I'm making hot chocolate!" Cal said from the kitchen as Evangeline shifted around pieces on the board they left permanently set up.

"I'm going to play black today!" Winnie sat, taking her seat opposite Evangeline and beginning to shift her pieces around.

"You play as black *every* day," Evangeline said, smiling as the clatter of silverware being dropped preceded Cal's grumbled swears. He was anxious to get to the talk with Winnie about what she'd done at school. If it weren't for their daily schedule and Evangeline's insistence that they stick to it, he would have already popped the lid on the big talk.

"Not *every* day," Winnie said, giggling a little as she pushed her bishops into place.

It felt good to defer the conversation. Cordon it off and hold her mind away from it. Evangeline liked the sense of control it gave her. The talk about Winnie's trouble at school would happen but on their own terms, in its appropriate place, and after the appropriate rituals were done. Mom Chess didn't get bumped.

"Ready?" Evangeline asked, squinting at her daughter with what she hoped was a calculating, intimidating look. The board was arranged, all pieces where they were meant to go—the only deviation from the regular rules found in Mom Chess was both Evangeline and Winnie had two queens on the board instead of a king and a queen. Winnie had found it deeply unfair, upon learning the game, that it was all about protecting a king who, according to her, "can barely move or do anything cool at all!"

They had made their own rules. Two queens, both powerful. And the goal of the game wasn't to capture any one piece—it was to capture *all* of your opponent's pieces.

They set to it, Evangeline moving first. The *click* of the wooden pieces on the wooden board was all comfort and joy. She loved watching Winnie think, seeing the quick flick of her eyes as she considered this piece or that piece, as she surveyed the board. She was bad at chess, and Evangeline, who had played seriously in high school and kept at it during her time at the Publix Harbor, saw the lines and exchanges that Winnie wouldn't uncover without years of practice and effort.

"What do you think is going on here?" she asked into the thoughtful silence, gesturing at one side of the board, where several pieces were on the precipice of a fight.

She loved this part: sitting back from the move-to-move immediacy of the game and taking it in instead from a distance, like a battlefield commander surveying her troops from a nearby hill, tracking larger undercurrents in the battle instead of individual bouts. *Who do you think is winning now?* she would ask Winnie. Or *Is this a good game?* Or *Does this game seem cramped or open?*

Winnie would scrunch her face up in thought and her eyes would take in the board. She would roll a captured pawn or rook between her palms, and after a moment, she would give her interpretation of the game. Sometimes, she was right. Often, she was wrong. But what did that matter? She was lifting her head from the fray and seeing the horizon beyond.

"I think we're both putting all of our energy into that side," Winnie said finally, reaching out to lightly touch the tops of the pieces in that area.

"I agree," Evangeline said, sliding one of her rooks across the back rank. "And do you think that's a good idea?"

"Probably," Winnie said, her eyes on the piece Evangeline just moved. She stuck out her tongue in thought for a moment before leaping in with one of her knights.

"What do you think— Thanks," she said, taking the hot chocolate Cal brought her. "What do you think a good player would do if she saw that all the energy was being put into just one side?"

Evangeline pushed a pawn one space forward.

"This is good," Winnie said, slurping up a mouthful of hot chocolate and melty marshmallows. She emerged from her mug with a mustache that she quickly licked away.

"What would a good player do right now?" Evangeline prodded again. She'd loved chess ever since she was a little girl and her own mom had taught her to play. She liked it as a game, as a chance to think, as a distraction, but she had always hated it as a metaphor. Authors and filmmakers and essay writers went to the chess well over and over to pull up their metaphorical water. Characters as chess pieces. Plot points as exchanges. Conversations as opening gambits.

Nonsense. Simplistic, heavy-handed nonsense.

Chess was chess. Let a thing be itself.

"A good player," Winnie said, staring hard at the impending collision, the knights and bishops backing the gridlocked pawns. Would she see it? Evangeline waited. Waited.

And smiled when Winnie's gaze slid over to the quiet side of the board, where lines were open and space existed for pieces to move freely.

Winnie brought one of her queens—Queenie, she called that one—over to that side of the board. Not a great move, and not the best square for Queenie to land on, but it had the spirit of a great move. It had the *beginnings* of greatness.

"You've got it," Evangeline said, grinning and sliding one of her pieces forward. "Nice one."

Winnie gave her own smile in return before slurping up more of the hot chocolate.

Fifteen minutes later, with the board cleared of all pieces save for Queenie and one of her pawns, Evangeline reached across and shook Winnie's hand—the closing gesture of their ritual.

"Good game, sweets," Evangeline said, standing quickly to shift around the board. She pulled Winnie close and tickled her. "I'll get you one of these days!"

Winnie screamed in laughter, one foot lashing out and sending a cavalcade of fallen soldiers to the carpet below. Cal shouted his own laughter, and Tennyson let out a low *woof* of playful pleasure.

When the pieces were picked up and the table on which the board permanently lived pushed back out of the way, they moved on to snack.

"Popsicle!" The sound of the freezer door sliding open with a *ca-thunk* and then closing again accompanied Winnie's triumphant crow, and Cal and Evangeline walked into the kitchen to find her already sitting at the little table, legs dangling, her mouth already staining red from the popsicle in her hand.

The book they'd been reading together, *A Wrinkle in Time*, lay on the table in front of her, and Winnie nudged it with the hand not holding the popsicle to her mouth.

Cal and Evangeline exchanged a look as they sat down opposite her. Cal took the book, running a hand over the cover but not opening it.

"Winnie, sweetie, we need to talk before we can do any reading," he said, bringing his eyes up to Winnie's. "It's about what happened at school today."

Winnie cocked her head, the popsicle still in her mouth. She was like her father in this: dramatic whenever the situation allowed for it. With one eyebrow raised and both eyes pointed at the ceiling, she looked like Cal, pretending to think hard about something for a gag.

Cal's annoyance showed as he turned to Evangeline. He could see how like him Winnie was, and it irked him endlessly. Evangeline cleared her throat and rubbed at her lower lip, trying to hide her smile.

She'd been surprised how much this situation with Winnie had been chewing on Cal all day. After their phone call with Mrs. Iverson, Evangeline had figured that was the end of it. Kids did weird shit. They were like little dice that the universe rerolled whenever it felt like it. Was it the die's fault that it rolled a one some mornings and woke up ready to fail?

But on the way home, Evangeline had sensed that something was bothering him. She'd figured it was Incident, who had performed just fine during the squad maneuvers but had piped up with more of her churchy nonsense during the lulls.

It hadn't been that, though, and when Cal, somewhat shamefully, told her what was really chewing on him, Evangeline had felt at first a curiosity and then a deep melancholy. He didn't need to say anything about his own father for it to be clear that Cal was thinking of his own upbringing and Cliff's cruel ministrations.

When they'd first started trying for a baby, Cal had oscillated between infectious bursts of hope and joy and deep periods of worry, and though it had taken him some time to open up about it, he'd finally confessed that he was worried he would be a bad father to their child, that she would grow up hating him like he had hated his own father.

"What if I'm like him?" he'd asked into the darkness of the night once, long after Evangeline thought he'd fallen asleep. She'd been listening to the sound of the wind in the trees just outside their bedroom, imagining them as waves on the ocean, and the soft wings of slumber had just begun to fold around her when Cal spoke to the night.

She didn't need to ask whom. Cal had spent some of the evening telling her about his father Cliff, the real Cliff, not the man who'd attended their wedding, cleaned up, breath free of both alcohol and the mints he'd used to cover the alcohol, the blue of his just-purchased button-up shiny and new. That man had been quiet and kind, if a little distant.

"He hated me," Cal had said after dinner. "When I was a boy, he hated me, and he made me hate myself. Other dads teach their kids what kindness looks like or how to read. I don't know if Cliff actually knew how to do either of those things. In the end, he taught me how to look for the cracks in myself."

In the liminal space of that night, entombed by the blankets and the darkness and the moonlight and the wind like ocean waves, Evangeline had turned to Cal and wrapped an arm around him.

"You won't," she said, shaking her head. "You won't be like him."

"How do you know?" He sounded like a little boy, and Evangeline imagined him in that tiny, drafty house where he'd grown up with Cliff, his mom having passed away early in his life. She could see young Cal—though, of course, she did not think of him as Cal but instead used his true name, the one removed from every mind but his own. It was one of his gifts to her when they were married, just as she had made a gift of her true name to him. It was against every rule the bureau had; they all knew the great pain and destruction that could happen if a fencer's true name was found out by the fae, the Wretched ones.

But they had been young and in love and sure in their belief, their deep knowledge, that it was the right thing to do. So, Evangeline did not think of Cal as Cal, not really. And he didn't think of her as Evangeline.

She saw that young boy in his upstairs room, covered by his one thin blanket on a bed without sheets. She saw his clothes contained within two plastic tubs pushed up against the wall, his small stack of library books nearby. Cliff snoring in a nearby room, the sound echoing around the empty wooden rooms.

This was Cal's father's real crime, Evangeline had thought then during that windy night and thought again this afternoon on the way home from work: his cruel instruction for his son was one that kept some part of Cal trapped forever as that scared little boy, sure he had done something wrong, sure that he had disappointed the man whose hand could be seen and felt in every part of his world.

"You won't be like him," Evangeline said, resting a cheek against the blemished skin of Cal's shoulder, "because he was a small person who thought himself big. You're a big person who worries about being small. You're not the same as him, and you won't be a father like him, Cal."

Except she didn't say *Cal*, not that night, not with only the wind as witness. She spoke his true name, and when he turned to her, the ambient glow of moonlight caught the tears in his eyes.

At the kitchen table, Cal took a breath and smiled at his daughter, who took a bite from the end of her popsicle and said, "I don't remember what happened at school today. Lunch?"

"I'm sure lunch did happen," Cal said. "But I want to talk about what happened on the playground with that classmate of yours—the one you pushed and threw sand at. Do you remember that?"

Winnie's face, still a comedic stretch of curiosity and bafflement, fell and she dropped her eyes down to the table.

"Yeah," was all she said.

Cal reached out a hand, taking hers. The popsicle began to drip a little on the table, but neither he nor Winnie took any notice.

"Can you tell us what happened?" Cal asked, and Winnie did, her voice sorrowful in the way only young children can manage, a kind of drama and oh-gosh sincerity that was the antithesis of her previous antics.

Tanner Ellman was the kid. Evangeline knew his father, who was a state senator, one of the few local legislators who was vocally anti-Harbor and against the huge funding the Fencing Bureau received each year.

When she'd finished, Winnie looked up, tears beginning to make her eyes swim.

"I told Tanner I was sorry a hundred times, and I promised I would never do it again, and I gave him both of my afternoon crafts and my afternoon snack and my afternoon milk, but he said he didn't like chocolate milk so I could just keep it, and I said are you sure but he was so I drank it, but only when he wasn't looking just in case he saw how much I was enjoying it and changed his mind."

"That's really kind of you, sweets," Cal said, nodding and smiling. He leaned over the table to wrap her in a hug before continuing. "It's important to say you're sorry when you do something wrong and do what you can to take responsibility for your actions."

Cal took a breath, his eyes rising to Evangeline's for a moment before focusing again on Winnie. *Don't make it such a big deal that it turns into something she can't move past,* they'd both said in the car. *Let her know it isn't okay, let her know we still love her, and talk about what she'll do if this happens again.*

"It's also important to not hurt people in the first place." He frowned as he said it, as if he were delivering bad news that couldn't wait any longer. "Your mom and I love you, Winnie, and we want you to be able to deal with big emotions and feelings without hurting anyone. Even when you're feeling surprised or upset or angry, hurting people can't be our solution, okay?"

"Tanner tried to grab the digger from me!"

"I understand that, and I'm sure his parents are talking to him right now about how that isn't okay," Cal said. *Unlikely*, thought Evangeline, but she said nothing. "It's you I want to think about, okay? If someone is doing something you don't like in the future, I want you to have some options for dealing with it that don't involve hurting them."

Winnie, glum now, nodded and ate the remainder of her popsicle in one bite, a good portion of it having puddled into red soup on the table.

"Hey, lovey?" Cal said, dipping his head to catch her eye. "I know this is a bummer, and I want to be really clear that this kind of behavior isn't acceptable. I also want you to know a secret, though, okay?"

A twist of curiosity pulled at Winnie's face as she looked at Cal, who leaned close and whispered, "I love you a whole bunch."

The almost-seven-year-old smiled and stage-whispered, "I love you a whole five bunches."

"Well, I love you a whole five hundred bunches."

"Well, I love you a whole infinity bunches."

Cal laughed and wrapped her in another hug.

"So," he said, "if this happens again, where someone is doing something you don't like or something that's making you upset, what can you do?"

"Tell my teachers?" Winnie said, turning the idea into a question.

"Definitely," Evangeline said, sitting forward as she entered the conversation. She'd wanted to let Cal have his moment with Winnie before jumping in herself. As someone without the big family baggage Cal carried around, she didn't see this conversation as the monumental one he clearly did. "Your teachers are there to help you, and I bet they would want to know if something was wrong."

"What else?" Cal prompted.

Winnie thought for a moment, her attention already beginning to wander from the conversation to the book still in Cal's hands.

"I could ask Tanner to stop?"

"Yes!" Evangeline nodded. "Talking with the person who is making you upset is a really important skill. And sometimes you might not be able to solve the problem by talking with them, but it's good to try at least before anything else."

"Okay, Momma." Winnie began to chew on the popsicle stick now, and Evangeline judged her emotional stamina as nearly extinguished.

Cal, who had the emotional stamina of a soap opera, looked ready to continue the conversation, but Evangeline caught his eye as she said, "Good; now let's do some reading before the pizza gets here!"

Winnie slipped from her chair—a sturdy thing made of dark wood with a flower pattern carved in to the vertical pieces—and came around to crawl into Cal's lap while he read. She was getting to be almost too large to sit in their laps, her limbs already foreshadowing the long, gangly things they would become in her awkward teenage years. Or could become, if she had those years.

Cal happily let Winnie settle in on his lap, resting his chin on the top of her head while she opened the book to the page they'd stopped on. He wrapped one arm around her in a hug and put out the other around Evangeline's shoulders, feeling that everything in the whole world had clicked together for just a moment, for just a breath.

The pizza arrived a short while later, carried in by the special guest.

"Oddry!" Winnie shouted as the head tech came into the house with his weekly announcement of "Fee fi fo fum, I bring pizza for Chrysanthemum!"

Chrysanthemum was Oddry's special nickname for Winnie, and it was a name no other person—Cal and Evangeline included—was allowed to use.

Winnie ran down the stairs and skidded around the corner to find Oddry depositing the three pizza boxes on the table, Evangeline entering from the kitchen with a beer for him.

"There she is," Oddry said, holding out his hand. He and Winnie had a secret handshake, one that seemed to grow and evolve with each week. They'd started the Monday pizza-party tradition before Winnie had arrived, back when the nights went longer and the number of beers far outpaced the number of slices they each had. It had grown into something more like a family night as time had gone on and their start and end times had crept earlier and earlier.

After a series of palm slides and finger guns and explosions made from clenched fists and spread hands, Winnie and Oddry bumped knuckles and broke off, each smiling. Around the rest of the world, Oddry Mulligan was a curmudgeonly genius, prickly in interviews and government depositions, erratic and odd in workplace encounters.

With Winnie, he was a laughing, happy man, as though the layers of cynicism and cantankerousness were clothes he put on to face the world, the equivalent of a business suit bought for an important meeting. But with Winnie—and with other children he ended up being around—Oddry's public persona fell away and what remained was someone kind, someone happy, someone joyous.

That person peeked through even in public if you were observant and patient enough, and it was this person Evangeline and Cal had become friends with, this person who they'd named godfather of their at-the-time unborn child.

"Let's play *Treetop Village*," Winnie said, racing off now to the board-game closet.

"Okay, but I want to be the wizard," Oddry said, calling after her as he took the proffered beer and slid into a chair at the table.

Winnie responded but had gone too far for any of them to make out her words.

"How was training today with the new squad?" Oddry asked as Cal came down the stairs and joined the two of them at the well-worn wooden table, which told a story of childhood in dents, small gouges, and stubborn marker stains.

"Things were going really great until Cal got in a fight with our newest member," Evangeline said, taking one of the plates they'd put out and helping herself to a slice of pizza. Cooley's had one standard pizza (pepperoni) and then two new ones each week, most of which were pretty good.

Evangeline eyed the slice on her plate critically, sniffing before taking a bite. Green curry pizza. Not bad.

"You didn't." Oddry took a slice of the famous pepperoni and fixed Cal with a long-suffering look.

"I was doing just fine," Cal said, raising his hands in despair. "We had all done our individual warmups and we were on to squad training, and I even paired up with Incident on a few tactics—I did!"

In response to Oddry's look of naked skepticism, Cal turned his wide eyes to Evangeline, who reached for another slice of pizza and said, "He did, yeah. They work surprisingly well together when they aren't trying to kill each other."

"But then," Cal said, "she had to remind us all that she refuses to directly attack any of the Wretched—whom she calls *the Blessed Few*— you know, the things that are going to be killing people, destroying buildings, and causing general mayhem in a few days. The Blessed Few."

"Incident has worked here for years," Oddry said as Winnie returned, the box for Treetop Village held with reverence before her. "You've heard her say all that nonsense before. This shouldn't be a surprise to you."

"But that was when she was just a weirdo on another squad," Cal said, taking a bite out of the other mystery pizza, which brought a grimace to his face after a moment. "Cranberry salad. Terrible."

"Daddy, you're the librarian," Winnie said, spreading out the board and beginning to pass around the pieces. "Oddry, you're the wizard, of course. Momma, you're the scientist. I'm the tinkerer."

"Thanks, sweets," Evangeline said, taking the tiny figurine, which was a bit of plastic shaped to look like a tiny man in a lab coat, a beaker of something green in one hand and a whole microscope in the other. "What Fencer Calidore is forgetting to mention is that, instead of ignoring Incident or steering the discussion in a different direction, he took it upon himself to insult her religion."

"Oh, sweet baby Jesus," Oddry said, slumping in his chair and dropping a look of deep disappointment on Cal. "I really do not need to deal with religious litigation right now, Cal—especially given your *sensitive assignment* tomorrow at the House of Always Giving." He eyed them both. "What did you say?"

"How does this game work?" Cal asked Winnie, squinting at his figurine—a woman holding a stack of books and wearing voluminous robes. "We're trying to build a treehouse or something?"

"*Dad*," Winnie said, dismayed. "We've played this like a hundred million times!"

"Don't worry; Daddy knows how to play," Evangeline said, winking at Winnie before turning back to Cal. "Go on, Cal. Let our boss know what you said."

Cal took another bite of his pizza, grimacing again, and finally said, "I just suggested to Incident that her religion wasn't old enough to make great claims over truth and history."

"Winnie, can you go grab some napkins for us?" Evangeline asked, and when Winnie pelted out of the room, Evangeline leaned forward and said, "No, you said, and I quote, 'I've had nights of sleep that lasted longer than your religion has, so let's leave the wisdom to a system of thought that's grown beyond the terrible twos.'"

"Oh, fuck off, Cal," Oddry said, groaning. "I don't know which of you is worse."

"She!" Cal said, looking around in horror. "*She* is worse. By a lot."

Oddry ticked the reasons out on the fingers of one hand. "You two are both dramatic, both set in your ways, and both temperamental as hell. I should suspend you both, and I should start with you."

"Here you go, here you go, here you go," Winnie said, dropping napkins next to each of them as she ran around the table and returned to her spot. "Now can we play?"

"You apologize," Oddry said, pointing first at Cal. He moved his finger then to Evangeline. "You make sure he does." He ended on Winnie. "And you roll that die, Chrysanthemum. The Forest Princess needs our help, and I mean to save the Treetop Village if I can."

For the rest of the evening, until Winnie's bedtime when Oddry read her a chapter from *A Wrinkle in Time* and offered poorly concealed criticisms of the science in the book, they played Winnie's favorite game and ate her favorite food, sharing stories and laughs. They worked together to defeat the forest trolls and save the Forest Princess, all while constructing the Greentop Castle high in the forest canopy.

At one point, Cal brought out ice cream—a surprise he'd gotten at the store the other day without telling anyone—and Winnie had let loose a banshee scream of delight, rising from her seat with arms outstretched. She'd followed Cal into the kitchen and helped him scoop the portions, putting the mounds of ice cream into four of her favorite coffee mugs.

"Penguin mug for Momma because she loves penguins. Red monster mug for Oddry because he loves scary movies just like me. Unicorn mug for you because unicorns are your favorite animal. And big green mug for me because I want a lot of ice cream."

It was the perfect night, and when Oddry left, he did so with a broad smile on his face, the cares and worries of the day forgotten in that oasis of time when they could all share joy without limit or requirement.

Later, after the equinox, after the banal horrors of the day and the true horrors of the night, Evangeline would think of this evening with a longing that hurt, that wrenched at the heart and tore at the throat. It would hang on the horizons of her memory, always out of reach, burning too bright.

A History of Fences and Fae by AK Senga, PhD

Published in 2027 by University of Minnesota Majestic Press
Excerpt from Chapter 3: "The Fencers"

Most famous of the fencers, of course, is the man who became known as Arthur Miracle.

Arthur Meyer was born in 1976 to Tom and Louisa Meyer, who lived then in Michigan. Tom was an electrician and an alcoholic. Louisa left when Arthur was only nine, taking her son to Georgia and remarrying a man named Burt. Although that marriage lasted for only a year, Arthur and his mother stayed in Georgia, where some extended family lived.

Historians, mathematicians, journalists, and novelists have spilled more ink than any would care to admit on Arthur Miracle's troubled upbringing, and I aim to spend as little time here as possible on those dark years of his life. Instead, let me summarize quickly before moving on to the true goal of my study: Arthur Miracle as a desperado symbol of the late nineties American zeitgeist.

Arthur did not graduate high school. Instead, midway through his tenth-grade year, he left Georgia to begin working for his father in Michigan. Tom Meyer had, the year before, opened a small-engine repair shop, and the promise of financial independence and a recovered relationship with his estranged father convinced Arthur to move, though he made regular visits back to see his mother.

On a late July afternoon in 1996, Arthur collapsed at work and, when he was able to get to his feet, found a tattoo had appeared on his chest. The number 2. The smallest prime, most powerful. While the appearance of new primes is most common on the equinox itself, world numbers show an average of ten to twelve newly primed fencers each month during the winter, spring, and summer months.

In half a year, Arthur's face—cleaned of the acne high on his cheeks and the threadbare goatee that had ringed his mouth—was on every news show and government promotional material as Arthur Miracle.

Unlike other fencers, who patrolled on the equinox in teams, Arthur Miracle was happy to work alone, and he seemed utterly unstoppable. Each equinox, he would stalk the streets of New York on his motorcycle, weaponless save for his primacy, which seemed to grant him power of just about any kind and shape he wanted. Fae fell before him, and New York reached levels of fae containment and neutralization not seen since.

During the off-season, Arthur was a worldwide celebrity, rich beyond anything that boy from Union City might have dreamed of.

But soon, the destruction of fae each equinox and the jet-setting of the off-season proved uninteresting to Arthur Miracle, and in 1999, he decided to make a run at the Threshold Tree—that strange, closed gateway at the center of each Harbor that, at the time, had been unopened and unexplored. Nearly every fencer at the time was either not strong enough or not in possession of a primacy that could break through the Threshold Tree.

Gathering a group of the strongest fencers from the United States to support him, Arthur Miracle trudged through the New England Harbor until he reached the Tree. Although Arthur was able to tear a hole into the Threshold with his primacy, the approach to the Tree and the act of gaining entrance resulted in four of the six members of his team dying. The other two were badly wounded.

Arthur Miracle went through the tear in the Tree anyway, which knit itself back together behind him.

One of the wounded fencers, Skyward Silas, succumbed to his injuries before he could get out.

The other, a fencer from Florida named WarSpeaker, only twenty years old, recounted what she'd seen:

Miracle went through that barrier and didn't come out—not as himself, anyway. I was running to get back to the fence, trying to carry Silas, when that barrier ripped again, and out he came. He'd changed, not into any faerie but into a monster, all covered in darkness and shadow, with shears big as my head. He wasn't Arthur anymore, and I ran. God forgive me, I dropped Silas, and I ran.

Today, of course, we know that entity as the Riparian.

Chapter 11

The bells clustered atop the towers of the House of Always Giving like silver faerie fruit hung just out of reach, and when they rang, they pealed their sweetness out in a rich, bright torrent.

"I hate those bells," Cal said as they neared the House on their two Oddry-given missions: the one that the rest of the squad and the bureau broadly knew about, and the one that only a necessary few knew about. It had hurt Evangeline and Cal to keep the secret from the rest of their squad, especially Nero, but Oddry's instructions were clear. When Aleph had delivered the bag of iron filings and the badly—and, if Evangeline's guess were right, hastily—photocopied blueprints for the church, he'd emphasized again the plan:

Plant the iron.

Get caught doing it.

In the ensuing tumult, steal their secrets, especially those referring to members and finances.

To Cal, Aleph had given a pleasurably malleable and heavy bag of iron filings, balls, and pebbles.

"Good mix of sizes and shapes in there," he'd said.

For Evangeline, Aleph had a small, nondescript camera made of black metal, smaller than any cell phone she'd ever seen. Just as the House of Always Giving allowed no iron to pass its doors, it also had a firm policy about technology developed after the Stone Age: as little as possible and none on its members. No phones, no radios, no computers were allowed inside.

The bag of iron filings was stretchy enough to expand across Cal's stomach, making him look as though he'd put on a little weight but not in an obvious way. The camera snugged into a small pocket sewn into the sleeve of the suit coat she'd be wearing. Cal would sneak the metal through the detectors before passing the camera to Evangeline.

Evangeline patted Cal's hand and continued looking out the window. He'd been like this all morning—restlessly picking and caviling at nothing, the sludge of his dark mood almost materializing around him.

"They get to ring out over the city and tell everyone to come in and worship the *actual* creatures that will be trying to kill people, ruin their lives, and destroy their homes in only a few days—and we just go along with our business as usual?"

There was an ugliness to Cal's anger, not because he was wrong but because it lied. Evangeline had phoned the office to let them know that she and Cal would take their own car and to have Incident, Nero, and the Stone Weaver arrive separately, knowing that Cal was likely to pick a fight with Incident on the way there.

Incident would see an insult to her faith from an unruly child.

Nero and the Stone Weaver would see a squad member whining and bickering about every little thing only a few days before the Long Day.

Evangeline saw the truth. The anger, the frustration, the hollow bitterness about every possible slight and injustice were all a shadow play put on by his grief, forms thrown onto a wall by a hand signing sorrow and showing petty rage.

Their car pulled up under the stone awning of the House, the pillars carved to show vining ivy and stacked stands of foxgloves; maple, oak, elm, and hawthorn trees climbed up to the marbled ceiling above.

Hiding behind these plants, carved with strokes almost gentle enough to be invisible, were the obscured forms of the fae—a slender arm sliding out from behind a tree trunk, a heel captured mid-run as the lithe figure slipped from view.

A pair of eyes, too wide and cunning, peering through the ivy.

Evangeline ran a hand over one of the pillars. The Sylvans imagined the fae to be at once otherworldly sages, bursting with wisdom and keen insight, and naughty children, capable of miraculous mischief and shattering innocence.

The truth, made obvious every equinox, was that the fae were neither sages nor children, neither holy mother nor holy father. They were nothing human, and every poetic metaphor and comparison that attempted to slot them into some stratum of human experience misunderstood the fae at grave risk.

Evangeline could feel her primacy raging inside her, wanting to be used. As the equinox waxed, Evangeline's power, her great gift from whatever force or being inked fencers and thrust them into the fight with the fae, grew harder and harder to control and keep inside. What was a gentle stirring in her chest in March became a second heartbeat by June and a cardiac hurricane by September.

As a young fencer—her prime had come in at fifteen, and she'd been pulled from school and begun her training—Evangeline had thought something was wrong with her. Doctor after doctor and test after test all confirmed that she was perfectly healthy, perfectly normal, and in possession of a perfectly average heart. She was not having a heart attack each fall, and any effects she was feeling were entirely the psychosomatic productions of her primacy.

Evangeline learned to manage the primacy. The effect was never painful, not in the way of a cut or a bruise or even a broken bone, of which she'd had many. Instead, it felt like an animal had burrowed inside her, something vicious and wild, and during the year, it made a home of her chest, hollowing out a lung for sleeping, another for dining. It made a hearth of her heart and warmed the winter there, growing strong and watchful, easing through spring and becoming unruly in the summer, throwing clawed hands against the prison bars of her ribs and slamming back against her spine.

And on the Long Day, when the world around her fell apart and the dead did not die, Evangeline would let the bright, angry monster inside her out.

"Welcome to the place of peace!" Incident, along with the Stone Weaver and Nero, was already at the House, standing in front of the closed double doors. She waved at Cal and Evangeline, whose car drove off to park. A few agents accompanied the group, though a collection of five fencers, even five so comparatively underpowered as these, even stripped of the iron weapons they could not bring into the church, would be more than a match for most national armies this close to the equinox.

Beside Incident, his hands disappeared into the folds of his robe, was Gregory Harp, still tan, still smiling, wearing a different set of robes that still sported the open hand of the Sylvans. Evangeline had learned during Cal's father's ceremony that the Sylvans didn't actually call such things "funerals." They had special names for everything, of course, each one purple and what she liked to call "faux-etic," a term that had made Cal cackle for several minutes when she'd used it to describe how some of his favorite writers sounded to her.

They'd called it a "Psalmody for the Lost," and though it had been filled with songs and poetry, with complicated rituals involving laying flowers of all kinds on the body and different dances with smoke and scents, it had been nothing more and nothing less than a funeral. A chance to say goodbye. A chance to mourn. And a chance to conjure up meaning for a thing as senseless and meaningless as death.

Evangeline had spent much of the service staring at the body—Cliff, she had kept reminding herself; a person, not just a body.

Standing there in front of the House now, Evangeline felt the thrum of nerves at what she had to do, but alongside that was the pleasure at getting to do it to these people.

Her primacy moved inside her again, singing along her bloodstream. *Soon*, she thought. *Very soon.*

"Welcome, respected fencers, to the House of Always Giving," Gregory Harp said. He smiled around at them, his gaze catching for a moment on Evangeline and Cal. "It is my great pleasure to receive you here, and to see some familiar faces, too."

His hands appeared from the folds of his robe as he stepped forward and shook hands with everyone but Cal, who kept his own hands stuffed into his pockets and offered Harp an empty look.

"Such a historical moment," he said, unperturbed, stepping back and disappearing his hands into his sleeves again.

After the funeral—the psalmody—Evangeline had looked up Harp and discovered that he'd been a high school history teacher in Missouri until he saw the light in 1989 and decided to become a priest in the House of Always Giving. She could imagine him, no longer grading tedious student essays about the Civil War or the Whiskey Rebellion, rising each morning and sliding his soft, unworked body into one of those thick robes. Would he run hands over the fabric, marveling at its quality, delighting in the whorls and ribbons of ornament that had been hand-sewn into its surface? Of course he would. Gregory Harp would stand in front of a full-length mirror, enrobed and enchanted by his own image, the sleeves of his robe conjoined to hide his hands. He would imagine himself as a wizard of old, a truth-sayer, a wielder of powers too strange and fae for the world to understand.

How it must grate on him to be in the presence of fencers who actually *did* have such powers.

"If you'll just follow me in," Harp said, turning and stepping through one of the heavy wooden doors, opened for him by Incident. Carved into the marble of the archway above were the words *She Waits Beyond the Grave*.

Easy to miss just under this eerie pronouncement was a thin band of metal tracing the entirety of the archway and the walls. A metal detector, one that any hungry devotee had to pass under. And just beyond, smiling pleasantly in their deep red robes, were two men prepared to enforce the prohibition of metals—iron, especially and specifically—in the House of Always Giving.

"They carry mallets made of reinforced plastic and stone," Oddry had told Cal and Evangeline. "And they don't fuck around. They look like pudgy, middle-aged deacons who say dumb shit like *TGIF* and *whoops-a-daisy*. They *aren't*."

The guards hadn't been visually present during Cal's father's funeral, and they hadn't brought any of their iron, anyway. Now that she looked at them, though, Evangeline saw the calculated looks in their eyes, the gentle sway of their hands to always be near those ugly, matte-black mallets, which hung from their hips and looked like badly made candle-snuffers. The way they held themselves, the way they moved, the way they *didn't* move—it reminded Evangeline of Aleph and the other agents, the threat of harm always within their reach, their every move and look calculated.

This should be fun, she thought, watching as first the Stone Weaver and then Nero walked through the doors, hands open at their sides. "*Be obviously compliant*" had been the official message from the administration before the trip. "*Be kind. Be courteous. Above all, demonstrate that we can be safe, reliable partners.*"

Evangeline nodded to Aleph, who walked forward and set off the alarm.

A clanging calamity of bells and sirens erupted all around them, rebounding from marbled wall to marbled wall. Maybe it was because of her training, or perhaps it came from what Cal called her "natural tranquility," but Evangeline had the presence of mind amidst the shouts of dismay and the sudden movement of the red-clad guards and their own bureau agents to notice how out of place—or out of *time*—those alarms were.

The inside of the House of Always Giving looked like a well-funded

Renaissance Festival—old-looking wood latticed across high, coffered ceilings, stones that might have been worked by hand from the fields of the rugged Highlands of Scotland emerged from the walls in ascending and descending patterns of grey, brown, and russet. The pews—the same ones she had sat in during the funeral—were low-backed, grim things reminiscent of a monkish past that had not existed in any form for nearly a millennium. It was both a tribute to and a resurrection of a romanticized past, one that its makers imagined sprang from storybook wonder and not from the darker pages of real history.

And now the verisimilitude of that happy play broke with each blare of twenty-first-century speakers embedded behind wooden beams in the ceiling or hidden at the base of intricately carved marble plinths. Lights previously invisible strobed in harsh, arrhythmic patterns, and deeper in the church, past the rows of pews and the raised dais where Gregory Harp had hectored the attendants of Cal's father's funeral, back in that shadowy part of the House where the tour today was meant to end—back there, a door Evangeline couldn't see slammed closed on hydraulic hinges and locked with a series of heavy *thunk*s.

The church guards were already en route to neutralize Aleph, who had stopped in the doorway, a look of surprise animating his normally impassable face. The guards were shouting, the other agents were shouting, Gregory Harp and Incident were shouting, and even Nero's voice could be heard above the tumult as she asked "What the fuck?" of the situation.

No one but Evangeline was paying any attention to Cal, who looked to her with a faint smile lighting his features.

She didn't blink and didn't look away—she loved watching Cal use his primacy, the way his primes seemed to swim along his skin like a school of fish agitated by the presence of a predator. Some fencers' tattoos flickered with light when using their abilities; some grouped in odd, unreadable patterns or grew large or retracted to tiny dots; some grew thorny and stylized, as though tattooed by a particularly artistic hand.

It was as though the uniqueness of the primes themselves had to manifest itself in every aspect of fencing, like the novelty of a fingerprint always making itself known.

Amidst the chaos and rush of the alarms, Cal's primes surged and schooled along his skin, and though she didn't blink or lose focus, Evangeline found herself staring at empty space, the afterimage of Cal still in her mind, like a sunspot seen after daringly glancing at a noonday sun.

She blinked, allowing her mind to catch up with reality, and there was Cal, standing beside Nero and the Stone Weaver, adding his own concerned shouts to the scrum of strong men under the archway. The bag of iron filings still hugged his midsection, hidden mostly by the slightly baggy shirt he wore but visible to Evangeline, who knew his shape better than any.

"You'll have to use your primacy to get through the metal detectors," Oddry had told Cal, who'd grinned at the prospect of further profaning the House of Always Giving with his fencing ability. "I'll talk to Aleph about causing a scene, which should allow you to hit the pause button on the world around you long enough to get through. Can you do that?"

Cal had started into an explanation of how it wasn't really like hitting a pause button but more like pushing the bubble of his time-slowing powers out around him while maintaining a tiny air pocket for himself to move through, but Oddry had waved it away and said, "*I don't care about that. Can you do it?*"

And Cal had said he could.

"Friends! My friends!" Gregory Harp stood at the edge of the action, waving his hands and baring his thin, hairy wrists, shattering another solemn and grand illusion, this one the sense that he was a wise and mysterious wizard of old.

"Enough!" Evangeline's shout cut through and was the signal for Aleph and the other agents to stop their struggle. Immediately they relented, giving up their own illusion that it had been a fair fight.

Aleph allowed his arms to be pinned behind his back by a guard who was bleeding from his nose, the trickle a near-perfect match to the color of his robe.

"It's my wallet," Aleph said, looking first at Harp and then Evangeline. "Jacket pocket, right breast."

Another guard stepped forward and found the offending token in Aleph's wallet—a thin band stamped with a few characters and the outline of a heart.

"It's iron, High Priest," the man said, offering the beat-up piece of metal to Harp, who took it as though it were a venomous bug perched on the end of a stick.

"You bring this into our holy House?" Harp said, turning his look of disgust on Aleph and then the fencers. "After our good-faith efforts to extend the hand of friendship, you do this?"

"It's from my son," Aleph said. "I just forgot to take it out—that's all. I forgot it was even there."

It was true that Aleph had a son, but Terry was twenty and hadn't ever given his father a piece of iron like that. Still, it made for a more believable story, and there was a sense of relief—small, but visible—that moved through everyone as Aleph mentioned his son.

"Gregory—High Priest Harp," Incident said, stepping forward to position herself between Harp and Aleph. "I'm so sorry. This is just a misunderstanding. Many of our agents and, indeed, many of us fencers, often carry iron as a necessary part of our job. Please don't let such a small thing spoil this chance for friendship and cooperation."

Did Incident notice Cal standing past the doorway? Did she realize he hadn't walked through before Aleph? When she looked around at those in attendance, did her gaze linger on Cal and then Evangeline, her eyebrows quirking in confusion and suspicion?

"I apologize, too, for this oversight," Evangeline said, stepping forward and catching Harp's eyes. "Our agents are so used to carrying iron at all times. This is so new for all of us, and clearly, we did not do a thorough-enough check before arriving."

With exaggerated care and transparency, Evangeline turned out her own pockets and went through her own wallet. By this point, someone had turned off the alarms, and the sound of the House returned again to its storybook glory, voices rising to get lost among the cathedral ceilings, the soft light of stained-glass windows rendering the rooms in idyllic stasis.

The agents, including Aleph, followed Evangeline's lead and ostentatiously demonstrated their innocence, but it was not enough for Harp, who, with a gesture, sent his people forward to pat down Evangeline and the agents. For a moment, she thought they might turn to the four fencers already through, and she could imagine how that might lead to a scuffle of an entirely different kind, but Harp seemed satisfied, and Incident, chewing on her lower lip and looking still at Evangeline, said nothing.

"Well," Harp said after Evangeline walked through the doorway and into the church proper without a blip or flash from the alarms. "That was exciting, wasn't it! Shall we try for a fresh start?"

He smiled around at them, patronizing and calm, and Evangeline had the sudden certainty that he had been the kind of teacher who'd loved the authority of the classroom far more than he'd believed in any kind of grand educational purpose. He'd probably said this same kind of thing to his tenth-graders: flashing his condescending smile at a group of pimpled young adults and saying *Tell us how you really feel* after some student shouted his anger and left for the principal's office. Swap his robes for a wrinkled button-up and ill-fitting slacks, and he could be there still today.

"Absolutely," Evangeline said, mimicking his smile. "We're grateful for the invitation, High Priest Harp, and I speak for everyone at the Midwest Bureau when I say how committed we are to this relationship being a fruitful one."

For us, anyway.

Inside, the House soared in beautiful stonework, every doorway an arch, every ceiling a broad-beamed, muraled thing. Stone floors sent sound up to stone walls crowded with statues set into recesses—likenesses of fae figures from storybooks and history, each one crowned with a delicate ring of foxgloves and rowan berries.

Set high above these statues, in an alcove greater than the others and lit by both stained-glass polychrome and cunningly hidden LEDs of soft gold, was the Faerie Queen herself, etched in light and shadow, the fall of her dress caught in masterfully carved stone, the wide, bright eyes cut into a face harsh and austere.

In one hand she held the mace of her station, a scepter said to be carved from the first tree and grown around the bones of the first being.

Her other hand extended forward, open and inviting, and Evangeline could almost see those long fingers curling in, could almost hear that silken voice calling her forward, toward the fence, toward the Harbor, beyond and beyond.

In her alcove, the Faerie Queen looked down upon her subjects.

For the academics the squad had met, the "Bloodless Queen Hypothesis"—a play on the Red Queen Hypothesis from evolutionary biology—was a cute idea to consider, one more theory for various academics to take out back and punch around.

But for the Sylvans, there was no hypothesis or theory to it—they believed, utterly and completely, that there was a Faerie Queen, that she ruled from the land of faerie beyond the Harbors, that the fae were her children or subjects (or maybe both), and that some day, if a churchgoing believer were very good and very faithful, they would be taken home to that strange castle of the Queen beyond the fence.

A chorus of Sylvans who had dispersed during the alarms but returned to their practice stood on the stone risers back behind the altar, swaying and clapping and chanting their way through rehearsal. They were known formally as the Fated Quire, but today they were dressed in casual clothes, jeans and T-shirts instead of the lavish robes they would wear on their holy day.

In that space, surrounded by walls, floors, and ceilings of stones sanded and polished to look and feel ancient, even the practice of the Fated Quire sounded majestic and ominous. Every clapped hand was a crack of thunder, and every run of song was a melody from beyond the grave, uncanny and beautiful, at least until one of the men in back, a tenor or baritone, lost the rhythm and clapped in a great pitfall of silence, jangling the rhythm and ruining the grave feel in the cathedral.

The Quire fell to laughter and shouts of mock anger, and Gregory Harp laughed with them.

"As you can see, we're still in the midst of our preparations for the equinox. It's always a busy few weeks in the lead up."

"We wouldn't know anything about that," Cal said, though just quietly enough so only Evangeline could hear. He'd sidled up next to her and she felt his hand slip inside her pocket, leaving the camera there.

"We are a *happy* bunch here," Incident said, waving at the members of the Quire, her accompanying guffaw a bright, boisterous sound. It sounded, even to Evangeline, who was trying hard to be generous with Incident, artificial.

They were led past the pews carved with yet more scenes of pastoral bliss, past the vast stone columns and through the archways, past the small rooms that led off to either side of the main walkway, each one set up with its own altar to one of the Queen's aspects.

Most were empty so early in the day, but a few held Sylvans, praying ardently to the Loving Queen or the Jealous Queen, the Watchful Queen or the Wrathful Queen. Each altar came with its own set of rituals and taboos, holy words and hidden words. A man in one—the

Melancholy Queen's altar—traced blocky sigils in the air with a stick of burning incense, chanting in a quiet, atonal voice. He did not wear shoes, and his arms showed thin lines of recently dried blood.

Evangeline had once tried to memorize the myriad minutiae of the Sylvan church but had stopped when she realized the labyrinthine titles and terms were *meant to be* convoluted. Nothing in this ridiculous religion, from the badly reimagined bits taken from Catholicism to the imaginings of the late-twentieth-century minds who spun Sylvanism out of nothing—none of that arcana was meant to make sense. The feelings evoked by the names of the rituals and the overwrought titles of the members—the Fated Quire and the Little Lord, the Spreading Branches and the Lady's Attendants, the Foxglove Knights and Her Majesty's First and Loveliest—the feelings pulled from those storybook syllables were the point, not any conscious understanding of hierarchy and order.

They're just like fencers, she'd realized once—hiding behind names and rituals that might have a little substance inside but were instead made and performed solely to create an illusion of solemnity and magic, as if the only response to an impossible, magical eruption in the real world was to recreate the real world as a place of magic and impossibility itself.

"*I'm* older than most of this stuff," Cal muttered, one hand coming to rest against his iron paunch, as he and Evangeline trailed behind the group and Harp, who was proudly describing the trip one of the stained-glass windows had taken to reach them.

". . . from a small hamlet in Yorkshire, where it was saved by an erstwhile member of our order, Bertram McCarthy, who dates it to over fifteen hundred years old! If you look here . . ."

The night after his father's funeral, as they lay in bed together, Cal had told Evangeline a story about visiting Yale as an undergraduate. He'd accompanied his advisor to a conference there, and during a particularly boring panel, he'd left the conference building and gone exploring.

"I was just a dumb kid from the Midwest," he'd said, laughing a little, his head nuzzled into her shoulder and his voice muffled. "The son of Dianne and Cliff, one dead of a drunk driving accident when I was three and now the other dead of a heart attack. I was amazed by all the architecture and the history, and I remember walking into this building and exclaiming about the stone steps and how worn down they were—you know, sort of thinner in the middle as you went up, and smoother there, too."

Cal giggled into her shoulder, the sound almost childish. The giggle of a kid who had just made a mistake and didn't yet have reason to fear laughing at himself.

"One of the students passing by told me that Yale sanded down the steps to look like that because they wanted to copy Oxford and Cambridge—one of those old schools in England. I never found out if that's true or not, but the idea stuck in my head. A school that so badly wants to seem wise and old that the people there would be willing to actually degrade the architecture to give the impression of hundreds more years of feet walking its steps or thousands more undergrad butts plunking down into its hallowed seats."

He'd emerged from Evangeline's shoulder and looked up at her, the humor gone from his eyes.

"That's what that fucking church was like today. Did you know that thing was built in the *nineties*? They're so desperate for you to think they've been around as long as any ancient cathedral from Rome or Istanbul or whatever. All the dumb robes and carved sconces and arches and what-the-fuck-ever else. They're playacting a history that isn't theirs and probably doesn't even exist."

Evangeline thought on this as Harp led them past the altar and the choir risers to point out a few tapestries that looked old and were probably made in the nineties, professionally distressed in the aughts, and were now pretending to be ancient in the twenties.

"Off to the east is our library wing, and I'm happy to show that off—we just had a visiting exhibit of the Auchinleck manuscript last year! Quite a treat for our humble church to host such an important document." Harp gestured toward an archway, beyond which a grand, well-lit hallway full of more paintings and more tapestries terminated at the grand library of the Majestic House of Always Giving.

"That's the manuscript with Orfeo, isn't it?" Cal asked, some of his gruffness gone. Even during the service, Cal had longed to look through the library, but to enter, a person had to be either a card-carrying member of the church or a scholar given special permissions.

"*Sir* Orfeo," Harp said, correcting Cal with a pitying glance. "And yes, the Auchinleck manuscript contains, among other works, the lai of Sir Orfeo, one of our central illuminative texts. Whoever wrote that strange, beautiful poem understood something of the fae and their realm."

Outside of Cal, none of the others in attendance seemed particularly interested by this information or the tour itself. In fact, Evangeline was working to keep her attention from drifting too obviously to the wing opposite the library, where the administrative offices were, at least according to the blueprint Oddry had shown her.

Down the hallway, left at the gargoyle statue, second door on the right. Should be a small, thin door.

From where she was standing, Evangeline thought she could see the gnarled wings of the statue, easily twelve or fifteen feet tall, but she didn't want to be caught staring, so she returned her attention to Harp and the tour he was leading.

This visit, such as it was, had no real stated purpose outside of the predictable and typical flexing of muscles and posturing that occurred between larger social bodies like the Bureau and the House of Always Giving—a chance for both sides to toe the line of their authority and sniff menacingly at the other under the guise of "open communication and goodwill efforts."

The same silly play was happening all across the country this week—a deal struck between the Central Bureau and the central mind of the House of Always Giving, whatever and wherever that was. In other states and in other cities, bureaus were sending a mix of fencers and/or staff to the local Sylvan chapter or chapters to eye up their arches, glare seriously at their pews and meeting rooms, and frown—without pretense or falseness this time—at the cavernous, circular room at the back of the building.

Were any of those other groups planning to poke their local Sylvans like Evangeline and Cal were? It would be just like the Central Bureau to orchestrate myriad small missions like this without any communication between or among groups. Despite Oddry's assurance that no legal consequences would ever touch them, Evangeline had doubts. Those bastards at the top would think nothing of distancing themselves from a mission gone wrong with phrases like *rogue fencers* and *not approved of or communicated to by any central authority.*

"And the Temple of Ascension, of course," Gregory Harp, former high school teacher, said, stopping at the doors—once again unlocked and held open now that the alarms were no longer blaring. "Here, the most sacred and important of our work is done."

Harp spoke in a hushed, awed voice.

Evangeline hated him.

She looked first to Aleph, who caught her eye and nodded, and then to Cal, who was staring ahead at the room with a look of unreserved hatred on his face. He wasn't the only one, either. Nero stood beside him, arms crossed, eyes slanted in anger. One half of her mouth had curled up to show her disgust at that place.

Even the Stone Weaver, new to the squad and to the world of fencing, sucked in a shocked breath when she saw the cavernous room inside, whispered about by many and reported on by a few of the braver news agencies but rarely opened to anyone outside of the Sylvan fold.

Harp was gesturing them inside, that hateful, placid smile puddled across his face, which glistened with a thin sheen of sweat. Apparently, those robes weren't breathable in addition to being grand and mysterious.

Finally, Cal found her eyes, his memory of their plan surfacing from beneath the thick layer of his rage at this room and what it stood for.

"I can't go in there," he said, voice loud and hollow. He turned eyes haunted by real disquiet on Gregory Harp, who seemed, if anything, pleased to have so upset a fencer. "I'll just stay out here on the pews, thanks."

"Of course, Calidore." Harp moved toward him, holding out his hands as if he might clasp Cal's, perhaps already calling up a line of his scripture to soothe and ease, but Aleph stepped between the High Priest and the fencer, one of his own hands out in a less-soothing way.

"I'll wait with Fencer Calidore," Aleph said in a way that suggested the matter was finished.

Harp shook his head at his own guards, their crimson bulk looming just outside the circle of the tour, before turning pained eyes on Cal's retreating form.

"Poor child. Still struggling with Cliff's passing, I imagine," he said, looking to Evangeline, "Such pain for the family. Cliff spoke of him, you know. Often during our individual meetings, which he attended *religiously*."

Harp paused to chuckle at his own joke before continuing.

"A simple and straightforward man, Cliff, who loved his Queen, his life, and his family. He spoke often of the son he'd felt he lost. Not with anger, of course. Not Cliff. A gentle giant of a man. Only sorrow for our dear Cliff. Only sorrow. He followed the Melancholy Queen's aspect, much as our sweet Incident does." He turned his beatific smile on the fencer, who blossomed beneath the attention.

Evangeline watched Cal go, watched him step around the raised dais without giving the Fated Quire a look, and she wondered how much of the set of his shoulders and the hang of his head was an act.

She was glad he had walked away before Harp started talking.

"Please, show us inside," she said, turning back to Harp and gesturing for him to proceed.

Inside, the room was a vertiginous shift from the rest of the House of Always Giving: simple white walls, sculpted as if by the hands of uncaring children, formed the uneven curve of a dome. A worn carpet, once thick and white, creaked under Evangeline's feet as she followed the others into the Temple of Ascension, forgetting for just a moment the mission.

Brown stains stood out against the white—sprays and handprints and smears on the wall and carpet, some telling a clear story of violence even as others invited stranger interpretations.

A long, thick band of dried blood running parallel to the floor for several feet at hip height, constant and with lines so defined, it might have been painted on by an interior designer of some note.

Arcane symbols traced by fingertips and surrounded by handprints large and heartbreakingly small, all perhaps banal in the context of a world gone mad if not for their location: high enough on the slanting white walls that they would need to have been done with a freestanding ladder that reached at least sixty feet, and Evangeline knew no such ladder had been used.

Dried puddles marooned and gone crusty. The remnants of fountains and sprays along the wall and coloring the carpet.

It was a page, once blank but now filled with the stories of rabid belief, tainted faith, and romanticized ignorance.

Simple wooden chairs—cheap fold-up numbers bought en masse

from the local big-box store—were set up in concentric rings around the circular, domed room, like a Quaker meeting room gone wobbly and strange. Some of these, too, bore the marks of brutality—the blood, which showed up as only shadows on the already-dark brown wood; scratches and chunks taken out of the legs, seats, and backs of the chairs; odd words in odder languages carved into the posts.

And numbers, of course—*4*s and *6*s and *8*s and *9*s and *10*s and *12*s and on and on, composites left around the room in small, shameful etchings. Each one hurt slightly to look at, like a pain so oft felt, it had become a deeper part of existence, like a sliver buried under her skin.

High on the wall, high enough that it might be the ceiling at that point, a finger had traced the hateful curve of a *2* without crossing it out.

Harp started talking about how they had ordered more chairs—"A fourth circle! We suspect we may even need a fifth for this year!"—but the fencers had all stopped listening to him, even Incident, who, because of her profession, had probably never been in this room or seen it.

"I hate this fucking room," Nero muttered as she stepped around Evangeline, hands clutched behind her, eyes darting from horror to horror.

They all hated this fucking room. The blood and the symbols and the numbers were bad enough, but for Evangeline, it was the places where the wall had been poorly repaired, the craters in the white curve, inexpertly filled and patched, each one large enough for a person to fit through.

"What were your numbers last year?" Evangeline heard herself ask, voice distant and reasonable. She knew the numbers, of course, but some part of her needed to puncture Harp's reverent wonder at this broken place, to bring their conversation back to something rational and tangible.

"Five hundred seventy-two souls gathered here last equinox," he said, eyes roving the chairs as if he could still see those poor fools, the elderly and sick—venerated among the Sylvans as those closest to saddling up on Death's horse—sat down in the cheap seats while children ambled about or played their small games, the parents and other adults chewing out banal conversations in amorphous groups. Teens lurked in their hateful huddles, and the devout college students—recently returned home from their hopeful holidays—did homework at one of the tables brought in for the twenty-four-hour-plus lock-in—hopeful that they might be taken by their Queen but not betting against tomorrow.

This was the room in which the Sylvans waited out the equinox. While the rest of the world was forced to stay in their homes for the entirety of the equinox save for a very few exceptions, the Sylvans were allowed to gather in their churches, locked inside their Temples of Ascension.

For the rest of the world, it was a day of terror, in which any death—save those caused by the fae themselves—would turn a person into a chaotic, destructive, violent creature, capable of impossible feats and weird magics. People dying of an accident or an illness would become beautiful and distant, fae and odd, before carving strange sigils into the wall and leaving a line of torn dictionary pages from the window to the bedroom. They would destroy furniture and devour pictures, frames and all. They would hurt without prejudice: family and friends, acquaintances and strangers, all powerless against this newly dead and newly born creature, faster and stronger and stranger than any human.

The fae broke bones and rent tendons; they tore limbs free and flensed skin; they harmed and hurt and killed without any real purpose or logic. It was not hunger, and it was not play, though every scholar and researcher and scientist and fencer agreed that the fae seemed to act with purpose.

Perhaps they possessed some strange logic and intent not yet understood by humans. Perhaps they were the product of their circumstances, and a better understanding of the human they had been could help decipher their actions as a fae. Or perhaps it really was pure chaos after all, no pattern or logic. Just noise, no music.

Or perhaps, and maybe worst of all, they acted under the guidance of a higher power, one that called to them from beyond the fences. The voice of their ruler. Their Queen.

Evangeline glared at one of the recessions in the wall, maybe some ten or fifteen feet up, a rough triangle big enough for a large kid or maybe a small adult to fit through. The joint compound or spackle or whatever it was that Harp and his people had used to fill in the hole served only to accentuate it, which was their point.

This crater—just like every other divot and poorly filled hole, just like every dried stretch of puddled, scribbled, and sprayed blood—was a tribute to one of their chosen ones. One of their lucky few.

It wasn't a horror story in here. It was a longing memorial.

"And how many of those five hundred–some died?" It was Nero this time asking the question. She stood over to one side, staring down at a patch of black-brown carpet.

"One blessed soul was taken by our Queen," Harp said, and did he look up at the same bit of patched wall Evangeline did? She thought so.

"Anthony Wicker," Nero said, looking down at some records she'd brought with her. "He had cancer. Aged forty-four."

"Anthony, yes."

"And how many did he kill after changing into one of the fae? Before he exited the Temple, I mean. I know how many he killed before we picked him up on West 12th."

"We . . . well . . . it's our policy," Gregory Harp began, clearly uncomfortable with the direction his friendly tour had taken. He looked around for help, mouth open and showing a glinting, gold-capped tooth back in the darkness there.

"Nero," Incident said, frowning over at her new squadmate, "this isn't really an appropriate—"

"Three," Nero said, the color rising high on her cheeks as she worked to hold in her anger. "That's how many people Anthony Donovan Wicker killed *after* escaping from the Temple of Ascension. Two EMTs who were responding to a call on Larch and 9th—he pulled their ribs out of their bodies, by the way. And a teenager who was looking down at the street from her window. She lived long enough for a different set of EMTs to arrive. They were too late to save her life, but this girl—"

Nero squinted down at the paper, as if she needed to read what it said there. As if any of them did.

Evangeline could still see the scene—they'd called all the fencers there, had them collapse on the position with all haste. Evangeline, Cal, and Nero had been the first to arrive.

The girl, Jessica Graeber, had been laid out on the lawn, roughly near the spot where the faerie had thrown her. Her limbs were a tangle around her, legs and arms bent at unnatural, awful angles.

Anthony Donovan Wicker—or the man who had been Anthony Donovan Wicker—had already begun its grisly work when they arrived, its hands wet with Jessica's blood. She had gone into shock, shutting herself off from the horrors of the world, perhaps waiting and hoping for the end. Her parents still slept inside the house, unaware of what had happened. The breaking of the glass on their daughter's window had not woken them.

Worse than Jessica's unseeing eyes and broken limbs, worse than the blood and the shattered glass—much, much worse was the song that the thing that used to be Anthony Wicker was singing when the three fencers cut around the corner and found it.

It had been a child's tune, a sideways lullaby, not one Evangeline ever sung to Winnie but close enough to send a shiver up her spine a year later.

All these months later, the melody, minor and lilting, was caught in Evangeline's memory, and she suspected it would be there until she died.

"*Peace*, Nero," Incident said, cutting in before Nero could describe the scene, the faerie's path of destruction, or the last words Jessica had mumbled out before dying.

I can't see anything. I can't see. Is my mom here? Mom? Can you hold my hand?

Cal had leaned forward and held the girl's hand—her parents would not wake for another few minutes. He'd held her hand and said nothing, and they'd all hoped Jessica Graeber died thinking she held her mother's hand.

"*Just* Anthony Wicker?" Evangeline asked, trying to keep her voice light. She peeked over at Nero's paper, as if she needed to consult it, and looked back up at Harp. "He's the only one who died and turned into a faerie?"

It was in the pause before he spoke that Evangeline saw the lie forming on Harp's lips. The way he blinked and sucked in a quick breath through his nose. The way he tilted his head just slightly to the left.

"We had twenty-two die during Anthony's trip home, if you must know. But he was the only one to be chosen by the Queen."

"Twenty-two is a lot, even for a fae attack in a crowded room like this one." Evangeline let the ghost of a smile cross her face. "You're sure that all of them were caused by the faerie? No one else turned?"

This was the point, Oddry had told them. This bit of information that the church had been concealing and lying about. The law—the flimsy bit of defense between the maniacs of the House of Always Giving and the rest of the world—allowed the Sylvans to gather in their church when no one else was allowed to be out, but it did so under strict rules. No one could take their own life. No one could be helped in taking their own life.

And all deaths—fae-induced and "natural"—had to be carefully and accurately noted. The bullshit religious laws that propped up all sorts of inequity and imbalance in America disallowed the installation of surveillance equipment in the House of Always Giving, and the fact that a handful of major senators were either official members of the House or flirting with the idea gave them extra cover.

But the Bureau had suspected for several years that the Sylvans had not been keeping good on their word, that they had been fudging the numbers between the two kinds of deaths.

"Find that evidence," Oddry had told Evangeline. *"There has to be some. Find it."*

"You know Anthony Wicker never made it, right?" Nero said after a moment, and Evangeline could have framed a picture of Harp's face—the off-guard sag of his lips, the arch of one eyebrow, the way he looked from Nero to Incident and then back to Nero.

"It's our job to shepherd the fae to the fence and the Harbor beyond," Nero said, nodding, as if she were giving a presentation to a group of schoolchildren. "And because they're so dangerous, our strategy is to almost never engage directly. We harry them, annoy them, get their attention, and encourage them along the major fae lines until they're pulled inexorably—that's the ten-dollar word my boss is always using—*inexorably* to and past the fence."

She raised a finger.

"But sometimes, a fae can't be maneuvered, and sometimes, you're rolling with a fencer badass enough to end those bastards where they stand." Nero swiveled her finger to point at Evangeline. "So, when Anthony Wicker rose from the massacre he'd made of that poor girl's face, we turned him into mulch. Less than mulch really, thanks to our squad leader."

"Stop this right now!" Incident said, her voice oddly resonant in the huge, domed room.

Harp, for his part, continued to stare slack-jawed at Nero.

From the sanctuary, Cal began to scream.

Chapter 12

The fencers moved first, their every muscle trained to react in situations like this. Nero was out the door, Incident close behind, their primacies already manifesting.

Incident's body was quickly obscured by the swarm of inky black particles she controlled, their origin as unknown as their identity. Every year, bureau scientists took their samples and did their tests and sent back reports peppered with the words *inconclusive* and *unknown*.

The black bits moved around her body like a murmuration of starlings, darting and swooping according to her will, until they formed into great gauntlets surrounding her fists, each as big as a car wheel and capable of absorbing a gunshot or smashing through a brick wall. Thin streams of the particles moved in a webwork a few inches from Incident's face, chest, and legs—a thin line of defense if she should need it.

Nero, for her part, had already manifested an amorphous bubble in one hand, the size of a beach ball and glinting with oily polychrome. As she moved out into the sanctuary, she wrenched at the perfect sphere until it had elongated into a ten-foot-long staff, topped at one end by the remaining curve of the bubble and the other by a hooked point that looked capable of doing serious damage.

Even the Stone Weaver looked ready for action. Though her primacy was nothing so outwardly fancy as Incident's or Nero's, and though she had no iron-laced sword to brandish, she followed her squad mates, prime tattoos aswirl along her skin, the numerals themselves unmoving but the color of them shivering along the spectrum, reds and purples and blues and yellows bubbling and boiling against one another and shining through the tattooed numbers on the Stone Weaver's body.

Evangeline felt a kind of pride, misplaced though it might have been, at her squad, even Incident, for leaping so quickly to action. Even deprived of their weapons and in the heart of such a hateful place, they moved to action without thought of consequence.

"The sanctuary!" Harp cried, crowding out of the Temple with his guards. Those same alarms were sounding now, and Evangeline had to move. She mingled with the group running toward the sanctuary, squinting against the reemergence of those strobing lights. Beyond the dais, which now held the statue-still forms of several members of the Quire, Calidore, a man who just that morning had paraded around the house with Winnie on his shoulders, each of their faces covered in Winnie's makeup, their necks garlanded with feather boas they'd won at the fair last year—that man, who had laughed so hard at one of Winnie's jokes the week before that yogurt sprayed from his nose, was holding ten or eleven people completely still with his primacy, ululating the words of his hollow grammarie loud enough for the nonsense language to echo and rebound in the open space.

With a single hand and the verbal gibberish he held them—a mix of brave Quire members and scarlet-robed guards who had responded to the iron filings he'd produced.

And with the other hand, he was still flinging handfuls of the metal around the sanctuary, the flakes and pebbles and discs of iron twinkling as they arced through the air before bouncing off the stone floor and wooden pews. Even with the sound of the alarms and the shouts of anger and confusion, the sound of the metal was an intermittent hailstorm, all *ping*s and *ting*s, the impacts leaving tiny divots where they hit.

"Calidore!" Incident shouted, her fight-ready gauntlets falling as she took in the scene. She stopped outside the ring of Cal's primacy, Nero, the Stone Weaver, and the Sylvans just behind her.

Oddry's instructions rang in Evangeline's head as she took a few deliberately slow steps to put herself behind the group before darting to the left, away from the sanctuary and the chaos—toward the administrative wing.

Once the chaos starts, they're going to start the alarms. But once they see the iron, they're going to close that place down. They have these big fire doors that can cut off every wing and the main sanctuary three different ways. You need to be in that administrative wing before those doors close.

Evangeline ran, dodging behind stone pillars where she could, though by the sounds of the scuffle and the direction of the shouting, it sounded as though no one had noticed her.

"The doors!" someone, maybe Harp, shouted, and Evangeline put on a burst of speed, rushing past a collection of displayed artwork along one wall, the paintings and sculptures all depicting the Faerie Queen and the imagined members of her twilight court.

A great grinding sound filled the church, and Evangeline had only passed the entrance to the administrative wing when the fire doors rumbled forth from the recesses in the stone walls in which they hid, another example of twenty-first-century technology always lurking behind the illusion of the ancient world.

Down the hallway, left at the gargoyle statue, second door on the right. Should be a small, thin door.

Ahead, the gargoyle loomed, larger and more foreboding up close. It had two sets of wings, one larger than the other, each tipped with horns, the scales expertly rendered by the artist who'd made it. Though its body was a mess of scarred flesh and pocked stretches, and though its legs were obscured by a wave of water cutting up from below—also expertly rendered—the face was human save for the juts of bone curling up from the end of the jawline and extending back behind the ears.

It was a face Evangeline had seen many times, of course, one every fencer had, from the cheery, new-hire smile of those early photos from before to the grainy, disturbing ones afterward.

The gargoyle—not a gargoyle really, but easier to think of him that way—held a pair of shears in one hand, the only bit of iron allowed in the House of Always Giving.

"Pyotr," Evangeline said, nodding at the figure before moving past. Although her pulse had climbed slightly with her run, it was the other heartbeat inside her chest she felt, the one that felt like a giant's footsteps shaking the frame of her body. The urgent thunder of her primacy longing to be used.

Despite the alarms and the muffled shouts of dismay coming through the fire door, Evangeline felt *good*. Like a spring held under pressure for too long and finally, *finally* given room to release.

All the time she spent being a leader for the squad, dependable and stable, was a function of her prime, and it was a function she resented. Because of luck or cosmic influence or fae magics or *something*, she'd woken one morning with a prime number tattooed on her body by an invisible hand. A prime number several hundred digits shorter than most other fencers', which gave her power and primacy and was assumed by the world to grant her authority as well.

All of that—the fame, the responsibility, the seniority, the *job*—was nothing next to this.

"What's happening?" The voice, belonging to a middle-aged woman emerging from one of the offices, brought Evangeline's headlong rush around the corner to a stumbling halt.

She was a classic Midwest church lady: greying hair done up in a sensible bun, wire-rimmed glasses connected to a shining golden chain that dipped down from the temple of her frames to her shoulders before looping behind her neck. This woman probably had a Tupperware filled with ground beef casserole waiting in a fridge somewhere, and she might have spent her lunch break reheating it in the communal microwave while talking about how fun the fair would be this year and how terrible it was that the workers had painted the lines out on County 12 too far over to the left.

"*It's just asking for trouble,*" she might have said to the other lunchtime interlocutors. "*Those county workers should know better.*"

She was a classic Midwest church lady in every way save for the gun.

She held the small, black handgun to her side, trigger finger extending forward over the guard, and she looked as though she had been trained in it. She might have been sixty or sixty-five and wearing the kind of clothy, overly modest dress that made Evangeline think of a floral garbage bag, but this woman, who was already raising the barrel, had clearly held and used this gun before.

"Fencer!" she shouted, taking a few quick steps back to put some space between them. Her voice might not have penetrated the fire door and soared above the alarms to alert Harp and the others, but Evangeline imagined most of the offices back there had some similarly corn-fed prairie kid in them, looking up from their tax-evasive church documents in concern.

The barrel of the gun rose until it was a black eye peering at Evangeline, in focus while the church worker behind grew fuzzy and distant.

"You shouldn't be back here, ma'am," the woman was saying. "This area is off limits to visitors."

The power that had been simmering inside of her all morning boiled now, and Evangeline lifted her hands in front of her, the numerals of her prime already dancing to the music that was to come.

She'd hoped to use her ability sparingly, if at all, and perhaps only for an emergency escape.

But without her iron swords, she had no other choice.

"I'm sorry," Evangeline said, the words almost inaudible over the roar of her heartbeats in her ears, one the sound of blood in her veins and the other the sound of some older, wilder, worse power rushing through her body and overwhelming her senses.

"It's all right, ma'am," the woman said, or maybe she said some other anodyne phrase, but she misunderstood. She thought Evangeline was apologizing for ending up back there, maybe, or apologizing for setting off the alarm.

Fencers didn't talk about their primacies much. A few of the especially obnoxious ones did, of course, but they stopped after describing the amazing leap they made from that burning building or the winds they calmed in order to hear that crying child. They never talked about the actual feeling of using their powers, the sense of extending that power inside of themselves out into the world. Even a showboat like the Tempest King, who would have taken the time for an interview while fleeing a burning building if it meant his getting some airtime—even that asshole had never described the feeling of his tattoos rising slightly from his skin, the feeling of his primacy wrenching him up to a higher order of being.

It was sacred. It was holy. It was the purest thing Evangeline had ever felt, at least until Cal and Winnie came along and they all learned what a family could be and could mean.

There in that obscene fae church, staring at the wavering muzzle of that ugly handgun, Evangeline experienced the rapture of her primacy.

The gun.

A foul thing, snub-nosed and compact, matte-black metal, cold and heavy. Her father had been a gun owner, a hunter, and Evangeline had grown up with guns around the house. But those had been made and used for food—deer and pheasant and elk and turkey, and her father had been cautious with the guns, keeping them carefully locked away in a thick safe when not in use.

This, though, was a bent piece of metal made for killing people. From the designer to the manufacturer to the distributor to the seller to the buyer to this woman, who would be lucky to end the day with enough of her mind left to put her pajamas on unaided, all the way down the line, the intention with this weapon was clear: *This kills people.* You might use it on an animal, and you might go target shooting with it, but that would be like using the handle of a screwdriver to pound in a nail. Just fine but not yet what it was designed for.

Evangeline scooped at the air and tossed a handful of stars forward, the gesture so calm and casual that the woman before her neither moved nor shot as the tiny shimmers of light flashed through the air, sliding sinuously forward until they wrapped around and swaddled the gun, obscuring its hateful shape.

"Is this . . ." the woman began, but said no more.

With her tattoos swaying along her skin like tiny dark dancers, Evangeline saw the world as it was: the woman before her a delicate instrument moved and struck and tuned by the busy, sad song trapped inside; the great stone pillars each a thin shell for the great resounding bass beats stretched like tendons from ground to ceiling; the artwork and the tapestries and the bulletin boards and the stone of the doorways and the stone of the floor and the soaring ceilings and the air, the very *air* itself a massive, multi-part orchestra, every bit of substance the world had to offer a tiny instrument waiting, just waiting, to be struck, its true song hidden inside.

The gun.

Evangeline gestured and the stars swathing the gun went supernova, flashing in a light array brighter and more arresting than anything the LED alarm lights could manage. The woman screamed and tried to drop the gun, but it was gone, disappeared when the stars lit and burned, and the song it had held inside, no longer caged by carbon steel and aluminum, burst forth.

At age fifteen, when her prime found her, Evangeline, like every American fencer, was taken by the Central Bureau's agents to a testing facility located in central South Dakota. There, she was subjected to a bevy of diagnostic and experimental tests to determine and assess any augments to her natural abilities as well as the particularities of her primacy.

After several weeks of tests, she was taken into a small office and a kindly man who introduced himself as only Louis told her that, to the best of their knowledge, her primacy was a kind of physical transformation of substance.

"It's a bit like when you boil water and it becomes gas," he'd said, hands clasped over one knee. "Because of the heat, the state of the matter changes. Your power lets you do that too, except you're converting matter to sound. It's extraordinary, really! I say this often with you fencers, but I've never seen anything like it. It's as though your thrown stars are starting some chemical or physical reaction in the substance of your target, and the reaction releases every bit of energy in the target as sound waves."

That man, Louis—who turned out to be Louis Byrne, a physicist of international renown—had developed a series of intensive tests for Evangeline to undergo closer to the equinox, once she had really come into her ability, the kind of stuff that was done for what one central administrator called "very promising cases."

Up to that point, Evangeline had managed to cantillate—a word used by Byrne for her ability that stuck in her head—small items or small portions of larger things, sending fist-sized chunks of stone or cloth singing, *cantillating*, off into the air, the sound waves not a blast of solid noise but always a haunting song, something melancholy and dark.

People nearby, scientists with their laptops and clipboards and notebooks, had all reported feeling affected by the music of Evangeline's primacy.

"It was dread," one of Byrne's assistants said, shaking his head as the effects finally passed after several minutes. "Pure dread."

"Just felt sick to my stomach and tired, I guess," another had said.

Very quickly, Evangeline had been set up to practice without anyone around, but when she returned nearer the equinox, one of Byrne's tests found him observing the effect from behind a panel of bulletproof glass. Perhaps he thought the melancholy effects, the dread, had not magnified with the equinox's approach, or perhaps he thought the inconvenience of nausea and dismay for an hour or two was worth the data he could gain by standing so near the reaction.

Evangeline stood in that small room and tossed her handful of stars at the cage, which held three small rabbits, pink noses pulsing with their quick breaths, and then the cage, the rabbits, the stand, the bedding, all of it was gone, and the room sang with Evangeline's power, the melody a great river of dread rushing and moving in the small space.

Technicians and scientists observing from the next room experienced the effects—intensified slightly—that Byrne had expected. Nausea, existential terror, waking nightmares, even a loss of speech for half an hour in one case. They all cleared up by the end of the day and had minimal recurring effects.

Louis Byrne, who, when he was awarded the Nobel Prize in Physics three years later for his astonishing advancements in understanding fencing phenomena, was wheeled to the stage by his husband Morgan, unable to stand and only speaking in strange, cryptic whispers in a language none but Evangeline could understand. He extended one trembling hand to receive the award, mumbling out some of the nonsense words that Evangeline would come to know and hate. Morgan read a short speech that, though it hadn't come from Byrne, communicated how grateful the physicist certainly was to receive such accolades.

Evangeline watched the ceremony from the government housing she was living in then, and she wept when Morgan finished the speech by looking up at the camera and saying, "And for Evangeline, who sang my husband his last song, Louis and I thank you for this award, and we curse you for this award." To his side, Louis Byrne stared down at his hands and whispered to himself.

In the House of Always Giving, held at gunpoint, Evangeline cantillated the weapon, and in doing so, she broke the mind of the woman holding it.

The melody that flooded out from the gun was a broken, twisted, terrifying tune, played in the same key as every other cantillation Evangeline had wrought, but unique still. Byrne had theorized her primacy as a chemical or physical reaction, a transformation of energy pure and simple. Like a solid sublimating to gas except with mass and matter and waves and all those other things that became too theoretical for Evangeline to follow.

But she had always thought of it as something simpler. Everything in the world—every *thing*—had a song inside it, something like a soul but not so religious. It was a melody that was at once part of the grand goings-on of the universe, a voice in the choir of everything, and a song totally and perfectly unique.

The gun's melody swelled out, a great glut of sound that pushed against Evangeline's chest and might have toppled her over if she hadn't been prepared for it.

The church lady who would never again heat her lunch in the communal microwave did fall over, and when Evangeline moved to walk onward, the echoes of the song already disappearing, the woman looked up at her with eyes gone a pale green, unseeing and wide.

The woman's voice was muted, and though she spoke in that nonsense language that any who experienced a cantillation did—the same language that Louis Byrne had whispered endlessly to himself after his experience—Evangeline could understand, and this woman said what they all said.

I see her. I see her. I see her.

Other office doors stood ajar on her way to the room she sought, but Evangeline saw no one else on her way, and soon she found the small, thin door, the one Oddry's nail-chewed finger had jabbed repeatedly on the blueprint.

It was made of some fragrant wood and had been painted a dark blue that accentuated the bright silver of the doorknob. Tiny dots of silver decorated the door, like lights in a night sky, and when Evangeline found it locked, she added her own stars to it, the door cantillating in a burst of sound.

Inside, the lie of the House of Always Giving was well and truly made apparent. A few computers sat blinking on lock screens. A full-sized fridge whirred quietly in the corner, and the remnants of a game of solitaire waited for someone to finish it on a table that looked more likely to have been purchased at the local big-box superstore than to have been carefully crafted by an elusive hermit in Wales.

An adjoining room told a similar story—desks covered in many-monitored computer setups and file cabinets with printed labels. Though the door to that room was closed, a pair of windows set into the dividing wall showed Evangeline a bank of screens set into the far wall that displayed various rooms and spaces of the church, feeds from hidden security cameras.

It was the nerve center of a twenty-first-century organization, and Evangeline felt sick looking at it, as though the fundamental wrongness of this place and everything it stood for existed there, lurking among the crinkled wrappers of candy bars floating atop the overfull wastebasket and the pair of slippers left neatly beside the desk chair.

One of the screens—NAVE 3/CHOIR, labeled with the modern, non-romanticized spelling, she noted—showed the ruckus Evangeline had left behind, Cal still holding his attackers at bay but in conversation with Nero and Incident, who had entered the static circle of his power and looked to be pleading with him. One of the Quire members had been frozen in the midst of a grand and heroic leap from the dais, a music stand held across her body like a bow staff. She hung in the air, motion arrested by Cal's primacy, the two ends of her hoodie drawstring caught floating up and away from her neck like delicate whiskers caught in a breeze.

Harp was a fuzzy head at the bottom of the screen, and she could see just enough of him to see that he was looking around with growing concern. If he hadn't realized Evangeline was gone yet, he would soon. Time to move.

The records Oddry wanted were surprisingly easy to find—the church member list and the list of equinox lock-ins were in a binder labeled *Members*. Nearby were *Budgets/Giving 2012–2016*, *Budgets/Giving 2017–2021*, and *Budgets/Giving 2021–*.

Evangeline took all of them, stacking the thick binders atop one another on the desk before stepping back and pulling out the tiny camera. Oddry had been insistent that she take photos—*The whole room, you hear? I want everything in there*—so she pointed and clicked, and clicked, and clicked, capturing the utter banality of the room.

When the great rumbling sounded again, Evangeline stepped toward that dividing wall and peered at the bank of surveillance screens, several of which showed the fire doors opening, and she had the errant thought that this must not be the only control room in the building. It was a thought that gave her pause, and despite the increasingly urgent need to move, she really looked at that group of screens.

Most showed the parts of the House she'd already seen—entryway and apse, nave in three parts, and the various alcoves. She saw in NAVE 3/CHOIR that Cal had released his captives and looked to be in disarmament talks with the agents, the fencers, and the Sylvans. But Harp was not present in that frame.

Instead, he was stepping through the opening fire doors separating the nave from the administrative hallway.

Evangeline took one more photo of the screens, frowning a little at the final few.

One was labeled CRYPTS and showed only darkness, though Evangeline thought for a frightening moment that she saw a ghostly movement on the screen there before she blinked and it was gone. Another—VAULT—was the same.

Several more frames showed other rooms and spaces that were not in this building, Evangeline was sure of it, but it was the last image that arrested her with its sheer impossibility, and fear clutched her stomach with cold, rough fingers.

This screen had no label and showed a long hallway, its seemingly endless length covered in intermittent patches of shadow and brightly pooled fluorescent light.

She'd seen that hallway before. She'd walked that hallway before, past the whiteboards and chalkboards punctuating its walls, talked down to by mathematicians, her prime poked and prodded and studied.

In the feed, the hallway was almost deserted save for a single person—wearing the mathematician's garb—walking well into the distance, the hallway before and behind them dark. Fluorescent lights, motion-activated, flicked on and turned off to allow a moving vehicle of light to accompany the mathematician.

The angle of the camera was such that the closest chalkboard was plainly visible, and on it Evangeline could read the number *572* written in a large hand.

But it was the message beneath that froze her.

TRANSFER SUCCESSFUL. SQUAD COMPROMISED. HARPOON IS GO.

"No," she muttered, and though she had already run out of time to escape, she dug the camera back out of her pocket and clicked a picture of those screens and the terrifying story they told. A desk set below them had several pairs of headphones on it and a notepad, as if waiting for some seemingly average church worker to show up for his surveillance shift, when he would settle into his chair, get his cup of coffee set before him, and tuck into hours of tape and possible transcription.

Harp's voice, no longer the at-ease host now but angry and shrill and jarring, preceded him as he moved with haste toward Evangeline, a rushing blur of pixels on the ADMIN HALL screen. Two other figures were there, huddled around the form of the woman with the gun, who lay on her back now, staring up at the ceiling. Even on the somewhat-grainy feed, Evangeline could make out the moving lips, forming and re-forming those same words in that slantwise, strange tongue.

I see her. I see her. I see her.

"It has to be you," Oddry had told her, his finger sliding across the blueprint to the white line showing the outside perimeter of the House of Always Giving—a white line representing a wall six feet thick that happened to run right near the records room where she was to steal their records and photograph their setup. *"You're the only one who can get out of there once you're caught, and you will absolutely be caught. Don't kill anyone. And try not to ruin too much of their dumb building."*

Evangeline waited until Harp stepped into the room with her, until his eyes found her standing near the back wall, and when she cantillated a great tunnel out of the thick stone and concrete, she watched the shockwave of sound send him toppling back over. She might have gone earlier so that he entered an already-escaped room, but the thought of Cal weeping during Cliff's funeral despite the judgmental hectoring of Harp gave her pause, and the small, hard part of her that wanted to use her primacy for immediate, urgent, overwhelming justice grew suddenly large and compelling.

So, she waited, and when he half sat up to stare at her with eyes already going empty, Evangeline smiled.

Outside of the tunnel, she found herself in a small courtyard—walled in—featuring a hip-height labyrinth made of carefully planted and cultivated foxgloves. Benches nestled into the tall grasses fanning up around a courtyard wall. A nearby sign, worn and weathered, described this place as THE FOLK'S PATH.

A toy plane, perhaps from a child allowed to wander the labyrinth during a church meeting, had been left on one of the benches. Maybe that parent had told the child to sit quietly there on that bench and not touch or eat any of the beautiful purple and pink flowers because they are poisonous, and little Oliver or Florence or Jasper had sat quietly on the bench while Mom or Dad casually worked the levers of religion inside the House of Always Giving.

It was peaceful and quiet and idyllic in the Folk's Path, and Evangeline cantillated it all, every individual foxglove plant releasing its own song until it was a royal chorus of melodies radiating out from that walled-in courtyard, a diapason that would have smoothed the mind and memory of a bystander with the same insistent power of a hurricane flattening homes and flooding neighborhoods.

The toy airplane remained unmoved and untouched, and Evangeline cantillated that, too, hearing in the striated melody the voice of the young boy who'd owned it, a tinkling pattern of notes that might have been his laugh buried away in the wash of tones and timbres representing every aspect of the airplane, the vast array of voices mingling and mixing with those of the foxgloves.

When Evangeline found herself in an empty, flat, dirt-covered courtyard, she strode forward and cantillated the outer wall itself, a thinner and weaker thing than the previous, which was good, because she was growing tired.

Even so close to the height of her powers, this much cantillation was a strain, and though her heartbeat remained even and her breathing was a steady in and out, she felt unsteady and disjointed somehow. Her head throbbed with an irregular, thundery pain, and her joints and gums ached with each movement and step.

Beyond the wall, visible now, was the street, happily empty save for the woman jogging across the street, her ears plugged by what looked like earbuds but were actually top-grade earplugs, and while anyone else standing so close would have fallen over into an empty and iterative comatose state because of the sound waves still percussing and dissipating through the air, this woman, who was an agent sometimes assigned to Evangeline called Dianora, was unaffected.

Dianora ran up, her hair pulled back into a simple ponytail, her workout clothes stained by the sweat of her jog. She removed the slim-profiled pack she wore and took the binders from Evangeline as she stepped through, and then she was off again without a word, up to the next street, where she stepped into a car and was gone, the grey sedan blending seamlessly into the traffic there.

For her part, Evangeline turned left and walked in the other direction, and after a moment, she got into another car, the melodies of her prime still singing in her ears.

She found Oddry in his office.

The music was loud, and when he moved to turn it down, Evangeline shook her head.

The office might have been large, but it was hard to tell through the sheer volume of stuff Oddry had packed into it. Shelves and stacked bins and cabinets of all kinds clung to the walls and metastasized in corners, each one filled with the strange books and artifacts Oddry trafficked in—shipbuilding manuals from the eighteenth century stacked beside comic books for superheroes Evangeline had never heard of, the stacks propped up by carefully gnarled twists of metal grafted to wood in shapes that spoke of intentionality despite giving no real hint of their purpose.

Above the rabbit's warren of overstuffed storage were the posters, laid out like tiles on the wall. There were images of fallen angels and demons, monstrous oozes and sneering skulls, pigs and goats, pools of blood and storm clouds bursting with garish lightning.

Speakers were mounted at the corners of the room, and they thrummed with the noise of a man growl-singing about Odin and his righteous war.

Evangeline set the camera, which she'd placed in a bag, on the desk.

"That was a shit show," she said, looking around the office and getting her bearings. "Did you get my report?"

"Report?" Oddry said, frowning up at her from the diagram of the fence he was staring at, the paper already full of his little notes and reminders.

"I wrote it up right when we got back. One of the agents was supposed to give it to you. Jesus, they're supposed to be dependable."

Oddry's look of gentle confusion had progressed into a dumbfounded silence. Evangeline never treated the government agents like secretaries or assistants like some of the bigger-deal fencers did—like Tempest King, who had regularly sent his agents out for takeout.

And Evangeline didn't write reports—none of them did. The bureau had plenty of paperwork to weigh it down, but reports written by fencers about their exploits was not any part of it.

"It's fine—I printed another copy," Evangeline said, pulling out a small wad of paper and unfolding it with one hand. She turned slightly to one side and raised the other hand high, as if she were stretching. She hoped the angle was right, but she couldn't be sure, so when she passed the paper to Oddry, she leaned over the desk with it.

In Evangeline's close, cramped handwriting, the note read:

The Shop is bugged and being surveilled by the Sylvans. Your office—camera in the left corner above the door somewhere. The cafeteria, vehicle bay, and at least one of the larger meeting rooms. They have a camera in the Sieve, too, and someone there is communicating with the Sylvans.

Below this, Evangeline had printed out one of the photos from the camera, the one she'd taken last of the screens. Visible on the bottom right of this image was the feed from the Sieve with its eerie message.

What the fuck is "Harpoon"?

Oddry's bafflement evaporated as he scanned the letter, and as he finished it, he sat up tall in his chair, his eyes flicking up to the left of his doorway. With a motion smoother than Evangeline would have expected from someone as regularly strange as Oddry, he slipped the paper from the desktop and into a drawer.

"Just drop it in my mailbox next time, Fencer Evangeline," he said, looking back down at the schematics for the fence. He tapped the paper with a pen. "And don't forget that I need you out at the fence tonight. The usual place. I don't want to hear any of your complaining about it, either—it's your responsibility as a squad leader."

There was no meeting at the fence tonight; Evangeline was sure of it. At least not one on the schedule. Why did he want to meet at the fence?

"Of course," she said, nodding and stepping back toward the door. "I haven't been able to find a sitter, so it'll just be me."

"You can bring your man-child husband if it means I get to see my goddaughter," Oddry said, not looking up at her, his voice once more returned to the usual and comforting levels of pleasant grumpiness. "Don't forget to leave your phone behind. I don't want you frying another piece of government tech. The budget can't handle your forgetfulness."

Oh. That was why. Oddry wanted to meet in the one place in the world where a conversation couldn't be bugged.

"Sounds good. See you then," Evangeline said, using every bit of will she had to not look up at the site of the hidden camera as she left Oddry's office.

A History of Fences and Fae by AK Senga, PhD

Published in 2027 by University of Minnesota Majestic Press
Excerpt from Chapter 4: "Autumn's Twilight Guard"

Not to be forgotten in any discussion of humanity's autumnal armament, the Newfoundland hounds that accompany so many fencing squads have become a regular sight. Though their true efficacy in the fight against the fae took several years to understand and implement, these dogs were suspected to be involved with the Harbors from the very beginning. Though initial reports seemed to suggest all dogs began acting erratically on that first equinox after the formation of the Harbors, it was ultimately revealed to be a phenomenon unique to *only a type* of Newfoundland: the Landseer.

Named for Edwin Landseer, the artist who made their coloring famous through his paintings in the nineteenth century, Landseer Newfoundlands were primarily oddity pets throughout the world for most of the twentieth century. Though they were originally used as livestock guardians and sailing dogs, Newfoundlands in general became domesticated pets, more likely to be found sleeping on a couch or next to their owners' feet at the dinner table than leaping into choppy waters to rescue a sailor overboard. Larger than most dogs and more expensive than the casual mutt rescued from the humane society, they became striking oddities in rural and suburban communities alike.

The other colorings of Newfoundlands—uniform brown, black, grey, or white; piebald white and brown or white and grey—all became just as desirable and present in ownership records for those people who could afford and accommodate such a large breed. Edwin Landseer's work looked to have been in vain; his paintings went out of vogue, and his subjects returned to a curious but banal breed.

All that—like so much else—changed on the autumnal equinox of 1987.

On September twenty-third, as a few seemingly random people woke across the world to find their bodies covered in prime numbers, and as the major governments of the globe closed, locked, and celebrated the construction of the Harbors, every Landseer Newfoundland changed, becoming almost supernaturally alert and protective, able to sense movement almost before it occurred and capable of leaping great distances, running too fast, barking impossibly loud. The colors of their coats moved and writhed to some unheard music, and veterinarians and animal specialists across the globe received increasingly frantic calls like this one, recorded on that first equinox and held now in the Landseer exhibit at the American Museum of Natural History. The speaker is Darlene Kepler of Hardin, Montana, and this is an excerpt from her 911 call that day:

"*It's Blitz—he's acting crazy.*"

"*Your dog, ma'am?*"

"*Yes, Blitz. He just barked and all the windows shattered. There's glass— Oh, god. There's glass everywhere.*"

"*Are you hurt, ma'am? Is anyone hurt?*"

"*He's just running all over, and his paws—they're all cut to shreds, but— Ooh, my god. Oh, my god.*"

"*Ma'am? I have help on the way. Can you please tell me if you or anyone in the house, any of the people in the house, are hurt?*"

"*It's his fur—it's changing. It's moving. He—Blitz! Blitz!*"

"*Ma'am? Ma'am, are you still there?*"

"*He just ran through the door—broke the damn thing down and ran out. Oh, god, send someone, send someone, please. Blitz is out there chasing one of those fools in the street. He's— Blitz! He's friendly! Just . . .*"

The call ends there, though the 911 operator continues to ask for

Mrs. Kepler for another twenty-two seconds. We would later learn that she exited her residence to stop her dog, Blitz, from attacking a person in the street. Unfortunately for Mrs. Kepler, that person was Donovan Tadeo, who had died three hours earlier and transformed into a faerie. Though Blitz ultimately succeeded in rendering the transformed Mr. Tadeo ineffective, Darlene Kepler passed away later that evening from injuries she sustained while trying to intercede in what she saw as no more than her dog interfering with someone's nighttime revels.

Like so much that occurred on that first equinox after the Harbors and the fences and the fae, it would be years before people understood the *what* of the situation if not the *why*. If the Wretched, those who should die on the equinox but instead turned fae and weird, were a kind of predator roaming the land on their way home to the Harbors, then perhaps the Landseers, with their fierce strength and supernatural senses, were natural competitors of a sort, a counterbalance to the upheaval of the natural world.

Chapter 13

Evening sent washes of color up from the horizon, filming the sky in pinks and purples, violets and reds as the sun went down and the fencers drove west along the wide gravel road.

"It's like a painting," Winnie said from the backseat, looking up from the book she'd brought. It was one Oddry had given her as a gift, *Twenty Essential Tools for Twenty Essential Tasks*. When asked if he'd thought it was too advanced for a six-year-old, Oddry had scoffed at the notion and said, "For you as a child? Maybe. For me as a child, probably not. For my goddaughter, no, definitely not."

And he'd been right. Winnie loved the book, first carrying it with her at all times and working through individual words during mealtimes and while in the car, until she'd read it so many times (and had it read to her so many times) that she had memorized it, and now she liked to hold the book closed on her lap or against her chest and recite parts of it.

As they drove toward the fence that evening, neither Cal nor Evangeline said much. The Shop had been abuzz with activity as various government agencies had begun their bureaucratic war over the events at the House of Always Giving. Senators had been on the phone and on the news, making increasingly bold statements, some about the overreach of fencing agencies and others about the obvious cache of secrets hiding in the Houses of Always Giving. The Director of the Central Bureau, a woman named Victoria Howl, had given a statement saying that she supported and would protect her fencers and her agency.

"These fencers are the last and only line of defense between the world's population and the fae cancer that appears every equinox. We cannot and I *will not* cast them to the wolves of public interrogation and inquiry. Their actions will be examined by our own internal investigators, and any and all responses will be carefully considered and fair," she had said, standing behind the podium out in front of the Central headquarters in New York. Standing behind her had been the two most recognizable faces in the fencing world, at least in the US.

Sister Hanka, director of the mathematician corps, stood silent and watchful, her face like a mask. She wore the black-and-white robes of her order, the same as Sister Marla and all the mathematicians working in the Sieve and in every other facility housing the prime seekers and number-crunchers employed to work alongside the fencers and techs.

Sister Hanka took her name—her title, really, since there had been several Sisters Hanka over the years—from the holy mother of mathematics, Johanna "Hanka" Grothendieck, mother of that dark and desperate prophet Alexander Grothendieck. Like Catholics who worshipped the Virgin Mary as the giver of life to their holy lord, so, too, did mathematicians vaunt the mother of their hallowed daemon.

To the other side of Director Howl, wearing a three-piece suit and shoes that probably cost more than some small homes, was a man Evangeline had hoped to never see again: the Tempest King.

"I guess he got promoted," Cal had said, looking up at one of the screens showing the press conference in the Shop. They'd been sitting around at their desks after the frantic debriefing, in which Cal and Evangeline had told Nero in quick, close whispers what the real mission had been; that no, they couldn't tell her beforehand for reasons of legal safety; that *no*, she couldn't tell anyone else including the Stone Weaver; that yes, Incident was still on the squad because who the hell else did they have? Nero's anger at the perceived betrayal had evaporated when Oddry told Cal and Evangeline about the hearings they would have to go through after the equinox.

"Nothing is going to happen," he'd said, cutting a hand through the air. "That is a promise. Some windbag senators will get their chance to whine about religious persecution, but I have a guarantee from the top—from Howl herself—that neither of you will face any more consequences than a few days' worth of congressional inquisition."

After that, Nero had been all smiles, and when the Stone Weaver had asked why, she'd only laughed and said she had vacation plans for the days after the equinox that she was really looking forward to.

Incident, on the other hand, had been furious, and her shouts rang out over the racket of the Shop's work. When she emerged from Oddry's office, her face had been wet with angry tears, and she'd stalked over to Cal and Evangeline to say that she was leaving for the day to help with the cleanup at the House of Always Giving.

"Don't," she'd said, raising a hand to stop Cal from speaking. He'd been about to leap without a parachute into the world of unsolicited and unwanted apologies, and he was happy to close his mouth and say nothing.

"You," Incident said, gesturing at Cal, "I understand. Your father died and you're sad, bitter, and confused. You acted out and will have no consequences for your actions, because the world needs fencers. You're a child acting childishly. But you."

She turned to Evangeline.

"Your story about 'getting lost in the church, panicking, and blasting my way out' is obvious horseshit. You were doing something back there, and I hope it was worth it, because that woman you turned into a mindless freak has a family. Kids and grandkids. And she was almost ready to retire. And High Priest Harp? He'll never take another step on his own again."

At that, she left, and when Oddry came out of his office a few minutes later, he looked like a man who had just run a marathon without any training.

"Wait a few hours to leave," he'd said, looking between the four remaining fencers in Evangeline's squad. The other squads were out at the training fields or on their own administrative visits with scholars or politicians. "The press should be mostly dispersed by then."

"Are you okay?" Evangeline had asked, peering up at Oddry. "Did she threaten to quit?"

"What?" Oddry turned to Evangeline and looked surprised at the question. "Incident? No, she'll never quit. She'd never be able to dress like that at another job."

He shook his head and turned to face the monitors again, where the press conference was going, but it was not that screen he pointed to.

Instead, his well-chewed nail directed their attention to the world map displayed on a smaller screen. The lines showing country borders were gone, and instead, the map showed only the outlines of the world's Harbors. Once more, the Belovo Harbor in Russia showed a blinking red dot inside its confines.

"According to all of our tech, the Riparian is still in Russia in the same Harbor," Oddry said, turning to them. "Add to that the fact that I had three separate confirmations in the last twenty-four hours by people who put eyes on the monster. What do you make of that?"

"It's *here*," Evangeline said, "or it was, at least. We both saw the signs."

"Maybe it came and left," Cal said, shrugging. "Like Santa. But I say it's a good thing if it's not here. We've got plenty going on without Pyotr of the Pools complicating things even more."

"You're not wrong," Oddry said, glaring at the press conference before stalking back into his office and slamming the door. The swell of harsh music emerged a few moments later.

Cal and Evangeline watched Director Howl, Sister Hanka, and the Tempest King respond to reporters' questions. Howl was brusque and businesslike in her answers, speaking with the confidence of a person who knows she will win. She did not smile, nor did she scold. She did not take follow-up questions.

Sister Hanka would not acknowledge the questions, saying only, "We can say nothing about this," to reporter after reporter. Only when one asked why she was there at all did she say, "The mathematicians share a great bond with the other branches of our fencing agencies, and I am here today to both show support and demonstrate our grave concern over this issue." She said nothing more and only shook her head in response to additional questions.

The Tempest King was another matter.

"I have some insight into the Midwest Branch," he said at one point before spinning a ten-minute answer about his time working at the Bluestem Harbor, how "personally and professionally challenging" he found it, and how he wasn't completely surprised at this breach of etiquette and professionalism.

"I like a lot of those little guys," he said at the end, flashing that surfer-bro grin at the camera. "Evangeline and Calidore were great supports for me when I fenced there, and I support them all the way. No doubt about it. But at the same time, those more-minor fencers—the ones with primes in the hundred thousands or more, I mean—they can be a little wild from time to time. Loose cannons, sort of. Again, it's all support from me, but something needs to get figured out down Bluestem way."

Cal and Evangeline had each offered a one-fingered salute to the screen at that.

Now, as their car crunched along the gravel road hemmed in on either side by fields of tallgrass prairie, the two fencers traced the labyrinths of their own thoughts, at least until Winnie spoke up from the back of the car.

"Are we going to the fence to fight faeries?"

"No, sweetie," Cal said, jolted from his thoughts. He'd been reliving the fight in the church, thinking again of those red-clad guards approaching and pulling out their weapons. In the moment, he'd felt like a secret agent, wise to the secret workings of the plan while the fools around him hadn't had a clue. He'd been burning with adrenaline and power, and each new guard or quire member he caught up in the hold of primacy had been evidence of his control.

But after, as exhaustion set in, the one question that wormed away inside him spoke again, and he wondered what if—what if he'd missed one of the guards and he'd been shot? What if he'd pushed on his primacy too far and killed someone, one of the quire members who had only been trying to get away? What if Evangeline had been caught unawares by Harp? Or found that surveillance room filled with highly trained, heavily armed guards, and even with her primacy at near-full strength, she'd been surprised and hurt? Or killed?

Fencers were not superhuman, not when it came to injuries. A knife could still pierce their skin; a bullet could still rip through their bodies. What if Harp had been ready for them? What if there had been too many people for Cal to hold?

On and on he worked at these questions, had been since that afternoon, pressing at them like a wound he couldn't let be, and the repetition of it brought him waves of pain and panic, yes, but also somehow pleasure, each jolt of fear like a spark inside him.

As a boy, long before his primes came in, Cal had been what his middle school therapist, a balding, heavily bearded man named Mr. Lenz, had called "A Straight-A Worrier," and the tendency had never gone away. His therapists, once he got older, called it "catastrophizing" or "generalized anxiety" or, once his primes came in, "intensive anxiety induced by high-stress vocational requirements."

When he'd met Evangeline, more than anything else, Cal had fallen in love with the way she did this job, which came with a near-guarantee of violence and a consistent possibility of death every single day. Evangeline understood the risks and understood that beneath every bit of government and agency precaution and safety measure, a simple and dark truth dwelled: fencers faced death every equinox.

Evangeline understood this and accepted it, and even after the wedding and the birth of Winnie, she had gone on accepting the truth without it staining the rest of her life with worry and terror and fear. She did not wake up from nightmares, and she didn't rush into Winnie's room at night in that first year to make sure she was breathing.

Cal, though, very simply, could not accept the nearness of death, and outside the noise of his own hollow grammarie, which seemed to block out the voices of his anxiety, he worried often and regularly about death. His own. Evangeline's. Winnie's especially.

He emerged from this morass of messy, clinging worry to Winnie's question, and when he turned in his seat to look at his daughter, he found her brandishing a spoon she must have pilfered from the drawer before they left the house.

"Oddry said last time at our house that all of the metal in our house has *some* iron in it," she said, holding the piece of silverware up like a sword. Beside her, lying down on the seat with his head on Winnie's lap, was Tennyson, who followed the slow menacing of the spoon-sword with sagging, tired eyes. He'd been forced to stay at the Shop during the operation at the House of Always Giving, and he'd spent the time running drills with some of the animal handlers there.

"Oddry was right," Evangeline said, looking at Winnie in the mirror. "But we wouldn't bring you to fight any fae, dearie. They're dangerous and no fun."

"And they're all trapped behind the fence anyway," Cal said, pointing out the window. As Evangeline took the road's final turn, the trees fell away and the fence came into view. "They can't get out of there, even if they wanted to. So, we'll be safe, but I feel even better knowing you're ready to fight if we need you."

He gave her a wink, and she tried to return it, first squinting both eyes and then shaking her head quickly before finally covering one with a hand and blinking rapidly at him.

"We'll stop here," Evangeline said, slowing the car and pulling off onto the thin grass growing alongside the road. "Winnie, can you get yourself out?"

"Yep!" came the response, and the small family emerged from the car, including Tennyson, who leapt from Winnie's door in a graceful arc. Another dog might have bounded away into the wide, open grassland bordering the fence, chasing bugs or sniffing at the library of delightful smells, but Tennyson took a careful look around before positioning himself next to Winnie.

He knew this place and what it meant. No bugs lived in those grasses, and no wild animals roamed this area. The mice and skunks and sparrows and snakes and hawks and all the other animals that should have been happily at home in a wide band of grassland bordering a forest were absent from this particular area, and they certainly didn't live in the area behind the fence nearby.

"There's Oddry," Evangeline said, pointing ahead to one of the small shacks placed near the Eastern Gate. Oddry stood with his arms crossed, wearing an old Minnesota Twins windbreaker and glaring at the fence as they approached. Nearby was the safety line that ran parallel to the fence, set exactly forty-one feet away from the fence itself. Beyond that line, the toxic effects of the Harbor were actively detrimental to anyone not protected by a prime. The safety line was a simple heavy rope strung from smooth stone pillars.

"You notice anything?" Oddry asked as they approached. The pocket of one of his cheeks distended with the pressure from sunflower seeds packed in there. His jaw worked for a moment before he spat a few empty shells out.

"Can you be more specific?" Cal asked, looking around.

"No," was all Oddry said.

"Is this place bugged too?" Evangeline peered through the open door of the shack but saw nothing more than a few heavy-duty plastic tables, the various supplies, and a map spread across one tabletop showing the

Midwest Harbor—probably the same one Oddry had been working on earlier.

"No."

"Do I notice a head tech being intentionally vague?" Cal asked, offering a beatific smile to go along with his sarcasm. Oddry did not respond.

"The ground is sinky and wet," Winnie said, one arm slung around Tennyson's back. She still held the spoon in her hand.

"Yes, exactly," Oddry said, breathing out a sigh of relief. "At least one of you has some sense."

"Did it rain?" Evangeline cocked an eye up to the sky, where tattered shreds of autumn clouds hung in the evening sky.

"I'm not a weatherman," Oddry said. "Let's get in the shack."

Inside, the wind was a gentle moan against the slats of the shack, and they took seats around the table, Winnie scrambling up onto Oddry's lap.

"You brought some iron," he said approvingly, glancing down at the spoon in her hand. "That's good. I don't suppose your superhero parents brought their swords?"

"They're in the car," Evangeline said.

"Then I'll expect you to protect us if there's a fence break and the fae come pouring out," Oddry said, leaning sideways to look at Winnie, who saluted him with her spoon and went back to pulling the coloring book and crayons out of the small backpack she'd brought. When Cal had told her that she would be accompanying them to a meeting with Oddry, Winnie had blazed up the stairs to her room to pack her version of a go-bag, which involved three different coloring books, crayons, colored pencils, pens, regular pencils, a yo-yo that she didn't know how to use and was knotted nine different ways, and three kinds of candy as a snack—"just in case the meeting goes for a long time and I get hungry, Dad!" she'd exclaimed when Cal protested that she'd already had dinner and didn't need candy.

In the end, as always, he'd relented, and now, as Oddry pulled out a folder from a bag of his own and got down to the business of their meeting, Winnie popped one of the pieces of candy in her mouth with a sly smile at her father.

"I printed out the photos you took, Evangeline," Oddry said, sliding several pieces of paper across the table to them. "It's good you took them, because the records you found were fake."

On top of the printed photos, Oddry plopped the binders Evangeline had taken earlier that day.

"Fake?"

"Look and see," he said, gesturing. "Those are recently printed records—I'd bet my false teeth on it."

"You wear false teeth?" Cal asked but was silenced by a deathly look from Oddry.

"I didn't even look inside them," Evangeline said, opening the nearest one—Budgets/Giving 2017–2021. Spreadsheets filled the binder, pages and pages of them, some showing giving patterns for individual members, some for families, some for businesses, and some for politicians. Other tables traced expenses for repairs, renovations, purchases. It was thorough, detailed, and Evangeline looked up with a frown.

"*Fake*," Oddry said. "I didn't realize it at first, and I was getting ready to forward it all on to the higher-ups, but then I thought about what you said when you got back, about how many people Harp said they had in their bullshit—sorry—their idiotic Temple of Whatever."

"So many people just waiting and hoping to go in that stupid room," Cal said, shaking his head at the thought.

"There I was, sitting on these spreadsheets like a dragon on his hoard, and I'm about to send them onward when I think to look at the photos you took, Evangeline, and look at that one, right there."

It was a portion of one of the photos Evangeline had taken, blown up to show just one of the screens. Oddry had done it with all of them.

This was the untitled screen, the one showing the hallway in the Sieve and the chalkboard with the writing:

572

TRANSFER SUCCESSFUL. SQUAD COMPROMISED.

HARPOON IS GO.

"I wanted to ask you about this one," Evangeline said, sliding the paper out to the middle of the table where they could all see it. "Clearly, they're sending messages here on the bottom, and I think they're talking about our squad, Oddry. Effie's transfer? Incident moved to our squad? You said yourself that the squad-reshuffle orders came down from above. It's about *us*, Oddry—my squad."

"Yes," Oddry said, nodding.

"What's Harpoon?" Cal jabbed the word with a finger. Beside him, Tennyson growled, and when Cal looked down at the Newfoundland, he found the Landseer pattern swirling in agitation.

"He doesn't like being so close to the fence," Evangeline said, sinking her fingers into his thick fur and comforting him until the growls eased.

"That's good," Oddry said, frowning at the dog. "It means his training is working."

"Harpoon?" Evangeline prompted.

"I don't know," Oddry said, spitting a few sunflower seeds to the side. "We have nothing in our databases with that name except reference to a very minor fencer who worked in ninety-two and ninety-three in Australia. He got almost no actual time working—he was almost sixty when his prime came in, and it was over twelve million digits long, so he wasn't much good even when he'd been trained. But his fencing name was the Harpooner."

"Seems like a stretch," Cal said.

"Okay, so you don't know what Harpoon is, but what about the rest?

They obviously know what's going on in the bureau, they're obviously working with someone in the Sieve to send and receive information, and they *bugged your office*, Oddry."

He swatted that last away like it was a fly buzzing around his head.

"You think they're the only ones to bug my office? Howl bugged my office my first day there! And she told me she was going to do it, too. The number badgers watch my email—even the semi-private one they think I think is hidden from them. I have at least six different senators who listen to recordings from my cell phone. I was a little surprised that the Sylvans had video of my office, but if they want to waste their time watching me design schematics and play air drums to Serpent of the Twilight every day, then good for them."

"Yeah, good for *them*!" Winnie said. She wasn't really listening to the conversation, but she had a habit of parroting back language to the adult conversations that happened around her. She was still entirely focused on her drawing—a tree that had pizza slices instead of leaves.

"What concerns me is that they knew we were coming today," Oddry said, returning their attention to the binder still open in front of Evangeline. He tapped the page. "These names? About one in three are people who aren't alive anymore or live in different states or, as far as I can tell, never existed at all. Some of those businesses haven't been around for years. They planted this for us to find because they knew we were going to raid them. Maybe it didn't go the way they expected, or maybe it did, but they knew."

"How . . ." Cal began, but Oddry tapped that same picture again, the one from the Sieve.

"You told me that Harp said they had around five hundred people in their Temple last year at the equinox, but that wasn't right, was it? Nero wrote it down—he said—"

"572," Evangeline finished for him, remembering how Harp had spoken that number with such solemn reverence.

"Right," Oddry said. "Harp gave us the lie that someone in the Sieve gave him. Once I realized that, I started looking more carefully at these records and realized how nonsensical they were. I can only assume they didn't expect you to see those screens back there—maybe someone was supposed to turn them off before you made it back there, or maybe you surprised them and they forgot. I don't know."

Evangeline was thinking of the woman she'd left murmuring nonsense. Was she meant to be the guard? Had it been her job to turn off the surveillance screens before the fencers arrived?

"So, it was a bust?" Cal asked.

"Not a bust," Oddry said, looking first at Cal and then out the small window behind him, which showed a stretch of the fence. "We know now that they have rooms in that building that don't show up on any of our blueprints, and we know they're lying about the numbers of people they take in each equinox."

He returned his attention to Cal and Evangeline.

"And we know they're working with someone in the Sieve. It might not seem like much, but it at least tells us where we need to be careful and who we can't trust."

"Our newest squad member Incident, for example," Cal said, but Oddry shook his head.

"She's not in on this," he said, holding up a hand to forestall Cal and Evangeline's rebuttals. "I know you don't like her, but Incident *does* have a moral compass. She's a true believer in that Sylvan nonsense, but she *also* is a believer in our mission, and she's a good fencer."

Cal grunted in response to that.

"And that brings me to the other things I need to tell you," Oddry said, spitting the remaining seeds in his cheek aside before replenishing the supply with a handful of them from one pocket. "You're going to have congressional hearings after the equinox that will make some military interrogations look like tea parties, and there's nothing I can do about it but promise that everything will be fine in the end. You'll get coaching from our people, and the majority of the committee will be favorable, so you won't get charged with anything."

"Oh, joy," Evangeline said.

"*Also*," Oddry continued, working at a seed for long enough that it became clear he was stalling, until finally he said, "as part of our attempts to *cooperate in the wake of this great breach of trust*, your squad is going to have an additional person, so Incident won't be the newest squad member anymore."

"Who?" Cal asked, spreading his hands. "We don't *have* any other fencers to add."

"Sister Marla," Oddry said quietly.

No one spoke for a long moment. Winnie's crayons against the rough paper let out a soothing white noise, and even Tennyson's growling had become a low burble.

"Sister Marla," Evangeline said.

"A *mathematician*?" Cal asked.

"I know," Oddry said. "We had to give them something, and the number badgers have always had the respect of the public *and* the politicians for some reason. Everyone trusts people who can do flashy, pointless shit—sorry, stuff—with numbers. It doesn't matter—she's going to ride with you on the equinox, and we know she can't be trusted because of what you found at the House of Always Giving, so you'll need to recalibrate your expectations, and we'll need to bring Nero in on this, too. You can trust her, and she'll— *What is that?*"

Oddry's eyes had been flicking between the fencers ahead of him and the window to the fence, and he leaned forward suddenly, aware enough of Winnie on his lap that he didn't disturb her work but had clearly focused beyond the conversation in the shack.

Cal was already up from his seat as he turned toward the window, one hand going instinctively to his waist, where he normally wore his swords, though they were in the car, brought along only as a formality, they'd thought.

Evangeline, too, moved quickly, the tattoo on her skin already beginning its dance. She would not cantillate in there, not so close to Winnie and the others, but perhaps she could draw the attention of whatever it was away to a safe distance where her music-making would be safe.

They found nothing—just the small window offering a glimpse of the fence and the Midwest Harbor beyond, the gentle hills of tallgrass prairie going russet in autumn's late evening light, coneflower colonies stunning in purple and pink and yellow, rising towers of many-flowered false indigo like caught cotton amidst the stems. It was beautiful and eerie, so still and quiet, but not any different from what the fencers had seen the thousands of other times they were near the Harbor.

"What did you see?" Cal asked as Evangeline opened the door and took a cautious look around.

"Nothing, apparently," Oddry said, wrapping his arms around Winnie in a hug. "Which means I need to either take a nap or drink some coffee."

"It's six thirty," Cal said, arcing one eyebrow. "PM."

"Coffee, then," Oddry said, waiting for Winnie to climb down before standing up himself.

As they exited the shack, Oddry having packed up his pieces of evidence again, they talked about the way forward.

Nero would be brought in and told everything. The three of them would keep an eye on Marla throughout the equinox when they could. Oddry would keep investigating this, especially whatever Harpoon might be.

"We can't go public with this until we know more, and we still have the equinox to deal with in a few days," Oddry said as they stood outside the shacks, trying to look anywhere but at the Harbor, which seemed to be watching them with alien interest. Below, the ground was still wet and swampy. "In the end, no one is going to let anything happen to you—you're too valuable, even to the people who don't like fencers. And we have a job to do that takes precedence over everything else. I'll do what I can before the equinox, but let's get through these next few days and then dismantle those Sylvans from the ground up."

"*That* is a plan I can get behind," Cal said, clapping.

"Tennyson, *relent*," Evangeline said, snapping her fingers and lowering her voice an octave, down where it got dangerous. She only used that voice with Tennyson when he was nearing trouble, and his growling cut out almost immediately.

"There's a big man over there by the fence."

Winnie spoke with calm curiosity, but the adults responded to her statement with panic. While the public wasn't technically prohibited from being around the fences, it was less and less common every year. At first, when the newly dead—the Wretched—fled into the Harbors, loved ones would gather at the fences, back far enough to avoid the radiation, each person hoping to see their lost friend or family member, their dead husband or wife.

In the days after the equinox, many of the Wretched might linger near the fence, laughing or whispering mysteries in their odd languages before finally running deeper into the Harbor in the following days or weeks. Some would sing well into the day, voices beautiful and haunting; others would stare out at the gathered crowds. In her time at the Publix Harbor, Evangeline had watched one of the Wretched sit on a tree limb nowhere near thick enough to bear the weight. The faerie had stayed there for almost thirty hours, totally still save for its hands, which moved in curious, repetitive motions, as though it were massaging the air itself.

And when it finally left, leaping the forty feet down to the ground in a graceful arc, a perfect sphere of glowing *something* remained in the space it had worked for those forty hours. Attempts to study or even recover the sphere had been discarded almost immediately upon design. It was much too far in for any telescoping grabbers to reach, and protocol for sending fencers into the Harbor almost entirely boiled down to *don't* in all but absolutely critical cases.

Each year, a smaller and smaller group of people understood the truth behind the message circulated about the fae: *Once they turn, they become something else. They don't know you anymore. They don't care about you anymore. Think of them as animals. Think of them as dangerous, dangerous animals.*

"Where is he, sweets?" Evangeline asked, scanning the fence line off to either side. Cal was doing the same.

Only Oddry understood right away, and he looked first at Winnie and the spoon she held up before her, a fence knight with her iron sword drawn, then at Tennyson, who had moved to stand beside the young girl, his coat aswarm with black and white shapes agitated into motion, his eyes locked ahead, the thunderous engine of his growl running again.

Oddry turned his eyes out, not to peer along the fence fanning out toward the horizon on either side of them but to the Harbor beyond, where on one slow rise of land, surrounded by flowers of stunning red and purple, a figure stood silent and still as the landscape itself.

Moving faster than his age and dress might have suggested he could, Oddry stepped close to Winnie and covered her eyes with his hand.

"Evangeline. Calidore. Look into the Harbor."

Evangeline swore under her breath, and Cal let out a huff of air as if he'd been socked in the stomach.

"But . . . Russia," Cal said.

The Riparian. Pyotr of the Pools. Zenithal. The Little Tear.

He'd had another name once, but no one said it anymore.

Around him, the flowers and grasses were dewed with drops of water that looked to be running upward slowly before flinging themselves into the air in gentle, patterned sprays.

The Riparian himself, *it*self, was perhaps a hundred feet away and looking not at the four people and dog but beyond them, toward the trees and Majestic in the distance. Two sets of wings arced behind its back, folded up now but each wingspan easily twenty-five or thirty feet when fully extended.

Despite the relatively clear skies and lack of trees or structures nearby it, a haze of shadow surrounded the Riparian, like finely shredded crepe paper stirred and held afloat by a gentle wind, thick enough that specific features of the creature were impossible to see, especially from so far away, but thin enough that no one could doubt who it was.

"Don't look into its eyes," Evangeline said as the group backed away from the fence toward where their car waited.

"Obviously," Oddry said.

"It's not even looking at us," Cal whispered.

"I can't look anywhere!" Winnie shouted, her voice piercing the silence of the evening in a way only children seem capable of.

"Quiet, Winnie," Cal said, leaning down to scoop her up. "Bury your head in my shoulder and don't look at that person out there."

"It's looking at us now," Evangeline whispered, dropping her gaze down but keeping the Riparian in her peripheral view.

"Just run now," Oddry said. "Just run."

They did, the sound of their footfalls providing a beat to the panicked barking of Tennyson as he followed them.

The adults and the dog were focused forward, but despite her father's advice, Winnie looked up from his shoulder at the strange man standing way out in the Harbor.

He must be big, she thought, because even though he was really far away, she could still see him pretty well.

But then that man, who looked like someone had smudged the drawing of him with charcoal fingers—that man stepped to the side and disappeared, and when he reappeared, he was right next to the fence, so close that he could have put a hand on it.

The fence was mostly solid but had big horizontal gaps in it, so Winnie could see him, and the big man kneeled down until his face was visible in one of those gaps.

He had four eyes, she would tell her parents that night. Two regular eyes and two sad eyes, and tears were running from that second set.

Just before her parents turned to reach their car, before her view was blocked, Winnie saw the Riparian raise a single hand, too many fingers clustered there but all of them extended in a wave.

Jumbled and jostled by her father's rapid running, Winnie was still able to manage a wave of her own in return.

The Riparian stepped again and was gone.

Chapter 14

With four days until the autumnal equinox, businesses and public institutions began posting reminders for patrons to get their shopping done early to avoid the long lines on the day before the equinox. Believers from the House of Always Giving, the Sylvans, walked the streets with signs proclaiming the day of deliverance was coming soon and promising forgiveness and friendship from the Queen for any who sought Her grace and joy.

A few carried signs denouncing the Fencing Bureau, and one or two even hoisted signs decrying the overreach of the fencers themselves.

With three days to go, schools sent coats and clothing home with students, grocery stores began to see runs on the necessities, and pharmacies started to sell out of first aid kits, bandages, and antiseptic. Metalworkers across the globe, their stores of iron pendants and iron blades long gone, moved to selling bits of cast-off iron, small strips and misshapen hunks that never became anything recognizable or sellable.

Governments issued and reissued warnings about the equinox:

Leaving your home was forbidden during the twenty-four hours of the equinox.

Taking or threatening your life or the lives of others was forbidden during the twenty-four hours of the equinox.

Only essential medical and infrastructural personnel were allowed on the streets during the equinox.

Lock your doors and windows and do not open them for anyone, even close friends and relatives. Do not listen to the laughter on the streets. Pay no attention to the rhyme and songs you will hear.

Stay in your homes. Stay in your shelters. Hold your iron close.

With two days until the equinox, the streets began to clear and businesses boarded up windows and doors, selling their necessary wares from makeshift tables erected on the sidewalks. Some cities, both in the US and around the world, housed their homeless population in shelters opened exclusively for the equinox, demonstrating what governments could do when they actually wanted to help. Majestic, along with most cities bordering a fence, had shelters.

Of course, other cities, many in the US and governed by somewhat different philosophies, had decided long before that the equinox provided a solution to their homeless problem. The fae could kill—and often did—but they could not create more of their own number. Just as some governments were happy to leave their unhoused citizens to fend for themselves on cold winter nights or during heatwaves, they were similarly comfortable allowing the equinox to play out as it would for those on the streets.

Winnie was sent home with the contents of her locker in her backpack and reading assignments to tide her over for the week-long break that would encompass and follow the equinox. She showed off the new series of books her teacher had given her: Mrs. Marble, the Marble Detective. She promised she would only read the first on the equinox and would save the other five books for when Cal and Evangeline came home once the Long Day was over.

Sealed jugs of clean water were delivered around to houses and left out for anyone who needed them, and packages of nonperishable food were sold at reduced prices for those who could afford them—and quietly given to those who couldn't.

On the day before the equinox, the world shut down one time zone at a time, the locks of doors and chains on gates tracking the sun's progress across the globe. Government agents in marked cars and bright vests drove the streets and walked the neighborhoods, checking on those not yet safely sequestered inside and confirming the safety of those who were. They doled out last-minute supplies to any who needed them and left bits of iron wherever they went.

Some catastrophes could be escaped by the privileged and selfish few who could find benefit in ignoring their fellow humans. In the end, of course, most catastrophes that effected the have-nots eventually reached the haves, but it would take time, and even then, a thick-enough layer of privilege and power could protect some.

This was no such catastrophe, so the government and the wealthy spared no expense in mitigating what risks they could. Like a sickness sliding through the cracks in the system, the horror of the equinox respected neither tax brackets nor degree status.

Only prime numbers, inked into the skin by some unknown hand, could offer any real protection, and despite the best efforts of mathematicians across the globe, none had as yet been able to reproduce the phenomenon.

With hours to go before the start of the equinox, the sun having set and the sky star-speckled, sirens wailed their warnings along empty streets. Businesses that just a week earlier would have been open, lights on and a steady clip of customers moving in and out of their doors, now looked abandoned, those windows now boarded up, empty of light or movement, the doors hung with thick chains, pure iron where the owner could get it, steel or another alloy where they couldn't.

Around Majestic, most homes went dark with the sun's setting, the people inside heeding the general advice to draw no attention from outside; make your home appear empty and lifeless. Do not pass by windows if you can help it. Do not make yourself a target to anyone passing by.

Like children on the playground who begin to understand intuitively what bullies look for, the people of the world had learned to make themselves small and uninteresting, silent and still and not worth the effort. The fae, the Wretched, the Blessed Ones, would happily stray from their inexorable movement toward the nearest Harbor if there were interesting and easy mayhem to be caused on the way. A riddle to be offered. A game to be played. A life to be toyed with.

A true name to be found.

So, most people turned their lights off and stayed quiet in the darkness of their locked homes, children held close, until morning, when the same precautions held but at least there would be light from the sun and the hope, the illusion, that everything was okay.

On their quiet street, in their quiet, surveilled house, Calidore and Evangeline were putting Winnie to bed, blessing her with kisses goodnight and promises for what was to come. They would be gone from the start of this sleep until the end of the next one, but then they would have a break from work and school, and then they would play. And then they would watch movies and color and eat snacks and read books. And then they would be together.

And then. And then. And then.

There is something of the grave in saying goodnight to a child.

"One more chapter?" Winnie asked as Evangeline closed the book. "Please?"

"We can't do it, sweets," Evangeline said, leaning in to kiss her daughter on the forehead. "Dad and I need to get in to work, and you need to get to sleep."

"But I'm not tired," Winnie said, stifling a yawn. Beside her, taking up most of the bed, was Tennyson. He lay completely still, as if he might be confused for a stuffed animal and left to sleep there with Winnie all night instead of joining Cal and Evangeline.

"You need to get lots of rest," Cal said, reaching out and taking one of Winnie's hands. She had the same long fingers as her mom. "How are you going to tire out your babysitters if you're sleepy the whole day?"

Winnie smiled at that, and she pulled Cal's hand to her face, snuggling it.

"Can we do a good-dreams list?" Winnie asked. It was one of their nightly rituals to ward off nightmares. The stories and snuggles and jokes and silliness helped, but so too did this: a list of the dreams Winnie wanted to have. Hopeful dreams. Happy dreams.

"I'll start," she said, holding up three fingers on Cal's hand, which she still held in her own. "Flying on the back of a dragon unicorn who only eats cupcakes, and she knows all the stories in the whole world and she tells them to us while we sit on her back."

Winnie folded over one of Cal's fingers and said, "Dad, you're next."

"A dream where we all live in a castle with whole rooms filled with ice cream of every flavor and you never get too full to eat it," he said, smiling down at her as she folded over another finger and then looked expectantly at Evangeline.

"A cold winter day where we're all together inside our house with a fire going and hot chocolate that makes anyone who drinks it sing in a funny voice."

Winnie giggled at this as she folded down the last of Cal's fingers, and then the three of them were all laughing.

After the lullabies and the stories of what had been, after quiet words in the secret language each family has as their own, the mother and father, Evangeline and Calidore, whispered a final farewell, gave her one last hug, and left their child to night's cares.

Downstairs, with Tennyson in tow, they loaded the rest of their gear as they went over the final details with the two babysitters who would take the first shift of the equinox. A married couple, Virginia and Alaric Stone, they were both trained EMTs who, along with the others who would take the next shift and the one after that, were part of the squad of babysitters hired by the Bureau each equinox for Winnie and any other children of fencers. They were people whose background checks and screening procedures made even top-secret clearance seem trivial in comparison. These carefully selected babysitters, along with the agents stationed in the house and the ubiquity of iron in the walls, the doors, the appliances, the floors, the windows—all of it promised safety and security for Winnie from any fae who happened to stray into this area, already an unlikely scenario.

Virginia, who was just emerging from a walkthrough of the basement—where Winnie would spend most of the day tomorrow since it had soundproofing and no windows—nodded to Cal and Evangeline before returning her attention to the clipboard in her hand.

"Everything looks good down there," she said. She was tall and white, her hair long and braided into a single, thick plait that fell down between her shoulder blades. Though her baggy clothing hid it, Virginia Stone had the muscle and tone of a formidable fighter, just as her husband, Alaric, did. All of the babysitters hired by the Bureau were required to have EMT training along with extensive self-defense skills and demonstrated care for children.

"On this level, too," Alaric said, checking off an item on his own clipboard. "You're good to go."

Cal and Evangeline had their swords in hand, their phones in their pockets, and anything else they could possibly need would be available for them at the Shop.

Aleph stepped out from the kitchen, looking odd in casual clothes instead of his usual suit. Like the other agents who worked the rest of the year, Aleph should have been home with his family on the equinox, sheltering from the possibility of death and destruction.

Instead, Oddry had worked the levers of administration and positioned Aleph—who would tag out in four-hour shifts with another agent, Steinbeck, currently sleeping in a small guest room downstairs—in the house with the government-approved babysitters.

None of them could say who was working with the Sylvans or how deep the layers of surveillance really reached, so Oddry made what concessions and implemented what safeguards he could without arousing too much suspicion.

"We'll justify it by citing the increased attention on you two from the investigations," he'd said, waving away their concerns and questions. "I want my goddaughter safe from any idiot Sylvan who decides to break the stay-at-home order and shows up at your house with a gun."

And they hadn't disagreed.

"Would you give this to Winnie in the morning?" Cal asked, picking up an envelope with Winnie's name on it from the table. "I leave her a note every year, and it has a page for her to color in there, too. She might need some help with the bigger words in the note."

"Of course, sir," Virginia said, taking the note and sliding it into her clipboard. "Happy to. That's very sweet."

Cal gave the stairs a last look, probably thinking he could pop back up there, give Winnie one more kiss, one more hug, but Evangeline put a hand on his arm. She knew him well enough to know what was going through his mind. It was the same worry he'd had every year on the equinox since Winnie was born.

Cal was dreading his own death, fearing it, not because he was worried for himself but because more than anything, he didn't want to leave Winnie without a father. *What if I don't come back?* he was thinking. *What if she's looking for me and I'm not there?*

So, he left her a note every year—presumably just a little something to get her through the day away from them, but Evangeline saw it for what it was. A goodbye letter, should it come to that. A note that, behind the jagged lines of Cal's handwriting, said very clearly: *I have loved you more than I thought possible, and you are a star in my night sky, and you will live a big, wonderful life, and I am so glad to have been in it at all, and I love you, and I love you, and I love you.*

Evangeline and Cal had talked about his notes and his deep fear of death early on in Winnie's life, back when the feelings were far more raw, and she'd realized that this was his way of putting his affairs in order, of doing what he could in the face of what he saw as a harrowing possibility. Her own note from Cal, of course, was snugged into the pocket of the coat she wore, just as it always was. She'd read the first one that first year but refused to read any after. He dealt with his fears by speaking and writing and worrying about them. She dealt with hers by refusing to give them power over her, now or in the future.

Her own mother, Roxanne, had been one of the baby boomers swept up in the craze for Eastern Buddhism that had swept up the west coast of America in the sixties and seventies. Before giving birth to Evangeline or meeting her to-be husband Gerry, Roxanne had spent her early years discovering herself over and over again at retreats, music festivals, spiritual adventures, and philosophy seminars. Most of the wisdom she'd found in those years had been burned away by the drugs and alcohol, and most of the pearls she'd retained sounded like gibberish to Evangeline even from a young age.

But one of them, from the psychologist-turned-guru Ram Dass and passed through her mother in response to one of teenage Evangeline's moments of difficulty and drama, had stuck with her.

"You know what Ram Dass says, darling," her mother had told her. "Emotions are like waves. Watch them disappear in the distance on the vast, calm ocean."

It had been from a book called *Be Here Now*. Evangeline had tried to read it and mostly found the ideas simplistic or stupid, but that image of emotions like waves disappearing on the ocean had stuck with her, and she'd spent much of her internal life striving to be that ocean. Vast and calm.

As she waved at the babysitters and followed Cal out the door, Evangeline sent her own fears, different in composition from Cal's but tuned to the same key, out onto that endless ocean inside herself.

A van idled on the street, black with wheels that looked capable of off-roading and a front end and grill designed to drive through barriers. The back door slid open, and Incident's face with its long, slim nose and wide smile, peered out at them.

"Welcome, knights of the Long Day," she cried, her voice disturbing the unnatural peace of the evening. The rest of the world had gone to ground, feigning sleep or at least stillness, but Incident looked alive, almost manic as she gestured them forward. "Our time has come and the Queen's call sounds for those who would hear it!"

In the immediate aftermath of what the press were calling "The Church-State Conundrum," Incident had been furious, refusing to talk directly to Cal or Evangeline and spending her usual training time away at the House of Always Giving to, according to her, "repair the grievous wounds inflicted upon my site of faith."

The previous day, though, she had arrived at work as though nothing had happened, greeting her fellow fencers, including Cal and Evangeline, with her usual dramatic aplomb. Not a word about the Conundrum. Not a word about the betrayal.

When asked by a curious Nero about it, Incident had smiled around at her squad and said, "Wrongs will be righted, and justice will be found, Nero. It is not for the Sylvan to judge but merely to await the unfolding of the Queen's plan."

"Neat," Nero had said, and that had been that. Training recommenced with the same vim and vigor it might have had if nothing had ever occurred at the House of Always Giving.

"I can't wait for this day to be over," Cal said, speaking through the fake smile he'd conjured. He gave a wave and then looked back, first at the window beside the front door where Virginia was watching them leave, and then up at the window to Winnie's room, which held only darkness.

"You and everyone else," Evangeline said, following his look back. Did she see movement in Winnie's window? It looked dark, bereft of even the thin purple illumination of Winnie's small night-light in the hall outside her room, but did Evangeline see the shape of a small face watching her go? A small hand raised in the darkness?

Or had the dark business of the night already begun?

Later, Evangeline would find the calm of her ocean turned turbulent and wild as she returned to these questions again and again, trying in vain to send them out onto that sea only to have them carried back in waves dark and unyielding.

"Welcome, welcome!" Incident said as she slumped back into the van, which had an open-plan, limousine design in the back half with benches around the outside. The Stone Weaver, who had already been picked up, raised a hand in greeting, the desperation in her eyes saying how very grateful she was that Cal and Evangeline had joined. During the recent training, Incident had undertaken a mentoring role to the Stone Weaver, pulling her aside after exercises or maneuvers to offer wisdom and knowledge, and as a result, the Stone Weaver had taken to escaping from rooms whenever Incident approached.

Tennyson leapt in first and, after receiving his pets from everyone inside, curled up and settled down in the center of the floor. Cal and Evangeline followed.

When they were settled and the van had resumed its course—to pick up Nero now—Cal said, "I saw the Russians have already moved over a thousand fae to their Harbors. And China has almost double that. Big numbers for so early in the day."

"Many are being chosen this day," Incident said, nodding and looking out the window.

"Not many secondaries despite the big numbers," the Stone Weaver said, looking down at the small tablet she would be traveling with that night. Given that she was still technically a fencer in training, it would be her job to serve as the primary point of contact with the people working in the Shop, relaying both updates about the world's fight throughout the day as well as locations the roving fencers should move toward. The Stone Weaver carried her own weapon—a macuahuitl that she felt most comfortable using, embedded with iron instead of the traditional obsidian—but she would be an emergency resource for the group, called on to fight only in the direst of situations.

"That's a relief," Evangeline said, and Incident nodded along at that. They might have differing ideas about whether the fae themselves were a problem—Incident calling them "the Blessed Chosen" while the others called them "the Wretched" seemed as good an example of this as any—but no one, Sylvan or fencer or Bureau administration or average citizen, wanted the number of those killed by the fae to climb.

To die by the soft hands of the Wretched, even on the equinox, meant only a mundane death. Fae could not create fae.

"And is *it* still here?" Cal asked, knowing the answer would be yes.

After the sighting of the Riparian, Oddry had returned to the Shop to ask what, precisely, the vast, worldwide array of machines and surveillance equipment and teams of monitoring mathematicians were doing if they could have missed the arrival of the Riparian at the Midwest Harbor. A bug in the software had been to blame, apparently, along with three eyewitnesses who had all fessed up to seeing what they assumed were signs of the Riparian and not the creature itself. No one could say when it had actually left Russian soil and shadow-walked to the United States, but there were clear reports each hour of each day since that it had not left the Midwest Harbor.

"Sighted at . . ." The Stone Weaver studied the tablet for a moment. "8:47 p.m. along the northern expanse of the fence. Our observers said it was studying one of the nearby trees for several moments before it turned to look at them."

"I'm sure the scholars and researchers have already developed a whole range of theories for how that particular subspecies of tree in those exact conditions has a deep and important connection to folk and fae histories," Evangeline said. She held her sword across her lap, drumming her fingers absently against its fuller.

"Hey!" Cal said. It was one of their old hobby horses, the sharp edges and poky bits of the disagreement smoothed away with time and much use. "Some of those scholars have been totally correct in their interpretations."

"Yeah, yeah," Evangeline said, chuckling out a little laugh that fogged a patch of the window against which she was leaning her head. "And how many of them have been wrong on the way to the five accidentally correct interpretations?"

"Evangeline is just upset because she never actually learned how to read," Cal said, turning to the Stone Weaver. "She actually isn't even allowed in libraries."

"Which one of us was a spelling bee champion three years running?" Evangeline asked, face alight with imminent victory. "And which one took five and a half years to get through college?"

"That was a misunderstanding between my advisor and the English department!" Cal said, whipping around to face Evangeline. "I was an innocent bystander!"

It was Evangeline's turn to mock-whisper to the Stone Weaver.

"If only that explained his GPA for the first two years."

Cal gave that a Bronx cheer, which brought a round of laughter from everyone in the van, including the agent driving.

"I like when you two fight," Incident said, her grin a bright slice in the evening gloam. "You seem less like toy models of fencers pulled straight from the box."

Nero emerged from her house as they pulled up, blowing kisses to the boys waving from one of the windows. Like Cal and Evangeline, she lived on a street occupied almost entirely by government agents tasked with keeping her safe.

Just before getting into the van, Nero manifested one of her bubbles—

the material of its surface having gone textured and rough, like sandpaper, in the last few days—and flexed it into a big heart. Her boys laughed at that, and her partner, June, gave another wave and a blown kiss from behind them.

"This van already smells terrible," Nero said as she climbed in. Cal and Evangeline both moved to make space near the door for her, which put Evangeline next to Incident.

So close in the back of the van, with the space lit by the moon's bright light and the rhythmic, regular flares of streetlamps, Evangeline saw the tiny crescent-moon scars that curled across Incident's face, arcing through her eyebrows and breaking the smooth plane of her cheeks, carved in among and over and around the chaos of her prime tattoo.

Her gifts from the House of Always Giving.

Evangeline had the sudden urge to reach out and run her fingers along those scars, to feel the topography and the history they represented, like a geologist walking a landscape and seeing what it had once been by the dips and rises, the scars and streams that marked it.

What could drive someone to such willing self-destruction? What kind of belief or hope could smooth such coarseness?

The conversation lapsed into small observations about the quiet of the streets, the orderliness with which Majestic—and, if reports could be trusted, the world—had prepared itself for the equinox.

As the van cut through the center of Majestic, the stillness of the world broke in a sudden cacophony of voices and movement as people streamed out of several buildings clustered along Main Street, each one carrying a sign and wearing black clothing, their faces covered by bandanas and masks.

They were the same protestors whose numbers had been steadily growing in Majestic over the past week, their signs, many of them familiar by this point, waving around in the night.

The van might have been an average make and model, unmarked

and black, but it was past curfew, and the protestors must have guessed—rightly—that it could only be ferrying people from the Fencing Bureau on their business.

What had begun as a small handful, "a pitiful pity party" as one of the more callous administrators had called it, had grown now into a sizable group, some thirty-five or forty strong, and they were keeping pace with the van, choking the street around it and even—

"They're going to block us in," the driver said, slowing the vehicle to a crawl as the protestors crowded in, shoulders and hips slamming into the sides of the van, hands and signs colliding with the windows.

Cal let out a yell as something solid hit the window by his head hard enough to send cracks radiating out from the impact point. Tennyson let out a sharp whine and then began barking in deep, subsonic woofs.

"Go!" someone screamed even as Evangeline leaned forward and shouted, "We're not running anyone over!"

The protestors had begun chanting and slapping their hands on the van in unison, and though the panic inside made it impossible to hear the words, every fencer and agent understood.

We need the tax money the government gives you, they said.
We need electricity, they said.
We need fresh water, they said.
Maybe the fae problem isn't so bad, they said.

"Tennyson—silence! Down!" Evangeline moved back through the van, and at her order, Tennyson quit barking and dropped back to the floor. His eyes continued to flick from window to window.

"Nero," Evangeline said, nearly shouting to be heard over the storm of the protestors. "Can you do anything with your bubbles?"

"Not unless you want me to kill a bunch of them," she said, frowning and shaking her head.

"Cal?"

"I can't move them with my primacy. I could get out, but—"

"Nobody is getting out," Evangeline said, her voice suddenly harsh. She had a vision of the doors opening and the fencers and agents being hauled bodily out of the van. People would die, and depending on how long the altercation took, those people might not stay dead.

"I can fire some warning shots," the agent in the passenger seat ahead said, although she looked doubtful about the efficacy of that plan.

In the tiny spaces between the protestors, Evangeline could see more people showing up.

They needed to figure this out soon.

"I can cantillate something nearby—a patch of the road or something," Evangeline said, shaking her head at the idiocy of the idea. "If you all are plugging your ears and shielded by the car, you would be okay, I think."

But the forty or fifty people outside wouldn't.

"I can do this," Incident said. The look of wild joy she normally wore had disappeared at Evangeline's suggestion, and she moved forward now, positioning herself in the center of the van, just ahead of Tennyson.

"You all get toward the back," she said, nodding at the fencers. "Take Tennyson with you."

They did, and after a quick conference with the driver, Incident called on her primacy.

A swirling tornado of black grains emerged around Incident, spiraling up and down her body and along her arms, until she was covered by a vast, writhing, whirling mass.

"Cover your eyes," she shouted before extending her arms and sending the horde of black out in either direction, punching holes in the windows and doors as she threw the protestors back, though not as hard or as far as she might have.

Incident angled her arms, and the black swarm, still writhing and moving, like a swarm of bees directed by a unified alien intelligence, moved forward along the line of the van, shoving back those protestors who didn't move away.

As the two extensions of Incident's power neared the front of the van, she brought her hands together in front of her, elbows bowed out, and the streams of black curved inward, denting the van and breaking both headlights as they did but forming a wedge between the vehicle and the protestors.

"Go!" Incident shouted, and the agent sent the van forward through the gap created in the protestors. As soon as they were in the clear, Incident sighed in relief and the endless motion of her primacy retracted back into the van and into her body.

Cal spun in his seat to watch the protestors disappearing in a motion eerily similar to the retraction of Incident's black extensions—black-clad bodies oozing from the street into doors and windows quickly opened and quickly shut.

Almost immediately, stillness returned to the world around them, and the only sounds were from the fire-hose-sized holes left in the van's sides from Incident's defense, the wind tearing raggedly through them as the agent behind the wheel urged speed from the vehicle.

"Contact the Shop—emergency number," Evangeline said to the Stone Weaver, who was already pulling out the squad's phone, a thick, tactical thing designed to survive far more than any of the fleshy bodies inside the van could. Evangeline had seen one of those phones run over by the tactical trucks the fencers used during the equinox, and it had survived without any damage at all.

"Where the sam hill are the cops?" Nero had slumped back into her seat. "What's the point of the curfew checks if a little army can go by unnoticed?"

"They did their last rounds almost an hour ago," Cal said, looking down at his watch. "Those protestors probably hunkered down with the lights off until the cops went by, and then waited for their moment."

"That's quite dangerous," Incident said, returned to her seat and looking about as if nothing out of the ordinary had just happened.

Which, for the equinox, was probably about right. "If what they wanted was to remain in fellowship and community with their like-minded comrades, they should have joined the other faithful at the House of Always Giving. We let in any and all on the equinox."

"I don't think they were interested in fellowship and community," Cal muttered, and to his surprise, Incident only shrugged and looked out the window.

While the Stone Weaver called in to the Shop to let them know what had happened, Evangeline got on another phone and called the police force to let them know. It was too close to midnight for them to do anything, probably, but they could start the investigation once the equinox was over.

"I don't mind some political agitation," Nero said, her arms folded over the standard tactical gear she was wearing, same as the rest. "But these fools are taking it too far. They really think we're the enemy."

They saw no more protestors on the road to the Shop, but they did see evidence of them—signs left out in yards and tied to stoplight poles calling for more oversight of the fencing authorities or stating the numbers of fencers' salaries next to average pay for teachers or nurses or sanitation workers. There were more signs about the electricity and water outages, about the rising temperatures in summer and the plummeting ones in the winter.

"I didn't know there would be so many of them," Cal said quietly.

"Me neither," the Stone Weaver said. She'd reported the incident to the Shop and now sat with the phone in her hands, as if waiting for an important call or waiting to make another one.

"New York and Florida both had to dispatch reserve fencers to manage the crowds of protestors," the Stone Weaver said, returning to the tablet.

"They got *reserve* fencers?" Nero said in disbelief at the same time Cal said, "*Crowds* of protestors?"

The Stone Weaver turned the screen out, and in its gentle blue glow, they watched video clips of these reserve fencers dressed in tactical gear, carrying not the iron weapons of their trade but riot shields and tasers, a few of them drawing on their primacies to manage the crowd.

A short, squat fencer breathed out some kind of pink, swirling gas that raced out in roping twists before splashing into the face of six or eight protestors, who all immediately dropped to the ground, motionless.

"That's Carver," the Stone Weaver said. "Don't worry—they're just rendered static for a few minutes. That's his ability—kind of like yours, Cal, except he has to be able to reach them with that pink smoke for it to work."

The scenes, and there were plenty of them to watch, were grim. Shots of signs snapping and breaking against the reinforced material of the shields; images of protestors flung to the ground or bound together and taken into custody.

"No way this gets better on its own," Nero said, sucking at a tooth and glaring at the screen. "Howl is going to have to address it."

"Director Howl doesn't have nearly the political power at the moment to solve a problem like this one on her own," Incident said, a comment that drew looks of surprise from the fencers around her. "Don't be so shocked. I pay attention."

"I guess so," Evangeline muttered.

The van rolled into the Shop and was immediately set upon by techs and medics of all kinds, checking to see if and how the fencers and agents had been hurt, marking the damage to the van, taking statements, and monitoring vitals. Behind the frantic assessment stood Oddry, watching the movement of his workers with grim attention.

"Any injuries?" he asked.

"No," Cal said, but Oddry brushed that answer away with a wave of his hand.

"I'm talking to the doctor who's examining you, doofus."

The doctor finished firing her pen light into Evangeline's eyes and shook her head.

"All good, sir."

"Good," he said, pointing first at Evangeline and then swinging his finger around to catch the whole squad. "You're late for the go-meeting. Move."

The room hummed with an energy it had not held during their last meeting. Every fencer wore their tactical gear, pockets filled with everything the techs, under Oddry's supervision, could imagine might be of use: flares and med kits, high-strength wire and fishing line, iron chains of thin, delicate make, energy gels and bars, salt pills. Some fencers, like the bomber pilots of World War II, took speed throughout the Long Day, pulling the government-issued pills, cut to doses designed for each individual fencer's body type, out of secret pockets throughout the night and day. Others asked for more weapons—iron-bladed throwing knives or loops of iron-laced razor wire.

Cal had asked for more of the iron bits and bobs and filings that he'd deposited at the House of Always Giving. That day had been a whirlwind for them all, but a memory he had not been able to lose was the feeling of that iron pressing in around his fingers as he'd plunged his hand into the bag and grabbed handful after handful.

He stood now next to Evangeline and the other members of the squad, one hand disappeared into one sturdy pocket of his jacket filled with the bits of iron. He had no intention of using it during the equinox, but just the feel of the cold, varied surfaces against the palm of his hand and wedged between his fingers was a comfort to him.

"It's been twenty minutes," Evangeline said, smiling and checking her watch. "And it's also past eleven-thirty. I'm sure she's asleep."

"You're probably right." Cal ran a hand through his hair, thinning already by thirty-five, before adding, "I just keep thinking of that night a few months ago. With the apple juice."

Evangeline's grin turned into a groan as the memory hit her.

"What six-year-old has a bladder that size?" she said, incredulous.

Cal laughed, glad to be there instead of pulling sodden sheets from a bed as Winnie shook and shivered in the slanted light of the stars projected onto the ceiling of her room. It had taken them half an hour to get her washed up and into warm pajamas—"dream dresses," as she often called them—and by that time, Winnie had been wide awake despite the owl-shaped clock in her room reading 3:47 a.m.

That night had ended with both Cal and Evangeline crowded into Winnie's bed, putting her into a snuggle sandwich, telling her stories of dragons and witches and every magical creature they or she could think of—except for faeries, of course.

It was a night Evangeline and Cal might complain about to friends or coworkers, but their smiles as they talked spelled out a deeper feeling: gratitude and a long-simmering, low-grade delight at the wonder of their lives.

What luck to know you are lucky.

Clipped to her jacket, Evangeline carried a radio that was linked with those of the other squad leaders—Gloaming, who stood nearby and was leading his squad in a last-minute consideration of the maps showing their routes to the fence and probable places for deaths they would need to respond to.

The other squad leader was Ordinal, who was sitting at a table on the other side of the room with their squad, holding a cup of coffee and laughing hugely at something one of their fencers had said.

Evangeline pulled out the radio and said, "Break, break, break for Ordinal; keep it down over there, would you?"

Ordinal wiped a few tears of joy from their cheeks and grabbed their own radio, finding Evangeline with their eyes as they said, "Roger and ten-four. Heard you hit some trouble on the way. Everyone okay?"

"All good here. Your squad ready?"

"As ready as we're going to get," they said, winking at Evangeline as they lowered the radio back to clip it on their belt and returned to the conversation.

Every other day of the year, the fencers moved and mixed among one another without care for who fenced on what squad, but this day, this night, the squads huddled together, building between themselves the fire and energy and love that would sustain them through the horrors of the Long Day.

The squads retreated into themselves, like teams preparing in the locker room for their final game, everything on the line and only these people, these other faces showing nerves and excitement, fear and worry and deep, profound hope—only they could understand.

They were brothers, sisters, siblings-in-arms, one another's final line of defense against all the dread the Long Day might bring.

"Fencers!" Oddry entered the room, followed now by a small army of his techs, all of them working at tablets or laptops or phones, relaying and synthesizing the mountains of information coming in from the other Harbors. Oddry wore a crisp, clean baseball jersey, new, if the shock of white fabric and the bright lines of the stitching were any indication. It looked several sizes too large and was worn over a silver turtleneck. Below, he wore jean shorts, their ends frayed into long wisps of blue, and combat boots done up tight to his calves.

"In your squads and your attention on me."

This was pageantry—the fencers were already in their squads, and when he'd stepped into the room, every conversation had quieted, every eye turned toward the front. They might joke and laugh during the rest of the year, but not now. Oddry spoke the first words of their annual prayer, and they would not disrespect it.

"The hour of the equinox approaches," he said, voice booming out and empty of its usual annoyance and sarcasm. Above him, the clock showed 11:38. "We are assembled to shield those who cannot shield themselves, and it is a charge pure and good and right. This day, when the Wretched rise from death's clutches and look to play their bloody, terrible games, they will find you, steadfast and strong, arm in arm with your squad. Your coterie. Your *knot*, and no force of fae or earth will undo your bonds. Trust in your powers, your primacies, and in the strength of your fellow fencers."

Oddry took a step forward, moving away from the retinue of techs who had, for the moment, stopped their work to watch their boss.

"Remember this: your enemies this day are not human. They have no family, no friends, no loved ones, and no love. They are creatures alien and unknown, who delight in carnage and ruin. Give them no mercy; they deserve none of it. Save your feeling for the mother who has watched her child die and change before her eyes. Save your feeling for the son who has seen his father die and become something else. Save your humanity for humans, and give to the Wretched nothing but hateful iron and prime as you drive them before you toward the fence and beyond.

"For reasons unknown, our Harbor has been chosen by the Riparian to walk during the equinox. This changes *nothing*. The Riparian cannot leave the Harbor, and no fencer should ever go past the fence. Let that monster leer and walk all it wants. This is *our* day. We have a responsibility, a task ahead of us, and we are very, very good at what we do."

From one pocket, Oddry pulled out a length of iron, long as his hand and misshapen by the years and much handling.

"Touch iron, fencers," he said, almost shouted, and as if on cue, the fencers in the room stood and put hands on their weapons—the iron swords and clubs, the iron axes and long knives, the iron knuckles and half-shields.

"Summer creeps into its grave," Oddry said, holding his iron high, "and autumn approaches. Let's meet that fucker and kick his goddamn teeth in."

The fencers roared their approval, and, squad by squad, left the room, touching the length of iron Oddry held out.

The equinox had begun.

Chapter 15

The first call came at 12:38 a.m.

Evangeline's crew was riding along the Grand Road. They had ditched the busted-up van for a vehicle that looked like a tank-truck hybrid.

Wheels designed by Oddry to deal with even the most treacherous terrain ripped up grass and gravel alike. An engine large and powerful enough to power a medium-sized navy war boat growled and screamed under the hood, responding to Nero's foot on the gas pedal with disconcerting acceleration. Wider than a road-legal vehicle and longer, too, with an open bed designed for a team of fencers to sit around its perimeter and a cab that could house six comfortably, the truck was built for battle, and the fencers inside were ready for a fight.

"Natural death reported at 225 West 9th in Majestic," the Stone Weaver said. She sat in the back row of the cab by Cal. Between them, curled up and snoring, was Tennyson. Up front were Nero behind the wheel and Evangeline. "Seventy-three-year-old man, Lawrence Kingston."

In the bed of the truck, buckled in and talking as quietly as they could above the wind and the truck's engine, were Incident and Sister Marla.

Filled with fire and drive from Oddry's speech, the fencers had left the meeting room and walked out to the street in the front of the Shop where their truck was waiting, only to find Sister Marla standing beside the vehicle, a notepad in hand and a long, winding chain of iron strung in loops about her body.

She'd given Evangeline a curt nod and climbed up into the bed of the truck.

At the news of a report, Nero cut a quick U-turn on the road they were on, not bothering to signal or look around for traffic. The roads, the fields, and the lawns were bare of people. The first time Cal had seen the equinox as a fencer, no longer hiding inside his house with his family but out on the streets with other fencers, he'd been struck by how wrong everything looked, like a vision of post-apocalypse in which nothing but the people had gone.

The squad was just outside of Majestic—driving the route that cycled between Majestic and the other surrounding towns. *Roving*, Nero called it—moving constantly but never far enough from any of the towns, especially most-populated Majestic, to be too far away from a call.

"I know that guy," Cal said over the scream of the engine as Nero sent them barreling down the road into Majestic at eighty or eighty-five and climbing. "He works at the grocery store as a greeter."

"Was he a high-risk case?" Evangeline asked. The government maintained a shoddy but oft-referenced list of people who were at higher risk than normal of a natural death. It wasn't much, and it had the accuracy of a toddler trying crayons for the first time, but it was something.

"Heart disease," the Stone Weaver said, nodding.

"How long ago?" Nero asked, taking a turn onto a residential street at sixty and gunning it up the road, straddling the center line as she did.

"Someone at the residence pressed the emergency button at 12:12. EMTs arrived at 12:17, worked on him for a little while, but they couldn't save him. The message just says: 'Attempted resuscitation, included administration of oxygen therapy and nitroglycerin. Efforts were not successful. Paramedics fled the scene as patient expired—approximately 12:34 a.m.'"

The Stone Weaver checked her watch—a wide-dialed, thick thing that looked nigh indestructible.

"So, that's four, now five minutes ago," she said as Nero banked left onto West 9th—a wide residential street overhung with the dark forms of old maple trees, the homes set back behind generous yards and lined by sidewalks that were probably decorated with chalk art from the neighbor's children.

As the truck, high beams like twin suns at its fore and traced by running lines of LEDs along its body, raced down the road, ignoring stop signs and yields, Cal watched the houses bleed by and thought of children biking along those sidewalks and down this road in the summer and fall, streamers from handles and playing cards in spokes, pilfered snacks from the pantry stuffed into backpacks and broken out once everyone got to where they were going.

He thought of Winnie, who had been slow to learn how to ride her bike, pedaling along with the other kids, her pink-and-purple princess-themed rig boasting a carriage-shaped basket at the front and stocked, absolutely *stocked*, with candy. He could almost hear her laughter, her shouts of joy.

"Next block," Nero said, downshifting and filling the quiet night with the engine's calamitous protest. "It should be . . . Oh."

The hooded streetlights offered intermittent halos of light on the dark street, like running lights down a theater walkway, but the neighborhood was swaddled in darkness, every home looking empty and abandoned, every lawn still and silent, every tree a dark mass suspended in the cold autumn air.

Except for the tree in front of 225 West 9th, which was on fire.

Tongues of purple flames devoured the tree, a huge maple that had probably just traded summer's greens for fall's beautiful coat of gold and red. Branches once broad and full of leaves now burned with abandon, the unearthly flame cracking and popping the wood in a chorus too merry and cozy to make sense.

Beneath the tree, stepping through a slow, careening dance, was the person who had been Lawrence Kingston, 73 years old, deceased.

Nero brought the truck to a stop in the middle of the street, leaving it running.

"Cal, point. Tennyson, stay and guard," Evangeline said, stepping from the truck and pulling out her weapon of choice—a sword modeled after the German long seaxes. Single-edged and multi-fullered, it had a long grip and a large, circular pommel.

Tennyson, who was awake and alert now, watched the fencers leaving the truck with obvious desire before moving back through the open window and standing beside Sister Marla, who looked less comfortable now that the equinox had actually begun. Her notebook and pen were nowhere to be seen, and she was cutting quick glances at the cab, perhaps thinking it might be safer in there.

Cal felt a thrill go through him as he stepped forward, the adrenaline and battle-fire devouring the nagging worries and fears that always moved inside him. The squad had many variations in their strategies, all drilled endlessly in training—a single fencer taking point with the others in support; fencers pairing off to deal with multiple fae; the whole group acting in concert without a single leader; every fencer for themself.

But for a single fae, especially one so close to the nearest fae line—the Grand Road cut through a neighborhood only a few blocks over on its way to the Harbor—a single fencer with a defensive primacy was best.

Lawrence Kingston stopped its dance and turned to the fencers midstep, arms still flung out akimbo. His—its—eyes were too large and too bright, even with the roaring purple fire above lighting the night.

"Knights of eld," the faerie said, pulling itself up to its full height and bowing to them. In life, Lawrence Kingston might have been a seventy-three-year-old man suffering from health problems that had thinned him out and made him weak or stooped, but as a fae, he—it—stood tall and proud. Hair black as the starless sky fell from its crown in thick, wavy tresses. Two intricate braids circled its head and formed a raven crown.

The cut of its eyes and its smile, the gentle cock of its head as it regarded them, the slow flex and release of its fingers—all of it spoke of a distant, uncaring cruelty. Its movements were like those of a spider—shutter-click quick and unsettling.

"*They are not human,*" the head trainer of the Fencing Bureau emphasized with each new collection of fencers. "*They were people once, yes. Him and her and they, but once the transformation begins, your language needs to reflect the reality of the situation. Grandma isn't 'she' anymore. Grandma has become 'it.' I don't want to hear any of you, even in training sims, even joking, referring to any of the fae by human pronouns. They are not people. They have no gender, no sex, no humanity. Do not make the mistake of giving them any.*"

The faerie beneath the burning tree spread wide its arms in welcome.

Cal reached for the nonsense language that always seemed at hand, as though deep down inside himself was a river of chattering voices, all spewing nonsense, a frantic, frenetic outpouring of his anxiety, his worry, his constant, chattering fear, and all he needed to use his primacy was to scoop a handful of the bitterly cold water to his lips and drink.

"A path lumned with punctility, slicker-slacked in an endless beginning is a play of the wind in turning elsewise—widdershins, that was—whiffle to wander. I, said with slender catchment, another category, disillusioned ontologies, a maze work of libidinal economies, running—*running*—with lollypop lackadais . . ."

As the words of his hollow grammarie spilled out, Cal gathered the tension and force of primacy to create an arrow-shaped buffer between him and the faerie, the air there turning slightly opaque with the manipulation of time.

On the equinox, fencers were given a directive, "a prime directive," Oddry often said, grinning around and laughing with the other nerds: whenever possible, ferry instead of fighting. The fencers' job was to encourage the fae to move toward the Harbor, to get the strange beings on the fae lines and past the event horizon, where no amount of civilians or potential destruction could distract them from the magnetic pull of whatever lay beyond those fences.

Lawrence Kingston cocked its head at Cal's nonsense language, the way the fae always did, its smile growing wider and mischievous.

"A poor boy with a poor story, tra-la-la," the faerie said, and it hunched down a little, the slump of its shoulders and back so obvious because its posture had been so perfect, almost balletic. It dropped its head, too, and brought its beautiful hands together, pressing and pressing the palms together in a too-familiar way.

Cal let the nonsense syllables run from his mouth and pushed forward the buffer of his primacy, knowing he could not catch the faerie in it but hoping it might push the creature back and toward the fae line. Faced with the pull of the Harbor and a squad of primed fencers, the fae typically ran.

When Lawrence Kingston brought its head back up, the odd familiarity of the posture and hand motion clicked for Cal just a moment before the creature began speaking, its voice a shocking approximation of Cal's father's.

"Hey, meathead, good to see you. You're looking good. Strong. Those numbers on your skin are freaky, though." The faerie laughed, and even Evangeline flinched at the sound, so close to being human and so close—dangerously, uncannily close—to being the laugh of Cal's father.

The fae played games with the world, games without purpose or goal, in which malice and kindness were interchangeable currencies to be swapped and spent at will. Cal knew this. He'd fought enough fae to understand that these creatures, who always seemed to know too much, would pick with casual cruelty at his mind even as they sought to rend and break his body.

But on some level Cal had expected an easing-in to the night's horrors, a kind of acclimation period. Some equinoxes were like that—easy calls consisting of just tailing a fleeing faerie as it rushed with more and more speed toward the Harbor. Some equinoxes, of course, were harder right from the go, but Cal found himself caught unprepared by the faerie's too-close, almost-perfect parody of his father.

The speed and volume of his hollow grammarie intensified as a voice inside Cal's head screamed at what he was seeing. A flush of blood blanketed his neck and the back of his head, warming him, and Cal took two quick steps forward, almost a hop, as he first spread his arms wide and then brought them together in front of him, ending with his splayed fingers lined up and pointing toward the faerie.

The buffer he'd been carefully maintaining followed his motion, the arrowhead inverting as the two lines slammed together around the fae, a pincer of time-stopping force that would have ripped it apart on a cellular level.

But Lawrence Kingston was not there when the two extensions of Cal's primacy came together.

Dropping the impression with a strangely tender look, one that snagged in Cal's gut like a fishhook, the faerie leapt, high and graceful. It arced upward like a diver being pushed by gravity instead of pulled, and landed among the burning branches.

The fire moved up and down its body freely, and though the flame had already eaten through many branches and devoured the leaves, it seemed to have no effect on the faerie, who crouched amidst the blaze on a half-burned bough and looked curiously down at the fencers.

It raised a single finger and grinned.

"Nero, defense!" Evangeline shouted, and Nero manifested a disc-shaped bubble only a moment before the faerie flung down a gout of flame, the same purple as the blaze in the tree. The fire splashed against the bubble, slagging the surface and causing it to run down in viscous rivers.

It was enough, though, and the fencers were able to scamper safely backward, down near the sidewalk.

"Incident, you're up." Evangeline was good at this, the managing of her troops, knowing who to tap when, what they would be best for. Cal respected that about her, admired it, and he was always proud to take her direction on the equinox. She might have the shortest prime among the Midwest fencers, but she was a leader because of her commitment to the job. She studied the research on fae behavior and tactics, talked with experts, and trained relentlessly.

She was a good fencer and a better leader, and when she called Incident, she knew what she was doing.

Yet the image of Lawrence Kingston hunched over, slumped down as Cal's father Cliff had always been in life, speaking as Cliff had—*just* like him, all the way down to the pet name Cliff had had for Cal as a younger boy, *meathead*—that image turned the river of frantic nonsense inside of Cal into a flood.

Before Incident could join the fray or do more than begin to call forth her inky tempest, Cal moved forward again, spitting his hollow grammarie, but now he reached to his hips and removed his own blades—one an updated and personalized Roman gladius that he carried in his dominant right hand, the other a short butterfly sword with a modified basket hilt that covered his left hand in a webwork of protective iron.

Someone was shouting behind him, but Cal could hear nothing beyond the empty language spewing from his mouth, which had reached the volume and pitch of a guttural scream. He could feel the tearing in his throat and knew it would be raw after this, but it didn't matter—so little mattered in that moment of freedom from fear or anxiety or terror. Rage was an emotion that covered all others, devoured them like kindling in a fire, and Cal fed that blaze.

The faerie stood and looked as though it might leap away from another of Cal's attempts to entangle it, but when the prime tattoos along his skin curved and swam—his own unique effect of using his primacy—it was not the faerie that Cal focused on.

Instead, he spoke his hollow grammarie into a thick, time-distorted haze around the branch on which the faerie stood, and instead of arresting or slowing the speed of the blaze, he pushed it forward—twice again as fast, thrice again, ten, twenty, fifty, a hundred, a thousand thousand times as fast—and the branch evaporated into the carbon bits it had been destined for all along.

The faerie, legs pistoning for a leap, fell to the ground in a clatter of limbs.

Cal strode forward, his ragged voice finally going silent, and slashed at the creature with his gladius, the iron blade humming in the air, its weight perfect and balanced in his hand.

The faerie flung up its arms, skin still alight with purple fire, and Cal scored its flesh with two long cuts that sizzled and flashed with eerie light in response to the iron. A howling, horrible cry rose from Lawrence Kingston's lips, a sound that no human ever had or ever could make. It was melancholy and haunting, and yet it pierced deep down inside Cal, causing his teeth to ache and his joints to hurt.

Still, he held on to the image of the faerie's imitation of his father, and when those well-slashed arms fell away, Cal stepped close and brought the large, heavy pommel of the gladius down toward the faerie's face in a hammerblow. The creature flinched away and so took the blow high on its cheek instead of dead center, but it was enough to wrench out another of those cries.

"Meathead," Cal muttered, grinding out the word between his teeth as he reared back for another blow. "Meathead."

A snarling bark sounded a moment before Tennyson cut in between him and the faerie, the dog using its sizable bulk to shove Cal back, hip-checking him off into the grass.

"Beast!" the faerie gasped out, but it was too late.

With brutal efficiency, Tennyson leapt atop the faerie, slamming it back to the ground as it was trying to rise. Paws the size of Winnie's bike tires landed on the faerie's chest, pinning it down, the black claws cutting into its skin. Tennyson's coat was a monochrome maelstrom, the movement too fast and hypnotic to consider for long.

When he growled, it was not the same sound as before but something deeper and cosmic, as though Tennyson the Newfoundland had become a mouthpiece for an entity bigger than himself, something etched out in the stars, moving through endless space and dark matter like a whale plumbing the deeps of the ocean.

To Cal, that cosmic growling had always sounded like a lullaby, an undercurrent of soothing depth to it. Evangeline talked about hearing strange, wild laughter in the rich texture of the sound. Nero refused to say what she heard, though Cal had once watched tears come to her eyes in response to a Newfoundland's fae growling.

As if no part of the madness of the equinox could happen without a perfect personalization of it, every experience unique and subjective, the powers and magics sui generis. One of a kind.

The growl continued and Tennyson held his position as Evangeline moved forward, holding out a hand to help Cal up.

"I—" he began, but Evangeline shook her head.

From a pocket at the back of her coat she pulled a long, delicate chain, the links worked and cut to look like teardrops, every bit of it iron. With movements practiced and quick, Evangeline looped and secured the chain around the faerie's wrists before stringing it back to wrap around its neck, until all that remained was an eight- or ten-foot lead, which Evangeline kept control of.

"Safe," she said, pulling a dog treat out of a pocket to give to Tennyson as he returned to her side.

Slower to rise was the faerie, whose face, beautiful and perfect only a moment before, now sported a brutal gash high on its cheek where Cal had struck it. Its arms, too, held out straight in front by the chain, were marred by two long slices on each from the gladius. The fire had gone from it, both literally and figuratively. No longer did it joke and sneer and sing. The iron acted like a dampener on its spirit, though if it were left on too long, any fae would find their internal fire returning.

The wounds did not bleed, and the continued presence of the iron prevented the naturally fast healing all fae seemed to possess. Instead, a soft shower of something dark fell from the faerie's face and arms, impossible to see in the night without the truck's high beams and the illumination of the fire from above. It was not gas nor liquid nor solid, and it disappeared entirely just before touching the ground; it had always looked to Cal like tiny bits of carbon from a bonfire cascading down through the air, but they fell as though moving through water, meandering and swirling and floating down more slowly than gravity's laws required.

"Nero," Evangeline said, and the other woman stepped forward to help Evangeline with the faerie, each of them grabbing an arm and hauling it to the bed of the truck, where they dumped it unceremoniously.

"I'll stay back here with it," Evangeline said, pulling out her seax and resting the blade on the chain collar Lawrence Kingston now wore. Its eyes were closed, and it was muttering under its breath, its only movement as it lay where the fencers had placed it.

"I should stay back with it," Cal said, craning his neck to look up at Evangeline standing in the back of the truck. It had been one of the responsibilities given to him in the parceling-out of equinox jobs. Evangeline as squad leader. Nero on the wheel. Cal on capture safety. Incident on rear defense and what Oddry had begrudgingly called "mathematician courtesy." The Stone Weaver on comms. And other responsibilities as ordered by the squad leader.

"Not this one," Evangeline said, not meeting his eyes. "Not after tangling with it. You need rest."

"I'm okay," Cal said, stepping on one enormous tire and pulling himself up to be closer to Evangeline. "He just got in my head, but I'm okay."

"*It* did," Evangeline said, her voice quiet. "I got this one, Cal."

Peeking around Evangeline, its eyes open now, the faerie said, "I am a part of all that I have met."

"You shut the fuck up." Evangeline still had her sword balanced on its iron necklace, and she edged the blade into its skin, pulling another of those bewildering cries of pain from it and causing a gentle spray of that dark, hazy matter to emerge. "And you, Cal, go sit in the truck and get yourself together."

This was not his wife speaking anymore, the woman the world knew as Evangeline, prodigy of the Publix Harbor, the woman whose true name he knew, just as she knew his. This was his squad leader, and he did what she said.

Nero was using a massive bubble to put out the blaze, sending it flying high above the tree and then bringing it crashing down like a colossal candle-snuffer. Only when the tree had been reduced to smoldering shards and the ground in a twenty-foot radius was completely ruined was she satisfied. Small flickers of purple flame still moved like spirits among the detritus, but it was enough.

"What happened to you out there?" she asked, opening her door and peering over at Cal. She clicked her seatbelt home and then they were rolling again, driving more slowly to accommodate Evangeline in the back.

"I wasn't ready; that's all," Cal said, shaking his head. He was keenly aware of the attention of Sister Marla, sitting in the back of the cab. Her notepad had returned, and she was scratching away at it, though when Cal shifted to put his back against the door and look around at everyone, the mathematician's eyes remained on him. "It caught me off guard by mimicking my father, and I couldn't help myself."

"They're monsters, you hear?" Nero pointed a finger over at him.

"Wild animals dead set on picking where they can pick and messing what they can mess. You respond that way because you have a heart—something they wish they still had. Nothing to be ashamed of."

Cal nodded and looked down, blinking at the tears starting to prickle at the corners of his eyes. The best fencers could do their jobs without feeling, as close to machines as humanly possible, and he strove for that now, pushing the grief over his father away, down into a well where it would not disappear but wait for him to pull it back up. This would not be the only faerie of the equinox—if it were mathematically possible, they would never be so lucky—and it would not be the last of the creatures to pry at his weakness.

"Thanks," he said, and nodded as first the Stone Weaver and then Incident reached up from the back to pat his shoulder.

"Grief is a bastard," Incident said, and for just a moment, Cal forgot what had happened between them, the snide words, mostly from him, and the highbrow condescension, mostly from her.

"Yeah, it is," he said, giving her a genuine smile for the first time.

"You're going to get through this," she said, holding his gaze. "You will."

Cal felt his grief well up, prickling the back of his throat and the corners of his eyes, and he found he could say nothing. He nodded his thanks.

"What did the faerie say to you?" Sister Marla's voice had none of the care or emotion the fencers' had, and her look was analytical. "I heard everything during the encounter itself, but it said something in the bed of the truck just now. What was it?"

"I'm not sure," Cal said, clearing his throat. "Something about being part of everyone it had met."

Sister Marla flipped back in her notebook several pages and said, "I am a part of all that I have met."

Cal peered back through the back window to make sure Evangeline and Tennyson were okay. Evangeline had moved up to one of the seats, but she still held out her sword, and Tennyson sat uncomfortably close to the faerie, his coat aswirl with agitation. They would be okay.

"Yeah, that's what it said. How did you know that?"

"*I am a part of all that I have met; yet all experience is an arch where-thro' gleams that untravell'd world whose margin fades for ever and forever when I move,*" Sister Marla read, snapping her notebook closed before bringing her eyes—bright green and wide with attention—back to him. Her hair, normally a jumble of curled grey and auburn pulled over to reveal the shaved side of her head, was held back for the equinox, the top and right side her of head a maze of tightly braided lines.

He knew those words. He'd shared them with Evangeline, and she with him, many times. How had he not recognized them out of the faerie's mouth?

"What the hell is that?" Nero asked, turning the truck onto a smaller side street, which would eventually run into the fae line, the Grand Road, cutting through this part of Majestic.

"A song?" the Stone Weaver asked, her face lit by the tablet's glow. Cal could see the mess of information the Central Bureau pumped through those tablets to each of the squads out for the equinox. They were as efficient as possible in communicating numbers and trends, links to major bits of news and systemwide notices, but the result was a headache-inducing havoc, one that he was glad to not be doing this year.

"Not a song, no," Sister Marla said, her eyes still on Cal, and he could hear the cadence and rhythm of the lines falling deeper and deeper in his memory and finally reaching good current.

"It's a poem," he said, back suddenly in his first-semester seminar in grad school, the windows of the small room showing the night sky, the light inside harsh and bright. His graduate classes had all met at night, a fact which Cal had loved. It had felt romantic somehow to talk about books and stories and poetry in the evening and into the night, long after most other students on campus had gone home and then out again to the nearest party.

That night, he'd been enjoying the discussion about *Paradise Lost*, an epic poem he'd read for the first time and absolutely loved, when another of the graduate students, a guy named Mike, had declared that he just couldn't bring himself to love poetry.

"*It tries too hard*," he said, grimacing as if the very thought hurt him. He was in the final year of his PhD and writing his dissertation on some kind of avant-garde technique used in a niche series of graphic novels, and had taken this class out of sheer curiosity.

The students went from shock to outrage in no time, but Mike had sat back in his seat, smug smile limp on his face, and nothing anyone could say could change his mind.

Until the professor, a woman Cal had adored named Aliette Durham, took her turn, saying first that it was fine if Mike didn't love poetry, that the course was about understanding it, not loving it.

Without preamble or explanation, Professor Durham had begun reciting a poem, one well out of fashion by that point in literary study, an old classic from Alfred, Lord Tennyson, a poem about Ulysses, the hero now aged and returned home, facing the end of his life and the approach of death.

Professor Durham had recited the whole of the poem from memory, first to surprise and then to silent awe. She had offered it exclusively to Mike, whose smug smile dribbled away against the relentless rhythm of the poem on Professor Durham's lips, the pleading and hoping of Ulysses made potent and powerful by this middle-aged Israeli woman, her hands clutched one moment at her chest and then held out in front of her. In that small classroom on the third floor of the English building, Professor Durham had resurrected Tennyson's "Ulysses," pulling it from history and letting it and its hero live again in her.

The final words, which she offered as a profound promise to the classroom, were ones Cal had never and would never forget: "*To strive, to seek, to find, and not to yield.*"

Smug Mike had offered no more thoughts that class period and returned the next day with a brighter outlook on the poetic form.

When their squad had been given the puppy that would become the mighty, massive dog sitting in the back of the truck now with Evangeline, the same dog who slept each night with Winnie and accompanied her about the house on weekends, Cal had been the one to suggest the name Tennyson, and it had stuck.

"A faerie spouting some poem? What's new?" Nero downshifted before wrenching the huge wheel over, bringing the truck out onto a larger road—two lanes heading east and two west—that happened to align neatly with the Grand Road.

"That poem was in mine and Evangeline's wedding vows," Cal said. Sister Marla continued to stare at him, her gaze intense and calculating. "It's 'Ulysses' by Tennyson."

"Tennyson?" Incident asked. "Like the dog?"

"The dog, yes," Cal said, "and the poet he was named after."

"Evangeline!" Nero shouted over one shoulder. "We're on the Grand Path—let me know when you're ready."

Evangeline flashed a thumbs-up.

"I don't understand why the poem matters," the Stone Weaver said. A sheen of sweat caught in the light from the device on her lap, and Cal made a mental note to check in with her once Lawrence Kingston was on his way to the Harbor. She hadn't been out of the truck for it, but that had been her first true encounter with one of the fae, and someone should make sure she was okay before the rest of the equinox steamrolled her.

"Not just the poem," Sister Marla said, tapping a pen against her notebook. "The line—'I am a part of all that I have met.' One faerie saying it is part of a larger whole. Yet more evidence for the Bloodless Queen Hypothesis."

"*Not* a hypothesis," Incident said, but without any malice or real disagreement.

"And not something I want to consider on the equinox," Nero said, saving Cal from responding. It seemed everywhere he turned, he found the Faerie Queen. Incident talked about Her constantly—praising Her for a glorious day, begging Her for luck or wisdom. Cal's father had too, and thinking of him, which Cal did regularly, brought to mind their final conversations, which were peppered with the Bloodless Queen and Her majesty, Her glory, Her infinite wisdom, all of which Cliff had suggested might help Cal with his work.

And now a mathematician, one of the cold, analytical, logical members of the bureau, was offering her interpretation of a half-heard snatch of what *might have been* a line from a poem to offer support for the hypothesis.

But you did hear that line, Cal thought with a certainty he couldn't escape, and it was an interpretation he might have offered himself if they were all sitting around a table in the Shop, the equinox a happy distance away, reports from bits of language caught on tape or recorded by fencers.

"*A line from a poem about an old king staring at death and thinking about trying to go on one last adventure?*" he would have said, mock shock lighting his features. "*And the Wretched quotes the line about being 'part of all that I have met'? Yeah, I'd say it's a little fishy, and that's not even saying anything about the next few lines about an 'arch wherethro' gleams that* untravell'd world.'"

The realization that perhaps he agreed with the mathematician sitting in the truck with him, and maybe he even agreed with the central premise of his father and the other Sylvans and the radical academics who all asserted, through literature and folklore and faith, that the Faerie Queen existed—the realization that he had begun to hold that premise too shocked and sickened Cal.

"We're good!" Evangeline shouted from the bed of the truck, and

Nero brought them to an easy stop there in the middle of the westbound lanes, the wide road eerie in its dark and stillness.

Cal was happy to step out of the cab and leave behind the robotic eyes of the mathematician, too wide and too knowing for his liking.

At the back of the truck, Evangeline stood on the road, the chain extending from her hand to the neck of the faerie, which crouched on the lowered tailgate, its eyes fixed westward, nostrils wide as it sniffed the breeze. Like a phantom, Tennyson stood behind it, ready to spring should anything violent occur.

But the time for that had come and gone. Whatever pull the Harbors had over the fae had hooked this one, and any power or agency it had, any individual autonomy, had disappeared. Like a ship crossing a black hole's event horizon, the fae had lost the ability to go any direction other than *in*.

Protocol indicated squad members should provide defensive support, so Cal, Incident, and Nero all got out their weapons—Incident with her triangular shield, the front etched with the open hand of the Sylvans; Nero with her iron-headed warhammer; Cal with his swords.

Evangeline tugged gently on the chain, and the faerie leapt down from the truck, landing light and soundless on the pavement. Still, its eyes were locked westward, toward the Harbor which lay, according to the Stone Weaver's map, 8.3 miles away.

With careful motions, Evangeline undid the chains binding the faerie, and as soon as the last link of iron left its skin, the creature bolted, racing off at a pace that would have been frightening if it hadn't been moving away from them.

"We just let it go now?" Sister Marla asked through the back window as the fencers all climbed back into the truck, which was still running. Evangeline nodded to Cal and then to the bed of the truck. They dropped into two of the seats there.

"We track it for a little while, just to make sure it's heading where we think it should," Evangeline said as the truck took off. She closed the back window with a *snap* before settling back into her seat.

The truck took off down the highway and soon enough caught up to the faerie, which was running faster than any Olympian had ever managed, but even that speed couldn't contend with the staggering amount of horsepower Oddry's techs had packed into the truck.

Nero kept them safely back from the faerie, pacing it at striking distance, and Cal could just see through the window that they were going around thirty-four miles per hour.

"They are going to keep poking about your father," Evangeline said, her eyes on the faerie ahead of them. "I know it's been hard, and I know he's been on your mind, but that can't happen again. You can't brutalize the fae like that."

"I can't . . ." Cal couldn't understand what he was hearing. "They're cruel monsters, Evangeline. That thing would have walked to the neighbors and made art with their guts if we hadn't gotten there."

"I know, Cal."

"So, I'm the bad guy for roughing it up a little bit? I got carried away, yeah, but they're the enemy, Evangeline."

She leaned over toward him, gesturing at a passing stand of trees. They had been speaking in near-shouts to be heard over the sound of the engine, but now Evangeline spoke more quietly, her face only inches from his.

"Marla is bugged and wearing a camera."

The trees moving by looked like men and women waiting in line in the rain, buttoned up and hooded, lit only by the moonlight.

"She . . . What?"

Evangeline pointed again at the trees, gesturing in a line across the top of them, as if tracing out a constellation for him.

"Oddry told me just as we were leaving. He thinks they want to discredit the fencers further—pile on to the media circus after the House of Always Giving. If they can show us as irresponsible or loose cannons, the government will have no choice but to restrict us. Investigations, fencers on leave, a reappraisal of all our protocols and standards—that's what Oddry thinks is on the line."

Cal felt a cold weight settle on his stomach. Not only were they bringing an un-primed mathematician around with them this equinox, one they could say with near-certainty was working with the Sylvans—but she was recording them? Had her poking at that poem been part of that? Some attempt to get the crazy fencer to lose his composure and say something awful?

He turned to Evangeline, but she nodded back out at the tree line.

"She's watching us right now, and I don't know if she can read lips," Evangeline said before laughing, the sound tinny and off but the expression right on. Marla would think it was just a husband and wife talking things over.

"I already thought this equinox was cursed when the Riparian showed up," Cal said, working to resurrect a smile in response to Evangeline's fake laugh. "And now this."

"Summer creeps into its grave," Evangeline said, her true smile appearing like unexpected grace as she let loose her Oddry impression. "And autumn approaches. Let's go be heroes."

Chapter 16

Nero let the faerie go on its way after a few more miles once its speed ramped up to a steady thirty-six miles per hour. It was hooked, well and truly.

The Stone Weaver reported that Ordinal's squad had already ferried four fae—one single and three in a group—to the Harbor. She played a message from Ordinal for them once Evangeline had opened the window again.

"Three twenty-year-old fools," Ordinal said from behind the wheel of another truck exactly like the one Evangeline's squad rode in. One of Ordinal's fencers—probably Daughter Courage, their resident in-training fencer—filmed from the passenger's seat. Next to Ordinal, curled up and panting, was their Newfoundland, Rocco.

"Suicide pact as far as we could tell," Ordinal continued, grimacing a little. They'd been around for a long time, almost since the beginning, and still, the grisly work fencers did each equinox affected them. It was one of the things Evangeline respected most about them. "A few of us got banged up in the encounter, but we're all right."

The camera—the same one attached to the Stone Weaver's tablet, which she had dutifully turned on to film Evangeline's version of this same message to deliver to the other fencers and admin back at the Shop—shifted to the backseat of the truck, where a fencer named Nineteen gave a wave and smile. His head bore a bandana of bandages and gauze, and one of his eyes was already shining toward a thick ring of bruising.

"I'm good," he said, flashing a double thumbs-up.

"We thought there were only two of them," Ordinal said as the camera returned to them. A nicotine patch was visible just behind their ear, and they were chewing what had to be nicotine gum. "Nineteen was covering our retreat when the third one jumped in. Couldn't transform fast enough."

Nineteen's primacy allowed him to turn into water. Simple as that. Three equinoxes earlier, Cal had spent their pre-equinox hype-up meeting demanding Nineteen transform from human to water and back again over and over, giggling like a child the whole time. Nineteen had stopped when Cal had asked, with straight seriousness, what would happen if someone drank Nineteen while he was transformed.

"Four in the bag for us and only minor injuries. That's the news from the best squad. Over and out." Ordinal stuck up two fingers in a peace sign just before the message ended.

With no more messages to catch up on and no calls for fae activity coming in, Nero took the truck once more onto their roving circuit, always staying close enough to the major population centers to remain relevant.

It was 2:30 a.m. when Cal turned to Evangeline, both of them seated inside the cab of the truck now, and said, "I'm going to call and see how things are going."

Evangeline rolled her eyes and grinned.

"What?" he said, already pulling out his phone. "It's a yearly pseudo-apocalypse and I want to check on our sweet child; what's wrong with that?"

"Not a thing," she said. It had been like this each equinox since Winnie had arrived—Who would break first? Who would reason themselves to calling before the other? Last year, it had been Evangeline. Winnie had had a cough, and Evangeline "just needed to check on that" around 1:45 a.m.

Nero shook her head and laughed in the front seat, and started telling a story about how she had called home to check on her twin boys every hour on the hour the first five years she'd been a fencer. She let out one of her big, boisterous laughs as she recalled how frustrated the agents on duty to protect her family had been.

"They finally said, all official, 'Ma'am, you just have to trust us,' and I swear I could hear their damn teeth grinding over the phone," Nero said before erupting into laughter again.

"Hey, it's Cal, just calling to check on how things are going there." Cal's voice beside Evangeline, his body half-turned toward the scrap of privacy the window offered, was quiet.

He paused, and Evangeline felt wires strung through her body go taut and still in that space, waiting to be struck.

"Pretty normal, I'd say," Cal said after a moment, the tone of his voice putting Evangeline at ease more than whatever he was talking about. She'd imagined for just a moment that pause stretching and stretching as bad news was delivered in halting, uneasy hitches, the wires inside her snapping one by one as she waited and heard only Cal's breathing and the happy natter of her squadmates.

The pressure inside her eased and she sucked in a breath, unaware that she'd been sitting so still with so little air in her lungs.

"Talking in her sleep again," Cal said, turning to Evangeline with a smile, phone angled away from his mouth. "Something about not finding the paintbrushes."

He brought the phone back and said, "Sounds good, Virginia. Thanks for the update. You all doing okay, too? Good, good. Yeah, everything good here. Quiet night so far. Okay, talk soon. Thanks. Bye."

"Your child remains safe?" Incident asked from the other side of the back bench, and Evangeline gave her a thumbs-up.

"Good," Incident said, holding Evangeline's eyes with her own. "She is far too young to be taken by the Queen."

"This is an unusually slow night for you, is it not?" Sister Marla asked, cutting across the conversation in her usual brusque style.

"Every equinox is different," Evangeline said, shrugging and looking out the front window at Majestic, lit by only the streetlights. It was beautiful, all low shadows and thin lights. Beautiful and lonely. And somewhere in there, back in that smudge of black too far and too dark to see, was the little fake neighborhood with their little government house, built like a fortress and holding a sleeping child.

"Still, a bureau total of only eleven so far, and it's nearly three a.m." Sister Marla had dropped her gaze to her notebook page, her pen once more busy on the paper. "Quite low, according to past patterns."

"What are you always writing?" Cal asked the question as if it had been bouncing around inside his chest for months, which, Evangeline knew, it had. "Do you have some theorem or formula you're plugging this tiny bit of information into over and over? Is it notes to yourself? I've met actual writers who don't write nearly as much as you."

"Excuse my colleague," Incident said, putting a pacifying hand on Sister Marla's shoulder. "He's rude."

Marla closed the notebook with a soft *snap*.

"Perhaps after the equinox, you could accompany me into the Sieve," she said, turning that empty gaze onto him. "My colleagues and I would be happy to offer insight into our work."

The thin wave of humor that had buoyed up Cal's question now receded, and Evangeline could see his thoughts running along the same path as hers, down into that memory of seeing the Sieve for the first time, being led down those hallways and subjected to tests and questions, made to stand still and alone in a vast dark room while *something* moved in that vast, lightless space. The strange, geometrically uncanny rooms. The mathematicians in their black-and-white lab coats shuttling along hallways, muttering endlessly to themselves. The sense that those hallways did not end but instead ran onward through earth and stone, under rivers and lakes, until arriving at another Sieve beside another Harbor where more mathematicians worried and worked at the endless problem of the hiding primes.

"Pass," Cal said, the good humor evaporated from his voice, and he turned back to the side window, pressing his forehead against the cool glass.

The next call came a little before sunrise, when the dark of the night had begun to soften at the edges, making the way for color and light to emerge.

"*Shit*," the Stone Weaver said, putting the phone to her ear even as she tapped at the tablet. "Multiple deaths in White Oaks. At least six Wretched. Paramedics arrived . . . Oh, no."

Nero had already pointed the truck toward White Oaks—the next town over from Majestic—and had set the truck blazing down the road.

"What?" Evangeline asked, feeling her body go taut and still again, those same strings stretching once more.

"There's no evidence they were able to flee before . . ."

"How many?"

"Three paramedics on one team, but another arrived just after them. Four in that one. I don't know why they would have sent two!" The Stone Weaver was jabbing viciously at the tablet, swiping from screen to screen and expanding what information she could. Her head swung in a slow, dumbfounded shake, back and forth and back and forth. "It looks like this was two separate incidents in two separate houses that both happened at the same time, and both households pushed their emergency buttons, which summoned two different paramedic teams."

"Arrival in three," Nero said, glancing at the GPS on the dashboard and bringing the truck hard around a right turn. The sound of squealing tires accompanied their acceleration down the next street.

"*You* will stay in the truck," Evangeline said, speaking first to Marla, who nodded, though she didn't seem particularly afraid. Evangeline turned to the Stone Weaver. "*You* are going to fight with us. With six Wretched, we'll need you. Backup and support only, understand?"

The Stone Weaver nodded, showing the fear Evangeline had thought to see on Sister Marla's face.

Tennyson, no longer sleeping, pushed himself up to sit and stretched as best he could in the confines of the truck. His coat had begun to shift and move in anticipation of the fight to come.

"Next street," Nero said, downshifting in a scream of protest from the engine and bringing them screeching around the corner. "Get ready."

"Cal, Nero, the Stone Weaver out the driver's side," Evangeline said, strapping on her weapons. "Incident and I will go out the passenger's side with Tennyson. Move as groups of three and don't be a hero."

"There it is," Nero said, and then after a moment, "My god."

The apartment building dominated the corner of the small, mostly residential block. No lights showed in the windows, and the small yard out front was still and empty save for the bodies.

Above, the fae were climbing the sheer face of the building, their forms aglow with dawn's first colors. As they moved, scuttling up or down, leaping in great, graceful bursts from one small, impossible hold to another ten feet up or twelve feet to the side, they sang a raucous, jolly song in a language that, even over the distorting noise of the engine and through the windshield, Evangeline could tell was no human tongue ever spoken.

"Go," she said even before the truck had come to a stop, and the cab was briefly filled with noise and agitated movement as doors were flung open and lead positions claimed—Nero in one and Evangeline in the other. Weapons were hoisted and battle cries sounded as the fencers leapt from the vehicle, because the Wretched were jumping down to meet them, fae magics already burning on their tongues and across their fingers.

Calm swept over Evangeline as she moved forward, her long sword in one hand, the chain of iron links wrapped around the fist of the other. She didn't long to fight the fae, and she didn't romanticize it as some other fencers did. The Tempest King had always talked about battle like it was sport, seeing himself as the hero aglow with victory and glory, his every action a line of poetry waiting to be sounded.

For Evangeline, a fight with the fae—a near-inevitability in almost every encounter—was not battle or combat, not really. She could never find within herself the fear or terror that the fae were supposed to inspire. Early in her career, she'd been praised for her clear-minded battle strategies, her calm demeanor in the midst of fae combat, but it had taken only three sessions with a Bureau-employed therapist—therapy was required for every fencer—for Evangeline to discover the truth.

"*You really believe that they're not human,*" the therapist, Dr. McCabe, had said. "*Unlike so many of your colleagues, you've actually done the radical thing of believing the training you're given. Fighting a faerie is the same as fighting a bear or a wolf to you—you might* struggle *against an animal, but you wouldn't think of that as combat, because you don't think of animals as combatants. They don't want to win a fight. If animals think, and every bit of research seems to suggest they do, they think about different things in completely different ways than we do. Such is it with the fae. That essential idea is embedded in your training. You're just odd because you actually believed it!*"

Evangeline stepped forward onto the apartment lawn, Incident behind and to her right, and looked up to see two fae falling down toward her, their paths sheering left and right, like autumn's leaves describing gravity's imagination.

On the cold grass nearby were the bodies of the paramedics, seven of them, arranged side to side, snug, like siblings cozied into bed on Christmas Eve. The fae had given each of the paramedics a bouquet of paper flowers, each petal and stem expertly folded, the text-covered paper clearly from a book of some kind.

The paramedics all lay in repose, faces slack and peaceful, hands brought together at the chest to hold the clutch of faux flowers. Each wore a crown of some dark, glittering material. Above them spread the branches of a maple tree, its leaves a miracle of autumnal color.

Above their heads and set into the grass were stone markers, like identification tags, that included each person's height, weight, descriptions of their skin, eye, and hair colors, and genus and species.

And like moths displayed in a bug collection for admirers, each one had a wooden sword pierced through their stomach, the handles of the long blades standing upright and still, pins through the abdomen of the specimens. The blades, conjured or created by the fae, bore intricate designs and were splashed in dark scarlet.

Cal's group moved out to the left side of the building, intercepting one of the falling fae, Nero already affecting its descent with a few of her bubbles, the beach-ball-sized manifestations first caught on the head of her warhammer and then flung upward with surprising velocity. The faerie dodged the first two with claps and melodic shouts of glee, but a third caught it hard on the shoulder and tumbled it end over end on its way down.

"Tennyson, ready," Evangeline said, and Tennyson moved up beside her, a foundation-shaking growl burbling from deep in his throat. The sound was like a discordant undercurrent to the bright melody spewing from the fae, and the swelling musical confusion might have ruptured some part of Evangeline's sanity if the fae hadn't landed and the fight—the *struggle*—begun.

Sweeping her seax before her to make space, Evangeline stepped in to the nearest faerie, a thing that looked to have once been a teenager, strands of blue hair still caught in the lush, thick waves of auburn that now puddled on its shoulders and flicked playfully around its face. A hair-product company had tried to use the fae in their marketing campaign in the late nineties, using stylized artistic renditions—no fae photographs were shared with the public save for a few images, each one carefully selected by government oversight committees—and the backlash had been swift and overwhelming. They'd gone out of business the next year.

In the space granted by her sword, Evangeline whipped the chain forward, unspooling it from her left hand with deadly accuracy and feeling the collision in her knuckles when the end slapped into the faerie's face and neck, sending the creature crashing backward into a stretch of brick wall next to a window. The shades, drawn as all shades in the nation—the world, really—should have been, twitched, and Evangeline prayed that was only from the impact.

"Knight of a broken order," the faerie said, a hand flashing to its face and the contusion already appearing there. It might have spoken again, but Evangeline lashed the chain forward, battering its hands away and eliciting a hiss of pain. The fae spoke as the wind blew. Endlessly and senselessly. Better to listen to the rain on a roof and call it language than transcribe the words of a faerie and call it meaning.

"Blessed Ones!" Incident cried, sending a wave of inky particles forward to intercept the second of the fae, who had been moving in on Evangeline's left side while she was distracted. The dark deluge lifted the faerie up, swirling and circling it like a harness, and though it thrashed and kicked, Incident held it safely away, floating six feet up in the air.

"You are become a name," the faerie in front of Evangeline said, its wide, bright eyes going suddenly cloudy and troubled. "Vext. Roaming. *Honour'd.*"

Evangeline brought her arm back for another lash of the chain at the same time the faerie extended its hands forward, palms out, fingers spread. The same gesture found in the House of Always Giving and carved on Incident's shield and cut forever into the face of Cal's father's gravestone.

The open hand. Imagined by the Sylvans as a gesture of kindness.

"Rot!" she shouted, leaping back, straight into Incident, who tumbled with her in a mess of limbs and black particles stripped of their governing purpose. They fell to the ground, and it was there, Incident's knee pressing uncomfortably into her side and her own leg twisted painfully beneath her, that Evangeline saw the faerie's eyes widen in something like ecstasy as it pushed its open hands forward, releasing from its palms two grey abominations, central whorls of something that shifted and writhed and expelled glistening strands that spun and twisted into awful fractals, math and mass perverted by whatever magic the fae possessed. The strands reached farther and farther out before twisting back into themselves along the path of the golden ratio.

Like endless hands stretching forward, the mass of grey consumed the space that only a moment before Evangeline and Incident had occupied. On and on it stretched, collapsing in on itself only to send out fresh, fractal tendrils that arced gently forward and curved back, arced forward and curved back, searching for substance of some kind to grab and hold and suffocate and devour.

This stuff, the "rot," had been the subject of endless briefings and meetings, its mechanics and significance and potential for various energy sectors tortured on the table of academic inquiry and technical investigation. It was oftentimes the last defense of the fae, though others seemed unwilling to use it regardless of the situation and their own safety. Like every other aspect of the fae, this awful ability seemed chaotic and unruled by anything resembling logic.

"It's a metaphor for capitalism: desirous of endless growth but doomed to fall back upon itself," one academic had once told a group of fencers.

"If we could only get a sample of it, we suspect we could solve perpetual motion," another had said.

"Military applications," a man in a suit from an unspecified branch of the armed forces had said. *"If you can bring a stable collection of the substance in, we would pay you handsomely for your effort."*

Once the efforts to capture and imprison faeries had ended so horrifically with the events of 1990 in Scotland, the world had turned to capturing and studying the leavings of the fae, and no prize was more sought after than the substance now expanding sickeningly in front of Evangeline in twin twisting trunks of grey. Every new strand was born and grew and died even as five or ten or thirty more strands unwound into existence around it.

During her time at the Publix Harbor, Evangeline had been asked a few times each year by various bureaucrats, politicians, and armed forces personnel if she would be willing to make a run into the Harbor to capture some of the rot. Often these requests, after being turned down, were occasioned by an additional query about whether she might be up for a run at the Threshold Tree. Nothing like what happened in ninety-nine, of course, nothing like the calamity of Arthur Miracle. It would be better done, more support, more research. "Your primacy almost guarantees you could get through," they would tell her, and inevitably, the conversation would end in the one-two punch of them showing her an astronomically large number that would appear in her bank account if she agreed and Evangeline walking out of the room.

After transferring to the Midwest Harbor and working for Oddry, the requests for her to capture some of the rot or make a run at the Tree had coincidentally ceased.

"Iron!" Evangeline cried, and rose, her seax flashing out before her, and where the metal met the rot, it flared with sudden light and heat, shearing through the slippery, writhing stuff without resistance. Cal had once joked that it must be what wielding a lightsaber was like.

Next to her, Incident sprang to her feet and struck with the edge of her shield, clipping off several arcing tendrils as they veered toward her.

"Why won't you just run?" Incident shouted, her elevated patter failing as she grunted and sliced and dodged. "Flee, fae!"

Nearby, Cal and Nero struggled against two faeries, working together to fling the fae back toward the road. Cal sounded like a madman, his nonsense language filling the air, what Evangeline's mother would have called "diarrhea of the mouth." But their strategy was working—Cal would catch one faerie up in one of his time lags, slowing the creature down, only for Nero to send one of her bubble projectiles flying at it. Back and forth they went, freezing and striking one fae and then doing the same to the other while the first picked itself up.

"Rear!" Incident shouted, and Evangeline turned to find the other faerie in their engaged duo wielding a green car door torn from one of the vehicles parked on the street, the oblong stretch of aluminum held before it like a shield.

"Oh, me," the faerie said as it swung the car door up and then down at her head, intending to flatten her beneath its smooth plane.

Evangeline threw up her sword, holding the long blade with both hands, extended fully above her just as the car door came down. Her wrists, elbows, and shoulders blazed with pain as her locked joints took the brunt of the door's momentum and power. The point of the seax shrieked against the door as it carved an angry curl of green paint and metal away.

But the force behind the blow was no earthly thing, and the top of the door seesawed down, pivoting against the fulcrum created by the sword tip, and when it clipped Evangeline's head, she felt her arms and legs go suddenly slack. The rest of the door came down on her, but she experienced it as if from a great distance, aware of the impact but too distant from the sites of pain to know what damage had been done.

Vision hazy but holding, she watched Incident holding the faerie's rotting spread at bay with her shield even as she flung a particulate whip at the other faerie, catching and dragging it away from Evangeline.

"Cover your ears," Evangeline tried to say, already summoning the power of her primacy. Cantillating a faerie was a harrowing, awful thing, but she could think of nothing else to do, especially since she could see the remaining two fae, the ones neither half of the squad had engaged, looking down from where they stood atop the building, preparing to jump down upon them.

Cover your ears were the words Evangeline heard inside her head, but her tongue felt thick, and what emerged was a slurry of nonsense, not even rising above the tumult of the skirmish to be heard.

Incident was a marvel, agile and steadfast in her defense against the still-spreading rot, which had eclipsed the faerie that had summoned it. Even as she cut and sliced and dodged and surged, she kept her grip on the other faerie, dragging it along behind her, the black rope of her primacy like a constricting serpent, slithering around and around the faerie, locking in arms and legs.

"Above you," Evangeline tried to say, but it came out as *ahv yuh*, and Incident kept her focus on the fae around her.

From the roof, the two fae leapt, chortling and singing as they did, and only then did Incident look up, too late.

They fell like stones.

Like bombs.

Tennyson took one in the air, the enormous Newfoundland leaving earth with a low *huff* and bounding up on a collision course that intercepted a thing that had once been a middle-aged woman, still wearing striped pajamas. The faerie's song cut out as Tennyson hit it hard, and the two returned to the ground trailing that smoky fae blood.

The other faerie dropped and would have landed directly on Incident, but around ten feet up, it was shoved roughly backward along a horizontal trajectory, all of its downward momentum arrested as it slammed into the wall of the building hard enough to crack bricks and send up a plume of dust.

Feeling began to return in Evangeline's extremities, and with it came pain—a good sign. Even her tongue felt less sluggish in her mouth.

The dust dissipated and the bricks fell in a soft, chuckling shower, but the faerie remained pinned against the wall, its eyes wide and roving.

With a painful shift of her hips and neck, Evangeline twisted over to see Cal and Nero still engaged with their fae, though nearing a victory.

Behind them stood the Stone Weaver, her eyes narrowed and intense, the primes along her neck gone a snowy white. Her primacy did not disturb the air or flash with light, and there were no lances of power that cut through the space along the line between the Stone Weaver's eyes and the faerie she held helpless against the wall.

The only physical manifestation of her primacy were the red tears that ran in thin rivulets from each eye. Evangeline had read the reports from the doctors and scientists who had studied the Stone Weaver, and though she'd thought nothing could surprise her any more after so long fencing, she'd had to read the pages several times to make sure she had not made a mistake.

It was blood running from the corners of the Stone Weaver's eyes. But it was not her blood. She was B negative, confirmed over and again, and the blood running even now down her cheeks, was O positive, also confirmed over and again.

Blood, Evangeline learned in those reports, could be used to identify a person. DNA swam around in there, or so she liked to imagine. And the blood that dripped from the Stone Weaver's eyes when she used her primacy to its fullest? Three separate analyses done by three separate groups of high-powered scientists and their high-powered labs came to the same disturbing conclusion.

It was the blood of the famous, the disgraced, the brilliant mathematician Alexander Grothendieck.

Cal and Nero left their fae tied up in iron chains against a tree and rushed over to offer relief. With their help, Incident was able to string up the faerie already caught by her primacy, and then she and Nero went to work on the faerie rot, using their iron weapons to cut and smash the spreading substance back. The chunks that fell away writhed and decayed at an accelerated rate, leaving behind silvery husks that caught and ran with the wind.

One part of the rot had extended far enough to reach a small tree, probably planted only a year or two before, and the fractal nightmare had exploded with activity upon finding something more substantial than air, racing up and down the trunk, curling around and around it before burrowing deep, the grey flesh of the faerie rot suddenly shivering with color and texture as it wrenched matter itself from the tree, stripping it of every bit of substance it had.

This quivering, roiling mass of rot had fallen to the ground and pulsed there until Nero stepped up and brought her warhammer down upon it, sending its contents out in a wave of running color and viscous fluids that dried up and disappeared almost immediately.

Evangeline had seen that rot latch on to a human being before, and while the results might have been roughly the same, that experience had been accompanied by the slow screams of the victim, which did not stop even after the rot had consumed him, voice and all.

"Are you okay?" Cal asked, kneeling down beside her and putting a hand on her forehead. When he pulled it away, the backs of his fingers were wet with blood. "Call for a paramedic!"

"I'm fine," Evangeline said. "Just get this door off me."

Without the weight of the door, blood returned to her arms and legs, and Evangeline bit back a cry of pain. Nearby, Tennyson had neutralized one faerie, and Incident, with the help of the Stone Weaver and Nero, was in the midst of neutralizing the others.

"Easy, easy," Cal said, helping Evangeline to her feet. Bruises were in order, and her head sloshed and swam as she gained verticality at first, but nothing seemed immediately broken, and outside of a probable concussion, Evangeline thought she would be all right.

"Help them first," she said, and when Cal didn't immediately move, she said again, "I'm *fine*, Cal. Once the fae are in chains, we can see about me."

With a doubtful look, he jogged over, first stringing Tennyson's pinned faerie with iron and then joining the other fencers as they took down the remainders. By the end, a collection of six fae sat, tied from tip to toe with binding iron links.

"My god, Evangeline, what the hell happened?" Nero asked when the work was done. She caught Evangeline's chin in one hand and peered into her eyes. "That cut on your head's a horror show."

"The rot surprised me, is all," Evangeline said, starting to shake her head and immediately stopping, the motion threatening to send up every scrap of food in her stomach. She took a breath and released it. "I wasn't ready for it. But I'm okay. Head wounds always bleed a lot."

"Paramedics here in two," the Stone Weaver said as she joined them. Color spiked high in her cheeks and on her neck, and she was still breathing heavily from the struggle.

"Hey—nice work, you," Evangeline said, putting a hand on the Stone Weaver's shoulder. "Pretty impressive, catching that Wretched mid-fall."

"Shame that the repairs have to come out of your paycheck," Nero said, frowning up at the wall.

"They . . . what?" The flush of pride on the Stone Weaver's face disappeared, but Nero was already chuckling.

"A joke—just a joke."

The fencers—Incident, too—all laughed, and in their eyes Evangeline could see the same desperate reach for humor and levity that they could surely see in hers. The small jokes and banter, the gentle slights and long-running laughs were a lifeline there, not just because of the cosmic wrongness of the equinox, and not just because of the six not-humans sprawled in a pile by that tree over there, each one silent and sluggish from the new iron.

These tiny bits of lightness were necessary when just there, in the spot where none of the fencers would look, were the bodies of the paramedics, untouched during the skirmish, each still clutching their funereal bouquet and resting peacefully.

The smiles and laughter faded from each fencer as those bodies pulled them back to ground. The fae they could chain up; they could use their primacies to harry and overpower and, in cases of particularly devastating primacies, even eliminate the fae. The Wretched. Evangeline did not, could not, see the fae as enemies on the battlefield, but they were creatures who could fit into her method and mission, pieces for exactly the game she was playing.

But human casualties like these, people who risked themselves on the deadliest day of the year without prime or primacy to protect them—what could any of the fencers do for them once their lives had been taken? They were the light shining on the lie so many fencers had to continue speaking—that this was a battle, that this was just another job, that this, strange and odd and fae as it could be, was "just the way things were." The celebrity and the money and the power and the immunity to consequences of any kind insulated fencers from this central truth: they were not heroes and they were not saviors.

They were natural aberrations, curiosities spat out by whatever arcane power governed the primes. They were not the main characters in this story, and apart from the very few fencers who died each equinox, they would all walk away from this day with their bruises and scrapes and broken bones and contusions seen to by the world's best doctors paid for by desperate-to-please governments.

Evangeline broke the circle of fencers and walked slowly over to the bodies of the paramedics, aware that more of them would be arriving at any moment to see to her own injuries. Both of her legs were feeling better with each passing moment, but her left shoulder continued to bother her, and the cut on her head would need seeing to.

"Why did they arrange them like this?" the Stone Weaver asked. She kneeled down beside one of the paramedics, a woman who couldn't have been older than twenty-five.

"Because they're fucking insane," Nero said at the same time Incident said, "Out of respect," and Cal said, "No one knows."

The fae didn't always arrange the dead, and they weren't always so respectful. There had been times in Evangeline's career where she'd assumed an intent behind fae activities that had seemed borne out by their actions. It was one of the many oddities about them—or perhaps one of the many horrors about them—that made the fae impossible to categorize or understand. Some fencers claimed to "know their enemy" on the various talk shows and in the high-profile interviews they often did, but, for her money, Evangeline thought they were all spitting bull. No one understood the fae. They existed slantwise to the world and minds of people. *Uncanny* was the word Cal often used for them—close enough to look and sometimes act like people but just distant enough to terrify with their differences.

Pareidolia was a better word for it. Like a kid looking at a cloud and seeing a face or a dragon or a car. It said nothing about the cloud to see that image and everything about the kid.

"We should do something for them," the Stone Weaver said.

"They'll be given burials." Nero kneeled down beside one of the bodies but would not look directly at it. "They'll all be put to rest tomorrow."

"We just leave them here for the whole day?"

"Only people allowed out today are emergency medical folks," Nero said, speaking the words as though they were distasteful. "Every additional person allowed out is another potential liability, needing fencing or medical help, which means others can't get help as quickly as they might need, and on and on."

"Can't we do . . . anything?"

The ambulance for Evangeline would arrive at any moment, but as she looked down the road for it, a shout of alarm ripped her attention back.

The fae writhed and flung their bodies about against the constraint of the iron chains, which had begun to dig into their skin and release more of that smoky blood, but still they moved and rocked.

The Stone Weaver was moving toward them, Cal and Nero just behind her, when one of the iron chains snapped with a bright, awful sound. The fae were interwoven with too many chains for the breaking of a single one to set them free, but it was enough for one of them to roll away from the morass of limbs. Gashes along its neck and arms coughed blood into the air, but its eyes were clear and its smile wide as it looked to the Stone Weaver.

Evangeline was up and moving, her body screaming in protest. The Stone Weaver had weapons and she had her primacy, but she paused at the sight of that faerie, broken free when it was supposed to be settled and sorted.

"Get back!" Evangeline roared, racing forward.

But the Stone Weaver stood still, enchanted by the fae who cut in toward her, moving with sinuous, snakelike charm, holding her eyes with its own gaze.

"Move!" someone shouted. Distantly, Cal began his nonsense-speak, but it would be too late. Tennyson barked, but where was he?

"Earplugs!" Evangeline cried, and she hoped they would understand. To fence on Evangeline's squad meant always having earplugs at hand.

She raced forward, hip-checking the Stone Weaver out of the way as the faerie leapt forward, the mass of its body colliding with Evangeline instead. She rolled with it, flinging the thing forward and uttering a low moan as the pain in her shoulder exploded.

The faerie sprang up, wounds surrounding it with a thin nimbus of black, smoky blood.

"Like a sinking star," it whispered to her, and Evangeline nodded, coming up to one knee and scooping from the air around her a palmful of bright stars. She tossed them at the faerie, the tiny blinking lights bouncing against its skin before setting off on an orbit around the creature, swirling and flashing in a beautiful cosmic dance.

Incident shouted something, but Evangeline could not hear it.

The faerie, she thought.

The stars pulsed once, twice, and then went supernova, the light too intense for the others to stare at, but Evangeline did not look away. This was her power, her ability, and its light and song and energy were hers.

To cantillate an earthly object was to release a song both beautiful and haunting, one that could destroy sanity and break minds with its power. From a grain of rice to a mountain, everything in the world had a melody all its own.

To cantillate one of the fae was something else altogether. Comparing the song that ripped out of the faerie body to the one Evangeline had pulled from that ugly gun in the House of Always Giving was to compare the roar of the ocean at dawn to the lapping splash of tepid water in a half-filled tub.

Sound powerful enough to send the fencers staggering back and the trees bending as if in a windstorm exploded out from the place the faerie had stood. It was a music of the stars played by an orchestra beyond time and without end. Passages from every major composer filled the air, each one turned odd and strange—Shostakovich reimagined as a lively march; Bach translated to a funeral dirge; Vivaldi and Wagner woven together into a big band sound; Chopin's hellish piano tune plunked out on a barroom keyboard as jig.

It was a tapestry woven from every bit of music the person who became this faerie had loved. In the explosion of sound and melody, Evangeline could hear the voice of that person humming along, singing along, their voice echoing in the shower before work or buzzing under their breath while doing the dishes. Earworm pop songs and labyrinths of jazz melodies swelled around the classical perversions, as though the cantillation did not simply release the energy and substance of the faerie as sound but more truly unearthed the sounds of a life, for soon enough, it was not just music but words—whole sentences and tiny snatches of conversation rising to the surface of the sound.

"I can't do this anymore." "I love you, Mama." ". . . said we shouldn't." "But it wasn't supposed to . . ." ". . . thought it would go on . . ." "I love you." "Why would you say that?" "Yes." "Bye." "Yes." "Nope, just me." "It was amazing." "Would you . . ." "This is the best day of my life." "I love you." ". . . ever come near me . . ." "Can you feel the wind, though?" "I miss you." "It's okay. I'm here." "I'm so proud of . . ." "You are my . . ." "I love you." "Two, please." "Did you see that?" "Hello." "It's too late." "I love you." "I'll wait." "What is this?" "Just returning these." "I love you."

It was at once a chorus of voices and yet all one, the person the faerie had been at age three and age thirty, in love and in loss, miserable and happy, bored and excited, joyful and despondent. The others could hear the song of this person through their earplugs, but it would be muted for them, the bright edge of the sound dulled but still able to cut. Tennyson wore no earplugs, and as the sound hit him, he howled and howled, whether out of sadness or pain or sympathy, Evangeline didn't know.

For her part, Evangeline heard it *all*, bore witness to it all, and when it stopped finally, the last echoes of words and music radiating off into the air, she fell back to the ground and wept for the person who had been and the people laid out on the ground who deserved better than this, and more, too.

A History of Fences and Fae by AK Senga, PhD

Published in 2027 by University of Minnesota Majestic Press
Excerpt from Chapter 6: "The Queen's Children"

After 1987, the world saw a sharp rise in new religions, many of them built around the fae.

One of these new religions, Sylvanism, began as all the others did: small meetings in restaurants and donations in small bills. But the early addition of a few influential members, including politicians of the US government and wealthy elites, gave Sylvanism the financial and social backing it needed to quickly become a strong institution both domestically and abroad. By the end of 1989, Sylvanism had houses of worship, known as Houses of Always Giving, in forty-two states and twenty-one countries. At the time of publication, Sylvanism is the world's third-most-practiced religion behind Christianity and Islam, and could surpass the latter before 2030.

Much ink has been spilled over the question of how a group of people could worship the fae—and their supposed Queen—when those same fae kill an average of 80,000 people each equinox[5] and destroy billions of dollars' worth of property. Academics, politicians, social critics, authors, athletes have all asked: why worship these creatures of chaos and ruin?

For the purposes of this project, which aims to be analytical and historical rather than speculative, let us simply say this: the reality of the fae shook the foundations of worldview, reason, and philosophy for everyone alive, ushering in a new era of fear, crisis, and wonder. That a new

---

[5] This number is slightly misleading; it is an average offered by the US government that takes into account numbers from 1987 up to the present. Average fae-related deaths, however, have dropped each year since 1991 as fencing strategies, government responses, and general awareness have improved. The projected number of deaths for 2026, for instance, is around 35,000—still a large number, but less than half the supposed year-to-year average.

religion should be born out of this tumult is no surprise—even, and especially, a religion that faces this new mystery on its own terms. A new faith system for a new world order. What could make more sense?

By 1988, the Sylvans had a draft of their holy text, *The Sylvan Scriptures*, circulating among faith leaders. Sylvans have maintained an official and unwavering stance that their holy book was communicated directly to several of their members by their Queen beyond the fence and, as such, that any identification of an author would cheapen the book and incorrectly understand its origins. However, internal documents and investigations have revealed early draft copies of *The Sylvan Scriptures* with comments, corrections, and critiques from such noted figures as Rose Friedman, Gilbert Harman, and Lowell Palmer Weicker, Jr., among others.

While much in the text changed over the eight months in which it was written and intensively revised, we do know that the opening of *The Sylvan Scriptures* has remained the same and received only one comment—a scribbled note by someone going only by the initials WB that reads, *but are we allowed to tamper with the rule of logic?*

Here is the opening of *The Sylvan Scriptures*, which is recited at each gathering of Sylvans in their Houses of Always Giving:

> *We cannot know.*
> *What does the Queen hope?*
> *Why does She move as She does?*
> *Why does She take some and not others?*
> *We cannot know.*
> *In our unknowing is all the truth of the world.*

The Sylvan Scriptures is deeply provocative, calling on its followers to "live in careful suspicion of your non-believing neighbor even as you love them with the Queen's own love" and "ponder thoughts of your earthly death as the equinox nears so that you might be closer to the Queen's hand when she chooses her followers." Though health care professionals have argued fiercely that sentiments like this one, which appear frequently through the *Scriptures*, encourage suicidal ideation and unhealthy behaviors, the Sylvans have never been forced to change or censor their holy book, due to the special protections they have as a religious institution. As of this writing, they are known to have members in many positions of political power and sitting on many advisory boards to major businesses. Recent years have also shown a concerning number of mathematicians counting themselves among the Sylvan orders, thereby raising questions of fairness and loyalty in their governmental work.

Chapter 17

Evangeline was getting her head wrapped in bandages by the newly arrived paramedics, all three of whom shot fearful glances at their fallen comrades. They were laid out like little soldiers, but it was the puddle of iron chain at their feet Cal couldn't stop looking at as he remembered the song of the faerie, the way it flashed with the light of those stars and then simply disappeared. He'd once asked Evangeline where the things she cantillated went when the song sounded.

"They *are* the sound," she'd said, cocking her head at him with a curious look. "That's where they go."

A chirp from his phone pulled his attention away, and Cal removed the indestructible brick to find a missed call flashing on the screen.

"Should we start moving them into the truck?" Nero asked, gesturing toward the five remaining fae. She was eating a nutrient bar, one of the many pressed on to them by the bureau. They boasted "a whole meal in five mouthfuls," which sounded both impossible and undesirable to Cal.

"Sure, let me just check this," he said, hitting Play on the voicemail and holding up the phone to his ear. "Missed call—I think it's from home."

"Probably calling to let you know your little lady is demanding candy for breakfast," Nero said, popping the last of the bar into her mouth and rubbing her hands on her pants.

The voicemail was silent for a moment, and Cal was ready to end the replay and chalk it up to an accidental call when Aleph's voice rasped from the phone.

". . . gone. All gone. Dead, I mean. They had a pact. They got her. It's coming for me now. It's—"

The call ended with an abrupt cry from Aleph, but it was the other sound in the background that sent tremors of fear and panic down Cal's legs, weakening his knees and almost bringing him down.

Singing, gentle but persistent, a soft *tra-la-la* haunting in its innocence even as Aleph's ragged scream rose and rose and finally cut off.

Cal flung the phone away, watching it spin through the air before cartwheeling across the sidewalk and up onto the grass. He felt breathless. He felt sick. He didn't feel anything at all.

"Cal?" Evangeline was looking around the paramedic in front of her, head half-bandaged and face starting to regain some of its color. "What is it?"

A gibbering voice had taken up the microphone in Cal's mind, filling the space inside his head with a raft of nonsense that sounded (*tra-la-la*) like a song, repetitive and endless and maddeningly simple.

"Home," Cal said, uttering the word with a force of will. It felt like that song (*tee-tee-tee*) might spill out of his head if he opened his mouth and wasn't careful. "Something's wrong."

Evangeline stood fast enough that she had to grab on to the paramedic for help, and her eyes fluttered briefly closed from the quick movement.

"What did they say?"

Cal could only shake his head, swallowing the idiot song thrumming in his throat and echoing in his mind.

"What's going on?" Nero asked from the bed of the truck, where the last of the chained fae had been deposited. Tennyson eased his growling to look over at Cal, cocking his head slightly in confusion.

He knows, Cal thought suddenly, with a shiver of certainty.

"Cal. What did they say?"

"We have to go home now," he said, and why was his voice so calm? "Virginia is dead, and Winnie . . ."

They drove.

Someone spoke. Something about no calls coming from that neighborhood. That house.

Someone else said, "This'll turn out to be nothing." Nero maybe.

Evangeline sat still and quiet, saying nothing, doing nothing. Her hands were clutched into fists, one on each knee, and she took tiny, quick breaths through her nose.

Cal felt like a tiny pebble bouncing around in a big, empty body. He saw limp hands in a lap, felt knees judder and shake with each movement of the truck, looked out through eyes like oculi cut into the dome of his head, distant and stony. He was in danger of going away, receding further and further from his body, from this place, this time.

Inside that empty husk of blood and bone and body, Cal was disappearing because that voice, that thready voice singing *tra-la-la* and *doo-doo-da* and *ta-lay-ta-lee-ta-tee-tee-tee* was the same voice that woke him each morning to ask for a clue. It was the voice that told him about school that day. The voice that called him "Daddy" and said "Look at my art" and "Will you play with me?" and "I love—"

Cal opened the door of the truck, which must have been going eighty-five or ninety miles per hour, and vomited onto the blur of road beneath them.

Nero punched the brakes, but Cal waved her on.

"Just go," he muttered. *Tra-la-lo.*

Twelve miles felt like a thousand. Every second was an hour.

The passing world blurred into wet watercolor wiped away and painted anew each moment, and Cal had the distinct thought that he was dead, that this was what death felt like—not the biology of his body ceasing but the thing that lived in his body going away. His body was a house made of muscle and tissue, with exposed bone-beams and blood in the walls, and Cal had been a ghost all along, haunting himself, moving from room to room, limb to limb, rattling the pipes and howling his joy and sorrow at the outside world. At some point, someone had come along and graffitied the house with numbers that moved and sang and shone, but it had changed nothing, not really.

And now he was moving on, off to haunt somewhere else because this world, this dumb fucking world, had revealed itself to be one where you could hear your own child singing on a phone, her voice still hers and yet already not, and somehow, some fucking way, that could just happen. To hell with a God who could or would or should prevent that kind of thing—what about the universe itself? What use were the laws of physics and the goddamn theorems that held the stars together and kept them spinning if they couldn't prevent this horror? What universe could at once sprinkle the night sky with a billion billion stars and allow this?

How could any equation balance when one side of it held Agent Dawnlove, reporting in for the next morning's mystery, and the other held a voice on the phone that sang *tra-la-la* without care? No beauty, no meaning, no significance could balance this. If this was love's opposite and equal number, then the scales had broken.

Watching the fall foliage pass by, Cal screamed his hollow grammarie into the quiet space of the car and sent a span of trees fleeing along time's path, aging a year, ten years, fifty years, a hundred, until they bent and curled and broke and became nothing.

"Put your earbuds in," Evangeline said as the truck neared their neighborhood, and everyone did.

The truck stopped askew in the driveway and Cal leapt from the door, his hollow grammarie already a steady drizzle from his lips, and he leapt over the body that lay across the threshold, noting absently that it was Alaric, the puddle of his blood staining the top step and doorway, and then Cal was into the house, into the living room, which was a panic attack, chairs and sofas turned over or ripped apart, half the carpet torn up in long strips that had then been braided, pictures punched in or throw down, and the large window that looked out over their picturesque front yard bore now a madman's screed penned with some substance that glowed and shed faint sparks, but the room contained no one living, and so Cal, swords in hand, moved onward into the kitchen where he met his first faerie, Virginia, her long hair free of its braid and wild now around her head, sitting at the dinner table and surrounded by a vast meal—bright red strawberries and rough green asparagus, turkey etched in browns, cups of milk, juice, and water, and bread in all shapes and all kinds and all of it, every bit of food and drink, all down to the cutlery, had been drawn on and cut from paper, Winnie's paper, a two-dimensional meal spread with care, and Cal strode forward as Virginia, as the faerie who had been Virginia, devoured a paper plate loaded with asparagus and bread, and when he shouted at her—the only question he could think of, the only thought he could hold in the tempest of his mind—"Where is Winnie?"—Virginia looked up and smiled and revealed a long, thin cut along one cheek still weeping that thin fae ash and she sang and she fell beneath the flurry of his swords and because Winnie was not there Cal moved on

down the stairs behind Evangeline, who held fistfuls of stars, and when she reached the bottom of the stairs she found the other two babysitters hired by the government, dead and become Wretched, and she blessed them both with starlight as she screamed out her question— "Where is Winnie"—and when their songs exploded out from their bodies, she was pushed back into the wall by the force, hard enough to jar her shoulder and pull at the threads of her consciousness, but she wouldn't disappear, not now, and she ground her teeth and shut her eyes against the wall of sound and turned to find Cal there, offering her a hand she didn't take, and upstairs or somewhere the dog was howling and barking, and the two of them pushed onward, into the safe room where Winnie was supposed to be but wasn't and they saw but at the same time did not see the play area with the toys she loved and the art supplies she loved and the small table she liked to organize and they saw but did not see the small chair Winnie loved that had been torn apart and then arranged in a hieroglyph neither of them understood and they saw but would not see the sheets of paper and the careful drawings and the spilled crayons and the red and they saw the room entire and yet saw nothing at all and they moved on

to the upstairs past Nero and Incident and the Stone Weaver and even Sister Marla who stood speechless in the living room and they might have spoken or they were perhaps weeping but they were the set for this play, well built and lifeless and meant to afford the story its course and direction and the players, mother and father, climbed the stairs and heard the faint singing, him barely through his earplugs and her fully and when she paused on the staircase leading to the hallway that split, one branch terminating in their bedroom and the other branch terminating in the child's, the mother felt a great yawning madness opening inside her and the father took her arm and said "we can't" and she said "can you hear it?" and he said "no" and then after a moment "yes" and they climbed the final stairs and they were weeping and they turned left and saw the door of their child's room shut and this gave them hope like poison, like cancer, and the mother turned the handle and pushed open the door to find Aleph, trusted guard, dying, maybe dead, the skin of his throat marbled into spots of purple and livid red, one hand still clutching a long iron knife and the other holding a chain, an iron chain, one that wound around his arm and then moved across the floor to the center of the room, and neither the father nor the mother would look there and they saw the bed where Winnie had started the equinox, the bed where the parents had bid her goodnight and goodbye, and there was the dresser filled with her clothes and the bookcase and there in the middle of the room, but no, and the artwork hanging on the walls, much of it torn now and ragged, paintings of unicorns and dragons and toads and snakes and all of it ruined now, even the untouched ones, ruined, because all over the wall someone—*someone*—had written the words of that poem, that same fucking poem, and around the lines strange symbols had been drawn, handprints too small to be Aleph's and figures that looked like people or crowns or eyes or broken-toothed smiles and cracks had splintered the solid walls of Winnie's room, cutting between and among the lines of the poem and undermining the drawings, separating *Yet all experience* from *is an arch* and running a line straight through the words *wherethro' Gleams that untravell'd world whose margin fades For ever and forever* and from the cracks in the wall a thick murgeon was beginning to run and in the center of the room but no, and above the light fixture had shattered and exposed the bare bulb that contained no filament and no burning light but a swarm of bees and they were stinging the glass of the bulb and stinging one another and they should have been dying or dead but they weren't and at their center was the queen and she was enormous, a grandeval monarch with too many wings and a bulging abdomen from which emerged more and more bees and into which flew the spent ones and she glowed sullenly and that light was madness and the father and mother might have fallen into it but in the middle of the room, touched only by that umbilical chain running from Aleph's limp arm to her—to *her*—arm, she sat with legs crossed beneath her and hands clasped to her chest and eyes wide and staring and mouth open and singing that nonsense, so like the nonsense still spilling idiot-quick from the father's lips and the mother cantillated the bed and the closet and the dresser and a ragged section of wall and the carpet and the body of the guard and the ceiling and the roof and the songs were discordant and overwhelming and the father felt he might go under those waves but there was his child, looking at him with eyes he recognized, eyes that undid the careful stitching of his training, and the mother saw too those eyes and she blasphemed against the god of her indoctrination and called out to her child with care and love and the parents fell to her, on their knees before their daughter, who stopped singing and held out her hands to them, fingers grown slightly too long and nails sharp, and she reached for them and the parents, father and mother, reached for her, and the dissipating sounds of the mother's work were ripples on the surface of the world running with calm persistence ever outward and with them went the sanity and care of the mother and the sanity and care of the father and they embraced their child and when she stroked her mother's hair with a single finger, running it like an archet over the long strands, and when she placed an open, spread hand against the back of her father's neck, pulling him in close, and while their child sang to them in a voice like rain and darkness and starlight and nothing, the parents wept over all that had been and could be and might be and would never be again.

Chapter 18

Decisions were made.

Nero and the Stone Weaver took the remaining faerie, Virginia, who was smoke and ash from Cal's fury, and promised to bring her—it—to the fence.

Sister Marla and Incident stayed, the first to wait for a car to bring her back to the Sieve, and the second for no reason Cal or Evangeline could think of if they cared enough to think about it.

At some point, Ordinal's squad arrived, but none of them knew what to say or how to say it, and there were more calls coming in, so they left after a little while.

Evangeline and Cal stayed with Winnie in the ruins of her room. To visitors brave enough to climb the stairs, they offered unyielding silence. For one another, they offered silence.

Tennyson lay just outside the room, his eyes on Winnie, his fur a swirl of black and white. He did not growl, but he did not come closer.

"Death closes all," Winnie said, smiling up at her father. "But something ere the end. Some noble work of note may yet be done."

Cal, who felt his own madness and purpose strung like guardrails around him, nodded and said, "Yes."

Oddry came.

Spitting invective and rage, he climbed the stairs and raced to Winnie's room, and there he stopped. Away went the cantankerous exterior. And away went the anger and the sarcasm and the impatience.

And all that remained was a broken, sad man who joined two other broken, sad people, and together they wept while Winnie recited the composite numbers from 1 to 125, singing them like a nursery rhyme.

"What happened?" Oddry asked finally, but there was no answer to give. It didn't matter what happened, nor did it matter how, which was what Oddry truly wanted to know.

It had happened. That was all.

"Incident said she could take . . . could take the faerie to the fence so you wouldn't have to."

"No." Cal and Evangeline spoke at the same time.

"Understood," Oddry said. He wasn't looking at Winnie. Maybe he couldn't.

"Red monster mug for Oddry because he loves scary movies," she said, leaning closer to him. "Just like me."

Oddry left the room for some time, and while he was gone, the parents began to speak, and their minds followed the pathways of the poem Winnie had written on her walls, the same pathways that wound through so much of the poetry the fae always seemed to recite. The continuation after death. Memory and its truths. The fickle fae and their inscrutable, amoral behavior. The glimmer of a world beyond this one.

The possibility that you, too, might go there.

"She isn't gone."

"No."

"I can't take her to the fence."

"I won't let anyone else."

"No."

"Some work of noble note."

"Nothing here can help."

"Senga, that professor, said there was more proof."

"For the hypothesis."

"The Bloodless Queen Hypothesis."

"The Faerie Queen."

Winnie, sitting between them, said, "How dull it is to pause, to make an end."

"If she's real—"

"The academics, the Sylvans, the fae, and the mathematicians all think she is."

"If she's real, then she has power over this."

"Over Winnie."

"Yes."

"She's beyond the fence."

"Beyond the fence and beyond the Riparian."

"Beyond the barrier there."

"You can rip a hole in that barrier."

"Yes, and you could slow its restoration long enough for us to get through."

"Yes."

"And this grey spirit," Winnie said, nodding along with this conversation, "yearning in desire to follow knowledge like a sinking star."

"And we what? Beg her for our daughter's life back?"

"Yes. And if that doesn't work, we kill her and take it back ourselves."

"We kill her?"

"We do."

"Beyond the utmost bound of human thought," the faerie finished with a clap of her hands.

"Okay."

"Okay?"

Grief had leveled their minds, remade them into moors howling with wind and empty of direction, landmark, path, or way.

This, though, was a bright, angry light beckoning them onward. Some noble work of note to remove that idle monarch on her throne. Steal her power. Make the world right again.

When Oddry returned, he found the fencers gathering their equipment, Winnie still held on the end of that chain.

Tennyson had finally entered the room and now occupied the space at the foot of the bed where he slept each night. The bed was gone, as was part of the wall nearby and the ceiling and roof overhead, but it was his spot. He curled his great mass into a circle from which his black muzzle and wide, brown eyes emerged. He watched Winnie and whimpered very softly.

"What's going on?" Oddry asked the room.

The mother and father exchanged a look, and then she said, "We're taking her to the fence."

Unthinkable to let that grammatical safety sneak into their speech, for the *her* to be rendered an *it*. Especially given what they meant to do.

"I'll call the squad. They can come with you."

"No," the father said, his voice flat and lifeless. "We'll go alone."

"Then I'll come with you," Oddry said. "Rules be damned."

"No," the father said again.

"We're not coming back," the mother said, and her voice was likewise dead and empty. "Or, if we are, we're all three coming back."

"What are you talking about?"

"Is she real?" the father asked. "The Faerie Queen."

"Why are you asking—" Oddry began but stopped, gasping at the sudden realization. "No. No way you're going in there."

"'No,' she's not real, or 'no' to us going into the Harbor?" Evangeline asked, though without any heat or argument. She'd finished her supply check and had hunkered down in front of Winnie, who was poking at the floor and making tiny shoots of some green-yellow plant rise from the floor. The stalk lifted a few inches into the air before wilting and curling back in upon itself. Maybe it was the iron preventing her from doing more. Or maybe that was what she intended after all.

"Both!" Oddry said, and he'd begun to cry now. "You know the numbers—most fencers that get into the Harbor don't come back—and *no one* has ever come back when walking into a Harbor where the Riparian is, and it's still here."

"Is she real, Oddry?" Cal asked again. "We're going after her either way, but if there's some information the Central Bureau has hidden away about her or whatever is inside the Harbors, then we'd like to have it."

"There's no—"

"I saw how you reacted to that report from the academics," Evangeline said, still not looking away from Winnie. "You weren't surprised, and you didn't do your usual sarcastic shtick about it. You at least think the Bloodless Queen Hypothesis is possible even if there's no strong evidence."

"But you also don't think *anything* without evidence, so what do you know?" Cal asked, dropping beside Evangeline and holding out a hand to Winnie, who stared at it without movement for a moment and then trailed one finger around in a spiral on his palm, leaving a trail of blotchy bruises in its wake.

Cal did not pull away.

Oddry said nothing for a moment, and both the mother and father thought he might have left the room again, the sounds of his footsteps hidden beneath the sounds of the song Winnie had begun singing softly once more.

"Central has compiled enough of these reports and enough evidence of things happening inside the Harbors that we can monitor just through human observers to believe that the Bloodless Queen Hypothesis is most likely correct," he said finally, keeping his voice low and speaking quickly. "Outside of Grothendieck's experience in the camp—which is *still* speculation, I should say—and the birth of the Riparian in ninety-nine, there have been four documented sightings of a figure we suspect is the Faerie Queen. Two of those sightings were verified by more than three observers."

"You didn't tell anyone about this," Cal said.

"It was and remains pointless to bring it up," Oddry said. "Whether she exists or not changes nothing of our work, and to give those shitbag Sylvans any more legitimacy would threaten the entire enterprise."

Cal nodded, and Evangeline let out a low, uninterested *hmmm*.

"We have no idea who she really is, what she can do, or what she wants," Oddry said. "Even if you could get to her—and there's not a single fucking reason to imagine that you could—what are you going to do? Ask her to bring your daughter back, pretty please? I love her, too, so understand I mean it and it breaks my tiny heart to say it: you cannot do this and survive, and you cannot do this and succeed."

When neither parent responded, Oddry huffed out a quick breath and spoke again.

"We're going," Cal said, rising and stretching toward the open ceiling, which showed the sky gone evening red. It was getting cold in the house without the wall and roof to hold in the heat. Winnie, in her tattered pajamas, would need a jacket.

"This can't work," Oddry said, walking around so he could see their faces, even if they wouldn't look at his. "You think she's going to give you Winnie back? It's a fucking moonshot. An impossibility. Even if she has that power, even if—"

"We're going to take Winnie back," Evangeline said, smiling grimly as Winnie produced a flicker of purple flame in one palm and then smothered it with her other. "We'll kill the Queen if we have to. Or maybe we'll die on the way."

"It doesn't matter," Cal said, nodding. "There's nothing left here for us. A moonshot is still a shot, and I'd rather run after the impossible than stay here and watch her walk away from me forever."

He looked up at Oddry for the first time, and whatever was in Cal's countenance made Oddry flinch and lean back.

"I can't do that," Cal said. "I can't let her go."

"No," Evangeline agreed, standing now and taking Winnie's chain in one hand.

For a long time, no one said anything. Oddry's phone began ringing, and he silenced it. It happened again, and then one more time.

The world spun on, and the equinox continued, and the machinery of the Midwest arm of the United States Fencing Bureau needed its helmsman.

Outside, in Majestic and in the Midwest and on the coasts and in South America, fencers were swinging iron and using primacies that let them hurl fire and sing darkness and cut consciousness. The European fencers would be just finishing up their work, as were the Africans, while most of the Asian countries would already be waking up to the day after the equinox, when the dead were mourned, the fencers were feted, and the fae problem deferred for another year, as though it were some natural cycle that everyone had agreed was normal and regrettable but ultimately natural.

How good it felt to detach from that delusion.

"I can get you the map," Oddry said. "And I can cover your tracks for a little while."

"We're not asking—" Cal began.

"She was . . . is my goddaughter and I love her too, so fuck your 'not asking' and listen to me. I can cover your tracks, but Central will not let you just disappear like this. They'll want to do an investigation as to what happened at your house, and they'll bury the Midwest in paperwork, but all of that will come *after* they recover you."

Evangeline shrugged.

"I'll take you to the fence," Oddry said, and when his phone rang this time, he took the call, snapping out a "What?" in greeting. His tone, though, changed when he next spoke, dropping low.

"When? When did you get that message?"

Pause.

"As far as you know, they delivered their daughter to the fence and hooked back up with their squad."

Pause.

"I don't care what the number pushers think."

Pause.

"Listen to me carefully. You need to stall them as long as you can. Delete those communications and tell them I'm on my way. *Keep* telling them that. And when the fencers get in, keep them there as long as you can. Do you understand? Good."

The parents' thoughts, those few they still had, moved as if under a heavy blanket, their shapes obscured and softened. Little they had seen or heard since that truck ride to the house had made it through that thick blanket swaddling their minds, but Oddry's growing panic as he talked on the phone did now, and they looked away from their almost-daughter to him.

"It's better for you if I say nothing about what I'm doing, but the official story is just this: I last saw them heading off to bring their daughter to the fence. Stall those mathematicians and the team when they arrive. That's it."

"What is it?" Cal asked. He found his hand had strayed to one of the swords held against his hip.

"A shitstorm," Oddry said, walking out of the room and gesturing for them to follow. "Despite no calls coming from this house and nothing appearing on our radar system, the Central Bureau has it on their system, and somehow, they know you haven't delivered Winnie to the fence."

"How?" Evangeline asked, and beneath that heavy blanket around her thoughts, a stirring of rage.

"I don't know, and I can't think about it right now," Oddry said. "Here's the situation: Central is sending in a team of fencers to contain you and settle the situation. They're already on a jet. We need to get to the fence now if you're going to do this."

They left the house at a run.

On the drive, no one spoke except for when Oddry said, "They must have known this was going to happen."

And then, a moment later, Evangeline's voice came from the back, where she sat with Winnie.

"Or they *made* it happen."

People dying on the equinox was an inevitability, and since the early years of the equinox, governments around the world did all they could to stop needless deaths.

As fencers, Cal and Evangeline were taught to deal with the consequences of an equinox death, and consequently, they were encouraged to ignore the causes of those deaths. Transport the fae to the fence and engage as little as possible—those were their orders each year, and so they thought little of the circumstances that might bring about a death beyond whether they might bring about more fae.

That training and the fact of their daughter's death had been enough to muffle Cal and Evangeline's suspicion of anything else, but now they questioned, and they wondered, and their fury grew.

"Aleph was in the room when we arrived," Evangeline said. "Dead. But he had Winnie already in chains."

"He was alive when she changed," Cal said, picking up the thread of logic and following it. "And he was holding that iron knife, which I bet was the one that had cut Virginia's face. She had a long gash on one cheek when I found her in the kitchen, already Wretched."

"Aleph was killed by a faerie. Alaric too," Oddry said. "They were the only ones."

"He fell as a tree," Winnie said. "And I, the woodsman of wrath and woe."

Evangeline turned away from Winnie at the thought and slammed one fist into the seat cushion.

"Who did this to you?" Cal asked, gritting his teeth in preparation for the answer.

"Come away, O human child!" Winnie said, eyes going wide.

"It had to be one of the babysitters," Oddry said. "When I got the call and before I left for your house, I scrubbed through the video feeds of your neighborhood and around your house perimeter, and I saw no one come in and no one come out."

"They . . ." Evangeline began but couldn't finish.

Someone had killed their daughter. Someone who had been there to protect her.

Winnie, strength sapped by the iron bound around her wrists, ankles, and abdomen, sang quietly to herself.

The fence road was quiet save for the gravel under the tires. Evening was becoming night, and the sky looked like water, awash in dark blues and purples. No stars yet and no moon. The trees were shaggy shadows held in black against the sky, stirred into motion by the constant wind.

Twice they'd had to stop so one of the parents could get out, needing the air and the ground and the space from that child who was not their child, that Winnie who was not their Winnie. She was an *almost*, a *nearly*, a *frighteningly close*. Her voice, her eyes, her gestures, her movements, her breath, her hair, her skin, her fingernails, her knees, her posture, her nose, her ears, her wrists, her feet—it all held a trace of Winnie, an echo of her.

When she said, upon their arrival at the fence, "Secret Agent Dawnlove reporting for her mission," the father gasped at the flood of pain, and not only because it reminded him of his daughter, sweet and curious and perfect and endlessly herself, but because she was there, she was in there, she had to be. Those words were hers, and so too was that voice, down at its core, stripped of the fae inflection.

Winnie was there, and they were going to get her back.

Oddry parked the car in the empty lot, killing the engine and lights and leaving them all looking out the front windshield at the fence, which was lit by spotlights set well back in the safe zone.

The tall grasses of the Harbor danced and swayed with the movements of the many Wretched even now running and leaping and dancing on their way to whatever existed beyond the sight and reach of the human world. There might have been thirty or three hundred of them, some dallying near the fence and others clearly moving deeper into the Harbor.

A more-immediate concern were the two enormous trucks parked in front of the gate—open, of course, to encourage the fae to use its entrance instead of scaling and damaging the walls of the fence itself.

The remnants of Evangeline's squad stood out in front of one—Nero, the Stone Weaver, and Incident. In front of the other was Ordinal's squad: String Theory, Cognatic, Daughter Courage, and Nineteen, his head still wrapped with bandages similar to Evangeline's.

"Oh, what the shit," Oddry said, sounding for just a moment like his old, curmudgeonly self. He wrenched open the door and leapt down from the truck. Evangeline and Cal got out too, pulling Winnie along behind them. Tennyson walked nearby, still looking nervously at the faerie girl he had once watched with adoration.

Nero spat on the ground and turned on her heel when she saw the two fencers, shaking her head and cursing. Ordinal turned to their squad and held out their hands in a *just wait* gesture.

"You're supposed to be out patrolling," Oddry shouted, striding forward. His baseball jersey, bearing the cursive scribble of the Minnesota Twins logo on the front and the name *Carew* on the back, was bright in evening's final light.

"Gloaming's squad is covering for us," Nero said, still looking away. "We had to be *here*."

"*Gloaming's squad*," Oddry said, twisting the words, "can't cover the entirety of our area by themselves."

"What are you doing here?" Cal asked, stepping around Oddry where he'd stopped on the hard-packed dirt lot.

"Oh, god," Nero said, her eyes dropping from Cal's to his side, where Winnie had appeared, hands held before her, the iron like a delicate piece of jewelry, complicated and fine, winding around her wrists and *tic-tic-tick*ing against itself as she walked.

It was Ordinal's turn to face away from the horror of what they all saw.

Cal didn't mind. Neither did Evangeline. Let them look away. Let them swell with their own pity, their own horror. Let them give thanks in the deep temples of their hearts that they were not leading their child, their only anchor in this world, to the abyss.

Cal and Evangeline couldn't care. They had become arrows shot at a target infinitely small the moment Winnie had died, and the shouts and cries and tears and rage of onlookers mattered little to them.

There was only air and movement.

"We came to pay our respects," Ordinal said, still facing away.

"And to support our colleagues," Nero said. "Our friends."

Oddry had begun looking back over the trees, maybe expecting that jet with the recovery team sent from Central to be hurtling toward them there in the sky.

"We're not sending her in there alone," Evangeline said.

"You're . . ." Ordinal said, staring at Evangeline without comprehension.

"Oh," Nero said, the sound guttural and pained. "No."

"You can't," one of the fencers on Ordinal's squad said, though not as a challenge. It was disbelief. Amazement.

"You're going for the Miracle?" Ordinal asked, stepping closer to them—stepping in front of them.

"Yes," Cal said.

"You know he became a fucking monster, right? You understand that?" Ordinal's voice was husky and broken. "I was a kid on a fencing squad when it happened—I met that arrogant bastard once, and I've seen what he became. I've been in there with that beast, and *it* is in there right now, waiting to cut you apart."

The night was quiet—this part of the world was still locked down, shut up safely and waiting out the remaining hours of the equinox. Roads empty, factories still, businesses shut down, and everyone watching the clock, waiting for midnight's relief.

So it was that the assembled fencers—a full two-thirds of the Midwest complement—heard the approach of vehicles from far off, engines raging into the quiet of the night.

"Who the hell is that?" Ordinal squinted off into the distance, chewing aggressively on the wad of nicotine gum in their mouth.

"Listen to me," Oddry said, turning around and facing the fencers. "Central knows what happened with Winnie, and they sent a team of fencers in to manage the situation."

"*Manage* the situation," Ordinal said, spitting the gum out onto the grass. "Better and better."

"Alerts coming in," Nineteen said, holding up the tablet, which was flashing with notifications.

"Us, too," the Stone Weaver said, showing her own screen.

"We don't have time for this shit," Nero said, stepping up beside Ordinal as, apparently, the newly deputized leader of Evangeline's squad. She turned to the parents. "You're going in there? Really?"

"Really," the father said.

"Trying to get past the Riparian and breaking through the barrier?" Nero asked. Every fencer dreamed of exploring the Harbor, and they grew up sharing those clandestine stories of the few who'd gone farther than others, taking tiny sips of those tales in secret, sharing them back and forth like the whispered words of lovers. "And then what?"

"Getting Winnie back," Evangeline said. "Or . . ."

But Nero understood. They all did.

Except.

"You mean to attack the Queen?" Incident said, stepping around Nero and putting herself in the path of Evangeline and Cal. She hadn't said anything during the entire exchange, and even now she wore a strange look, one neither Cal nor Evangeline could or cared to read. "You mean to wrest her power away and use it bring your child back?"

"If it comes to that."

Incident looked past Cal and Evangeline, to Oddry.

"You're allowing this?"

"I am," he said, looking back again, where the trees lining the long, serpentine road leading to the Harbor from Majestic were aglow with headlights. "And they need to move now."

"I can't—" Incident began, her face collapsing into resolution of some kind, but Cal had begun speaking under his breath already, the story of a none-prince from the dropped world of Bellona winding out in his thin voice, and he did not wait to find out what Incident wouldn't allow or couldn't abide. He caught her up in a web of his hollow grammarie, freezing the look of decision on her face and catching, too, the start of her own primacy emerging around her body, the black particles suddenly stilling. What the scientists at Central would have given to study those prime particles this way—simultaneously in motion and frozen. Speed without time's confusions.

"Oh, hell," Oddry said, throwing up his hands. "Let her out of there! She's not . . ."

Cal and Evangeline, though, were moving forward, stepping around Incident's suddenly still form, resolute as she was.

And the team from Central was growing close.

"This is insane," Nero said, putting a hand on Evangeline's shoulder—

not to stop her, but in comfort. "Are you sure—both of you—that you want to do this?"

The other fencers had shuffled closer, like the last people left at a farewell party, everyone wanting to get their last look and word.

"Yes," Evangeline said, and Cal nodded. What else was there to say?

"Do you want us to come with you?" Nero asked, and every fencer there, each one down to the interns, nodded their willingness to go, too, to be the support squad.

Knowing full well what had happened to Arthur Miracle's support squad and to Gogaji's and to every other squad of fencers sent in as support for whichever hotshot hundred-digit fencer wanted their run at the barrier—knowing it meant an almost-certain and grisly death even in the case of nigh-impossible success, they nodded and murmured their willingness to go.

Tears stung at Cal's eyes, and Evangeline pulled Nero into a rough hug before looking around at the other fencers.

"Thank you," she said. "All of you. But this is ours. Go back to your families. Your kids."

Ordinal wiped at their eyes as they grabbed first Cal and then Evangeline into quick hugs.

"We'll do what we can from this side," they said, giving Cal a push toward the gate and turning to face the oncoming team—the chase team—from Central. "We'll slow them down, though I'm guessing they picked a few heavies to oversee this."

"You need to go now," Oddry said, pushing his way into the group. "They'll be here any second." He was beginning to turn away and caught himself, eyes on the faerie standing silent and still just outside the scrum of fencers, her own eyes trained on the fence and what lay beyond it.

"And you, Chrysanthemum," Oddry said, voice so quiet and low, he might have been talking to himself. "You're the best part of my world."

"They're here," Nero said.

Three black sports cars emerged from the trees, rooster tails of gravel dust hanging behind them in the night air.

"Go!" Oddry said, stepping away and setting off toward the cars at a jog.

Cal's throat had gone raw and painful from the amount of crying he'd been doing, and the effort to maintain his hollow grammarie grew too much for him. As they ran for the gate, he released his hold on Incident and heard, amidst the other voices raised in alarm and defiance, her voice as she finished her sentence.

But that was part of the previous world, one they were leaving behind. Purpose ahead, simple and awful, and the mess and banality of life behind.

Now the air and the movement.

The curved metal and wood of the gate was a portal, and as the family ran beneath it, the sounds of the world died away, angry voices and the clang of iron against iron replaced suddenly and absolutely by the sound of the endless wind.

"The mourners mourn and depart," Winnie said, snaking a hand into Cal's and pulling him in the direction of the Harbor, the attraction of that place working on her. And though his every muscle recoiled at that cool, smooth touch, he did not pull away. "The dead one lives awhile in our heart, alas, and is dead again."

The mother, the father, and the child ran into the Harbor.

PART 3

Some Work of Noble Note

A History of Fences and Fae by AK Senga, PhD

Published in 2027 by University of Minnesota Majestic Press
Excerpt from Chapter 6: "The Queen's Children"

A note on the Queen's aspects, a term which refers to the orders within Sylvanism for its most dedicated members. Very early in the conception of Sylvanism, one of its founders—Shaun Powell—offered in a letter to the governing board the notion that the Faerie Queen was "possessed of nine unique aspects (Wrath, Forgiveness, Melancholy, Joy, Love, Jealousy, Watchfulness, Innocence, and Uncanniness), which might provide an organizing principle for our members seeking advanced enlightenment and engagement with the Queen's grace." Perhaps Powell and the board of directors were taking their cue from the Romans, who worshipped all the gods but were happy to give votive offerings and special attention to a single god when it was necessary or beneficial. After the incorporation of these aspects into their doctrine, the Sylvans encouraged their followers to worship their Queen holistically but to "become intimately acquainted" with a particular aspect of their deity.

Similar to confirmation in Catholicism or the levels of Operating Thetan in the Church of Scientology, the aspects of the Queen provide a kind of structure through which a member of Sylvanism can show their devotion. After a certain number of years or a sizable-enough gift, Sylvans can choose to enroll in one of the aspect-affiliated "Orders of the Queen." These are "The Orders of the":

1. Loving Queen
2. Jealous Queen
3. Watchful Queen
4. Wrathful Queen
5. Melancholy Queen

6. Joyful Queen
7. Innocent Queen
8. Uncanny Queen
9. Forgiving Queen

Each of these orders has its own rules, expectations, guidelines, imagery, titles, and aspirations for its members. Some of the orders are quite secretive. For instance, the Order of the Uncanny Queen, though we can say with certainty that it maintains a member list in the thousands, is almost completely unknown. Its representation of the Faerie Queen shows her standing knee-deep in a river crowded with dead fish. In one hand, she holds a book—thought to be *The Last Thylacine*—and in the other she holds what appear to be several small, dead humans. One large fang extends from the right side of her mouth, and her hair is on fire.

Members of this order—who call themselves the Foxglove Knights—refuse to say what these images represent or how their order is distinguished from the others.

Other orders, of course, are more forthcoming. The Order of the Melancholy Queen, for instance, is quite open about their structure and efforts. They follow a three-tier structure: the Little Lords, the Forlorn, and the Seekers of Melancholy.[6] With each move to a new tier, members of this order are required to give something up: financial, social, and finally physical. Seekers of the Melancholy are quite distinctive for the small scars that cover their entire bodies. This scarification is done over the course of several weeks, and though it is supposedly monitored by a team of doctors, it remains a highly divisive practice socially and scientifically. The scars, it is said, are meant to symbolize a Sylvan's "utter and

---

[6] For an insightful and thorough analysis of what he calls the "rampant, fantastical jargonism" of the Sylvans in their effort to be seen as both more reputable and more ancient, see Wenzel's 2012 deep-dive study of the Queen's aspects, *The Ninefold Path*.

complete offer of self to the Faerie Queen." The cutting ceremony is accompanied by recitations from *The Sylvan Scriptures* and displays of Sylvan imagery. Critics of the ritual have likened it to psychological and physical torture.

Seekers of the Melancholy are supposed, if we take their scripture and stated creeds seriously, to revel in sadness, both the spreading and discovery of it.

Chapter 19

The family raced through grasses dancing to the rhythm of a fae wind. Gone were the statue-still stands of strange plants.

Behind them, the sounds of fighting slowly faded, though the light show thrown by the clash of primacy-wielding fencers followed them for a long time.

More immediate was the chaos of the Wretched as they ran, some following a crow's-flight path straight through thick grasses and close-grown bushes; others leaping and racing in circles, colliding with one another and springing back up to surge forward again. Some wore smiles. Some wore solemnity. Some let their mouths hang open and others bared their slowly lengthening teeth.

And all laughed.

Like hyenas. Like blue jays chittering to one another. Like kookaburras aping human laughter. Like none of those, not truly, the fae laughed. They tittered. They chortled. They guffawed and sniggered and howled.

A cachinnation that pulled at the loose threads of Cal's mind. The leaping, laughing shapes in the darkness, the sky above filled with strange stars, and the sway, sway, sway of the grasses around—it was too much.

Cal felt himself spreading out, like a drop of paint fallen into a vat of water, pulled in every direction, all thin tendrils reaching for nothing as they expanded.

He needed to focus on the plan. The plan like a rope pulling them through the darkness. The plan like a story, easy to understand, simple in its near-hopelessness.

Find the Faerie Queen.

Make Her give Winnie back.

If She won't, kill Her and *take* Winnie back.

The impossibility of it, the scant slant of hope's light peeking along one edge, made it somehow easier to cling to. Worries and concerns buzzed around his consciousness like flies, grown stupid and lazy in autumn's chill, unable to reach him. Nothing else mattered but this, and if it was a chance so small that it barely existed, then he would give to that chance everything of himself, and the rest be damned.

It was a plan of grief. Of desperation. Of horror.

And there was relief in that, an easing of some tension that Cal had not, until that moment, realized he'd held. Doors were closing in his mind that would probably never open again, and lights were ticking off, and in his heart, wells of emotion were being capped off and forgotten, one by one.

In that simplicity, in that grief, in that ending, there was an emptiness that could never be confused for peace but, for now, was enough.

They ran, and Cal listened to the sounds of this place. The music of this cruel universe was laughter, high and percussive, and Cal swam in that manic melody, losing his grip on the plan for a moment as he fell and stretched and thinned and—

The iron in his hand, coiled around his knuckles, wrenched hard and sent a segmented bolt of pain up from his wrist to his elbow to his shoulder to his back and neck and all the way down his spine.

Winnie stood at an angle, leaning away at the end of the taut iron chain, her hands pulled into her tiny stomach, feet set apart. She'd left the path and stood chest-deep in the thin, swaying film of switchgrass.

Standing before her, strangely still amidst the chaos of the Harbor, two fae shocking in their progressed transformation. People only ever saw the beginnings of a person's fall into their fae form, the thickening of the hair, the bright growth of the eyes. Smooth skin and long, graceful fingers. Every movement executed with a dancer's perfection and art.

The public held an image of the fae, propped up by old children's stories and kept alive by the Sylvans, as perfect, ageless, graceful beings.

"*Imagine the life cycle of a butterfly,*" Oddry liked to say. "*We begin as caterpillars—humans—a little gross and weird but functional. And then we transform into this big, stupidly beautiful thing—what the public sees of the fae. But then imagine that what you and I usually see of butterflies is only the beginning of their transformation, and as they fly away, their wings keep getting larger and grow sharp edges and bones, and their feet split and split and develop cracked nails, and soon they have five eyes, ten, twenty, each one unblinking, and when their proboscis emerges, it's wet and thorned and riven up and down.*"

These fae standing before Winnie had moved past that initial phase of beauty, trading in grace for terror. One stood eight or nine feet tall, its features once beautiful but now stretched beyond beauty's lines, its chin going pointed and sharp, its forehead tall and spiked with bone spurs poking through its dark skin. The other had been stretched diagonally, its left arm trailing onto the ground and its right lifted high by a shoulder that curved up to a point above its head. A lopsided sneer cut along its face, and its left eye looked in danger of dribbling down its jaw and onto its chest.

The Sylvans worshipped the fae as emissary angels. The public imagined them as beautiful, chaotic, sometimes murderous gods or terrible, pristine monsters.

But they were none of that. They were something else.

Something stranger.

One of the fae held out a hand, split over and over with too many fingers and nails that themselves split and branched into tiny coraline trees. It uttered a noise low and untouched by the shape of language, but Winnie responded at once, her tiny body arcing against the pull of the chain, every muscle in her arms and legs straining to get to the fae.

They're calling to her, Cal realized. Jealousy stroked long fingers across his back and neck. *They think she's one of them.*

"No," Evangeline said, her voice rough and tear-choked. Her long seax in hand, Evangeline stepped forward and cut down in a blur of motion, bare slivers of moon and starlight describing the slice that separated the faerie's arm just below the elbow, neat and clean.

The creature threw itself back, its voice now high and keening. The other ambled forward, its lopsided eyes fixed on Evangeline, mouth agape in crosswise howl.

"Get back, Winnie," Cal said, pulling her back and sliding an arm around her, aware of but unwilling to fathom her shuddering, bucking motion and the way she struggled against him.

Evangeline might have diced the other faerie—its partner had retreated to a point where the pull of the Threshold Tree was again too much, and it raced off into the darkness, less an arm, the stump drizzling that same shadowy, smoky blood of the fae. Her sword flicked before her, carving out space in which she might do her sharp work, but Tennyson moved first.

Loosing one of his huge, cosmic growls, Tennyson sprang forward in the darkness, the swirling white patches of his coat releasing their own melancholy light. His teeth snapped and his huge paws, nail-tipped, exploded against the fae, which fell beneath his fury with barely a sound.

Tennyson was trained to apprehend and detain the fae, but like Cal and Evangeline, the thick weight of his training had slid away like it was nothing, less than nothing, when Winnie had died and not died. The weeks and months and years of repetitive instruction, of reward and punishment, of scheduled indoctrination evanesced against the reality of true, personal dread.

But if their new eyes and new minds saw Winnie not as the enemy, not as a wretched burden to be moved and released, then what did that mean for all the other fae? If Winnie was still in there, still recoverable, were the other fae the same? Was the creature below Tennyson another person waiting to be saved?

The dog's growl continued and grew, shaking the foundations of the world as the flashing of his fur became a light show at once entrancing and blinding, and when he was done, the faerie was a scattered mess of unrecognizable parts, strewn here and there, all spewing shadow.

These questions were shears threatening to cut the only strings holding Cal together, and he pushed them away even as the enormity of what they meant threatened to overwhelm him. He needed purpose now. Awful, impossible, clear purpose.

Let there be questions after if they were lucky enough to get an after.

"Good boy," Evangeline said, putting a hand on Tennyson's head as he rejoined them.

"We need to keep moving," Cal said, looking back over his shoulder at the gate in the distance. He grasped again for the plan. Get to the Queen. Kill the Queen. Save Winnie.

Evangeline nodded, and they went, stepping around or over the shadowy remains.

Around them, the fae laughter continued, as though the death of one of their own, and the dismemberment of another, was all part of the natural, hilarious order of things, all cause for joy and festival.

As they passed the book tree, the one with leaves grown into the shape of pages and covered in swirled, incomprehensible language, Winnie cried out and would have fallen if Cal hadn't caught her. The chains around her legs had grown tangled, not just teardrop links twisted against teardrop links but clogged and choked with grasses and plant matter, the iron tight and restrictive against her skin.

"I cannot rest from travel," Winnie said as Cal lifted her, gently as he could, up from the ground and into his arms. She turned to him and smiled, her bright eyes finding his. "I am become a name."

Cal squeezed his daughter against his chest, clenching his teeth against the revulsion, the grief stringing his muscles into tight ropes and roiling his stomach.

"It's okay, Winnie," he said. "It's okay. It's going to be okay."

"I know, Daddy," she said, the iron clinking heavily as she raised a hand, the fingers long, and placed it against his cheek. He looked back down to see her smile, the one he knew, Winnie's smile. The teeth were different, no longer those of a child, the shapes all slightly wrong, and then she scratched him, the nails of her long fingers furrowing the plane of his cheek.

The pain was sharp and bright and welcome, and though he pulled back with a hiss, he did not drop his daughter, and if anything, he pulled her closer, and when he found her eyes again, he mirrored her smile back.

"Okay?" Evangeline asked, eyes wide.

"Okay."

They ran, Cal clutching Winnie, Evangeline the tip of the spear ahead of them, her long blade out. When the chortling fae happened to get too near their winding progress, she menaced them away with threats or deliveries of violence. None of them took it personally—they were all being pulled inexorably toward the center of the Harbor, the Threshold Tree, and like marbles sent down a wide chute, all pulled on an inevitable path to the bottom but careening into one another along the way, slamming into the sides and articulating chaotic, innumerable routes from point Anywhere to point Bottom.

"I might have been an arborist," Winnie said in a near-whisper. "Planting thousands of trees and saving more from disease, destruction, death."

"What are you saying?" Cal looked down into Winnie's face, where familiar eyelashes lined familiar brown eyes. Eyes that studied clues in the morning before school. Eyes that stared down at crayon drawings of giants and turtles and flowers and stars after school. Eyes that widened on pizza-party nights, that crinkled in anticipation and delight when Cal stalked forward with tickle fingers at the ready. Eyes that closed in satisfied delight at the first bite of ice cream on a Saturday evening.

"I might have been," Winnie said again. "I might have."

"Leave it, Cal," Evangeline said, pushing ahead over a hill, the path below their feet cutting a shadowed line ahead. It might have been a half mile more to the Threshold Tree, or it might have been five.

The fields before them were aswarm with fae, myriad monstrous shapes in the darkness, hooting and hollering and leaving swaying wakes in the grasses they ran through.

"We redeth oft and findeth y-write," Winnie said, extending one hand out to the streaming fae. "And this clerkes wele it wite . . ."

She trailed off, eyes going wide, extended hand curling into a clawed mess.

"What is it?" Cal stumbled over a hairy root arcing up from the ground and barely held on to Winnie and his balance. His foot came down hard in a thin puddle.

"We need to keep moving," Evangeline said from ahead, turning and looking back. Her face was wet with tears, and her mouth hung open in a silent cry of pain. Her lower teeth were dim and shadowed in the darkness of her gaping mouth, and Cal had the sudden horrifying realization that she was far away from him. There was the plan, which might not work but also *might* work, and they had to cling to it. Everything else was ocean and wave and swell and undertow and storm and darkness and churn and rip and this was their rope. This was all they had, but there was no "they" anymore. No "we." No "us." They had splintered.

Both of them looking at Winnie, both of them parents, both of them loving her, and yet there was a gulf between Cal and Evangeline. He knew it. He saw it. What was she thinking? What was she feeling? When she looked at Winnie, cradled in his arms, her features her own and yet not, her body like a costume she wore over her own—what did Evangeline see? A monster? Their daughter, too far gone? A faerie? Or did she see the ghost of a daughter that Cal didn't know, a person only Evangeline had ever seen, had ever known, had ever loved. Was she mourning her own daughter just as he was mourning his?

Ahead, the fae shrieked and went still, their eyes rising first to the stars before turning to fix on Cal, Evangeline, and Winnie. Hundreds, maybe thousands of them, all turning lamplight eyes on the fencers and their child.

Cal took out a sword, his gladius. He moved to set Winnie down, but she clutched at him, bringing her face close to his.

"Layes that ben in harping," she said, her voice going soft and fearful. "Ben y-founde of ferli thing." She bucked and seized in Cal's arms, and he almost dropped her. A fleeting thought ran through his mind: *I remember when you were born, and I could hold you in the crook of one arm for hours. And did. When you snuggled there like you were born for it, or I was.*

"Is it the chase team?" Evangeline asked, looking around. "Did they break through our people?"

"The fae don't care about fencers so close to the Threshold Tree," Cal said. That poem Winnie was reciting caught at his memory. The lilt and rhythm of Middle English, the slide of the consonants against the vowels; all of it was a muddled shape in the darkness of his mind.

All around them, the fae had turned into watchful statues, stone-still limbs and chests and fingers and mouths. Only eyes, lit by the moon's hazy Harbor light, showed any sign of activity and life.

When she spoke, Winnie's voice had dropped to a whisper.

"Sum bethe of wer," she said, reaching out and pressing the palms of her hands against Cal's face, stretching the skin of his cheeks back. "And *sum of wo.*"

Rain splattered against them, gentle and easy, accompanied by the chorus's applause as raindrops came down around them.

"Sir Orfeo," Cal said, meeting Winnie's eyes. One of the poems the Faerie Queen had recited to Grothendieck at the beginning of it all.

Winnie nodded, her recitation coming fast now.

"And sum of joie and mirthe also, and sum of trecherie and of gile."

"It's here, Cal," Evangeline said, and Cal looked around Winnie to see the Riparian standing beside a tree nearby, one hand buried into the flesh of the wood, sunk wrist-deep and held there.

"He's here," Cal said. Let it be a him now. Hope for it.

Evangeline cut wild eyes at Cal, but she did not correct him.

The plan, like a thread noded by knots, tore apart before Cal's eyes, cut by those scissors held in the Riparian's free hand. How had they forgotten about this?

Winnie dropped from Cal's arms and skittered behind his legs, peering around him at the Riparian like a frightened child. Like the frightened child she still was.

A low moan escaped from Cal's lips, barely audible over the rain's susurration.

Louder was Tennyson's growl, which grew and doubled and rebounded upon itself, as though a team of tattooed, angry, violent bikers were revving their rigs in a mounting display of power and potential.

Tennyson took a few steps forward and placed himself between Cal and Winnie and the Riparian.

And did Winnie reach out a hand toward Tennyson's fur? Did she sink her fingers in deep to the monochrome swirl of his fur like she used to?

Cal opened his hand, letting the lengths of teardrop-shaped chain fall to the ground in a serpentine hiss.

"Tennyson, guard," Evangeline said, her voice taking on the weight of authority, and his growl shifted in pitch slightly in acknowledgment.

So close, the Riparian was a horror dressed in moonlight, the sooty rain obscuring its face aglow with pale illumination, the long lines of its arms and legs set off from the darkness of the Harbor by the moon's soft radiance. Though Cal could not see its eyes, he could feel its attention on them, its alien curiosity.

In its hand, those scissors, the blades as long as Evangeline's sword, opened and closed, metal grating against metal. Open. Closed. Open.

"Keep your earplugs in," Evangeline said.

They had fallen out at some point—in the car? Sometime in the house? Cal couldn't remember, but he fumbled through the pockets of his jacket until he found another pair.

"Do not fight it," Evangeline said, and Cal could hear one of their old trainers in her voice, an old iron woman, a fencer two years retired, named Augury. "Do not engage."

"If you see it, run," Cal said, joining his voice to his wife's and feeling, for a moment, that perhaps they weren't so far apart after all. "If it sees you, run."

The Riparian stepped back from the tree, its hand emerging from inside the trunk and clutching a fistful of splinters, which it tossed into the air like confetti.

"I'm not waiting anymore," Evangeline said, and in a motion as fluid and beautiful as any dancer in perfect tune to the music around her, Evangeline pulled those destructive stars from the air around herself and flung them at the Riparian.

Cal hunched against the cantillation, but the blast of music did not come. No explosion of sound and energy and force and *being* emerged when the stars flared and died against the Riparian's skin. A tiny haunting melody, what a child might sing to herself under her breath, floated out, but it was nearly impossible to hear with the earplugs in.

Tiny craters revealed themselves on the Riparian's skin where the stars had landed, but the creature known once as Arthur Miracle seemed unbothered.

"Swords it is," Evangeline said, and Cal followed her lead.

Together, the mother and father moved forward, and their adversary, once the greatest fencer the world had ever seen, moved against them.

Cal let the frenetic nonsense of his hollow grammarie fall from lips wet with faerie rain and flashed the two swords before him.

"There is a child, torn-grown and thither-run, and material, ductile and endless, springing soundlessly from a world of time's pyramids, where stairs carved in pearlescent pulchritude pulse and waver, a cool kindness from night hawk wings that . . ."

The Riparian moved like a kite whipsawing in the wind, unpredictable and chaotic, herk-jerking through the darkness toward them. Its great shears sounded like a whip as they opened and closed.

Around the fight, fae like deer, all eyes and stillness, watched.

Cal let his eyes go as unfocused as his speech as he tracked the Riparian, intensely aware of Evangeline moving forward on his right. He sent his primacy forward, releasing the buildup of tension and time, imagining the force like a net. There would be no stopping the Riparian in its tracks; he knew that much. But if he could slow it down, cause it to stumble, catch an arm or a leg in some of his hollow grammarie, then perhaps Evangeline could do her violent work.

The nets of his sludgy grammarie slithered through the darkness, missing the Riparian, whose movements were too chaotic to predict until there—the creature slammed to the left, almost as if it were leaping *into* the path of Cal's attack instead of dodging it, and the grammarie slapped against its arm, halting its movement.

Cal felt the catch in his chest, where it slammed into his sternum and drove the air from his lungs. He screamed and fell to the ground, one knee driving hard into a pool of fetid water. Broken ribs, a shattered breastbone, punctured lungs, his internal organs ripped and torn by the bone fragments sent exploding out by the force of his primacy being used on something too large and too powerful—Cal was sure his chest and abdomen were totaled, but he gasped in a heaving lungful of air and felt the pain recede. Not gone, but not as bad as he'd thought.

The Riparian was not so lucky. It lunged forward, ripping across twenty, thirty, forty feet of space with frightening speed, but it left its arm behind, the sound of its tearing a great, wet rip. It shifted its attention for a moment—Cal felt that focus slide away from him—and turned back to see his own elbow, forearm, and clawed hand hanging in space, the last tendrils of Cal's power holding it up for a second before giving in and letting the slab of muscle and meat and hair and bone drop with a thick onto the wet ground.

A gush of shadow from the stump of the Riparian's right arm swung in a wide arc as the creature turned back to Cal and Evangeline. It did not scream. It did not roar. It did not shout in pain or anger or challenge.

With one of its arms already cooling on the grass behind it, the Riparian advanced, and the only sound was the continued *snnnnit, snnnnit, snnnnit* of its shears.

It devoured the distance between itself and the fencers, and Cal had to throw himself backward to avoid the Riparian's lunge, those shears snipping together in the space where Cal's neck had been.

Tennyson let loose a great bark, like thunder on an open plain, and the Riparian turned toward the dog. Next to an ordinary person, Tennyson was a bear of a dog, large enough to impress and frighten.

Before the Riparian, he was a toy. And behind him, her eyes lifted up in wonder, was Winnie, and when she smiled, and when she laughed, and when she raised iron-banded hands up, and when she moved to step around Tennyson—

"Arthur," Evangeline shouted, making her own lunge forward, any attempt at defense and care gone. The Riparian made another of those odd lunges and put itself directly in front of Evangeline. She drew a great line across the creature's abdomen with her blade, her battle shout turning to a scream of agony that chilled Cal to hear. Her prime tattoos swayed along her exposed skin as she leapt back, dodging away from the Riparian's swipe.

He couldn't let her fight alone.

"Arthur Miracle!" Cal screamed and threw himself up and at the Riparian, whose attention swung to him.

His training, the hours of swinging his swords and practicing cuts and strikes and parries, moved Cal's muscles on a level his conscious mind had long since abandoned, and when he sprang forward, it was that training that flung up one arm to deflect the swinging shears, the basket-handled butterfly sword rising to catch the cut of the shears.

The collision echoed along Cal's bones, immediately numbing his fingers, hand, wrist, and arm up to his shoulder. Worse was the damage to his sword, which shattered into bright iron shards and delicate, broken curls of steel. Blood, too, spattered the air, and even as he struck a blow with his gladius on the Riparian's shoulder, Cal saw but did not feel the chicken-scratch cuts on his palm, fingers, and wrist, their clean lines already disappearing beneath the welling blood.

Thrown back again and struggling again to his feet, Cal realized the Riparian fought without sound. No beastly grunts or demonic screams. No wild fae laughter or humanoid shouts. It did not cry out in pain nor did it bellow a challenge to its enemies.

Would they become this way? The plan, scattered now but still recoverable, followed Arthur Miracle's path, and if whatever turned him into *this* horror happened to them, would Cal and Evangeline spend the rest of time haunting these Harbors, transformed into huge, silent creatures that acted and moved and attacked and ran without even the slightest trace of logic or pattern in their actions?

To Cal, it didn't sound like such a bad existence. In a world without his daughter, the endless silence would be a relief.

Evangeline slashed and moved, slashed and moved, flinging out an empty hand to counterbalance the relentless, reckless swipe of her sword, but the surprising fury of their attack on the Riparian had lost its bite, and now the creature, one-armed as it was, stepped close to Evangeline, its height making it a giant so close, and caught the cut of her sword in the jaws of its shears. A wrench of one huge hand, and Evangeline's blade went tumbling off into the tall grasses.

Still, the fae in the Harbor watched, gone as silent as their profane guard dog.

Snnnit, snnnnit, snnnit went the shears as the Riparian whipsawed left, paused, and then surged forward, kicking Evangeline hard in the side and toppling her over and down the hill.

"Evangeline!" Cal cried before letting his tongue slurry out yet more of that nonsense, flinging forth those webs of thickened time again. The Riparian, as though it could see the invisible webbing of Cal's primacy, slid left and bounded back, moving faster than anything so large should have been able, even leaping high into the air at one point.

Cal felt his attempts growing sluggish and weak, and when he spoke again, it was not nonsense that emerged, but a story. Shaped and given purpose. Given meaning.

"Once, it all was good. Not perfect, but good. A child was born and life became a tale to be lived and not told, and dreams gained purpose and hope grew unbearably light and all was good. Even the bad was good. Even the silence sang and even the fear was golden and when loss came it was like scooping a handful of water from the endless ocean."

Cal threw a web of power, slinging it forward and watching it hit and catch on the Riparian's shoulder, but whatever potency he'd had was used up. The Riparian shrugged off the attempt and bounded forward again, feinting this way and that. It looked ready to close on Cal but it stumbled again, and he thought it might fall over, so precarious was its balance, but in an instant the Riparian righted itself, and then it was in front of Cal—*above* him, hanging in the air over him, and though he heard Evangeline shout for him, and Winnie, too, her voice rising with an inflection he didn't understand, Cal could do nothing but look up at his doom.

The chaotic swirl of shadow and darkness around the Riparian's face stilled and dispersed, and there he was, Arthur Miracle, features as they were in life. A weak chin lined with an asymmetrical scar. A long, thin nose. Cheeks rough with beard growth, dark as the mop of hair on his head.

But the eyes.

Those are my eyes, Cal thought, and impossible as it was, he knew it was true. He'd looked at those eyes in the mirror every morning, every day when washing his hands or brushing his teeth, shaving or flossing. They were wide and staring and sad. *He has my eyes.*

Blink.

He was looking at Evangeline's eyes now, beautiful brown and empty of the emotion he was used to seeing. The playfulness. The joy. The frustration. The way she watched the world around her with a calm, easy peace. All gone as those eyes peered at and into him.

Blink.

Winnie, frightened and then joyous and then angry and then sleepy and then curious and then suspicious and then

Blink.

His father, bloodshot and half-closed.

Blink.

His mother, eyes Cal would have sworn to have forgotten years and years past, weeping.

Blink.

Oddry, haunted and hungry.

Blink.

Blink.

Blink.

When the shears sliced into him, Cal was lost in memory's museum, and the pain came from far, far away.

Chapter 20

The Riparian was going to kill Cal, and Evangeline couldn't stop it.

Her primacy, like an ugly, ravenous beast, not yet sated by the events of the equinox and the cantillations of fae and object alike, demanded more, and when Winnie reached for the Riparian, when Evangeline's daughter reached for that monster in the same way she would reach for her Evangeline herself, eyes up and hands open and all childlike trust—something twisted in Evangeline's gut, and she wanted to kill the Riparian, to feel its flesh in her hands as she pulled muscle from bone and tore skin like paper. She wanted it to die, and she wanted it—*him*—to know it was her who had done it.

The Riparian fought in silence, and she wanted to hear his song.

She moved forward, shouting his name, and was rewarded with a furrow running along the creature's abdomen, but it was not enough, and when Cal screamed Arthur's name, she barely heard him, so complete, so overwhelming was her rage. Winnie was safe with Tennyson, and this was her purpose now. Destroy. Kill. Ruin.

End.

She used the long seax as a butcher might use a cleaver, hacking and swinging from the shoulder, missing more than she struck, but the true attack was in the emptiness of her other hand.

"Arthur," she said, as she pulled a handful of stars from the air, the primacy inside her howling with pleasure. A handful of destruction, but not yet enough.

"Arthur Meyer," she said, feeling a frisson of fear as she scooped more and brought her blade down on flesh and bone.

Not yet enough.

"Art," she said, the words still under her breath, so quiet she could hear them only in her head. She scooped more, and again, and again, saying the name—his true name—over and over, letting the words accompany the song of her violence.

The flash of the Riparian's shears in the almost-dark of the night put Evangeline on the back foot, and when she sliced again, it was those selfsame shears catching her blade instead of skin and tissue. The creature wrenched her sword from her hand, and she watched it go, stunned into stillness until she was following it, the impact of the Riparian's kick still shaking her body.

The hill twisted and roiled around her as she tumbled, striking her hip and her neck and her head and her arm, which sang with a pain so bright, so sharp, that she thought she might disappear into it entirely.

But Winnie needed her, and when Evangeline landed at the bottom of the hill and came to a rest, she did not let the waves of pain from her arm—broken, severely—carry her under. Teeth clenched and lungs laboring and arm screaming, Evangeline overcame a second, two, five. She rose, aware on some distant level that Cal was screaming her name before his voice cut out.

Silence.

The hill before her swam in and out of focus for a moment, and when it finally collapsed into something solid again, so too did the situation atop it.

Cal, arms slack at his side, face upturned, was a mirror image of what Winnie had looked like. Childlike. Innocent. Lost.

He stared up, eyes wide and mouth hanging slightly open, into the revealed face of the Riparian.

That monster was going to take Cal.

"No!"

Her arm, the one kicked by the Riparian, hung sluggish at her side, but the other was still in her power, and Evangeline felt a thrill of shock when she realized the densely packed stars still burned and shone in the seams of her tightly clutched fist. More than she'd ever thrown, more than she'd ever taken, and waiting now to be used.

Above, Cal let out a soft cry.

Evangeline took the hill, and when she reached its peak, she didn't stop running, instead transferring her speed to a leap, and did Winnie look up at her mother in the air as she'd once done, not as a fae, not as a child on the path to becoming a monster but as a child on the path to becoming more human?

Perhaps she did, and a flush of something like hope overtook Evangeline as she drove her fist, burning now and glowing like a full moon hung too low, into that long gash she'd laced down the Riparian's abdomen.

Her knuckles parted flesh still coughing smoke before breaking on something hard and unyielding. Evangeline felt her fingers go slack, felt the bright power of the stars disperse, and then all was sound.

Not music. Not melody.

What emerged was chaos, atonal and discordant. And light, too. Flashes of green and grey, the sickly blue of day's defeat and the washed-out brown of leaves dried and curled in a gutter.

Memories, not her own, rose and fell in Evangeline's mind as these sounds and lights struck her, and she knew as Arthur Miracle's short life and long death took her, that Cal was seeing this, too, and Winnie as well, and somehow the thought brought her peace. There they were together.

They saw a young boy—Art—picked on in school.

They saw Art push back, a bloody nose his punishment and sore knuckles his reward.

Cal laughed as they watched Art's first dance at prom, unsure where to put his hands and feet, smiling anxiously at the girl he didn't really want to take.

And later, Evangeline felt Cal sigh as they watched Art climbing a tree full of summer's vibrant green to meet a boy named Leo.

Winnie, still herself—*still!* Evangeline thought with wonder and hope—and yet not herself, shouted in fear when Art fell down at work and rose with a strange feeling on his chest. In the bathroom, he lifted his shirt to find a single number tattooed there. 2. The smallest prime. The only even prime.

They watched Art become Arthur Miracle. He grew strong under that early Bureau's training regimen, which imagined fencers as military special forces, all muscle and grit and pent-up violence. He learned to use his prime without so much destruction and death, and Evangeline almost felt sadness as she watched him write those letters of condolence to the people killed, mangled, and disappeared during his practice.

Arthur, no longer Art, wore fame for the first time and found it fit nicely. He traveled. He grew rich. He slept with anyone he wanted, men and women both, never for more than a night, and never with anything resembling love.

They watched as he destroyed fae each equinox and looked with increasing challenge at the Threshold Tree. They watched as he assembled his support team. They watched as he swaggered into the Harbor for the last time and knew, as if these were their own memories, that deep down he felt fear.

And when he tore the tree asunder with his power, Cal, Evangeline, and Winnie followed as he walked through.

Beyond is the hill, came a voice in their minds. Arthur's voice. Art's voice. *And on the hill is the castle which holds nothing. The Queen lives there, and she is a jealous lady. Before the entrance to her castle is a great courtyard. There, upon the stones, would-be fae arrive to purge themselves of their humanity. When I stepped through the Tree and climbed the hill, I found the courtyard full of these disgusting beings.*

And seated above them on her throne is the Faerie Queen.

To her I brought my arrogance and weakness, and she was displeased. I had nothing to offer but destruction, and so destruction is what she gave me in return.

I took my place in the courtyard. I stood upon a broken stone and became clean. Simple. Unending.

The Queen gave unto me a new form, a new life, and a new purpose.

Seek her.

She is waiting for you.

The noise of the Riparian's—of Arthur's—story died away, and Evangeline, who hadn't realized she'd been closing her eyes, opened them to find the Harbor engulfed in slowly dispersing smoke, all that remained of the Riparian.

Or maybe not.

As the world became clear again around her, Evangeline saw first Winnie and then Cal and then Tennyson, all looking around as she must have been, confused and uncertain.

And between them, still looming over Cal, was a man the world had not seen since 1999.

"Arthur Miracle," Evangeline said.

He turned, and Evangeline recoiled at what she saw.

The skin of his face was a mess of scars laid over and across one another. His neck, too, was covered in the raised, painful-looking wounds, and as more of him came into view—he was not clothed—Evangeline could see the rest of his skin bore those same badly healed cuts, a palimpsest of puckered skin.

Twos. They were all twos. His prime in life cut into him over and over and over again.

And amidst those furrows and troughs and piles of raised flesh, there on his chest, was his prime, disfigured as his face but visible.

Cal held a hand to his side, where the shears had caught him, but he looked steady enough. Those shears were supposed to separate a person from themselves, body broken from mind, vessel from self.

But it was Cal, still whole.

Arthur looked at Evangeline for a long time and then whispered,

"Nothing." He placed a hand on his chest, the skin of the fingers, knuckles, and hand similarly scarred.

"You're nothing?"

He shook his head.

"No." He put a hand on his chest again. "Nothing."

"You're . . ." Cal began, his voice heavy with pain.

"No!" When he spoke this time, Arthur's scars glowed with an eerie light, and the fae all around the Harbor flinched backward, their first movement in some time.

Winnie, too, flinched back.

"You are." He gestured toward Cal, Evangeline. "Even she still is." He pointed toward Winnie.

He again placed his hand on his chest.

"I am *not*."

He began walking, not toward the Threshold Tree but toward the Gate in the distance, and when he moved, so too did the fae, like dogs held at bay until finally, finally they could run.

And they did, all mad leaps and wild laughter, cutting through the grass and leaping over hills again toward the Threshold Tree as though nothing had happened.

Tennyson barked once as Winnie tried to go with them, the thick *clink* and *clack* of her iron giving away her attempt, and though her arm still hung limp and painful at her side, Evangeline stepped close to her daughter and wrapped her in a hug, shivering at the horror and joy of it.

"We're going to save you," she said into Winnie's hair, which had grown thick and waxy. She was changing, and they didn't have much time. "Cal, are you okay to walk?"

"Yes," he said. "I'm okay."

"Are you sure?" Everything in Evangeline urged her to move. Already Winnie's features were changing, like a distorting mirror pulling Evangeline's little girl into curious shapes, uncanny and frightening.

Cal looked uneasy. If the shears had gotten him, he'd be dead, worse than dead. She'd seen fencers separated from their souls by the Riparian's shears. They looked and acted a lot like Arthur Miracle had, though with more injuries and making even less sense.

It couldn't have been the Riparian's stare, either. That look undid people, separating their bodies into constituent parts, like carefully organized toys. Organs over here. Bones there. Tissue in a pile that way. Blood in this puddle.

But hadn't she seen him staring up into the Riparian's unobscured face? Maybe it had been the pain, or maybe the confusion of the moment, or maybe—

"He had my eyes," Cal said, staring at Arthur's retreating form. "And then he had your eyes, both of yours, and everyone I've ever known. I could hear their voices in my heads. Yours, too. And yours, Winnie. And I couldn't move. I couldn't do anything."

"What happened to you, Cal?" Evangeline stepped toward him, but he held up a hand.

"*Nothing*. That's the thing. When I met his eyes, I felt suddenly like I was a big ball of thread, knotted up and tangled around, and it—he—the Riparian, I mean, was rooting around to find the part of me he could cut to make everything come undone. When he clipped me with those shears—"

"He what?"

"It's okay, Evangeline," Cal said, and when he smiled, it was a ghastly thing. "His power, his and the shears, they're the same—to render something into nothing. That's what I'm trying to say. He cut me with those shears—not my body but in here." Cal clapped a hand to his chest, and Evangeline saw Arthur Miracle doing the same thing only a few moments before, the same motion, the same message. "He wanted to cut away all the lives that I might lead, all the possible futures I might have had, but that already happened."

He turned to Winnie, who was watching him with curious attention.

"I just have one future now, and so his power was nothing for me. He wanted to hollow me out, but . . . I'm already empty."

Evangeline felt the shadow of who she used to be pushing her to go to Cal, to hug him, to take his hand, to whisper something to him.

But she too had been hollowed out. Made clean and purposeful. There was a thread inside her still, the same inside Cal, but only one, unbreakable, and it pulled them both forward. Perhaps there was a tangle of maybes ahead of them, a mess of possible futures, but for now, there existed only this. The Tree. The Queen. Winnie.

"His shears didn't even cut me," Cal said, lifting his shirt to show his side. A black line was burned into his skin there, wrapping around from his navel to his spine, but the skin remained unbroken. Tennyson nosed forward to smell at it. "It's like I'd already lost the only thing he could use to hurt me."

He looked again at Winnie, and then shook his head.

"Let's go. If the chase team broke through our people, they'll be coming along soon."

The fae, set into motion once again, raced off into the darkness toward the Threshold Tree. Cal, Evangeline, Winnie, and Tennyson became just four more bodies pulled along in the current.

As they walked, the parents took turns carrying Winnie, saying little as they passed her back and forth. Even Tennyson took a turn, whimpering only a little as Winnie climbed onto his back. His coat went pure white as she sat atop him, the black retreating to his paws and snout.

The sun broke along the horizon as they crested the hill and followed winding paths toward the Tree. The fae streaming around them began to thin out, and they also didn't laugh so much. Instead, they spoke, and though most were too far away to hear clearly or moving too quickly by them to make out, the soft chatter of their words chilled Evangeline.

"I might have planted a small garden in my backyard as an older woman," Winnie said as they walked. "In it, potatoes. Peppers and tomatoes. Raspberries! Squash and pumpkins. A stand of corn. I might have tried and failed to plant carrots, and when I spoke to my neighbors of this, we could have talked about the clay-like soil. Planting cycles. Starting from seed."

"What are you saying, dear?" Evangeline asked, putting a hand on Winnie's hair and sliding it down to the back of her neck. She rode easily on Tennyson. A tiny knight on her mighty steed.

A prisoner moved against her will.

"I might have," she said, turning to her mother. "I might have risen with dirt under my fingernails and the smell of soil in my nose."

"Yes" was all Evangeline could say.

"We'll plant that garden together," Cal said, his eyes ahead, his cheeks wet.

"*No!*" Winnie said, her voice sharp and hard. Tennyson jerked from the sudden twisting pull of her hands in his fur, but he did not throw her off, and he did not alter his path forward. "I *might* have. I *may* have not."

"Okay, sweets. Okay," Cal said, still not looking.

A few steps later: "I might have lived on the coast in a small house with a person who loved me. We might have gone for walks together, holding hands, and I might have looked out over the ocean and thought many things. I might have felt sand in between my toes."

And then: "I might have worked as a dishwasher. Long hours. My hands might have grown wrinkled and arthritic from it. I might have seen doctors and applied salves and struggled my whole life with it."

And later: "I might have collected stamps. A philatelist!" She giggled in delight at this, and Cal, those haunted, dead eyes turning toward her, giggled too. A dreadful sound. "I might have put together whole books of my stamps, showing them off to my parents, my friends, my spouse, my children. I might have been so proud."

Winnie grew more talkative as they approached the Tree, refusing to stop with her maybes and might-bes.

Every word from her anchor and lift at the same time. It was rain hitting already-soaked clothes. It was the song of the wind on a lazy afternoon. When she said "I might," Evangeline's sadness stirred like a great beast inside, poked and prodded before settling down for a long winter. When she said "I could have been," Evangeline wanted to die and felt like she could live forever. And somehow, those two feelings were the same, not pulling in opposite directions but in one. Forward. On to the Tree.

"Please stop," Cal said at one point as Winnie described how she might have been an English teacher.

"Just let her talk," Evangeline said. Her arm, still slack by her side, had begun to send sharp, painful signals up into her shoulder, where she was sure something was badly broken. Her few attempts to move it had almost blinded her with pain, but it was the feeling of something grinding in there that had been hardest to stomach.

"I can't . . ." Cal said, looking over at her, his eyes sunken and watery in dawn's orange and red glow.

"It's not hurting anything," she said.

"It's killing me." He said this without emotion or inflection of any kind. As though he were already dead. The Cal who would squirm away from moments of uncertainty or tension with easy, pat phrases—"We'll just see" or "Who knows?" or "What a world, huh?"—was gone.

Good.

"I don't know how many more words I'll ever get to hear from her," Evangeline said.

Cal said nothing, and Winnie began again.

"I might have played piano." She giggled. "Badly."

The Threshold Tree rose into the clouds.

The ground around it was no longer the soft grass and dirt of the paths and fields. Their boots crunched against what Evangeline first took to be a twenty- or thirty-foot-wide band of stones.

"They're shells," Cal said, squinting down at them.

And so they were. Some were coin-sized and might have housed tiny snails, while others were the shells of great turtles and tortoises. And others were bigger yet, and odd, home to no animal or creature Evangeline had ever seen.

And nearby, rising like burial mounds from the flattened mess, were shells large as cars, large as small homes.

Though the Harbors had been open for fewer than fifty years, the shells were bleached a bright, uncompromising white and covered in a tiny script, inked in a deep black that had not faded and looked—

"It's fresh." Cal held up three fingers, the pads shiny with black ink smudged from a triangular shell big enough that Evangeline might have crawled into it and had room to spare.

"Leave it," Evangeline said, training her eyes on the great Tree before them.

It was tall—taller than any tree she'd ever seen, and its many boughs wove together in an intricate braid, impossible to follow and impossible to sort out. It was said Arthur Miracle, when he went through to that castle on the hill, used his power to unknot the Threshold Tree, pulling out the braids and untangling the branches and boughs with brutal, total control, as he did everything in those days.

Evangeline wasn't going to bother with any of that.

She was going to rip a gateway out of the Tree. And if it hung open forever, a gaping wound between Faerie and the Harbor and the world beyond, then so much the better. She didn't care. The single remaining thread of her life ran through those bone-white boughs.

"I'm ready," Cal said, gripping his sword in one hand and Winnie's chain in the other. "We're ready."

Tennyson had begun to growl, the sound liquid and violent, and Evangeline realized that it was the *only* sound she could hear now.

"They're gone," she said, looking around at the tree-dotted fields of the Harbor.

Empty of fae.

"The equinox ended hours ago," Cal said, following her glance. "We're probably the last ones."

Somehow, the thought gave Evangeline a chill of fear.

She swung her arm forward, scooping stars from the air, but her motion was stopped by Winnie, who leaped forward and slung her chains along Evangeline's wrist, pulling down viciously.

The stars tumbled from her hand and burst against the shells at her feet, releasing dry, dusty melodies that dispersed almost immediately.

"Treachery," Winnie said, her eyes—the colors shifting and changing now, blue to purple to green to grey to brown to maroon to—holding Evangeline's.

"What is this?" Cal said, but he was not talking to Evangeline or Winnie. He was looking back toward the Harbor, toward the Gate now many miles distant.

At the people shambling up the pathway toward them.

Nero, walking with a limp and bleeding badly from her shoulder.

Ordinal, seemingly whole and visibly unhurt but clutching at their stomach.

And Incident, sporting two shining black eyes and a badly cut lip.

"No," Cal said, stepping forward and holding up his sword. "Not her."

Treachery, Winnie had said, and Evangeline found herself staring down into those shifting eyes and wondering who was holding the knife.

"Cal, just listen," Nero said, holding up a hand, the bandages there turned into bloody rags. She must have lost a finger. Maybe a few.

"She's a Sylvan," Cal said, pointing his sword at Incident, who stopped, her eyes moving between Cal, the sword, and the Tree behind him.

"She is," Ordinal said, taking a position beside Incident. The three of them stood, half on the path and half obscured by chest-height grasses, and outside of Ordinal holding a long iron rod—their equinox weapon of choice—they were unarmed. "But she's on our side."

"We're going through," Evangeline said. "Right now, we're going through."

"You can't!" Incident said, her voice a ragged thing. The group sent by Central must have done some serious damage. Evangeline felt concern and worry like phantoms inside her mind. Had fencers been hurt worse than this? Killed? If these three had followed them, where were the others? And what had happened to the chase team?

"Evangeline can get us through," Cal said, letting the point of his sword drop. He felt as she did, Evangeline was sure. All of this was unnecessary.

The concerns of a different world.

The concerns of the people they used to be.

Tennyson's growl revved up, growing throaty and rougher. He stepped in front of Winnie.

"No," Nero said, ambling forward with hisses of pain. "Listen to me. Just listen. We thought those Central people were here to just manage the disaster. But they were in on it. They orchestrated this whole thing."

Tennyson barked once.

"What are you saying?" Cal stepped forward, his sword forgotten now.

"Central, and the mathematicians, and the fucking Sylvans made all of *this*," Nero said, gesturing around them at the Harbor and then at Cal, Evangeline, Winnie, and Tennyson specifically, "happen. All of it. *This* was part of their plan. *This* is what Operation Harpoon is."

"What is?" Evangeline asked.

"You." Incident spoke this time. "You both, you *three*, are Operation Harpoon."

"What are you saying?"

"I've been gathering intelligence inside the House of Always Giving for years," Incident said. "My job was to play a sycophant. I went farther than anyone else. I played my part perfectly." She touched at the crescent scars on her neck, her jaw. "Oddry put me up to it. He knew they'd been planning something. And he was right."

"You were always a shit fencer," Cal said, "but what you're telling us now is that you were a shit double agent, too? Your job was to stop *this* from happening?"

"They've been wary of me for the last few months," Incident said, and gone was her usual drama, her usual over-the-top affectation. "Something had spooked them. But our visit to the House last week blew my cover totally. They started feeding me bad information. The mathematicians did too. I was an agent in the Sylvan ranks, but they have Sylvans among *the mathematicians*. Marla is one. *Hanka*, the *head* mathematician is a Sylvan! They knew I was a leaky line, and so they—"

"I don't care about any of this," Evangeline said, and Cal nodded beside her. "The only chance for me to have a daughter anymore is beyond that Tree. If we survive, and if she does, then I'll come out and kill you myself—you and everyone else who orchestrated this or let it happen."

"That's what we're here to say," Ordinal said, their voice raspier than usual. That was not the gravel of a lifelong smoker. Evangeline squinted, and yes, there were the marks around their throat. Someone or something had been choking them. "Their plan wasn't just to kill Winnie. It was to get you here. To this point. So you'd open up the Tree for them. That's why they sent the team. That's why they made all of this happen."

"Sum of trecherie and of gile," Winnie said, and Evangeline was jolted by the shape of her daughter's face, which had begun to stretch, her chin arrowing down into a point. The iron had slowed the process, but this was inevitable without some intercession. They didn't have much time.

"It doesn't matter what they want. We're going through there to get Winnie back." Cal jutted his chin forward, defiant. It was the look he had when he decided he'd found the hill he would die on, a phrase that caught and snagged in Evangeline's mind, given their situation.

"That *is* what they want," Nero said, hissing the words through her pain. "That primed-up walkie-talkie you all brought in was their final test for Operation Harpoon. Now that they can find and capture live primes, they can send whatever they want in here. Do you know who headed up the chase crew? Our old friend, the Tempest King. And he's in here, right now, with a fucking bomb, all primed and ready to blow."

"A *bomb*?" The thought was so impossible, so wrong. That scratched walkie-talkie had worked, yes, but a bomb?

"For what?" Cal looked just as confused as Evangeline. "To blow up some grass?"

Incident looked around the Harbor, maybe scanning for errant fae, before speaking.

"Only five fencers today have a primacy and the power capable of opening a way through the Tree. Two are too old or frail to make the trip. One is just starting her third-grade year. One worked for Russia, and he died twelve days ago. The fifth is you, Evangeline. How many times have you been asked to make a run at the Tree in your time? Ten? Twenty? And always you said no, and your direct superiors rightly supported that decision. This is their attempt—their masterstroke—to force your hand. And when you open the door, they'll throw the bomb through."

"And that would accomplish . . ."

"They want to disrupt the Harbors. I called in every last favor and burned every last bridge I had to figure out what was going on after . . ." Incident gestured awkwardly toward Winnie, standing back beside Tennyson, behind her parents.

"After they killed our daughter," Cal said. When the truth arrived, it was not cowardice to avoid it or bravery to speak it. Only a choice between two different kinds of dreaming.

"Yes, after that, I went to the church, and after some pressure, they gave up records and schematics and plans. Powerful people want to draw energy from the Harbors to power a new grid. They want to capture and experiment on fae. They want to send in fencers beyond the Threshold Tree. 'Missions ranging from raiding to conquering,' they said."

"And the Sylvans?" Cal asked. "What do they get out of this? A bomb in the doorway to their faerie heaven?"

"The Sylvans have to wait and hope for a chance to die on the equinox each year," Incident said, grimacing. "But they've been promised primes and a free trip past the Threshold Tree once all of this is done. The mathematicians know there are infinite primes—they proved that years ago. So, why not dole some out to the Sylvans—infinite supply and finite demand. The Sylvans give them money, power, and the backing of every senator and prime minister and CEO they have in their pocket."

"And in return, they get to play fencer and walk through the Tree," Evangeline said, shaking her head at the perfect, awful logic of it.

Tennyson let loose a series of phlegmy, angry barks, the patterns on his coat atomizing into perfect grids of black dots on a sea of white before exploding and reassembling all over again. About forty yards away, a pair of fae ran, silent and watchful, up to the Tree and through, leaping into the yawning darkness between the branches with liquid ease. The Tree closed around them without a sound.

"This is the start of their attempts to fracture the system," Incident said. "And they're not going to stop. Public opinion is shifting, and so is political will. They want to use you to open the door, Evangeline, but they want to use your story—the bereaved parents driven to a desperate act by the lack of protection offered by the bureau."

Evangeline was shaking her head. This was wrong. Not the story Incident was spouting—that was probably right. It had the stink of systemic truth to it. The whiff of bureaucratic cogs cranking and corporate goal-setting machines whirring.

It was wrong because her purpose—and Cal's and Winnie's and even Tennyson's—was there. It was simple. It was the Tree and the castle and the Queen. It was getting Winnie back at all costs. Only that.

All of this was the problem of a world Evangeline had departed the moment she'd stepped into Winnie's room the previous night.

She opened her mouth to say so.

And paused.

Cal, too, was shaking his head but unable to speak.

"I . . ." Evangeline began, but what could she say? The messy, meaningless concerns of the world were spreading in her mind, infecting that perfect purpose to which she'd been clinging, loosening her grip and poisoning her focus.

Tennyson snarled and let loose a full-throated bark, the kind of sound that had teeth and claws and blood and violence.

"I really thought you were going to do it."

The voice was familiar, and even as she turned, Evangeline placed that smug tone, so that the sight of the Tempest King standing there was no surprise. His clothes, the dark black and blue of the New England fencers, had seen better days, and Evangeline found herself hoping that some of those tears and rips, with the bloodied wounds underneath, had been given to him by the Midwest fencers at the Gate. "The little guys," as he liked to call fencers with longer primes and lesser primacies than him.

A backpack bulged behind him, a massive thing. *The bomb*, Evangeline thought, though her true attention was on the long knife he held to Winnie's neck, the iron edge so close to skin that had gone too smooth, too even, but was still Winnie's.

"Let her go," Cal said, taking a step forward but stopping there.

"*It*, fencer Calidore," the Tempest King said. "One death and those years of training just disappear? Just like that?"

"Don't move, Winnie," Evangeline said, the words springing from instinct rather than thought.

"See the great Achilles, whom we knew," Winnie said in reply, one of her eyebrows curving into a suggestive crescent, a look so familiar to Evangeline, so true to the daughter she'd had—*still* had—that she felt the urge to vomit twist her stomach.

"You two are supposed to be the great hope to open the way through the Tree," the Tempest King said, a sneer on his face. "Do you know how many fae I had to cut down to help you get here? Or even better, how many times the Riparian would have obliterated you if I hadn't knocked it off course or into one of your clumsy attacks? It's pathetic that it's come down to this. To you."

His primacy was speed at a blinding rate, and Evangeline saw their journey there, their fight with the Riparian, anew—the fae who seemed to avoid them; the Riparian, so clumsy and wrong-footed. The whole thing, every step of it, even before the equinox, had been so carefully planned to maneuver them to this place.

The Tempest King pulled on Winnie's chain, still keeping her between himself and Tennyson, who stood at perfect attention, his great tail swishing back and forth, back and forth behind him. Every muscle under that shaggy, thick coat was tensed, ready to launch all hundred and fifty-plus pounds of him forward at the slightest opening.

Or at a command from Evangeline.

"Even with the full report from the remnants of your coterie," the

Tempest King said, eyeing up the three bedraggled fencers standing nearby, "I thought you'd still go through with it. And you want to. I know you do. So, here's what's going to happen," the Tempest King said. "Fencer Evangeline, you open that Tree. Fencer Calidore, you use your ability to stop the way from closing up. I'm going to throw this backpack in there, and then you can let it close. We're all going to count to fifteen. After that, you can go through there. Talk to the Queen. Barter for Winnifred's life. I won't stop you."

"And that bomb isn't going to disrupt our chances to talk with Her?" Cal spoke in the calm, even tone he used when truly angry.

"This might *help* your chances," the Tempest King said, and he looked genuinely confused, as though Cal had said something particularly stupid. "I'm trying to make the way between the Harbor and Faerie *permanent*. No more of this depending on one or two fencers in a generation to make an impossible run at an impossible task. If this goes off, I expect that tree will have a hole blown in it big enough for you two, your faerie kid, and that big horse of yours to traipse through any time you want."

"How can you be so sure it'll work?" Evangeline asked, eyeing the backpack. "That's the second piece of tech the mathematicians have sent in *ever*. No one could predict what's going to happen."

The Tempest King was shaking his head, those surgically perfected teeth dazzling in his billboard-ready smile.

"You still haven't figured it out yet. This isn't the second piece of tech we've brought in—mathematicians have been running these tests for months. Years! They ran prototypes of this thing"—he nodded back at the pack behind him—"every day these past four weeks in Russia. That's why the Riparian was there. It's attracted to this artificially primed shit—like hornets swarming an intruder to their nest. Those Russian mathematicians were going through fencers like they were nothing, running them at the Tree to drop bombs and throw bombs and plant bombs."

He laughed, his cheeks dimpling.

"The Riparian must have chewed through ten or eleven fencers these last few weeks alone."

Eleven fencers. Even under the dome of her trauma, Evangeline still felt shock at that. To lose a fencer on an equinox—one fencer—was cause for memorials and inquiries and days of mourning. But ten? Eleven?

Incident was nodding, though she didn't look happy to be agreeing with the Tempest King.

"He's right. The mathematicians, along with certain members of the Central Bureau, high-ranking officials in the House of Always Giving, and government officials okayed the plan, and after some preliminary attempts, it looks like they sent the Red Tiger at the Tree to rip it open."

"A serious waste," the Tempest King said. "She opened the Tree with her primacy—she could do something with cutting space-time in small amounts, apparently. She cut it open and then tossed the bomb through. It blew, ripped the Tree open, but it wasn't big enough, and eventually the Tree stitched itself back up, as it always does, although it took a long time. A few fencers took down some measurements, and the mathematicians think this thing"—he gestured to the bag again—"is plenty big enough to overcome whatever force puts the Tree back together. At least until we can get a real team in here to make the opening more permanent."

"We'll stop that team, too," Ordinal said, though they didn't look like they were in any shape to stop anyone.

"You're feeling big about that skirmish at the gate?" The Tempest King huffed out a laugh through his nose, a noise Evangeline knew well and had hoped to never hear in her life again. "They were supposed to distract you so I could get through, and they did. You thinking it was a success is perfect proof that it worked."

"Oh, shut the fuck up," Nero said, drawing up one of her bubbles and holding it at the ready. "This is not happening. Let the girl go, and we'll let you go."

Ordinal, too, gripped their iron rod, though their other hand still pressed firmly against a stomach wound Evangeline couldn't see.

And Incident had clothed herself in the swirling raiment of her primacy, the black particles moving and rippling like a school of fish.

They wanted to fight.

A great and significant battle at the border between worlds. One for fence historians to write about.

Evangeline looked at Cal, who shook his head slightly, and in that gentle motion, she felt the two of them aligned again.

The drive to fight hung before them both, and the parents *together* beheld it, not from their own positions in the world but from a shared one. They looked with four eyes that were two, with two minds that were one, as though consciousness were a closed system they had finally, *finally* found a way to breach and connect.

To Evangeline, it felt like looking out at the stars and realizing she was part of them and they her. Like she'd climbed a mountain only to understand that she was the mountain and the space outside it, that the distance and the vastness and the glory of it all were inside her just as much as she was inside them.

It felt like love. Not *like* it. It was love.

And it felt like hope, which was to say love.

And joy, which was to say love.

And power, real power.

Which was to say love.

Chapter 21

Incident struck first, and for any other enemy, the fight would have ended a moment after it began.

A line of her inky primacy, like ants busy at their work, had been moving out along the ground as they'd been talking, creeping through grass and along dirt.

Cal and Evangeline had seen this before, her ability to control her primacy with such surgical precision. Lining up those tiny black particles in a perfect line, one particle wide and almost invisible. A lance if she needed it to be. A whip if the situation called for it. A line of razor wire.

Or a distraction.

Like perfectly spun thread, the line of particles slowly rose behind the Tempest King.

"You three are already injured," the Tempest King said, looking between Ordinal, Incident, and Nero. "And these two are in no state to fight. I don't want anyone else to die, okay? If we do it my way, there's no skirmish, no more good blood being spilled, and everyone can get at least a little of what they want."

"You want to mess around with the world," Ordinal said, their breathing growing shallow. "That's what got us into this spot. The Harbors. The fences. All of this shit. We thought this place was a sandbox just waiting for our hands."

"It *is*." The Tempest King softened as he spoke. "This is ours. Every bit of this Earth is ours. And thanks to some crazy mathematician in the past who was probably controlled by the Faerie Queen, we gave half of this place over to *nature*."

The word twisted in the Tempest King's mouth, becoming a sniveling curse. He continued.

"All of the designs and plans the mathematicians have are about helping people in the short term—energy, security, safety. But the bigger plan is to reclaim this land. For people. Living people. To disrupt and end whatever spell Ronald Reagan cast in 1987. All of this land that we could use for agriculture and housing and energy—and instead, it's all fenced-off toxic graveyards. Imagine all of this land given back to actual people. Family farms and homesteads. Energy fields—solar and wind and hydroelectric. Homes in the mountain ranges currently fenced off and polluted by the toxic shit in the Harbors."

"You're an idiot," Ordinal said. "You're *their* idiot. None of those number pushers can know what a bomb could do in this place or what goes on on the other side of that Tree. And even if they could know, and even if this plan goes off without a hitch, then you're playing a mug's game if you think that idyllic future is really in the cards. They'll chop up that land and sell it to the highest bidder. *Family farms?* How many times did men in suits spoon-feed that shit to you until it tasted just right?"

The Tempest King opened his mouth to respond, but the fight had already started.

That particle-thin line of thread, which had risen throughout the conversation, like a cobra drawn skyward by the cloying notes of a flute, struck.

Perhaps it was Incident's quick gesture as she clutched her hands into fists, her breath hissing through suddenly clenched teeth.

Perhaps it was Cal's eyes, which flicked between the Tempest King and the shadowy serpent rising hypnotically behind him.

Perhaps it was simply the Tempest King's reflexes, which were to the average person's what a supercomputer was to a beaten-up calculator low on batteries.

The strike, which should have pierced the Tempest King through the center of his chest, like a thread connecting his spine with his sternum, instead cut just along the edge of his side as he moved.

Blood hung in the air, a small spray of it, the only remnant of the Tempest King in that space. Winnie's chain, too, rested unnaturally in the air for a moment, a linked arc refuting gravity. Only the blade he'd been holding to Winnie's neck went with the Tempest King when he blurred to the right, away from Incident's surprise attack.

Tracking his movement was nearly impossible, and an offensive against the Tempest King was just as easy, so the fencers fell into defensive maneuvers—Incident wrapping herself in a thick sheath of tight-knit black; Nero pulling the fabric of a bubble all the way around her.

Ordinal was the Tempest King's first target, but just as the blur reached them, they exploded into confetti, the pieces smaller and finer than even Incident's primacy. Glistening and shiny, the bits of Ordinal expanded out into an archway through which the Tempest King moved, swinging his blade through air that only a moment before had been occupied by the aging punk fencer.

Tennyson was barking and someone was screaming. Cal felt echoes of a past urge to join such a fight, now barely heard in the vast cavern hollowed inside himself.

When Ordinal collapsed back into themself, though, it was not with the usual smirk that accompanied uses of their primacy. Instead, they returned, shimmering for a moment, to where they had been, standing just as they had, before dropping to the ground, both hands clutched to their stomach now. When they bared their teeth in pain, the tobacco-yellow was smeared with a film of blood.

The Tempest King, too, stopped, to survey the field, and when he saw Ordinal on the ground, and Nero and Incident stepping in front of them in defense, he paused.

"I have orders to kill as many of you as I need to for the mission," he said, slicing at the air with his sword. "But I don't want to. Let me do this, and I'll bring Ordinal to the gate for medical help myself."

The bubbles—small as baseballs and flung just as hard—were answer enough, and the Tempest King smeared away into motion again, cutting forward and slamming into Nero and her armor. The blade he brought down on the bubble surrounding her shattered, but his true attack was in the air itself.

Compression heating, Oddry had called it when the Tempest King was with the Midwest fencers. For an object moving as fast as the Tempest King did, the air he moved through couldn't get out of the way fast enough, so it was instead compressed, and when gasses were compressed so quickly and brutally, they grew hot.

Which meant the Tempest King's greatest weapon, and the one he had grown skilled in using, was the heat shield that he created ahead of him, one that, under the guidance of whatever logic or force gave fencers their abilities in the first place, didn't affect him.

Nero's bubble melted around her, molten and dripping, and when she screamed, it was a full-throated, horrifying thing. She fell beside Ordinal, writhing in the dirt, her cries growing duller as her movements slowed.

Only Incident stood now, her primacy a swirling maelstrom around her, at times coalescing into tendrils that snapped out or long blades that cut the air defensively. Even for the Tempest King, Incident would be hard to fell.

A soft clinking beside him pulled Cal's attention away, and he found Winnie taking small, restrained steps toward the Threshold Tree, her eyes grown too wide, the pupils slitting like a cat's as she beheld the white branches.

Beside her, Evangeline scooped stars from the air with one hand, the other still hanging lifeless at her side, and tossed them at the Tree.

Bough and branches shuddered and shook and exploded in a burst of song. Melodies as countless as drops of water in the ocean filled the air and might have thrown Cal backward if he hadn't been ready for it, hadn't leaned forward instinctively into the blast, one hand going to Winnie's back to hold her against it.

In those songs were whole lives bound. People, some from the past, some the future, some the present, and some who were still only possibilities. Children and parents and widows and brothers and aunts and friends and lovers and enemies.

"I am part of all that I have met," Cal whispered, feeling the tiny light inside himself spark and flare. Great bolts of something brighter and more beautiful than anything he could have imagined hiding in his heart shot out, connecting him to Evangeline and Winnie and Nero and Incident and Ordinal and the Tempest King and Tennyson, yes, but also to every would-be and had-been and might-be person loosed by Evangeline's cantillation.

It was a communion, holier than anything that had ever happened in a building of stone or wood, more sacred than any act performed before altar or icon.

And when it ended, when the song of Evangeline's cantillation dispersed into the Harbor, Cal found himself hand in hand with Winnie and Evangeline, staring ahead at the way through the Threshold Tree.

At Cal's feet, Tennyson whimpered.

Like looking through a window at winter's frozen set while sitting inside, entombed in thick blankets and grateful for walls and insulation and heat, the family looked through the Tree at the land of Faerie.

A lightning-scarred sky hung thick and dark above, the towering turmoil of thunderheads shaded in bruised blues and sublime purples. The song of thunder rolled as though from far away and sounded like men singing in a mine, and when lightning flashed above, the bolts unfolded along slow, languorous paths, sometimes jagging and cutting, and other times curling in on or out of themselves, like whirlpools thick with light.

The bone-white of the shells around the Tree did not continue on the other side. Instead, the land of Faerie was all thick moss and slow, sloping hills climbing inevitably to a castle in the near distance. As Cal looked, a line of goldenrod lightning unwound in the sky above the castle before terminating on one of the many towers rising from the castle.

"Home," Winnie whispered, the word a knife in Cal's gut.

She leaned forward, and so too did Cal, and so too did Evangeline, but between that lean and their first step, a wave of heat flashed over their faces.

The Tempest King stood there, the bag already removed from his back and set on the green moss of Faerie. Beyond him, on the hills just before the Queen's castle, a few fae leapt and bounded and raced for home.

"Enough now," he said. Cal was pleased to hear how winded the Tempest King sounded. "It's over."

He pulled a small remote from the bag and pressed the button.

"In ten seconds—" he began, but Cal interrupted him.

"Such easy lines," Cal said. "Over and not over."

"What?" the Tempest King said, cocking his head. He hadn't even been speaking to Cal or Evangeline, but to Incident behind them, who still stood in her full battle dress, the tentacles and blades of her primacy extended around her like the arms of an exploding galaxy.

"We're born and we live and we breathe and then we die," Cal said, floating on the residues of that light, that communion still burning inside him. "We work and we love and we dream of tomorrow—*tomorrow!*"

He laughed, and the sound must have been even more jarring to the Tempest King than his speech, because the other man took an involuntary step back.

"We remember yesterday and we reach for tomorrow and we live in time's debt. I had a daughter. I might have a daughter again. And you a bomb! In a bag!"

The Tempest King watched with disgust as Cal began laughing again. The edges around the doorway Evangeline had made were already beginning to heal themselves, the space beginning to slowly shrink.

"What's wrong with you?" The Tempest King took a step, two, toward the opening.

"I'm afraid I can't explain myself," Cal shouted, feeling the dance of his primes on his skin, the light of that fire inside him burning and burning and burning. "Because I am not myself, you see?!"

The Tempest King understood too late what Cal was doing, and when Cal caught him in the senseless, meaningless drivel of his hollow grammarie, it was with a look of dawning horror on the Tempest King's face, one knee already driving forward to get back, his form a frozen blur of movement.

Cal let the slurry of his nonsense continue to fall, speaking faster and faster, louder and louder, leaping carelessly between bits of his favorite books, truths about his life, worries and fears, and the garden variety nonsenses he usually spoke. He understood, for the first time in his life, how essentially meaningless it all was, how fundamentally nonsensical.

Not unimportant. Not incapable of holding or having meaning, sense. Just this: the bare facts of a life, like the scratches of a novel on the page or the arrangement of leaves fallen to the ground in fall, carried no meaning to be found, no sense of their own. They were, all of them, waiting to be found and *filled* with meaning. To be made sensical. To be turned on the wheel of human imagination and shaped into significance, importance, value.

Even as his voice frayed and his vocal cords grew painful, Cal pushed on the limits of his primacy, extending it beyond the Tempest King, out and out to catch and hold that bag and the ticking contents.

"Get it, Cal!" someone shouted, but Cal knew only the nonsense truths streaming from his mouth, their every syllable extending the area of his grammarie, and with a final scream of disconnected sounds waiting to be made meaningful, he caught the bomb up his web—just as it exploded.

As it froze, the bag became a sun, its rays the rags its fabric became in the explosion, its heart a thing too bright to look at directly. Heat waves bent light and turned the space around the blast into a haze.

Still spewing his hollow grammarie, Cal gestured toward Evangeline, pantomiming scooping stars from the air, but when he looked to her, she was not preparing to cantillate the bomb.

Instead, she was watching in horror as Winnie, having used the distraction to shuck off her chains, scurried through the opening and ran forward toward the castle, the tattered, dirty purple of her nightgown a swirl around her.

"Winnie!" she screamed, and she too was through the Tree, and just behind her was Tennyson, loosing a series of deep, chesty barks. Evangeline looked back once, eyes wild, panic on her face.

Cal almost lost the thread of his hollow grammarie. Panic thrummed inside him. His family was disappearing, the way through the Tree was still closing, and he couldn't keep up his hold on the Tempest King and the bomb for much longer.

"Get through, Cal," came a voice beside him, and he turned to find Incident, the chaos of her primacy compressed in a tight ball orbiting her body in slow arcs. "Get through before it closes."

Cal nodded, the slurry of his nonsense still tumbling from his lips but slower now and growing fainter. His voice would break soon, and then the bomb would go.

The pathway Evangeline had cantillated in the Tree had been enormous, but when Cal clambered through, it had lost half of its area, maybe more. They didn't have long.

"Hold it as long as you can," Incident shouted from the other side.

Beyond her, Nero was stirring and moaning. Ordinal sat up long enough to vomit once before dropping back to the shell-strewn ground. "Get back but hold the bomb as long as you can!"

Cal nodded, casting a quick glance over at Winnie, Evangeline, and Tennyson, who were growing distant. With her arm as it was, Evangeline wouldn't be able to manage Winnie, and so deep into the heart of the Harbor—into Faerie itself—who knew what Tennyson would do.

Five steps back. Ten. Fifteen and his hold on the fencer and bomb grew weak.

Cal held up his fingers. Five of them.

"I was born to a mother and a father who did their best but often did their worst," he said, dropping one finger.

Four.

"Like a ribbon of weed I am flung far every time the door opens. The wave breaks. I am the foam that sweeps and fills the uttermost rims of the rocks with whiteness."

Three. Incident was flinging those inky particles forward in huge waves, more than Cal had ever seen, more than he knew she was capable of.

"Agent Dawnlove is reporting and I have no riddle other than my love and my fear of tomorrow."

Two. His control was fraying and so was his voice, and the words that came out next were a husked whisper, barely audible and even less intelligible.

"I love you and I love you and I love you and I love you and I love—"

One.

Incident, her primacy surging forward in onyx waves that swirled and formed layer after layer around the bomb. A tomb for the explosion. A sepulcher.

One connected all the way back through the Tree to Incident herself. No matter how far she flung her primacy, it always stayed attached to her.

"Go get her back," Incident said as Cal brought down his remaining finger and stopped, finally, the flow of words.

A muffled blast punched the heavy blanket of silence that hung over Faerie, and a light shone from inside that dark tomb, a light that flashed bright along the line of Incident's primacy, flaring like a long fuse burning its way to a stick of dynamite, all the way back through the Tree and to Incident, who screamed in pain and fell out of sight as the Tree knit itself back together, the window blinking out of existence from this side.

The Tempest King, released from Cal's power, did not speed away or leap forward but instead fell to the ground, still and almost unrecognizable. Cal had caught him in the act of moving, and the stretch of his hollow grammarie had been too slow to catch the Tempest King all at once. Instead, the back half of his body had, at impossible speeds, run into the stilled front half.

Cal paid him no mind as he raced after his family.

Go get her back, Incident had said, and he would. No matter what, he would.

Chapter 22

Through the delightful land of Faerie he ran. Weary. Worn.
Under his feet, green moss strung over stone and soil. Around him, air thick with humidity but cold and unmoved by wind.

Trees grew along the hills, their branches like the curled fingers of hands. Leaves like flowers and leaves like faces and leaves like falling water and even leaves like the pages of books, like the tree Cal had loved in the Harbor—leaves like every sort of thing in every sort of color grew from the branches.

Tremors of jittering movement ran up and down those leaves, like a body shivering to regain warmth or in response to fear.

And hidden inside those trees, behind the veils of the leaves and behind the bars of the branches, were beings. Animals, maybe. Birds or monkeys or people. They moved too quickly for Cal to see, and when they flung themselves at the bars of their prisons, they swam in that same shadow that had cloaked the Riparian's face. Talons and long-fingered hands and sucking tentacles reached out to grip those upturned, close-grown branches, but beyond them, obscured by shivering leaves, was only darkness.

"Onward, onward, onward," these beings whispered, and Cal found sense in what they said.

Over hills he ran, up and up and up toward the castle above.

And Faerie ran along with him, out and out and out in every direction, moors and swamps and plains and forests and deserts and what looked like habitations in the distance, all of it spreading from the castle, which sat at its center, a pin planted deep in its heart to hold it together, to give it shape and structure and meaning.

He caught his family on the final slope before the castle, his lungs heaving, his heart a heavy thud in his chest. From a comfortable distance, he wondered if he was going to have a heart attack. Like father, like son. Collapse so near his high, holy goal.

Evangeline had wrestled Winnie back into chains and installed her once more on Tennyson, whose fur had gone pure black save for his head, which glowed with sudden traceries of white, perfect parallels to the lightning in the sky.

"I'm here," Cal said.

"The bomb?" Evangeline asked, hugging him with her one good arm. How had she managed to get Winnie back in chains and up on the dog with one arm?

"It's done," he said, shaking his head. If there would be a later, he would tell her then.

"Good," she said.

Winnie, for her part, had grown stranger, more fae. Her hair was still that chestnut brown but now shifted and shivered with suggestions of other colors, blue and white and grey and red, the shades there and gone again. Spurs of bone, like flowers waiting to unfurl their petals, had pushed up through the soft skin along her clavicles and above her ears, still curled tightly in on themselves but promising more.

When she turned to Cal, her eyes were a soft crimson, the pupils swelling and shifting in shape. Slits and circles and stars and the curious, smooth rectangle of a goat.

"Red eyes suit so few," he said before he could stop himself, his voice a ragged tatter.

Winnie smiled, revealing teeth grown sharp and long and wicked.

When she started the litany of lives she might have led, people she might have been, Cal smiled and reached out for her hand, ignoring the pain of her nails as they dug into his skin.

With his other hand, he took Evangeline's, nodding to her.

"Let's go."

The gates of the castle had been left open. Like a huge maw carved into the dark grey stone of the front wall.

And through that opening, a panoply of voices emerged, all talking in the same endless monotone, speaking over one another. It was a slow susurrus, a murmuring multiplied by thousands and thousands of participants, and though Cal could separate none of the individual voices or understand what any of them were saying, the effect sent waves of gooseflesh racing down his arms.

"I might have woken on a Sunday morning to see spring rain falling outside my window," Winnie said, her voice almost wistful. The family walked forward through the gate, which brought them through the thick outer wall, its width easily forty feet. Inside that tunnel, the murmur of the voices beyond grew louder and louder, and Winnie's words joined with them in a way that caused a spire of anger to rise inside Cal. She was his daughter. Even in her transformation, even in this new oddity, she was Winnie, she was Agent Dawnlove, she was his child who had taken her first steps on that old red rug they'd had in the living room. She was his child who had called broccoli "little trees" and tried planting them in the yard.

She was his child who had watched him with big, staring eyes those first few months, sometimes crying but sometimes just watching. The doctors had said she couldn't really see much, just vague shapes and blurry outlines, but Cal had been sure they were wrong, that when he brought his face close to hers, she saw him as he did her—whole and complete and clear as can be. And somehow in that seeing, he'd seen himself, too, not as he was but as he might be. A father. Dependable and honest and loving and kind and all the things she would need, all the things he'd found in himself in greater reserves than he'd ever thought possible.

She was his child, and if those were faeries in whatever part of the castle lay beyond this tunnel, then she was nothing like them.

And how many of those faeries have parents or spouses or children or friends who would say the same about their lost loved one? a voice whispered in his mind.

On the other side of the wall was a courtyard, the floor huge, uneven slabs of rose-red stone.

In that courtyard, perfectly spaced apart, like dots on a grid, were faeries. Cal felt a sudden vertigo as he looked around at them, sure at first that there were no more than a few hundred and then, as though something in the world or his mind shifted, equally sure that he was looking out at many, many thousands, maybe hundreds of thousands, of faeries, all equally spaced in this courtyard that might have stretched forever.

One and all, the fae stood totally still.

Their eyes, grown too large and uneven, many-colored and inhuman all, were cast up and up, not to the sky's dramatic play but to the being seated upon a throne on a ledge above them.

She, too, was totally still, looking down on her subjects with cold attention. A crown of braided wood the same color as the Threshold Tree rested on her head. The tall back of her throne rose behind her, first a simple wooden thing, adorned with a rough star, and then, as that same shift happened again in Cal's perception, it was an ornate golden throne, carved with a scene Cal couldn't make out but that seemed to be moving and shifting as he watched.

The Queen, too, changed before his eyes. At first, she was a ruler carved from hard ivory, eyes of tranquiline blue, her hair falling in tresses of gold under the crown, but a moment later, her skin was a dark shade of brown, and she looked down upon the courtyard of fae with deep brown eyes.

And then again, she was a huge cat, sitting upon her throne of onyx stone, that same wooden crown perched upon the fur of her head, her coat a beautiful, startling grey.

And then a bird, her enormous claws wrapped around a perch made of bone.

And then a child.

And then a stone creature.

And then a being of water and will.

And then.

And then.

It was like the collapse of the wave function, though instead of the various states of being collapsing finally into something stable and unchanging, the Faerie Queen collapsed and exploded into possibility over and over and again. She was, and then she might be, and then she was again.

And her subjects sang to her a paean of loyalty and honor.

All of them, all hundred or thousand or hundred thousand or million, spoke endlessly in the various potentials their lives might have followed.

"I might have been a stonemason," one faerie claimed, speaking in that iterative, plaintive voice of the fae. "I might have felt well-worked granite beneath my hands and known peace."

"I might have lived in a large apartment and fallen into debt," another said, her mouth a ragged scar along the lower half of her face. "I might have taken a second job to pay for my home."

"I might have," said faeries large and small, once-men and once-women and once-children and once-adults and once-people. All of them, voices overlapping and blending together, reciting the litany of maybes and might-haves and could-bes. Resurrecting the cloud of their possible lives for the Faerie Queen above.

Winnie's voice twinned with the crowd, and she made to get down from Tennyson.

"No," Cal said, holding out his hands to stop her. Near them, he saw, a place had opened in the grid, a place he was sure hadn't been there before, and it was toward this space Winnie struggled.

"You have to stay with us, sweetie," Evangeline said, using her one good arm, and Cal saw now the cuts and scratches along her neck and arm she'd received while wrestling Winnie back onto Tennyson. Winnie added to them now and offered Cal some of his own, her eyes trained on the Queen above.

Below, Tennyson whined and whimpered, taking anxious, quick steps back and forward.

"I might have been," Winnie wheezed, straining against the strength-sapping iron around her wrists and body and against the restraint of her parents.

"Please," Evangeline said, weeping now.

"Don't go," Cal said. "Stay here. Come on now. Those stairs over there."

Ahead, through thirty or forty rows of confessing fae, was a series of switchback stairs leading up to where the Queen sat.

They walked through the fae, and though Cal clutched at his remaining sword, ready should any of them attack, it was for naught.

They might as well have been walking through fields of tallgrass prairie again. Or among statues, speaking but unmoving.

The stairs rose before them, but Tennyson took the lead, climbing quickly, and though Winnie still spoke her possibilities to the Queen above, she had stopped struggling. Cal and Evangeline took the stairs two at a time to keep up with Tennyson's climbing.

When they reached the ledge above, the song of the fae grew distant, as though the Queen sat a mile or more above her subjects instead of forty or fifty feet.

Behind them, an army of fae, ridding themselves of all the futures they might have walked.

Before them, the Faerie Queen, a cloud of possibilities, never settled.

When she spoke, it was in a voice like dried leaves swaying against one another in autumn's chill wind. It came from the Queen, but it also came from the air and the sky and the stone under their feet. It was as if the entire land of Faerie conspired for its Queen to speak.

"You are here," she said. "Eidolons from another land."

"I might have grown to love the feel of snow underfoot," Winnie said. "I might have found joy in the *crunch*."

"And you come with a little star," the Queen said, a shade of disapproval in her voice. "Bound and held."

"She is our daughter," Evangeline said. "She . . ."

"We've come to ask for her life," Cal said, rasping out the words as best he could. He let his vision unfocus so that the shifting form of the Queen couldn't distract him. "She was taken. She's only a child. She—"

"You are here," the Queen said again. "Marked with those hateful numbers to beg for the life of your child."

Not a question.

Evangeline helped Winnie down from Tennyson.

"We are."

"Our last visitor to this land brought nothing but his arrogance with which to barter. Of him we made the nothing he longed for in his heart of hearts. What do you bring to trade?"

"We have already saved your land," Evangeline said, iron and anger in her words. "A scheme to blow a hole in your Threshold Tree would have brought more fencers here, sent by people whose aim is the end of you, this land, and the process that brings our dead here."

A shock of sound, so loud it threatened to stave in the barrel of Cal's chest. At first, he thought it was the angry shout of the Queen, but as it faded, he understood it for what it was: laughter.

"Let them come. It is an event deferred, nothing more. You offer me time, of which I have no need. Is this all?"

Desperation tightened screws along Cal's spine, and he patted his pockets, feeling for anything that might be a gift, that might sparkle and shine in this world. Nothing.

"What would you have?" he asked, trying to speak above Winnie, who continued her recitation. Tears welled in his eyes.

Fae had begun to climb the stairs, their transformations complete, and when they passed by, they paid no attention to the humans or the dog standing before their Queen. They did not speak any more of their might-bes or could-haves, and Cal had the realization that they'd said them all, had cleaned themselves completely of that messy human future.

So perfected, they walked by their Queen and into the doorway behind her. Onward.

"Am I to bargain for you as well? Have you so little to offer?"

"You can take me," Cal said. "A trade. One for the other."

"No."

"What, then? What do you want?" He shouted the words as best he could, his throat afire with pain.

And then it came to him.

The poem Winnie had been reciting—Sir Orfeo—featured a version of the Orpheus myth where the boy, Orfeo, travels to Faerie to get his wife back with only a harp to aid him. He succeeds by playing music so beautiful that the King of Faerie grants Orfeo any prize he wants.

"What about music?" Cal said, shifting his eyes from the Faerie Queen to his family.

"Yes. Which of you brings such a gift?"

"My wife, Evangeline," Cal said.

Evangeline looked at Cal. Her eyes, red and swollen as his, held so much, and he knew, somehow, that this was the end. That gone were the mornings of riddles and laughter. Gone were the stories at bedtime. Gone were the stolen kisses while Winnie wasn't looking. Gone were their working lunches together. Gone was waiting to hear about Winnie's day at school. Pizza parties and game nights and movies snuggled on the couch and walks and coloring together and learning together and singing together and being together and simply being. Gone was being.

She nodded, and Cal did too.

Evangeline moved quickly, pulling a handful of stars from the air around her. She paused for a moment, holding that unbearable brightness in her hand before flinging the stars directly at the Queen.

Cal stepped forward, bringing his blade up, bracing himself against the explosion of sound and power, but it didn't come.

Instead, the stars fell through the Queen like dust motes floating through the air. One by one they flared and died on the throne beneath her.

Silence, save for the shuffling feet of the fae moving on.

"We would have music," the voice repeated. "None of these tricks or tries. A fair exchange."

Evangeline's primacy, like a fire, needed fuel to burn and dance and crack. And everything in Faerie, including the Queen herself, had been stripped clean of such substance.

All gone. The mornings and the nights and the days. The Sunday naps together. Gone, the pull of a comb through Winnie's hair after a bath. Gone, the smell of her shampoo in his nose. Gone, the sound of her slow breathing as she slept.

"It has to be me," Cal said, dropping his sword with a clatter and putting his hands on Evangeline's shoulders. "A fair exchange."

"What are you— No. Cal, no."

He was crying now, the tears falling freely, but he didn't care.

"Your primacy won't work on yourself," he said, shaking his head to forestall her arguing. "And I couldn't get out of here without mine. It has to be me, Evangeline."

Tennyson released a deep bark, confused by what was happening but sure that something was wrong.

"Cal—"

"Don't call me that—not now," he said, smiling through his tears. "Not here at the end."

"It's not the end, Cal," she said, but he shook his head again.

"It is. For me, it is. But it won't be for you, and it won't be for her."

"Cal—"

"Please," he said. "Please don't call me that."

Evangeline nodded and leaned forward, wrapping him in a one-armed hug, the best she could manage. Sobs began to hitch at her shoulders and shudder along her chest.

"There has to be another way," she said, but without conviction.

"There isn't," he said into her thick brown hair, sweat-smelling and dirty and flecked with dried blood and more beautiful than anything he'd ever seen. "Take her, bring Tennyson, and go home. Tell her every day how much I love her. And remember every day how much I love you."

She pulled in a harsh breath and wept into his shoulder for a moment, as he wept into hers.

"Soon," the Queen's voice said, its vibrations moving along their bones, "your little star shall burn out, and I will have no more power with which to barter."

"Joseph," she said finally, a rough whisper in his ear. "I love you. You're my—"

"I know," he said, shaking his head and pulling back. "I know. Me, too."

He kissed her, their wet lips meeting for too short a time.

Gone, their nights beside one another. Gone, her heat next to him. Gone, her eyes in the morning.

"Winnie," he said, turning from his wife before he lost the strength.

He found his daughter, changed but still there, still muttering through her possibilities. Maybe it was the Queen's power or maybe it was the spark of her still inside, but when he said her name, she stopped and looked up at him, and they were her eyes again, that brown that he could have looked at every day for a lifetime and never grown tired of.

He kneeled down before her, wrapping his arms around her thin frame.

"Agent Dawnlove. Your task today is to take your mom back home and live a big, wonderful, loving life with her. Climb trees to find clues and read books to find clues and look everywhere to figure out what it's all about. Sometimes, you might be sad or unsure or confused or scared, but I have a secret weapon for those times, and I'll give it to you right now."

He pulled back, meeting her eyes again. He held up a hand, cupped it below his mouth, and whispered, "I love you, I love you, I love you, I love you," into it. Clutching his fingers into a tight fist, as though his love might escape, Joseph took his daughter's hand and passed the secret weapon into it.

"When you need it, you'll always have it. They'll refill with just a little time, too, so don't be shy about using them."

He leaned forward and kissed her on the forehead.

"I love you more than I thought it was possible to love anyone. And no matter what happens, you'll always have that love, whenever you need it. Day or night. Right there."

He tapped her hand, which she'd clutched into a fist.

"I love you, sweets."

Winnie stared at him as he stood, and he kissed her hand before letting go of it.

"It must happen now," the Queen's voice said, and Evangeline was shaking her head, her face a blur through the tears in Joseph's eyes, but he said, in as firm a voice as he could, "You can do this. I love you."

"I love you," Evangeline said, and Joseph, blinking away the tears, watched her scoop those stars from the air.

The last thing he saw was Winnie turning to face him, the fae transformation already beginning to reverse, her eyes finding his.

The last thing he heard was his daughter, voice hers again, that melody one he would recognize and heel to in any storm, saying, "Daddy, what—"

The stars hit him and memories flashed before his eyes: Winnie crawling into bed with them on a cold Saturday morning. The three of them making pasta together and spilling sauce all over the floor. Winnie meeting Tennyson when he was just a puppy and hugging him close. Evangeline taking his hand as they walked together on one of their first dates. The rain sounding against an umbrella he held while Winnie shouted with laughter at the impossibility of staying dry in a rainstorm. Winnie opening presents on Christmas, her hair askew and her smile wide. Evangeline sitting beside him in the morning, both of them reading, the silence like their own language. Winnie and Evangeline playing Mom Chess after school, giggling and talking and strategizing.

Winnie and Evangeline reading together.

Winnie and Evangeline sitting together.

Winnie and Evangeline laughing together.

Winnie and Evangeline together.

Joseph, Calidore, went out and out and out and was no more.

A History of Fences and Fae by AK Senga, PhD

Published in 2027 by University of Minnesota Majestic Press
Excerpt from Chapter 7: "Grothendieck's Long Promise"

While the events of the disaster that journalists have named the Midwest Tragedy are still in the process of being sorted through over five years later, any serious history of Harbors, the fae, and the fencers of the world must touch upon the US fencers Evangeline and Calidore, as well as their daughter Winnifred.

While Calidore was a fencer of middling ability, Evangeline was several degrees stronger, both in terms of her primacy (the transformation of matter into sound waves) and her prime number (a 3053-digit prime, $2^{10141} + 2^{5071} + 1$). These two were working the equinox at the Midwest Harbor when their six-year-old daughter died suddenly.[7] Calidore and Evangeline broke official protocol and brought their daughter, already well into her fae transformation, into the Harbor.

This book is a work of academic vision, and I have no aspirations of entertaining conspiracy theories or speculating on the personal lives of anyone. However, I had occasion to meet Calidore and Evangeline, and I happened to advise them of recent scholarly discoveries and arguments only a few days before the equinox when their worlds fell apart. I discussed the Bloodless Queen Hypothesis with them, and I cannot help but feel some responsibility for their efforts.

---

[7] Recent reports from several governmental whistleblowers, all of whom cite "a source high up in the Fencing Bureau administration" who has suggested "with evidence" that Winnifred did not die of natural causes and may have been intentionally killed under government orders. Three of the five government agents tasked with protecting her had also transformed into fae by the time fencers arrived on the scene, and investigations have revealed that at least two of these people, if not the third, intentionally induced the transformation in themselves just after killing Winnifred. The remaining agents not involved in the plot were unable to hold out against so many fae and expired before help arrived.

It is my hope in this chapter to imagine these two fencers as long-promised variables in an equation imagined by that most mysterious mathematician and writer, Alexander Grothendieck. But before exploring this idea, I offer two pieces of documentation that might shine a light on these fencers.

The first is a recovered transcript of a psychological session done for Calidore almost seven years before the equinox in question.

```
From the psychological interviews of Fencer Ca-
lidore.
Prime: 81*2^5600028+1
Q: What feelings do you have about your job?
A: Fencing? At first, I thought it was amazing,
you know? I finally had a purpose. It was like
I'd been preparing for it all my life, too. All
those books I read as a kid about heroes and wiz-
ards and magic. And then it ends up being true!
A little true, anyway. I felt great at first.
Q: And then?
A: Well, then, the memory stuff has to happen,
you know? They pull your name out of the world,
and it's like popping out a drain plug. Other
memories start to go. Cousins didn't remember me
very well, aunts and uncles too. Them I didn't
mind so much, but my dad—he barely knows me. It's
like he's seeing me and my memory through a fog
every time we talk, and we didn't talk all that
much even before I got my primes. Now? If we
didn't have Winnie, I think he might just let
himself forget me.
Q: Do you have regrets about becoming a fencer?
```

A: I might if I'd had a choice! But it's not like we have a surplus of people waking up with primes, so even though the nice government men who came to visit me said I didn't have to join up with the Fencing Bureau, it was pretty clear that I did. And at the time, I didn't mind—I thought it was cool, and death seemed impossibly far away to me. I was in my twenties, in a graduate program in English and thinking I was going to end up as a cashier at a big-box department store or something. I wasn't worried about physical injury or anything like that; I was worried about a meaningless, pointless existence, and WHAM—in came my primes and gave me a ready-made purpose. Fight the fae! Escort the fae! Do weird shit with your magical superpowers! I know, I know—we're not supposed to call them magic or superpowers, but come on. The Tempest King is basically the Flash but more of an asshole, and there's that woman down in Argentina who can throw stone lances that she conjures from inside her bones. If that's not magic, then I don't know what is.

Q: You mentioned death feeling far away when you started, Calidore. Does it still feel that way?

A: (pause) Not so much.

Q: Do you want to talk about that?

A: Not really. But I suppose it's good for me, right?

Q: (silence)

A: Yeah, okay. I'm sure Oddry probably told you about our conversation?

Q: Would you tell me about it?
A: Sure. He told me a few days ago—and this is a direct quote from my government boss, so feel free to report him—he told me that I "looked like shit smeared on a side street." Exact words.
Q: (silence)
A: I told him I haven't been sleeping well recently, and he said obviously, but then he asked me why. And it's because of Winnie.
Q: How old is she now?
A: (laughter) Evangeline keeps saying half a year, and I keep saying six months. Let's go with half a year.
Q: Noted. You were saying?
A: Ever since Winnie was born, I've had trouble sleeping. Nightmares, taking forever to fall asleep, waking up throughout the night—all of it. I know it's normal for parents of an infant to be tired, but this seems different.
Q: How so?
A: Every time we put Winnie to bed, even when it's the middle of the night and she's just pooped her pants for the third time and we're all exhausted and nothing seems better than falling asleep for even thirty minutes—even then, when I walk out of her room, I have this fear that I'm never going to see her alive again. That she'll die in her sleep. SIDS, you know. But not just SIDS. We have this kid, this little bundle of possibility, and all I can think of, all day and especially all night, are the awful possibilities,

the ones where she chokes on something when we're not in the room and dies. Or where she gets caught on something in her bed—and, look, there's nothing in her bed, right? We follow all the rules about no stuffies and no blankets—but still! I have these awful fears before I fall asleep of her getting tangled in something and dying.

So, what do I do? Rationalize that these are impossible fears brought on by my anxiety and go to sleep? Fuck, no. I creep back into her room to make sure she's breathing, or I watch her on the monitor until she moves a tiny bit. I'll creep down the hallway and wait just outside her room until I can make out her breathing over the sound of the noise machine—which sounds exactly like breathing. How messed-up is that? Who thought that was a good idea?

Q: These fears of death coincided with the birth of your daughter?

A: Seems like it. Or maybe they were already there and Winnie just brought them to the surface. I don't know. But now I think about her dying all the time. I know that sounds messed-up, like I'm fantasizing about it or something. Is it possible to obsess over a fear instead of just a desire? Because I don't want my daughter to die. That's not what I'm saying. It's like my fear of it is so great and all-consuming that it's taken up room in the places where my happiness and pleasure usually go, and now it's driving their cars and operating their machinery.

Q: Of course, we can become obsessed by and even dependent upon our fears or worries. What you're describing sounds completely normal, Calidore, especially for a new parent who loves his child as much as you obviously do. Does this fear of dying relate to your own life as well? Are you afraid of dying?
A: Maybe.
Q: Maybe?
A: Do you know what's nuts? I'm afraid of dying, yeah, but I think everyone probably is on some level. But I have this worry it might be the only thing keeping me alive. That if I would just let go of all this anxiety and worry and fear and dread, that I wouldn't have enough energy left inside me to turn the cranks and keep the wheels spinning. I know that can't be right—I know it up here in my head, but somewhere deeper, I fear it's true. Down there, I KNOW it's true.

And the second, an excerpt from a short interview Evangeline gave to Tim Russert when she began at the Publix Harbor in Florida. This was her first fencing position, and even then, she was seen as a potential prodigy, nothing on the level of Arthur Miracle, Gogaji, or Jiangshi Chaoren, but still easily in the top 5% of fencers in terms of power levels, and perhaps even higher, given the curious and puissant nature of her primacy.

Russert: How does it feel, knowing all of these high expectations people have for you? Does it scare you? Are you excited by it?
Evangeline: I'm nervous, yes, but I feel great

about the training I've received and the support here. I know I'm young, but I want everyone to know they can feel safe with me patrolling this equinox.

Russert: I'm glad you brought up your age. Only twenty-five and starting as a lead fencer at one of America's highest-profile and population-rich fences. But also—only twenty-five and already one of America's highest-grossing fencers. You've got to be one of the richest 25-year-olds in the country, if not the world! What's that like?

Evangeline: (laughs) I don't really know. I don't have much to do with all of that money. I bought a new car with it, and I got my mom a new house.

Russert: But jets? And Paris for the weekend? And houses around the world? We see fencers all the time hanging out with actors and athletes and models. That doesn't appeal to you?

Evangeline: Not really. My mom always says I'm an old soul trapped in a young body, and I think that's probably true. I just want the simple things, I guess.

Russert: And what are the simple things for Florida's newest superstar fencer?

Evangeline: A nice little house. Someone to love. Maybe a whole family. Saturday mornings with doughnuts and board games. That sounds pretty good to me.

Russert: And a couple thousand neutralized fae every equinox, right?

Evangeline: Sure. Of course. Yeah.

Chapter 23

The makeshift cemetery glittered with frost in the early morning, and though dawn was a few hours gone, the hooked moon still hung above the horizon.

Winnie kneeled before the tombstone and ran her fingers along the new-cut words there.

"They're smooth," Winnie said, her voice quiet. "Really smooth."

Beside her, Tennyson was a mountain of black-and-white fur, his eyes trained on Winnie.

A chill wind moved like a soft spirit through the field where they'd set up the grave marker, and Evangeline drew the collar of her coat up around her neck. Near the small gravel turn-in, not even a proper parking lot, two government agents waited by the car, giving Evangeline and Winnie their privacy.

October's light and color were nearly gone, and in a few days, November would be upon them. Snow would fall and temperatures would plummet. Evangeline would pull out Winnie's heavy winter coat and the thick, well-insulated boots she liked, the grey ones with the frogs on them. The ones Cal liked to pretend gave her the ability to hop like a frog through the snow.

The weeks since the equinox had passed with awful, excruciating sluggishness. Evangeline often found herself simply watching the clock during the endless meetings and hearings, sure that time's wheel had slowed in its turning. Worse still were the quiet afternoons at home, Winnie still at school, Tennyson asleep on the rug nearby, a cup of tea going slowly cold beside her. Everyone at Winnie's school, including the very-sorry administrators and the quiet, gentle school therapist who had held Winnie's hand while showing her the toys and art supplies in his office after telling her she could come there anytime for any reason—all of them had left the choice about when Winnie should start back completely in Evangeline's hands, who had in turn left it to Winnie herself. And after five or six days at home, Winnie had declared that she would return to school, leaving Evangeline to the slow turnings of melancholic mornings and long afternoons.

Yet that slow, constant pain was somehow preferable to the insistence of one day turning into the next, one week rolling over to another, and now this season ending. Autumn offered a kind of safety for her. It said all of this was still happening. It said Cal had only just gone. It said, *You are still in the present and so is Cal, and so still you are two together.*

Winter was a new chapter. It turned present into past, and Evangeline was not ready for that.

"I brought this for you," Winnie said, and Evangeline stepped forward to watch as Winnie took out a small envelope from a pocket. On the front, in her tall, wobbly handwriting, she'd written *Secret Agent Calidore* in green marker. Evangeline had helped her with the spelling.

Winnie tipped close to the stone and whispered something Evangeline couldn't hear as she leaned the envelope against the marker. She'd been clear that the directions inside were secret, "for Daddy only." Evangeline took a step back while Winnie spoke her quiet instructions.

A small, silver car thudding with frame-shaking music pulled in off the abandoned country road, arresting the attention of the agents until Oddry stepped out. He gave the two suited men a nod but otherwise ignored them.

Oddry's apparel was still the haphazard, mismatched effort Evangeline had always known it to be, but he was different now. He carried himself with less energy, less enthusiasm, and where before there had been a genuine, caring spirit behind his snarky eccentricities, now there was something harder, something brittle. His eyes moved more slowly from their hollowed, sunken caves, and Evangeline wondered, not for the first time in recent weeks, how much he was actually sleeping.

"Sorry I'm late," he said as he stepped up beside Evangeline.

"It's okay," Evangeline said. "More hearings about . . ."

"Yeah," he said, his voice low and his eyes on Winnie, who was still confiding in her father's tombstone. Tennyson had looked up as Oddry approached but, judging him to be the non-threat he was, the dog had settled himself back down to his primary task.

"I think the president finally has her head around what *actually* happened. Which means she finally understands why the entire Mathematician Corps leadership team was axed and why Congress will soon be dealing with a pack of high-profile lawsuits and investigation and subcommittees and blah blah blah. She asked again about meeting with you."

Evangeline nodded. She'd given her official recounting to Oddry the day after emerging from the Harbor, allowing him to record the whole thing, wanting to just get it done. And ever since, the requests had come from every quarter to poke and pry at her.

"I can—" Evangeline began, but Oddry shook his head.

"Fuck, no. I told her she can watch the tape like everyone else, and if she still wants to meet with you in a year, then we can talk. But once the news gets out that a fae transformation was reversed, it's not just going to be politicians who want to get at you. You don't have to speak to anyone you don't want to, and I'll keep them all away for as long as I can, but I don't think they're going to go away."

Evangeline felt the dutiful assurance rising in her chest once more, felt the words—*It'll be okay, really; I can do it*—already on her tongue, but she pushed it all down and simply nodded at Oddry. Memories of that day struck at her with odd, random intensity, bringing her up breathless and sweating while reading on the couch or suddenly and without warning during a run. She felt entirely at the mercy of her own fickle grief.

She would go a whole day or two without thinking of the Harbor or the Riparian or the Faerie Queen, and then she'd be watching a movie with Winnie and have to rush to the bathroom, holding back sobs or vomit, her body wracked with chills and convulsions.

"Have you thought more about transferring?" Oddry asked after a moment. He twisted a few fingers through the puff of hair at his crown.

Evangeline shook her head.

"No. Sometimes. It's just too soon." It was an easy lie to tell, and Oddry took it with a sympathetic nod. This was what the world expected: time to process, time to mourn, no need to rush into things. The polite requests about when she might like to return to fencing, where she might like to be, if she'd prefer a job training fencers, if she even wanted to fence at all—all were really nothing more than tepid attempts to test the waters with her, and each came with this little exit clause. "If it's not too soon" or "If you are feeling up for it" or "We, of course, understand if you need more time." On and on.

The truth was harder, of course. Cal haunted every room in their house, every park where they played, every window and hallway and bit of carpet at the Shop, and Evangeline wasn't ready to leave him behind.

Yet.

"The new stone looks nice," Oddry said.

Evangeline nodded, feeling the hurt stirring in her chest, reaching its long claws up her throat. She'd wanted to put Cal's name on it—his true name, the one he'd had before he was Fencer Calidore. But it was absent from her memory. She'd given it away, and once given, it was gone.

"It's smooth," Winnie said, turning to look at him. "The letters are so smooth and cool."

"Can I feel?" Oddry asked, stepping forward and squatting beside Winnie. The mass of his too-large dress shirt pooled on the ground and over his knees.

Winnie nodded and guided his fingers through the recessed letters and numbers. She whispered them as she went, as though they were the words of an incantation that might conjure Cal once more by articulating the bookends of his life.

After the shock of that day had left her, Evangeline had found in its place love and grief both, twined and knotted together.

In the first weeks, she had done her best to disentangle them, pulling at the strands of her love for Winnie, her solace and relief in the tiny joys of Winnie's hand in her own, Winnie sleeping beside her—it had not even been a question of whether Winnie would sleep in her own bed or with Evangeline. The nearness of her daughter, the heat of her, even her tears and behavioral chaos and all the other things the psychologists had warned her about and termed "perfectly normal"—every bit of it was another thread of such great and profound and redemptive happiness that Evangeline felt overwhelmed by it.

But then the grief. It twisted through all things, sometimes hidden under the surface and other times as obvious and obstructing as a blindfold over Evangeline's eyes. The memories of what had happened at the fence and beyond still tore at her, but there was little of grief in them. That was disgust, revulsion, horror.

Instead, each day she saw what could have been in every hollow and curve and movement of their life. She would walk through their house—*her* house—and see the shadows of imagined futures she had held for her life with Cal and Winnie, projects they might have done in that room or games they might have played at that table or books they might have read on those chairs. She saw the place where Cal had sat for breakfast and saw his shadow, his afterimage, sitting there all the way into the future, his middle-aged shuffle to his spot and his old-aged creaks.

When the autumn winds, already threaded through with winter's chill, slapped against the windows and pulled the remaining leaves of the trees down, she saw the three of them, their little team, their little *coterie*, reveling in their three lives all braided together in their warm house, talking or laughing or simply being near one another.

It was as if every day, Evangeline was expected to mourn another handful of futures they would never have together. In the wide-eyed wonder of Winnie's smile, she saw glimpses of the person she might become, and she felt grief anew that Cal would never see it—that the two of them together could never share in their daughter's growth. Each future shone just out of reach, too bright and too far.

Her present was a tiny boat on a vast ocean, the stars slipshod and myriad in the sky above, but the future—once a wind in her sails, a glimpse of land on the horizon—had become the leaks punched into her ship, threatening to pull her under anew each day unless she kept at the work of bailing water. Steadily, endlessly, constantly bailing.

Grief, Evangeline had learned, could be momentous and climactic, could be a midnight sob and screaming on the side of the road and acting erratically, but mostly it was this: the slow, the steady, the constant effort of tossing out the water to stay afloat one more day, to gaze at the stars above one more night.

Grief, it turned out, could be boring and ubiquitous. When friends or family asked how she was doing, some through the haze of their modified memories, she found more and more that she had nothing to say. No revelations. No great truths. No discoveries. No stories to tell.

I'm bailing water, she wanted to say. *I am bailing water I love to stay alive in this life I also love.*

On Winnie's first day back to school, Evangeline had dropped her off. They'd walked in, hand in hand, flanked by agents, all the way to Winnie's teacher's room. It was early, and the few students who had arrived were out on the playground. *Sounding their barbaric yawps*, Cal might have said.

Winnie's teacher, Mrs. Iverson, was inside, and she kneeled down before Winnie upon seeing her, wrapping the girl in an embrace and whispering her apologies. Winnie gave her a hug and, as her teacher leaned back, said, "My daddy died."

Nothing else. Just that. Said simply and honestly. Mrs. Iverson had nodded and said again how sorry she was, how she had been thinking about Winnie, how everyone in the class had been thinking about her.

But for Winnie, the conversation was over. She had said all she would say—all that *could be* said. Everything else was so much air stirred and moved and left to rest again.

"Only if your mother says it's okay," Oddry said, pulling Evangeline back into the moment. He was still squatting in front of Cal's stone but looking back over one shoulder at her now.

"Pizza party, Momma?" Winnie asked. Since the equinox, Evangeline had done her best to maintain the barest skeleton of a normal life for Winnie whenever possible. Breakfast and dinner each weekday plus lunch on the weekends, time for homework and reading, an evening walk around the neighborhood with Tennyson, and some time goofing around in the yard with balls or hula hoops or whatever.

But when Winnie asked to stay up late for a movie night or miss school or spend her morning coloring quietly or invite a friend over, Evangeline said yes. Always yes. Not because some therapist had told her it would be best but because she wasn't ready for no yet. A time was coming, maybe soon and maybe not, when Evangeline would have to shake her head sadly at Winnie's request for "Just one more chapter, please?" but that time was not now.

Evangeline was in the business of saying okay to whatever her daughter needed or wanted, and when, a few days after being back in their house she'd spotted Winnie reading Cal's note to her, the one he'd left before the equinox, she'd asked if Winnie would let her read it.

Winnie had thought for some time on that, sliding her splayed fingers along the page, and finally said, "Not yet. It's still just for me."

And Evangeline had said, "Okay."

I am bailing water, she had thought then, *bucket by bucket, because we fought for this life and because it is worth it.*

"Pizza party at ten a.m.?" Evangeline asked, feeling warmed by the small smile fighting its way on to her face. "Okay."

Winnie clutched a victorious fist high in the air before angling it toward Oddry, who nodded and bumped knuckles with her.

"But we have to have pepperoni and onions," Winnie said, suddenly serious. "It was my dad's favorite."

"Of course," Oddry said, solemn as Evangeline had ever seen him. After a minute, in a quiet voice, he said, "I miss your dad."

"Me too," Winnie said, and then she scowled at the stone in front of them. "He would have really liked how smooth these letters are. I'll tell him in my next message."

She sat back and sank one arm into Tennyson's thick fur. The dog, his tail sweeping a slow back-and-forth in the cold, crinkly leaves behind him, nuzzled his wet nose into Winnie's jacket in return.

Oddry pulled a small paperback from a pocket and leaned it against the tombstone.

"I finally read that book you told me about last year," he said, speaking to the marker. "It was weird, but I see why you liked it so much. I guess I did too."

He reached out, tracing the letters of the name on the stone once more before standing.

"I'll get the food," Oddry said. He pushed a fist into his side and twisted until his back cracked. "I'm sure somewhere is open by now."

"We'll meet you back at the house," Evangeline said. "Should we do it, Winnie?"

"Yeah. I'm ready," Winnie said, putting her hand on the stone one more time before stepping back to stand beside her mother. Tennyson, obedient as ever, followed her. He had always been attached to Winnie, much more so than Evangeline or Cal, but since their return from Faerie, his commitment to Winnie had grown almost desperate, as if simply losing sight of her opened the door once more to the horrors they'd lived through.

Evangeline found herself feeling the same way.

"Bye, Daddy," Winnie said. "See you next time."

This was their seventh stone. After buying this bit of land—a stretch of fallow-grown field Cal had liked to run by, she had paid a stone mason two huge sums of money: one for the stones, almost as many as she could ever want, and two for a new installation each time she asked, on the same land, in the same spot. The man had wanted to ask questions, but the money Evangeline had given him had been answer enough.

"Until next time, buddy," Oddry said, kissing a hand and holding it out toward the stone.

Evangeline's primacy had grown weaker each week, dimming in power the further away they got from the equinox, and perhaps there would come a week, some cold March day, where she reached for her ability and found it had waned so completely as to be almost gone.

But that was a long time away, somewhere in the next chapter of their lives.

I am bailing water, Evangeline thought as she felt tears hot on her face. She scooped a handful of stars from the air and, with a small, tight smile at the grave marker, tossed them forward, garlanding the stone in a bright constellation for a moment before it erupted into sound and music.

With her power waning, there was no danger for the others, so they stood there, pushed back slightly by the great wave of sound that rolled on and over and through them, looking at the space where Cal's marker had been, where the letter from Winnie and the book from Oddry had been.

The music, if it was music, was many things at once: sweet and trilling, low and haunting, bright and marching, sad and swaying.

Beside Evangeline, Winnie laughed at the sound, swept up by it, and she flung her arms out as if it might carry her into the air. Tennyson added his bass-boom bark as he watched Winnie.

Oddry, for his part, wept.

"Thanks, love," Evangeline said, though quietly, just for herself and Cal, her voice fitting neatly into the last arching remnants of the song.

The small group of them headed back to the cars, the song still cycling softly in their ears. Winnie ran and so did Tennyson, and Evangeline smiled at the sight.

Her daughter, hair afire with autumn's sunlight, wearing joy like shield and sword both. Wild and laughing and alive.

Acknowledgments

This book would not exist without the help and goodwill of many people. My deep thanks to Sara Megibow, Katie Hoffman, Leah Spann, Josh Starr, the good people at DAW and Astra, Richard Shealy, Myra Gross Schoen, Elisha Zepeda, Ben Wheeler-Floyd, Janet Schrunk Ericksen, Barry McQuarrie, the monks at the Saint John's Abbey Guesthouse, and the University of Minnesota Morris. I am a lucky person to have so many wonderful people in my life.

The dog in this story, Tennyson, is based on my own Newfoundland, a Very Good Girl named Mabel. If you see us out on a walk, come on over and give her a snuggle.

Finally, I am forever grateful to my family. To Rachel and Agnes: thanks for giving me a reason to write. Our little coterie of three is my favorite.